**Mills & Boon is proud to present
three super novels in one collection
by an author we know you love
and have made an
international bestseller**

Enjoy these three books by rising star

Caitlin
CREWS

One Reckless Decision

Contains

Majesty, Mistress...Missing Heir
Katrakis's Last Mistress
Princess From the Past

May 2014

June 2014

July 2014

August 2014

Caitlin
CREWS
One Reckless Decision

Published in Great Britain 2014
by Mills & Boon, an imprint of Harlequin (UK) Limited,
Eton House, 18-24 Paradise Road, Richmond, Surrey, TW9 1SR

ONE RECKLESS DECISION © 2014 Harlequin Books S.A.

Majesty, Mistress…Missing Heir © 2010 Caitlin Crews
Katrakis's Last Mistress © 2010 Caitlin Crews
Princess From the Past © 2011 Caitlin Crews

ISBN: 978 0 263 24658 2

024-0714

Printed and bound in Spain
by Blackprint CPI, Barcelona

Caitlin Crews discovered her first romance novel at the age of twelve. It involved swashbuckling pirates, grand adventures, a heroine with rustling skirts and a mind of her own, and a seriously mouth-watering and masterful hero. The book (the title of which remains lost in the mists of time) made a serious impression. Caitlin was immediately smitten with romances and romance heroes, to the detriment of her middle-school social life. And so began her lifelong love affair with romance novels, many of which she insists on keeping near her at all times.

Caitlin has made her home in places as far-flung as York, England, and Atlanta, Georgia. She was raised near New York City and fell in love with London on her first visit when she was a teenager. She has backpacked in Zimbabwe, been on safari in Botswana and visited tiny villages in Namibia. She has, while visiting the place in question, declared her intention to live in Prague, Dublin, Paris, Athens, Nice, the Greek islands, Rome, Venice, and/or any of the Hawaiian islands. Writing about exotic places seems like the next best thing to moving there.

She currently lives in California, with her animator/comic-book-artist husband and their menagerie of ridiculous animals.

Majesty, Mistress...
Missing Heir

CAITLIN CREWS

CHAPTER ONE

JESSA glanced up from her desk automatically when the door to the letting agency was shoved open, and then froze solid in her chair.

It was like a dream—a dream she had had many times. He strode inside, the wet and the cold of the Yorkshire evening swirling around him like a great black cape.

She found herself on her feet without knowing she meant to move, her hands splayed out in front of her as if she could ward him off—keep him from stepping even further into the small office. Into her life, where she could not—would not—allow him to be, ever again.

"There you are," he said in a deep, commanding voice, as if he had satisfied himself simply by laying cold eyes upon her—as if, unaccountably, he had been looking for her.

Jessa's heart thudded against her ribs as her head spun. Was he an apparition, five years later? Was she dreaming?

"Tariq," she said, dazed, as if naming the dream could dispel it.

But Tariq bin Khaled Al-Nur did not look like a dream. He was nothing so insubstantial, or easily forgotten in the light of day. When she had known him he had claimed to be no more than a wealthy, overindulged member of his country's elite class; she knew that he was now its ruler. She hated that she knew—as if that knowledge was written across her face and might suggest to him that she had followed his every move across the years when the truth was, she had wanted only to forget him.

But she could not seem to pull her gaze from his.

Jessa found that all these years later she could re-member every detail about Tariq with perfect, shocking clarity, even as the evidence before her made it clear that he was far better—far much *more*—than she had allowed herself to recall. His features were harder, more impene-trable. He was more of a *man,* somehow. It seemed impos-sible, but her memories had diminished him. The reality of Tariq was powerful, alive—dazzling.

Dangerous.

Jessa tried to concentrate on the danger. It didn't matter that her heart leaped when she saw him, even now. What mattered was the secret she knew she must keep from him. She had foolishly begun to hope that this particular day of reckoning would never come. She looked at him now, clear-eyed thanks to her shock, though that was not the im-provement she might have hoped for.

He was hard-packed muscle in a deceptively lean form, all whipcord strength and leashed, impossible power beneath skin the color of nutmeg. Time seemed to stop as Jessa stood in place, cataloging the harsh lines of his face. They were more pronounced than she remembered—the dark slash of his brows beneath his thick black hair, the masculine jut of his nose, and the high cheekbones that announced his royal blood as surely as the supremely confident, regal way he held himself. How could she have overlooked these clues five years ago? How could she have believed him when he'd claimed to be no one of any particular importance?

Those deep green eyes of his, mysterious and nearly black in the early-evening light, connected hard with a part of her she thought she'd buried years before. The part that had believed every lie he'd told her. The part that had missed, somehow, that she was being toyed with by a master manipulator. The part that had loved him heedlessly, recklessly. The part that she feared always would, despite everything.

When he was near her, she forgot herself.

He closed the door behind him, the catch clicking softly on the doorjamb. It sounded to Jessa as loud as a gunshot, and she almost flinched away from it. She could not allow herself to be weak. Not with so much at stake! Because he must know what had happened. There could be no other reason for an appearance like this, here in the forgotten back streets of York at an office that was surely far beneath his imperial notice.

He must know.

With the door closed, the noise of the evening rush in York's pedestrian center disappeared, leaving them enclosed in a tense, uncomfortable silence. The office was too small, and felt tinier by the moment. Jessa's heart hammered against her chest. Panic dug sharp claws into her sides. Tariq seemed to loom over her, to surround her, simply by standing inside the door.

He did not move, nor speak again. He held her gaze with his, daring her to look away. Challenging her. He was effortlessly commanding even in silence. Arrogant. Fierce.

He was not the easygoing playboy she remembered. Gone was his quick smile, his lazy charm. This man was not to be trifled with. This man was the king who had always lurked within the Tariq she'd known, who she'd but glimpsed in passing here and there. A shiver traced cold fingers down her spine and uncurled in her belly.

He must know.

Her pulse sounded too loud in her ears. She could feel their tangled history and her secrets all around her, dragging at her, forcibly reminding her of the darkness she'd fought so hard to escape back then. But she had more to protect now than just herself. She had to think of Jeremy, and what was best for him. Wasn't that what she had always done, no matter the cost to herself?

She let her eyes travel over Tariq, reminding herself that he was just a man, no matter how fierce. And for all his regal bearing now, back then he had disappeared without so much as a word or a backward glance or a forwarding address. He was as treacherous and formidable as the exotic desert that was his home. The exquisitely tailored clothes he wore, silk and cashmere that clung to the bold, male lines of his body, did nothing to disguise the truth of him. He was a warrior. Untamed and wild, like a shock of brilliant color in the midst of grays and browns. He was a predator. She had known it then, on some deep, feminine level, though he had smiled and joked and concealed it. Her body knew it now, and horrified her by thrilling to it even as she fought for control. Her lungs felt tight, as if he sucked up all the air in the room.

She had never thought she would see him again.

She didn't know how to react now that he was in front of her.

"No," she said, astonished to hear that her voice sounded calm even when the world around her seemed to shimmer and shake. It gave her the courage to continue. It didn't matter how compelling he was. His being so compelling had been the problem in the first place! She squared her shoulders. "No. You cannot be here."

His dark brows rose, haughty and proud. His hair, thick

and black and a touch too long for civility, seemed to sparkle with the autumn rain from outside. He kept his impossible, haunting eyes trained on her face. How she had once loved those eyes, which had seemed so sad, so guarded. Tonight they seemed to see right through her. His expression was unreadable.

"And yet here I am." His voice was low, husky, and held the barest hint of the foreign lands he'd come from, wrapped in something both chocolate and smooth. *Dangerous.* And once more—a blatant, unmistakable challenge. It hit Jessa like a fist to the midsection.

"Without invitation," she pointed out, pleased her tone was just this side of curt. Anything to seem stronger than she felt. Anything to look tougher than she was. *Anything to protect Jeremy.*

"Do I require an invitation to enter a letting agent's?" he asked, unperturbed. "You must excuse me if I have forgotten British customs. I was under the impression places such as these encourage walk-in clientele."

"Do you have an appointment?" Jessa asked, forcing her jaw to stop clenching. It was what she would ask any other person who appeared off the street, wasn't it? And really, why should Tariq bin Khaled Al-Nur be any different?

"In a manner of speaking," he said, his tone hinting at some significance that was lost on Jessa, though she sensed he expected her to understand his meaning. "Yes."

His eyes traveled over her, no doubt comparing her to his memories. Jessa felt her cheeks flame, in some combination of distress and fury. She had the sudden worry that she fell short, and then could have kicked herself. Or, preferably, him. Why should she care about such things? Nothing would change the fact that she was an ordinary girl from Yorkshire and he was a king.

"It is nice to see you again, Jessa," Tariq said with a dangerous politeness that did not conceal the ruthlessness beneath. She wished he would not say her name. It was like a caress. It teased at the back of her neck, swirled through her blood, and traced phantom patterns across her skin.

"I'm afraid I can't say the same," she replied coolly. Because she had a spine. Because she needed to get rid of him, and make certain he never returned. Because their past was far too complicated to ever be brought out into the present. "You are the very last person I would ever wish to see again. If you go away quickly, we can pretend it never happened."

Tariq's dark jade eyes seemed to sharpen. He thrust his long, elegant hands into the pockets of his trousers with a casualness Jessa could not quite believe. The Tariq she'd known had been nonchalant, at ease, but that man had never existed, had he? And this man in front of her was nothing like the man Tariq had pretended to be. He was too hard, too fierce.

"I see the years have sharpened your tongue." He considered her. "What else has changed, I wonder?"

There was one specific way she had changed that she could not possibly share with him. Did he already know it? Was he baiting her?

"*I* have changed," Jessa said, glaring at him, deciding that an offense was better than any defense she might try to throw up against this strangely familiar man, who was much more like steel than the lover she remembered. "It's called growing up." She lifted her chin in defiance, and could feel her hands ball into fists at her sides. "I am no longer likely to beg for anyone's attention. Not anymore."

She did not see him move but she had the sense that he tensed, as if readying himself for battle. She braced herself, but he only watched her. Something too ruthless to be a smile curled in the corner of his hard mouth.

"I do not recall a single instance of you begging," Tariq replied, an edge in his dark voice. "Unless you mean in my bed." He let that hang there, as if daring her to remember. Mute, Jessa stared back at him. "But if you wish to reenact some such scene, by all means, do so."

"I think not," she gritted out from between her teeth. She would not think about his bed, or what she had done in it. *She would not.* "My days of clinging to pathetic international playboys are long past."

She felt the air tighten between them. His dark green eyes narrowed, and once again she was reminded that he was not a regular man. He was not even the man she had once known. He was too wild, too unmanageable, and she was a fool to underestimate him—or overestimate herself. Her weakness where he was concerned was legendary, and humiliating, and should have left her when he had.

But she could feel it—feel him—throughout her body, like nothing had changed, even though everything had. Like he still owned and controlled her as effortlessly and carelessly as he had years before. Her breasts felt tight against her blouse, her skin was flushed, and she felt a familiar, sweet, hot ache low in her belly. She bit her lip against the heat that threatened to spill over from behind her eyes and show him all the things she wanted to hide.

She knew she could not let this happen, whatever *this* was. She wanted nothing to do with him. There were secrets she would do anything in her power to keep from him. Chemistry was simply that: a chemical, physical reaction. It meant nothing.

But she did not look away.

* * *

She had haunted him, and Tariq bin Khaled Al-Nur was not a man who believed in ghosts.

He stared at the woman who had tortured him for years, no matter where he went or with whom, and who now had the audacity to challenge him with no thought for her own danger. Tariq considered himself a modern sheikh, a modern king, but he understood in this moment that if he had one of his horses at his disposal he would have no qualm whatsoever about tossing Jessa Heath across the saddle and carrying her away to a tent far off in the desert that comprised most of his homeland on the Arabian Peninsula.

In fact, he would enjoy it.

He was right to have come here. To have faced this woman, finally. Even as she called him names, and continued to defy him. Just as she had done so long before. His mouth twisted in a hard smile.

He knew that he should be furious that she wished to keep him at arm's length, that she dared to poke at him as if he was some insipid weakling. He knew that he should feel shame that he, Sheikh Tariq bin Khaled Al-Nur, King of Nur, had come crawling back to the only woman who had ever dared abandon him. The only woman he had ever missed. Who stood before him now in an ugly suit that did not become her or flatter her lushness, unwelcoming and cold instead of pleased to see him again. He should be enraged at the insult.

But instead, he wanted her.

It was that simple. That consuming. He had finally stopped fighting it.

One look at the curvy body he still reached for in his sleep, her wide eyes the color of cinnamon, her sinful, lickable mouth, and he was hard, ready—alive with need. He could taste her skin, feel the heat of her desire. Or he remembered it. Either way, he needed to be deep inside her once again.

Then, perhaps, they could see how defiant she really was.

"A pathetic playboy, am I?" he asked, keeping his tone light, though he could not disguise the intent beneath. This woman reminded him so strongly of his other, wasted life—yet he still wanted her. He would have her. "An intriguing accusation."

Temper rose in her cheeks, turning ivory to peach. "I can't imagine what that means," she snapped. "It is not an accusation, it's the truth. It is who you are."

Tariq watched her for a long moment. She had no idea how deep his shame for his profligate former existence ran within him. Nor how closely he associated her with all he had been forced to put behind him, and now found so disgusting. He had fought against her hold on him for years, told himself that he only remembered her because she had left him, that he would have left her himself if she'd given him the opportunity, as he had left countless other women in his time.

Still, here he was.

"It means that if I am a playboy, you by definition become one of my playthings, do you not?" he asked. He enjoyed the flash of temper he saw in her face much more than he should have. The warrior inside him was fully roused and ready to take on his opponent. "Does the description distress you?"

"I am not at all surprised to hear you call me a *plaything*." Her mouth twisted. "But I was never yours."

"A fact you made abundantly clear five years ago," he said drily, though he doubted she would mistake the edge beneath. Indeed, she stiffened. "But is this any way for old friends to greet each other after such a long time?" He crossed the room until only the flimsy barrier of her desk stood between them.

"Friends?" she echoed, shaking her head slightly. "Is that what we are?"

Only a few feet separated them, not even the length of his arm. She swallowed, nervously. Tariq smiled. It was as he remembered. She still looked the same—copper curls and cinnamon eyes, freckles across her nose and a wicked, suggestive mouth made entirely for sin. And she was still susceptible to him, even from across a desk. Would she still burn them both alive when he touched her? He couldn't wait to find out.

"What do you suggest?" she asked. Her delicate eyebrows arched up, and that sensual mouth firmed. "Shall we nip out for a coffee? Talk about old times? I think I'll pass."

"I am devastated," he said, watching her closely. "My former lovers are generally far more receptive."

She didn't like that. The flush in her cheeks deepened, and her cinnamon eyes darkened. She stood straighter.

"Why are you here, Tariq?" she asked, in a crisp, no-nonsense voice that both irritated and aroused him. She crossed her arms over her chest. "Are you looking to let a flat in the York area? If so, you'll want to return when the agents are in, so they might help you. I'm afraid they're both out with clients, and I'm only the office manager."

"Why do you think I'm here, Jessa?"

He studied her face, letting the question hang there between them. He wanted to see her reaction. To catalog it. Her fingers crept to her throat, as if she wanted to soothe the beat of her own pulse.

"I cannot imagine any reason at all for you to be here," she told him now, but her voice was high and reedy. She coughed to cover it, and then threw her shoulders back, as if she fancied herself a match for him. "You should go. Now."

And now she ordered him out? Like a servant? Tariq

shifted his weight, balancing on the balls of his feet as if readying himself for combat, and idly imagined how he would make her pay for that slight. He was a king. She should learn how to address him properly. Perhaps on her knees, with that sinfully decadent mouth of hers wrapped around him, hot and wet. It would make a good start.

"If you won't tell me what you want—" she began, frowning.

"You," he said. He smiled. "I want you."

CHAPTER TWO

"ME?" Jessa was taken aback. She would have stepped back, too, but she'd locked her knees into place and couldn't move. "You've come here for *me?*"

She did not believe him. She couldn't, not when his dark eyes still seemed laced with danger and that smile seemed to cut right through her. But there was a tiny, dismaying leap in the vicinity of her heart.

She could face the unwelcome possibility that she might still be a fool where this man was concerned, on a purely physical level. But she had absolutely no intention of giving in to it!

"Of course I am here for you," he said, his eyes hot. One black eyebrow arched. "Did you imagine I happened by a letting agent's in York by accident?"

"Five years ago you couldn't get away from me fast enough," Jessa pointed out. "Now, apparently, you have scoured the countryside to find me. You'll forgive me if I can't quite get my head around the dramatic change in your behavior."

"You must have me confused with someone else," Tariq said silkily. "You are the one who disappeared, Jessa. Not I."

Jessa blinked at him. For a moment she had no idea

what he was talking about, but then, of course, the past came rushing back. She had gone to the doctor's for a routine physical, only to discover that she had been pregnant. Pregnant! She had had no illusions that Tariq would have welcomed the news. She had known he would not. She had needed to get away from him for a few days to pull herself together, to think what she might do while not under the spell his presence seemed to cast around her.

Perhaps she hadn't phoned him. But she hadn't left him.

"What are you talking about?" she asked now. "I was not the one who fled the country!"

His mouth tightened. "You said you were going to the doctor, and then you disappeared. You were gone for days, and then, yes, I left the country. If that is what you want to call it."

"I came back," Jessa said, her voice a low throb, rich with a pain she would have said was long forgotten. "You didn't."

There was an odd, arrested silence.

"You will have heard of my uncle's passing, of course," Tariq said, his gaze hooded. His tone was light, conversational. At odds with the tension that held Jessa in a viselike grip.

"Yes," she said, struggling to match his tone. "It was in all the papers right after you left. It was such a terrible accident." She took care to keep her voice level. "Imagine my surprise when I discovered that the man I'd known as simply the son of a doctor was, as it happened, a member of the royal family and the new king of Nur."

"My father *was* a doctor." His brows rose. "Or do you think I impugned his honor after his death merely for my own amusement?"

"I think you deliberately misled me," she replied evenly, trying not to let her temper get the best of her. "Yes, your father was a doctor. But he was also the younger brother of a king!"

"You will forgive me," Tariq said with great hauteur, "if your feelings did not supercede legitimate safety concerns at the time."

How could he do that? How could he make her feel as if she had wronged him when *he* was the one who had lied and then abandoned her? What was the matter with her?

"Safety concerns?" she asked with a little laugh, as if none of this mattered to her. Because none of it *should* have mattered to her. She had come to terms with her relationship with Tariq years ago. "Is that what you call it? You invented a man who did not exist. Who never existed. And then you pretended to be that man."

He smiled. Jessa thought of wolves. And she was suddenly certain that she did not wish to hear whatever he might say next.

"I'm sorry about your uncle," she murmured instead, her voice soft. Softer than it should have been, when she wanted only to be strong.

"My uncle, his wife, and both of their sons were killed," Tariq said coolly, brushing off her words of condolence. The wolf smile was gone. "And so I am not just King of Nur now, but the very last of its ancient, founding bloodline. Do you know what that means?"

She was suddenly terrified that she knew exactly what that meant, and, more terrifying, what *he* would think it meant. She could not allow it.

"I imagine it means that you have great responsibilities," Jessa said. She couldn't think of any reason he would drop by her office in Yorkshire to discuss the line of succession in his far-off desert kingdom, save one. But surely, if he knew the truth, he would not be wasting his time here with her, would he? Perhaps he only suspected. Either way, she wanted him gone. "Though what would I know about it?" She spread her hands out, to encompass the letting office. "I am an office manager, not a king."

"Indeed." He watched her and yet he made no move. He only kept that dark green gaze trained upon her while the rest of his big, lean body seemed too still, too much raw power unnaturally leashed. As if he was poised and ready to pounce. "I am responsible to my people, to my country, in a way that I was not before. It means that I must think about the future." His voice, his expression, was mocking, but did he mock her, or him? "I must marry and produce heirs. The sooner the better."

All the breath left Jessa's body in a sudden rush. She felt light-headed. Surely he could not mean…? But there was a secret, hidden part of her that desperately hoped he did and yearned for him to say so—to make sense of these past lonely, bittersweet years by claiming her, finally, as his. To fulfill the foolish dream she'd always held close to her heart, and fervently denied. *His wife. Tariq's wife.*

"Don't be absurd," she chided him—and herself. She was nothing. A no one. He was the King of Nur. And even if he had been a regular, accessible man, he was also the only one with whom she had so much tangled history. It was impossible. It had always been impossible. "You cannot marry *me!*"

"First you mock me," Tariq said gently, almost conversationally. And yet the nape of Jessa's neck prickled in warning. "You call me a pathetic playboy. Then you order me to leave this place, like some insignificant insect, and now you scold me like a child." His lips curved into a smile that did not reach his eyes. "Perhaps you forget who I am."

She knew exactly who he was. She knew too well what

he could do to her. What he had done already. She was much more afraid of what he might do now.

"I have not forgotten anything, Tariq," she said, glad that her voice was calm yet strong, as it ought to be. Glad that she sounded capable and unmoved, as she should. "Which is why I must ask you to leave. Again."

Tariq shrugged with apparent ease, but his eyes were hot.

"In any case, you misunderstand me," he said. He smiled slightly. "I am not in the habit of proposing marriage to ex-lovers who harbor such disdain for me, I assure you."

It took a moment for his words to fully sink in. Humiliation followed quickly, thick and hot. It was a dizzying reminder of how she had felt when his mobile phone had come up disconnected, his London flat vacated, one after the other, with her none the wiser. Mortification clawed at her throat and cramped her stomach. Had she really imagined that he had appeared out of nowhere because he wished to *marry* her? She was unbearably foolish, again, as if the past five years had never happened.

But they had happened, she reminded herself. And she had been through far worse than a few moments of embarrassment. It was the memory of what she'd survived, and the hard choices she'd made, that had her pushing the humiliation aside and meeting his gaze. There were more important things in the world than Tariq bin Khaled Al-Nur, and her own mortification. Her cheeks might still be red, but her head was high.

"Then what is it you want?" she asked coolly. "I have no interest in playing games with you."

"I have already told you what I want," he said smoothly, but there was still that hard edge beneath. "Must I repeat myself? I do not recall you being so slow on the uptake, Jessa."

Once again, the way he said her name nearly made her shiver. She shook it off and tried to make sense of what he was saying but then, abruptly, gave up. Why was she allowing this to happen? He had waltzed in after all this time, and cornered her behind her desk? Who did he think he was?

With a burst of irritation, at herself and at him, Jessa propelled herself around the side of her desk and headed for the door of the office. She didn't have to stand there and let him talk to her this way. She didn't have to listen to him. He was the one who had had all the choices years ago, because she hadn't known any better and hadn't *wanted* to know any better, but she wasn't that besotted girl any longer. That girl had died years ago, thanks to him. He had no idea what she'd been through, and she didn't owe him anything, including explanations.

"Where do you imagine you can go?" he asked, in an idle, detached tone, as if he could not possibly have cared less. She knew better than to believe that, somehow. "That you believe I cannot follow?"

"I have some ideas about where you can go," Jessa began without turning back toward him, temper searing through her as she stalked toward the door.

But then he touched her, and she had not heard him move. No warning, no time to prepare—

He touched her, and her brain shorted out.

His long fingers wrapped around her arm just above the elbow. Even through the material of her suit jacket, Jessa could feel the heat emanating from him—fire and strength and his hard palm against her arm, like a brand. Like history repeating itself. Like a white-hot electricity that blazed through her and rendered her little more than ash and need.

He closed the distance between them, pulling her up hard against the unyielding expanse of his chest. She gasped, even as his other hand came around to her opposite hip, anchoring her against him, her back to his front, their two bodies coming together like missing puzzle pieces.

She could feel him everywhere. The sweet burn where his powerful body connected with hers, and even where he did not touch her at all. Her toes curled in her shoes. Her lungs ached. Deep in her belly she felt an intoxicating pulse, while between her legs she felt herself grow damp and ready. For him. All for him, as always.

How could her body betray her like this? How could it be so quick to forget?

"Take your hands off me," she demanded, her voice hoarse with an emotion she refused to name. At once, he stepped back, released her, and all that fire was gone. She told herself she did not feel a hollowness, did not feel bereft. She turned slowly to face him, as if she could not still feel the length of his chest pressed against her.

She thought of Jeremy. Of what she must hide.

Of what Tariq would do if he knew.

"Is this what you think of me?" she asked, her voice low, her temper a hot drumbeat inside her chest. She raised her chin. The hoarseness was gone as if it had never been. "You think you can simply turn up after all this time, after vanishing into thin air and leaving me with nothing but your lies, and I'll leap back into your arms?"

"Once again, you seem to be confused," Tariq said, his voice hushed, his gaze intent. Almost demanding. But there was something else there that made a shiver of silent warning slide along her spine. "I am not the one who ran away. I am the one who has reappeared, despite all the time that has passed."

"You are also the one who lied about who he was," Jessa pointed out. "Hardly the moral high ground."

"You have yet to mention where you disappeared to all those years ago," Tariq said, his voice sliding over her, through her, and making her body hum with an awareness she didn't want to accept. "Exactly what moral high ground are you claiming?"

And, of course, she could not tell him that she had found out she was pregnant. She could not tell him that she had suspected, even though she had loved him to distraction, that he would react badly. She could not tell him that after days of soul-searching, she had come back to London to share the news with him, only to find him gone as if he had never been. As if she had made him up.

And she certainly could not tell him that he was a father now. There was absolutely no doubt in her mind that Tariq's reaction to the news would be brutal. She sucked in a breath and forced a serene expression onto her face.

"The truth is, I have no interest in digging up the past," Jessa said. She shrugged. "I got over you a long time ago."

His eyes were like jade, and glittered with something darker.

"Is that so?" he asked in the same quiet voice, as if they were in the presence of something larger. She shoved the notion away, and had to restrain herself from reaching out and shoving *him* away, too. She knew better than to touch him.

"I'm sorry if you expected me to be sitting in an attic somewhere, weeping over your picture," Jessa said, trying to inject a little laughter into her voice, as if that might ease the tension in the room and in her own body. Tariq's eyes narrowed. "But I've moved on. I suggest you do the same. Aren't you a sheikh? Can't you snap your fingers and create a harem to amuse yourself?"

She thought for a tense, long moment that she had gone too far. He was, after all, a king now. And far more unnerving. But he looked away for a moment, and his mouth curved in something very nearly a smile.

"I must marry," Tariq said. Then he turned his head and captured her gaze with his. "But before I can do that particular duty, it seems I must deal with you."

"Deal with me?" She shook her head, not understanding. Not wanting to try to understand him. "Why should you wish to deal with me now, when you have had no interest in me for all these years?"

"You and I have unfinished business." It was a statement of fact. His eyebrows rose, daring her to disagree.

Jessa thought for a moment she might faint. But then something else kicked in, some deep protective streak that would not allow her to fall before this man so easily. He was formidable, yes. But she was stronger. She'd had to be.

Maybe, on some level, she had always known she would have to face him someday.

"We do not have unfinished business, or anything else," she declared, throwing down the gauntlet. She raised her chin and looked him in the eye. "Anything we had died five years ago, in London."

"That is a lie." His tone brooked no argument. He was the king, handing down his judgment. She ignored it.

"Let me tell you what happened to me after you left the country," Jessa continued in the same tone, daring him to interrupt her. His nostrils flared slightly, but he was silent. She took a step closer, no longer afraid of his nearness. "Did you ever think about it? Did it cross your mind at all?"

How proud she had been of that internship, straight out of university that long-ago summer. How certain she had been that she was taking the first, crucial steps to a glittering, high-powered career in the city. Instead, she had met

Tariq in her first, breathless week in London, and her dreams had been forever altered.

"You were the one who left—" he began, frowning.

"I left for two and half days," she said, cutting him off. "It's not quite on a par with what you did, is it? It wasn't enough that you left the country, disconnected your mobile phone, and put your flat up for sale," she continued, keeping her gaze steady on his. "Actually telling me you no longer wished to see me was beneath you, I suppose. But you also withdrew your investments."

His frown deepened, and his body tensed. Did he expect a blow? When he had been the one to deliver all of them five years ago, and with such cold-blooded, ruthless efficiency? Jessa almost laughed.

"What did you think would happen?" she asked him, an old anger she had thought she'd forgotten coloring her voice. She searched the dark green eyes she had once artlessly compared to primeval forests, and saw no poetry there any longer. Only his carelessness. "I was the intern who was foolish enough to have an affair with one of the firm's biggest clients. I had no idea you were *the* biggest client. And it was smiled upon as long as I kept you happy, of course."

Jessa could picture the buttoned-up, hypocritical investment bankers she had worked for back then. She could see once more the knowing way they had looked at her when they thought she was just one more fringe benefit the firm could provide for Tariq's pleasure. Just another perk. A bottle of the finest champagne, the witless intern, whatever he liked. But then he had severed his relationships—not only with Jessa, but with the firm that handled his speculative investments, all in the span of three quick days following the September Bank Holiday.

"I thought it best to make a clean break," he said, and there was strain in his voice, as if he fought against some strong emotion, but Jessa knew from experience that his emotions were anything but strong, no matter how they might appear.

"Yes, well, you succeeded in breaking something," she told him, the anger gone as quickly as it had come, leaving only a certain sadness for the girl she had been. "My career. Into tiny little pieces. They sacked me, of course. And once they did, who do you think wanted to hire the promiscuous intern who'd lost her previous firm so much money along with such a high-profile client?"

His mouth flattened and his eyes flashed that dark jade fire. But Jessa remembered the look of disgust on the senior partner's face when he'd called her into his office. She remembered the harsh words he'd used to describe her behavior, the same behavior that had received no more than a wink and a smile the week before. She'd stood there, pale and trembling, unable to process what was happening. She was pregnant. And Tariq had not only left her so brutally, he had left England altogether, to become a king. On top of all that, he had never been the person he'd claimed to be, the person she'd loved. It was all a lie.

"And that was the end of my brilliant career in London," Jessa said in a quiet, matter-of-fact manner. She tilted her head slightly to one side as she considered him. "I suppose I should thank you. It takes some people a lifetime to figure out that they're not cut out for that world. Thanks to you, it took me only a few short months."

"My uncle was killed," Tariq said in a low, furious voice, his body seeming to expand as he stood in the middle of the office floor, taking over the entire space. "I was suddenly thrust upon the throne, and I had to secure my position. I did not have time to soothe hurt feelings half the world away."

"They don't have notepaper or pens where you come from, then," Jessa said sarcastically, pretending she was unaffected by his magnetism, his power. "Much less telephones. Perhaps you communicate using nothing save the force of your royal will?"

He looked away then, muttering something harsh in a language she was just as happy she didn't know. In profile, he was all hard edges except for his surprisingly mobile mouth. He looked like the king he was. Noble features, royal bones. The sort of profile that would end up stamped on coins.

When she thought about it that way, the absurdity of the situation was almost too much for her. They should never have met in the first place—it was all too fantastical. It was one thing to dream of fairy-tale princes when one was fresh out of university and still under the impression that the world was waiting only to be bent to one's will. Tariq bin Khaled Al-Nur had always been too sophisticated, too dangerous, *too much* for the likes of Jessa Heath, and that was long before he became a king. She was a simple person, with a simple life and, once, a few big dreams, but she'd quickly learned the folly of dreams. She knew better now.

"Never fear," she said, folding her arms over her chest. "I'm a survivor. I picked myself up, dusted myself off, and made myself a life. It might not be the life I wanted when I was twenty-two, but it's mine." She lifted her chin and fixed her eyes on him, unafraid. "And I like it."

There was another silence. A muscle worked in Tariq's jaw, though he was otherwise motionless. Jessa had said things she had once only dreamed about saying, and that had to count for something, didn't it?

"There is no apology I can make that will suffice," Tariq said then, lifting his head to catch her gaze, startling her with his seeming sincerity. "I was thoughtless. Callous."

For a moment Jessa stared back at him, while something seemed to ease inside of her. Almost as if it was enough, somehow, that he had heard her. That he offered no excuses for what he had done. And perhaps it might have been enough, if that had been the end of what his abandonment had cost her. But it had only been the beginning. It had been the easy part, in retrospect.

"Congratulations," she said sarcastically, thinking of everything she'd suffered. The impossible decision she'd made. The daily pain of living with that decision ever since, no matter how much she might know that it was the right one. "You have managed to avoid apologizing with such elegance, I nearly thanked you for it."

"It is obvious that I owe you a great debt," he said then. If she hadn't been staring straight at him, she might have missed the flash of temper that came and went in his eyes. And she couldn't shake the strange notion that he meant to say something else entirely.

"There is no debt," she told him, stiffening. If he owed her something, that meant he might stay in the area, and she couldn't have that! He had to go, back to his own world, where he belonged. Far away from hers.

"I cannot make up for the loss of your prospects," Tariq continued as if she hadn't spoken. His voice was both formal and seductive. An odd mix, yet something inside her melted. "And perhaps there is nothing you wish for that I can provide."

"I've just told you I don't want anything," she said, more forcefully. "Not from you."

"Not even dinner?" He didn't quite smile. He inclined

his head toward her. "It is getting late. And I have wronged you. I think perhaps there is more to it, and the very least I can do is listen to you."

She didn't trust him for a second, much less his sudden gallantry and concern. She knew exactly how manipulative he could be. He'd lied to her for months and she'd bought it, hook, line, and sinker! And she had not forgotten that he'd said they had unfinished business between them. She should refuse him outright, demand he leave her alone.

But she didn't do it.

She was still buzzing from the unexpected rush she'd gotten when she'd told him exactly what he'd done to her. When she'd laid it out, piece by piece, and he'd had no defense. She had no intention of sharing the rest of it with him, but she'd be lying if she didn't admit that she liked being the one in charge. Perhaps she wasn't quite ready to dismiss him. Not quite yet. Was it that she felt powerful, or was it that melting within?

It was by far the most terrifying moment of the day.

"I'm afraid that's impossible," she told him stiffly, appalled at what she had nearly done. Was she mad? "I already have plans."

"Of course." Something passed through his eyes and made her catch her breath. "I understand. Another time, perhaps."

"Perhaps." She was noncommittal. Surely there could be no other time? Surely he would simply vanish back into the ether as he had before?

"Until then," he murmured, and then he turned and let himself back out of the office door. Jessa had the sense of his body moving like liquid into the night, and then she was alone.

He was gone as abruptly as he had come.

Jessa let out a breath, and sagged where she stood,

finding herself on her knees in the center of the industrial blue carpet. She pressed her hands against her face, then let them drop.

The room was again just a room. Just an office. Without Tariq crowding into it, it was not even small.

Jessa stayed where she was until her breathing returned to normal. She had to think. She was not foolish enough to believe that he was gone for good, that he might have hunted her down in York for a simple conversation most regular people would have on the telephone, or via the Internet, or not at all. The crazy part of her that still yearned for him swelled in the knowledge that he would, inevitably, return, and she felt something like a sob catch in her throat. She had come to terms with having loved and lost Tariq years ago. She had had no other option. But she had never expected that he would swing back into her life like this. She had never dreamed she would see him again, unless it was on the television.

She excused herself for being so uncharacteristically overwhelmed. He was an overwhelming man, to say the least! Jessa climbed to her feet and smoothed her hands over her skirt, straightening her ill-fitting suit jacket with a quick tug. If only she could set her world to rights as easily. It was one thing to mourn the man she had loved so much she'd let him change the course of her whole life while she was on her own these past years. It was something else again when he was in front of her. But she couldn't allow any of that to distract her from the main point.

Because all that mattered now was Jeremy.

The child she had fiercely and devotedly cared for while she'd carried him inside of her for nine long months. The baby she had kissed and adored when he'd finally decided to greet the world after so many hard, lonely hours of painful labor, his face red and his tiny fists waving furiously in front of him.

The son she had loved so desperately that she'd given him up for adoption when he had been four months old despite how agonizing that decision had been—and how hard it continued to be—for her. The son she still loved enough to fight with everything she had to maintain his privacy, his happiness, no matter the cost.

No matter what she might have to do.

CHAPTER THREE

JESSA was not surprised to find Tariq at her front door the following morning. If anything, she was surprised he had waited the whole of the night before reappearing. It might have lured her into a false sense of security had she not known better.

Perhaps she did still know him after all.

She opened the door to his peremptory knock because she knew that simply ignoring him would not only fail to deter him, it might also rouse her neighbors' interest and Jessa didn't want that. She didn't want someone noticing that the King of Nur was lounging about outside her otherwise unremarkable terraced house on a quiet Fulford side street just outside York's medieval walls. What good could come of drawing attention to the fact they knew each other? She needed to get him to go back to his own country, his own world, as quickly as possible.

She cracked the door as little as she could, and stood in the wedge, as if she was capable of keeping him out with her body if he wanted to come in.

Their eyes caught and held. Time seemed to halt in its tracks. Jessa felt her heart quicken its pace to thud heavily against her ribs, and her breath caught in her throat.

She was aware on some level that the morning was gray and wet, but the weather faded from her notice, because *he* was all she could see. And he was distressingly, inarguably real. Not the figment of her imagination she had half convinced herself he had been, conjured from the depths of her memory to torture herself with the night before. Not a dream, not even a nightmare.

"Good morning, Jessa," he said, as casually as if he spent all of his Saturday mornings fetched up on her doorstep, looking impossibly handsome and as inaccessible as ever.

He was no hallucination. He was flesh, blood, and all male, packed into one deceptively lean and powerful body. Today he wore black jeans and a tight black jersey that hugged the muscular planes of his chest and announced that whatever else the King of Nur might do while enjoying his luxurious lifestyle, he kept himself in top physical condition. His jade eyes burned into hers, nearly black in the morning gloom.

"I didn't make you up, then," Jessa said in as even a tone as she could manage. She wanted to order him to leave her alone, but she suspected he would pounce on that and use it against her, somehow. Best not to hand the warrior any weapons. "You're really here."

"How could I stay away?" he asked, with one of those predatory smiles that managed to distract her even as it unnerved her. She did not believe that he was here simply for her, no matter what he claimed. What was the likelihood that the lover who had had no qualm discarding her so completely would have a sudden drastic change of heart five years later, apropos of nothing? *Slim,* she had decided sometime in the early morning hours, long after she'd given up on sleeping. *Slim to none and bordering on less than zero.*

He had to know about Jeremy. Didn't he?

"You do not believe me," he murmured. He leaned in closer, taking up far too much space, blocking out the world behind him. "Perhaps I can convince you."

The good part about this situation, Jessa thought as he moved closer, close enough that she could smell the familiar, haunting scent of sandalwood and spice and his own warm skin, was that it made her choices very simple. There was only one: ease his fears and suspicions however she could, and send him on his way.

She told herself she could do this. Her head felt too light, her knees too weak. But she would do what she must, for her son's sake. She could handle Tariq. She could. She stepped back and opened the door wider.

"You'd better come in."

Tariq let Jessa lead him inside the house, which felt dark and close as all English dwellings felt to him. This whole country of low clouds and relentless rain made him crave the impossibly blue skies of Nur, the horizon stretching beyond imagining, the desert wide and open and bright. The fact that he was not where he was supposed to be, where he needed to be—that he was still in England when he should be at the palace in Azhar handling the latest threat of a rebel uprising near the disputed border— reminded him too much of his playboy past. Yet he had still come to find her.

He had no time for this. He had no patience for ghosts or trips through the past. It was finished. He was no longer that self-indulgent, wasteful creature, and had no wish to revisit him now. Yet she had haunted him across the years, as no other woman ever had. He could recall her smile, the arch of her back, the scent of her skin, in perfect detail. He had

had no choice but to find her. He had to exorcize her once and for all, so he might finally get on with his life as he should have done five years ago. Marriage, heirs. His duty.

Jessa walked before him into her sitting room, and came to a stop beside the mantel. Slowly, she turned to face him, her tension evident in the way she held herself, the way she swallowed nervously and pulled at her clothes with her hands. He liked that she was not at ease. It made his own uncertainty less jarring, somehow. She could deny it all she liked, but he could feel the awareness swell between them.

Tariq's eyes swept the room, looking for clues about this simple woman who made him feel such complicated things, so complicated he had tracked her down after all this time, like a besotted fool. The sitting room was furnished simply, with an eye toward comfort rather than glamour. The sofa seemed well used and neat rather than stylish. A half-drunk cup of tea sat on the coffee table, with the remnants of what he assumed to be toast. There were a few photographs in frames beside her on the mantel-piece—a family of three with a mother he took to be Jessa's sister. Others of the sisters together, as small children, then with Jessa as a gawky teenager.

Her eyes were wide and cautious, and she watched him apprehensively as he finally turned his attention to her. If she thought to hide her responses from him, it was much too late. He was as attuned to her body as to his own.

Tariq reminded himself that he could not simply order her to his bed, though that would be far simpler than this dance. He did not know why she resisted him. But he was not an untried boy. He could play any games she needed to play. He picked up the nearest photograph and frowned down at it.

"You resemble your sister," he said, without meaning to comment. "Though you are far more beautiful."

Jessa's cheeks colored, and not with pleasure. She reached over and jerked the photograph from his hand, leaving him with only a blurred impression of her less attractive sister, a fair-haired husband, and their infant held between them.

"I won't ask what you think you're doing here," she said in a low, controlled voice. But he could see the spark of interest in her eyes.

"By all means, ask." He dared her, arching his brows and leaning closer, crowding her. He liked the lick of fire that scraped across his skin when he was near her. He wanted more. "I am more than happy to explain it to you. I can even demonstrate, if you prefer." She did not step away, though her color deepened.

"I don't want to know how you justify your behavior," she retorted. She tilted her chin into the air. "We have nothing to discuss."

"You could have told me this on the doorstep," he pointed out softly. "Why did you invite me into your home if we have nothing to discuss?"

She looked incredulous. "Had I refused to answer the door, or to let you in, what would you have done?"

Tariq only smiled. Did she realize she'd conceded a weakness?

"This game will not last long if you already know I will win it," he said. His smile deepened. "Or perhaps you do not wish for it to last very long?"

"The only person playing a game here is you," Jessa retorted.

She put the photograph back on the mantel and then crossed her arms over her chest as she faced him. He moved closer. He stretched one arm out along the mantel and shifted so that they were nearly pressed together, held back only by this breath, or the next. She stood her ground, though he could see it cost her in the pink of her cheeks, hear it in the rasp of her breath. He was close enough to touch her, but he refrained. Barely. He could see her pulse hammer against the side of her neck. It was almost unfair, he thought with a primal surge of very male satisfaction, that he could use her body against her in this way. Almost.

"You keep testing me, Jessa," he whispered. "What if I am no match for it? Who knows what might happen if I lose control?"

"Very funny," she threw back at him, her spine straight though Tariq could tell she wanted to bolt. Instead, she scoffed at him. "When is the last time that happened? Has it *ever* happened?"

Unbidden, memories teased at him, of Jessa sprawled across the bed in his long-ago Mayfair flat, her naked limbs flushed and abandoned beneath him. He remembered the rich, sweet scent of her perfume, her unrestrained smile. The low roll of her delighted laughter, the kind that started in her belly and radiated outward, encompassing them both. The lush swell of her breasts in his hands, her woman's heat against his tongue. And the near-violent need in him for her, like claws in his gut, that nothing could satiate.

He didn't understand all the ways he wanted her. He only knew that she had burrowed into him, and he had never been able to escape her, waking or sleeping. She was his own personal ghost. She haunted him even now, standing so close to him and yet still so far away.

He looked away from her for a moment, fighting for control. She took that as a response.

"Exactly," she said as if she'd uncovered a salient truth. "You are not capable of losing control. No doubt, that serves you well as a king."

Tariq turned his head and found her watching him, color high on her cheeks and her cinnamon-brown eyes bright. Did she mean to insult him? Tariq did not know. But he did know that he was more than a match for her. There was one arena where he held all the power, and both of them knew it.

"You misunderstand me," he murmured. He reached over and slid his hand around the back of her neck, cupping the delicate flesh against his hard palm and feeling the weight of her thick, copper curls. She jumped, then struggled to conceal it, but it was too late. He could feel her pulse wild and insistent against his fingers, and he could see the way her mouth fell open, as if she was dazed.

He did not doubt that she did not *want* to want him. He had not forgotten the days she had disappeared, which had been shockingly unusual for a girl who had always before been at his beck and call, just as he had not forgotten his own panicked response to her unexpected unavailability, something he might have investigated further had history and tragedy not intervened. But there was no point digging into such murky waters, especially when he did not know what he would find there. What mattered was that she still wanted him. He could feel it with his hands, see it in the flush of her skin and the heat in her gaze.

"Tariq—" she began.

"Please," he murmured, astounded to hear his own voice. Astonished that he, Sheikh Tariq bin Khaled Al-Nur, would beg. For anything, or any reason. And yet he continued. "I just want to talk."

Was he so toothless, neutered and tame? But he could not seem to stop himself. He had to see this through, and then, finally, be rid of her once and for all. If there was another way, he would have tried it already. He *had* tried it already!

"About us."

* * *

Us. He'd actually said the word *us*.

The word ricocheted through Jessa's mind, leaving marks, much like she suspected his hand might do if he didn't take it off her—if she didn't burst into flame and burn alive from the slight contact.

As if there had ever been an *us* in the first place!

"You have to get on with your life," her sister Sharon had told her, not unkindly, about two weeks after everything had come to such a messy, horrible end in London and Jessa had retreated to York. Crawled back, more like, still holding the secret of her pregnancy close to her chest, unable to voice the terrifying truth to anyone, even her sister. And all while Tariq's face was on every television set as the tragedy in Nur unfolded before the world. The sisters had sat together in Jessa's small bedroom while Sharon delivered her version of comfort. It was brisk and unsentimental, as Sharon had always been herself.

"I don't know what that means," Jessa had said from the narrow bed that had been hers as a girl, when Sharon had taken the reins after their parents died within eighteen months of each other. Eight years older, Sharon and her husband Barry had taken over the house and, to some extent, the parenting of Jessa, while they tried and failed to start their own family.

"It means you need to get your head out of the clouds," Sharon had said matter-of-factly. "You've had an adventure, Jessa, and that's more than some people ever get. But you can't lie about wallowing in the past forever."

Tariq hadn't felt like the *past* to Jessa. Or even an *adventure*. Even after everything that had happened—after losing her job, her *career*, her self-respect; after finding herself pregnant and her lover an unreachable liar, however little she might have come to terms with that—she still yearned for him. He'd felt like a heart that beat with hers, louder and more vibrant inside her chest than her own, and the thought of the gray, barren life she was expected to live without him was almost more than she could bear. She had choked back a sob.

"Men like him are fantasies," Sharon had said, with no little pity. "They're not meant for the likes of you or me. Did you imagine he'd sweep you off to his castle and make you his queen? You, little Jessa Heath of Fulford? You always did fancy yourself something special. But you've had your bit of fun and now it's time to be realistic, isn't it?"

Jessa had had no choice but to be realistic, she thought now. But Tariq was back and there was far too much at stake, and she still couldn't think straight while he touched her. And he wanted to talk about *us,* of all things.

"There is no *us*," she said crisply, as if she was not melting, as if she was still in control. She met his gaze squarely. "I'm not sure there ever was. I've no idea what game you thought you were playing."

"I have a proposition for you," he said calmly, as if what she'd said was of no matter. He lounged back against the mantelpiece, letting his hand move from her skin slowly. He was every inch the indolent monarch.

"It is barely half-nine and here you are propositioning me," Jessa replied, determined to get her balance back. She kept her voice dry, amused. Sophisticated, the way she imagined the glamorous women he was used to would speak to him when he propositioned them. "Why am I not surprised?"

If her heart beat faster and her skin felt overheated, and

she could still feel his hand on her like a tattoo, she ignored it.

"Am I so predictable?" His hard face looked cast in iron in the low gloom from the front windows. And yet Jessa sensed that the real shadows came from within him.

She stood ramrod straight because she could not allow herself to move, to back away from him. She thought it would show too much, be too much of a concession. She laced her fingers together in front of her as tightly as possible.

"It is not a question of whether or not you are—or were— predictable," she said coolly. She raised her eyebrows in un- mistakable challenge. "Perhaps you were simply like any other man when things got too serious. Afraid."

He stilled. The temperature in the room seemed to plunge. Jessa's heart stuttered to a halt. She knew, suddenly, that she was in greater danger from him in that moment than ever before. Something dark moved across his face, and then he bared his teeth in something far too wild to be a smile.

"Proceed with care, Jessa," he advised her in a soft voice that sent a chill snaking down her spine. "Not many people would dare call a king a coward to his face."

"I am merely calling a spade a spade," Jessa replied, as if she did not have a knot of trepidation in her stomach, as if she was not aware that she was throwing pebbles at a lion. She shook the loose tendrils of her hair back from her face, wishing her curls did not take every opportunity to defy her. "You were not yet a king when you ran away, were you?"

"Ran away?" he echoed, enunciating each word as if he could not quite comprehend her meaning.

"What would you call it?" she asked coolly. Calmly. She even smiled, as if they shared a joke. "Adults typically have conversations with each other when an affair is ending, don't they? It's called common courtesy, at the very least."

"Again," he said, too quietly, "you have forgotten the sequence of events. You were the one who disappeared into thin air." He stood so still, yet reminded Jessa not of a statue, but of a coiled snake ready to strike. Yet she couldn't seem to back down.

"I merely failed to answer my mobile for two days," Jessa replied lightly. "That's not quite the same thing as quitting the country altogether, is it?"

"It is not as if I was on holiday, sunning myself on the Amalfi Coast!" Tariq retorted.

Jessa shook her head at him. "It hardly matters now," she said carelessly, as if her heart hadn't been broken once upon a time. "I'm only suggesting that perhaps it was a convenient excuse, that's all. An easy way out."

Tariq was so still it was as if he'd turned to stone. He studied her as if he had never seen her before. She had the sudden, uncomfortable notion that he was assessing her as he might an enemy combatant on the field of battle, and was coldly scanning her for her weaknesses. Her soft points.

And all the while that awareness swirled around them, making everything seem sharper, brighter.

"I will not explode into some dramatic temper tantrum, if that is your goal with these attacks," Tariq said finally, never looking away from her. She felt her cheeks heat, whether in relief or some stronger emotion, she didn't know. "I will not rage and carry on, though you question my honor and insult my character." His hard mouth hinted at a curve, flirted with it. "There are better ways to make my feelings known."

She refused to feel the heat that washed through her. She would not accept it. The tightness in her belly was agitation, worry, nothing more. But the desperate, purely feminine part of her that still wanted him, that thirsted for his touch in ways she could not allow herself to picture, knew better.

"What, then?" she demanded, unable to pull her gaze from his. What was this intoxicating fire that burned between them, making her ask questions she knew she did not want the answers to? "What is your damned proposition?"

"One night." He said it so easily, yet with that unmistakably sensual edge underneath.

Somewhere deep inside, she shuddered, and the banked fire she wanted to deny existed flared into a blaze.

His gaze seemed to see into her, to burn through her. "That is all, Jessa. That is what I want from you."

CHAPTER FOUR

Tariq's words echoed in the space between them, bald and naked and challenging. Jessa swallowed. He saw her hands tremble, and a kind of triumph moved through him. She could not control what would happen. Perhaps she even knew it. But she did not back down. She still thought she could fight him. It made him want her all the more.

He knew, even if she did not, that she was going to end this confrontation in his bed. Beneath him, astride him, on her knees before him—he didn't care. He only knew that he would win, and not only because he always won. But because he would accept no other outcome, not with this woman. Not when she had been in his head for all these years.

Because he already knew how this would end, he could be patient. He could wait. He could even let her fight him, if she wished it. What would it matter? It would only make it that much better in the end.

"I don't want to misunderstand you again," she said after a long moment. She searched his face, her own carefully blank.

He realized that he liked this grown-up, self-assured version of Jessa. He liked that she stood up to him, that she was mysterious, that she was neither easily read nor easily intimidated. When was the last time anyone had defied him?

"One night of what?" she asked.

"Of whatever I want," he said softly, pouring seduction into every syllable. "Whatever I ask."

"Be specific, Tariq," she said, an edge to her voice. He interpreted it as desire she would have preferred not to feel.

"As you wish," he murmured. He leaned toward her, pleased with the way she jerked back, startled, and the way her breath came too quickly. "I want you in my bed. Or on the floor. Or up against the wall. Or all of the above. Is that specific enough?"

"No!" She threw one hand into the air as if to hold him back, but it was too late for that. Tariq moved closer and leaned toward her, until her outstretched palm pressed up against his chest. Her hand was the only point of contact between them, her fingers trembling in the hollow between the hard planes of his pectoral muscles.

She did not drop her hand. He did not lean back.

"No, what?" he asked with soft, sensual menace. "No, you do not wish to give me that night? Or no, you do not want to hear how I will sink inside you, making you clench and moan and—"

"Don't be ridiculous!" She whispered the words, but her eyes glazed with heat and something else, and the hand she held between them had softened into a caress, touching him rather than holding him off.

"It is many things," Tariq said in a low voice, "but it is not ridiculous."

He took her hand in his and, never looking away from her, raised her wrist to his lips. He tasted her, her skin like the finest silk, and her pulse beneath it, fluttering out her excitement, her distress. It was like wine and it went to his head, knocking into him with dizzying force.

She made some sound, as if she meant to speak. Perhaps she did, and he could not hear her over the roaring in his ears, his blood, his sudden hardness. He had not expected the surge of lust so sharp and consuming. It barreled through his body from their single point of contact, making him burn. Making him *want*.

It was worse now that he touched her, now that he was before her, than it had been when he only remembered. Much worse.

"I want you out of my system," he told her, his voice urgent and deep. Commanding, because he meant it more than he had just moments before. Because he was desperate. He needed a queen and he needed heirs, and she was what kept him from doing that duty. He had to erase the hold she had on him! "Once and for all. I want one night."

One night.

Jessa stared at Tariq in shock for a moment, as the impossible words shimmered between them like heat. The breathtaking strength of his hard chest against her palm made her whole arm ache, and the ache radiated through her, kicking up brushfires everywhere it touched. Her mind could not seem to process what he'd said, but her body had no such difficulty. She felt her breasts swell in reaction, her nipples hardening into tight, nearly painful points that she was grateful he couldn't possibly see beneath the wool sweater she'd thrown on earlier. Between her legs, she ached, even as her body readied itself for him. Awareness, thick and heavy and intoxicating, thrummed through her. She was electric.

And he was watching her.

Jessa could no longer bear his proximity. And why was she still touching him? Why had she let the moment draw out? No longer caring that he might see it as a victory—only needing space between them—she snatched her hand away from the heat of his body and moved to the other side of the room. There was only her coffee table between them when she stopped, but it was something. It made her feel slightly less hysterical, slightly less likely to pretend the past five years had never happened and fling herself into his arms. How had she lost control of herself so quickly?

"I beg your pardon," she began in her stiffest, most formal tone.

"Do you?" he interrupted her, leaning so nonchalantly against her mantel, so big and dark and terrifying, with all of that disconcerting, green-eyed attention focused intently upon her. He was like her own personal fallen angel, come to take her even further into the abyss. She had to remember why she could not let him. "Do not beg my pardon when there are so many more interesting things you could beg me for."

He was so seductive even when she knew better. Or perhaps it was only that she was so susceptible and weak where he was concerned. She could feel his hands on her, though he had not moved. Her palm itched with the need to soothe itself against the steellike muscles of his chest once more. How could her body want him, still? She had been so sure she was over him, finally. She had been certain of it. She had even, recently, begun to imagine a future in which Tariq was not the shadow over her life, but a bittersweet memory.

"You must be joking," she said, because that was what she might say if her body wasn't staging a full-scale revolt—if, in fact, she felt as she ought to feel toward this man. It had taken her five years to get over him once. What would it be like a second time? It didn't bear considering.

"I assure you, I have no sense of humor at all where you are concerned," he said.

Somehow, she believed him. And yet there was a certain gleam in his dark eyes that convinced her she was better off not knowing exactly what he meant by that remark.

"Then you are insane," she declared. "I would no more spend one night with you then I would prance naked down Parliament Street!"

As she heard it echo around her lounge, it occurred to her that a wise woman might not have used the word *naked* in front of this man, in defiance of this man. Tariq did not seem to move, and yet at the same time he seemed to grow larger. Taller, darker, *more*. As if he blocked all the exits and kept her chained where she stood, all because he willed it. How did he do such a thing? Had he always been so effortlessly irresistible? In her memories, he had taken over every room he had ever entered with the sheer force of his magnetism, but she had supposed that to be her own infatuation at play, not anything he did himself.

"What I mean," she said when he simply studied her in that hawkish, blood-stirring way that made her mouth go dry and made her wonder if she might be more his prey than she knew, than she wanted to know. "What I mean is that of course I will not spend a night with you. There is far too much water under the bridge. I'm surprised you would ask."

"Are you?" He looked supremely unconcerned. Imperial. A brow arched. "I did not ask."

Of course he had not actually asked. Because he was the King of Nur. He did not need to ask. He needed only to incline his head and whatever he desired was flung at his feet, begging for the chance to serve him. Hadn't she done the same five years ago?

He had no more than glanced at her across the busy office that fateful day and Jessa had been his. Just like that. It had been that immediate and all-consuming. She had not even waited for him to approach her. As if she was a moth drawn inexplicably and inexorably to the flame that would be the death of her, she had risen to her feet and then walked toward him without so much as a thought, without even excusing herself from the conversation she was taking part in. She had no memory of moving, or choosing to go to him. He had merely looked at her with his dark sorcerer's eyes and she had all but thrown herself at him.

And that had been while he was playing his game of pretending to be a doctor's son with some family money, but otherwise of interest to no one. Now he was no longer hiding—now he was a king. No wonder he seemed so much more powerful, so much more alluring, so much more devastating.

"Then you have saved me the trouble of refusing you," Jessa said, fighting to keep her voice calm, with all the tension ratcheting through her. "Good thing you did not bother to ask."

"Why do you refuse?" Tariq asked quietly, straightening from the mantel. It was as if he stepped directly into her personal space, crowding her, though he was still all the way across the room. Jessa eased away from him, from the powerful energy he seemed to exude like some kind of force field, but she had to stop when the backs of her knees hit the couch.

You cannot run, she warned herself. *He would only chase you. And you must think of Jeremy. You must!*

"Why do you want one night?" Jessa retorted. She

shoved her hands into the pockets of her trousers, trying to look calm even if she didn't feel it. "And why now? Five years is a bit too long for me to believe you've been carrying a torch." She laughed at the very idea, the sound dying off when he only looked at her, a truth shimmering in his dark gaze that she refused to accept.

"I told you that I must marry." He shrugged, as if a lifelong commitment was no more interesting to him than a speck of dust. Perhaps it was not. "But first I wanted to make sure you were no longer a factor. You can understand this, can't you?"

"I would have thought I ceased being any kind of factor some time ago," Jessa said. Was her tone the dry, sophisticated sort of tone she'd aimed for? She feared it was rather more bitter than that, and bit her lower lip slightly, wishing she could take it back.

Tariq rubbed at his chin with one hand, still watching her closely, intently, as if he could see directly into her.

"Who can say why certain things haunt a man?" He dropped his eyes. "After my uncle died, my life was no longer my own. My every breath and every thought was of necessity about my country. It was not enough simply to accept the crown. I had to learn how to wear it." He shook his head slightly, as if he had not meant to say something so revealing. He frowned. "But as it became clear that I could not delay my own marriage further, I knew I could not marry with this history hanging over me. And so I resolved to find you. It is not a complicated story."

This time, when he looked at her, his dark green eyes were even more unreadable than before.

"You expect me to believe that you…" She couldn't bring herself to say it, it was too absurd. "There is no history hanging over us!"

"You are the only woman who has ever left me," he told her. His tone was soft, but there was a hard, watchful gleam in his gaze. "You left an impression."

"I did not leave you!" she gritted out. There was no way to explain why she had gone incommunicado for those days—she who had rarely been out of his sight for the wild, desperate weeks of their affair.

"So you say." He shrugged, but his attention never left her face. "Call it what you wish. You were the only one to do it."

"And this has led you to track me down all these years later," Jessa said softly. She shook her head. "I cannot quite believe it."

The air around them changed. Tightened.

"Can you not?" he asked, and there was something new in his voice—something she could not recognize though she knew in a sudden panic that she should. That her failure to recognize it was a serious misstep.

Satisfaction, she thought with abrupt insight, but it was too late.

He crossed the room, rounded the coffee table in a single step and pulled her into his arms.

"Tariq—" she began, panicked, but she had no idea what she meant to say. All she could feel were his arms like steel bands around her, his chest like a wall of fire against hers. And all she could see was his hard face, lit with an emotion she could not name, serious as he looked down at her for a long, breathless moment.

"Believe this," he said, and fitted his mouth to hers.

CHAPTER FIVE

JESSA'S world spun, until she no longer knew if she stood or if she fell, and the mad thing was that she didn't much care either way.

Not as she wanted to. Not as she should.

Tariq's hard, hot mouth moved on hers and she forgot everything. She forgot all the reasons she should not touch him or go near him at all. She forgot why she needed to get rid of him as quickly as possible, so that he could never find out her secrets. So that he could not hurt her again as easily as he'd done before.

None of that seemed to matter any longer. All she cared about was his mouth. All she wanted was *more*.

He knew exactly how to kiss her, how best to make her head spin in dizzy circles. Long, drugging strokes as he tasted her, sampling her mouth with his, angling his head for a better, sweeter fit.

"Yes," she murmured, barely recognizing her own voice.

Sensation chased sensation, almost too much to bear. His strong hands moved over her, one flexed into the thick mass of her hair at the nape of her neck while the other splayed across the small of her back, pressing her hips against his. His clever, arousing mouth moved slick and hot against hers. Fire. Heat. Awe. The potent mix of vibrant memory and new, stunning sensation. Touching him was the same, and yet so very different. He tasted like some heady mix of spices, strong and not quite sweet, and she was drunk on it, on him, in seconds.

She could feel him everywhere, pumping through her veins, wrapped around each beat of her heart as it pounded a hectic rhythm against her chest. How had she lived without this for so long? She could not get close enough to him. She could not breathe without breathing him in. She could not stop touching him.

She let her hands explore him, trailing down the length of his impossibly carved torso, like something sculpted in marble, though his skin seemed to blaze with heat beneath her hands. He was nothing as cold as stone. He was so big, bigger than she remembered, and huskier. His strong shoulders were far wider than his narrow hips, his muscles hard from some kind of daily use. She traced patterns across the breadth of his lean back, feeling his strength and his power in her palms.

Tariq muttered something she could not understand. His hands stroked down the length of her back to cup her bottom, urging her closer until she was pressed tight against his thighs and the rock-hard maleness between them. She gasped. She felt her core melt and tremble against him. He sighed slightly, as if in relief. Jessa heard a distant crooning sound and realized, only dimly, that it came from her.

And still, he kissed her. Again and again. As if he could not stop. As if he, too, remembered that it had always been this way between them—this dizzying, terrifying rush of lust and need and *now*. Jessa could not seem to shake the memories that scrolled through her mind, each more sensual than the last, or the shocking fact that this was real, that they were doing this, all these years later.

She could not think. She could not imagine why she *should* think.

She twined her arms around his neck, arching her back to press her swollen, tender breasts against the hard planes of his chest, tilting her head back to give him better access. He did not disappoint. He broke from her mouth, his breathing harsh, and kissed his way down her cheek, her neck. His mouth was like a hot brand against her skin.

"More," he whispered, and his hands went to the hem of her sweater, pulling it up past her hips, then pausing when he uncovered her breasts. He looked at them for a long moment, as if drinking them in. Then he caressed each puckered nipple and tight globe in turn, shaping them through the camisole she wore, while Jessa moaned in mindless, helpless pleasure. Her sex ached, and she could feel an answering heat behind her eyes. She felt burned alive, eaten whole. She wanted more than his hands. She *wanted*.

Muttering a curse, Tariq stripped the sweater from her body, guiding her head through the opening with his strong, sure hands. He tossed it aside without glancing at it, and then paused for a moment to look down at her, his hard eyes gleaming in the gray morning light. The expression she read there made her belly clench, and pulse to a low, wild drum within.

Jessa's nipples stood at attention, tight and begging for his mouth. She could feel the hungry, restless heat in her core, begging for his mouth, his hand, his sex. Even her mouth was open slightly and softened, swollen from his kisses, begging for more of the same.

Could actual begging be far behind? How soon before she was right where she swore she'd never be again—literally on her knees, perhaps? Clutching desperately at him as he walked away once more?

The thought was like cold water. A slap. Jessa blinked, and sanity returned with an unwelcome thump, jarring her.

She staggered backward, away from him, out of reach of his dangerous hands. How could she have let this happen? How could she have allowed him to touch her like this?

Again, she thought wildly. *How can he do this* again*?*

"Stop," she managed to say, pushing the word out through the hectic frenzy that still seized her. He had broken her heart five years ago. What would he do this time? What else could he break? It had taken all these years to come to a place of peace about everything that happened, and here she was, tumbling right back into his arms again, just like before.

She hadn't believed that he could want her then, and she didn't believe it now, not deep inside of herself. She had never known what game he had been playing and what had led a man like him to notice someone like her. And here she was, much older and wiser, about to make the same mistake all over again! Just like last time, he would leave her when he was finished with her. And he *would* finish with her, of that she had no doubt. The only question was how much of herself she would turn over to him in the meantime, and how far she would have to go to get herself back when he left her, shattered once more.

No. She could not do this again. She would not.

"You do not want to stop," he said in that dark, rich voice that sent her nerve endings into a joyful dance and made her that much more resolute. "You only think that you do. Why think?"

"Why, indeed?" she asked ruefully, trying to pull herself together. She stood up straight, and smoothed her palms over the mess of her hair. She was afraid to look into the mirror on the far wall. She felt certain she didn't wish to know how she looked just now. Wanton and on the brink of disaster, no doubt.

"Whatever else passed between us, there is still this," Tariq continued, just short of adamant. "How can we ignore it?"

His voice tugged at her, as if it was something more than sex for him. As if it could ever be anything more than that, with this man! Why hadn't she learned her lesson?

"I won't deny that I'm still attracted to you," Jessa said carefully, determined that her inner turmoil should not come out in her voice. That she should somehow transmit a calmness she did not feel. "But we are adults, Tariq. We are not required to act on every last feeling."

"We are not *required* to, no," Tariq replied smoothly, a perfect echo of the easy, tempting lover he had been before, always willing to pursue passion above all else. It was how he had lived his life. He even smiled now, as if he was still that man. "But perhaps we should."

Jessa took a moment to reach over and draw her sweater toward her, trying to take deep, calming breaths. She pulled it back over her head as if it were armor and might protect her. She smoothed the scratchy wool material down over her hips, and then adjusted the heavy copper spill of her hair, pushing it back over her shoulders. Then she realized she was fidgeting. He would read far too much into it, and so she stilled herself.

How could she want him, as if it were no more than a chemical decision, outside of her control? Yes, of course, he was a devastatingly handsome man. There was no denying it. If he were a stranger and she saw him on the street, Jessa would no doubt find him enthralling. Captivating. But he was not a stranger. He was Tariq bin

Khaled Al-Nur. She knew him too well, and she had every reason in the world to be effectively allergic to him. Instead, she melted all over him and had to bite the inside of her cheek to keep from asking for more.

Begging for more, even.

She wanted to be furious with herself. But what she was, instead, was terrified. Of her own responses, her own reaction to him. Not even of Tariq himself.

"I thought perhaps you wished to talk about something of import," she said, sounding merely prim to her own ears, when she wanted to sound tough. She cleared her throat and then indicated the two of them with her hand. "*This* is not something I want. It's not something I need in my life, do you understand?"

"Is your life so full, then?" His dark eyes bored into her. His mouth was serious, flat and firm. "You never think of the past?"

"My life is full enough that the past has no place." She raised her chin, a bolt of pride streaking through her as she thought about how she had changed since he had known her. In ways both seen and unseen, but she knew the difference. She wondered if he could see those differences, but then told herself it hardly mattered. "It would not seem so to a king, I imagine, but I am proud of my life. It's simple and it's mine. I built it from scratch, literally."

"And you think I cannot understand this? That I cannot grasp what it is to build a life from nothing?" He shifted his weight, reminding Jessa that they were standing far too close to the sofa, and that it would be much too easy to simply fall backward and take him with her, letting him crush her so deliciously against the sofa cushions with his—

Enough! she ordered herself. *You cannot allow yourself to get carried away with him!*

"I know you cannot possibly understand," she replied. She moved then, rounding the coffee table and putting more space between them. She had always thought her sitting room was reasonably sized, a bit roomy, even. Now it felt like the inside of a closet. Or a small box. She felt there was nowhere she could go that he could not reach her, should he wish to. She felt trapped, hemmed in. *Hunted.* So why did something in her rejoice in it? "Just as I do not pretend to understand the daily life of the ruler of a country. How could I? It is beyond imagination."

"Tell me, then," he said, tracking her as she moved toward the window, then changed direction. "Tell me what it is like to be Jessa Heath."

"How could I possibly interest you?" she demanded, stopping in her tracks. She threw him an incredulous look. "Why would you want to know anything so mundane?"

"You would be surprised at the things I want to know." He slid his hands into the pockets of his dark jeans and considered her for a moment. Once more, Jessa was certain there was more going on than met the eye. As if, beneath those smooth words he hid sharp edges that she could only sense but not quite hear. "I have told you that you have haunted me across the years, yet you do not believe it. Perhaps if you told me more about yourself, I would find you less fascinating."

"I am a simple woman, with a simple life," she told him, her voice crackling with a kick of temper that she did not entirely understand. She didn't believe that he was mocking her. But neither did she believe that she could have fascinated him. With what? Her utter spinelessness? Or had he truly believed that she had left him and was one of those men who only wanted what he thought out of reach?

"If you are as proud of this life as you claim, why should

you conceal it?" he asked, too reasonably. Too seductively. "Why not seek to sing it from the rooftops instead?"

Frustrated, Jessa looked away for a moment, and felt goose bumps rise along her arms. She crossed them in front of her and tried to rub at her shoulders surreptitiously. She just wanted him to leave. Surely once he did, everything would settle back into place, as if he had never been.

"I would think you as likely to be interested in watching paint dry as in the life and times of an ordinary Yorkshire woman," she said in a low voice.

"It is possible, I think, that you do not know me as well as you believe you do," Tariq said in a haughty, aristocratic voice. No doubt he used this exact tone when ordering his subjects about. No doubt they all genuflected at the sound of it. But Jessa was not one of his subjects.

"My life is not a great story," she threw at him, daring him to judge her and find her lacking, yet knowing he could not fail to do so. "I wake up in the morning and I go to work. I like my job and I'm good at it. My boss is kind. I have friends, neighbors. I like where I live. I am happy." She could feel the heat in her eyes, and hoped he would think it was nothing more than vehemence. She wished she could convince herself of it. "What did you expect? That my life would be nothing but torment and disaster without you?"

His mouth moved, though he did not speak. It was tempting to tell him exactly how much she had suffered, and why—but she knew better. If he did not know too much already, then he could not know about Jeremy, ever. What was done was done. Tariq might think she did not know him, but she knew enough to be certain that he would handle that news in only one, disastrous way. And if he was only going to disappear again—and she knew without a single doubt that he was—she knew she couldn't risk telling him about Jeremy.

"Please go," she said quietly. She couldn't look at him. "I don't know why you came to find me, Tariq, but it's enough now. We did not require a reunion. You must leave."

"I leave tonight," he said after a moment, and her gaze snapped to his, startled. "You seem skeptical," he taunted her softly. "I am devastated that you find me so untrustworthy. Or is it that you did not expect me to go?"

"I hope you found what you were looking for here," she said, unable to process the various emotions that buffeted her. Intense, all-encompassing relief. Suspicion. And a pang of something she refused to call loss. "It was not necessary to dredge up ancient history, however."

"I am not so sure I agree," Tariq mused. His mouth looked so hard and incapable of the drugging kisses she knew he could wield with it. "Have dinner with me, tonight." He paused. Then, as an afterthought, as if he was unused to the word, he added, "Please."

Jessa realized she was holding her breath, and let it out.

"I don't think that's a good idea," she said, frowning, but more at herself than at him. Why did something in her want to have dinner with him—to prolong the agony? What could she possibly have to gain? Especially when there was so much to lose—namely, her head and her heart?

"If it is a good idea or a bad one, what does it matter?" Tariq shrugged. "I have told you I am leaving. One dinner, that is all. Is that too much to ask? For old time's sake?"

Jessa knew she should refuse him, but then what would he do? Show up here again when she least expected it? Somehow, the idea of him in her house at night seemed far more dangerous—and look what had happened already in broad daylight! She could not let him come back here. And if that meant one more uncomfortable interaction, maybe it was worth it. She was a grown woman who had told herself for years now that she had been an infatuated child when she'd met Tariq, and that the agony of losing him had been amplified by the baby she had carried. It had never occurred to her that seeing him again might stir up such strong feelings. It had never crossed her mind that she could still harbor any feelings for him! Maybe it was all for the best that she finally faced them.

And anyway, it was in public. How dangerous could even Tariq be in a roomful of other people?

In the back of her mind, something whispered a warning, but it was too late. Her mouth was already open.

"Fine," she said. It was for the right reasons, she told herself. It would bring closure, no more and no less than that. "I will have dinner with you, but that is all. Only dinner."

But she was not certain she believed herself. Maybe she could not be trusted any more than he could.

Satisfaction flashed across his face, and his mouth curved slightly.

Jessa knew she'd made a terrible mistake.

"Excellent." He inclined his head slightly. "I will send a car for you at six o'clock."

CHAPTER SIX

IT WAS only when Jessa found herself seated at a romantic table out on the fifth-story terrace of one of the finest houses she had ever seen, improbably located though it was in Paris, France, not far from the Arc de Triomphe, that she accepted the truth she had known on some level from the moment she'd so thoughtlessly agreed to this dinner: she was outmatched.

"I am pleased you could make it," Tariq said, watching her closely for her reaction. Jessa ordered herself not to give him one, but she could feel her mouth flatten. Had he had any doubt she would come?

"I was hardly given any choice, was I?" she asked. He had played her like the proverbial fiddle, and here she was, out of the country and entirely within his power.

Tariq only smiled arrogantly and waved at the hovering servant to pour the wine.

They sat outside on the terrace that circled the top floor of the elegant home, surrounded by carved stone statuary and wrought iron, the Paris night alive around them with lights and sounds. Yet Jessa could not take in the stunning view laid out before her, much less the beautiful table set with fine linen and heavy silver. Her head still whirled until she feared she might faint. She stared at Tariq from her place across from him while conflicting emotions crashed through her, but he only smiled slightly indulgently and toyed with the delicate crystal stem of his wineglass. And why should he do anything else?

She had taken care to wear her best dress, there was no pretending otherwise. If it was within the realm of possibility for someone like her to impress him, she'd wanted to do it—and now the royal-blue sheath dress she'd felt so pretty in earlier felt like sackcloth and ash against her skin, outclassed as it was by the splendor of Paris and what she knew was simply *one* of the homes Tariq must own.

How had she ever dreamed she could compete with this man, much less fascinate him in any way, no matter what lies he told? And the most important question was *why* had she wanted to do so in the first place? What did she hope to win here? She knew that he desired her, but she had already learned exactly how much stock he put in such things, hadn't she? As her sister had told her years before, *at the end of the day you're not the type a man like that will marry, are you?*

Whatever happened tonight, Jessa could never tell herself she hadn't known better.

Of her own free will she had stepped into the car he'd sent. She hadn't complained when, instead of delivering her to some appropriately luxurious hotel in the York area that might live up to the expectations of a king, whatever those might be, it had taken her instead to the Leeds Bradford Airport. She hadn't uttered a sound when she was handed aboard the impressive private jet by his ever-courteous, ever-solicitous staff. She'd told herself some story about Tariq's self-importance and had imagined she would make cutting remarks to him about his having to fly down to London for dinner. She had even practiced the sort of urbane, witty things she might say as she relaxed against the deep, plush leather seats and accepted a glass of wine from the friendly and smiling air hostess.

But then one hour had turned to two, and she had found herself emerging not in London at all, but in Paris. France.

To whom, exactly, should she complain? Tariq hadn't even been aboard the plane to compel her to come here. The scary thing was that Jessa knew full well that she had compelled herself.

"You cannot be angry with me," Tariq said softly, his voice low but no less intense. Jessa could feel the rich, slightly exotic sound of it roll through her, as if he'd hit some kind of tuning fork and her body was springing to attention. He nodded toward the view of stately buildings and glittering monuments in the cool night air, then returned his dark gaze to hers. "Such beauty forbids it."

"Can I not?" Jessa folded her hands in her lap and resolved to keep the hysteria at bay no matter what else happened. And if she was honest, what she felt when she looked at him was not hysteria, or anger. It was far more complicated than that.

"You agreed to dinner," Tariq said with a supremely arrogant shrug. A smile played with the corner of his mouth but did not quite take root there. "You did not specify where."

"Silly me," Jessa said. She met his eyes calmly, though it cost her something. "It never occurred to me that one was required to designate a preferred country when one agreed to a meal." *Under duress,* she wanted to say but did not. It wasn't entirely true, was it?

"There are many things that have not occurred to you, it seems," Tariq replied. Jessa did not care to explore the layers or possible meanings in that remark.

"You mean because of your vast wealth and resources," she said instead, as if she was used to discussing such things with various members of assorted royal families. "It is only to be expected when one is a king, isn't it? Surely these things would be much more impressive if they were the result of your own hard work and sweat."

"Perhaps," he said, a dark, affronted edge in his voice, though he did not alter his position. He continued to lounge in his chair like the pasha she supposed he really was. Only his gaze sharpened, piercing her, reminding her that she insulted him at her peril—and only because he allowed it.

"Do you find royalty offensive, Jessa?" he asked in a drawl. His brows rose, mocking her. "You English have a monarch of your own, I believe."

"The Queen has yet to whisk me off to a foreign country for a dinner that would have been uncomfortable enough in the local chip shop," Jessa retorted.

"It will only be uncomfortable if you wish it so," Tariq replied with infuriating patience, as if he knew something she did not. This time he really did smile, and it was not reassuring. "I am perfectly at ease."

"Somehow, that is not soothing," Jessa said, with the closest thing to a real laugh that she had uttered yet in his presence. It surprised them both. He looked startled as their eyes met and held. The moment seemed to stretch out and hover, locking Jessa in the green depths of his eyes with the glorious shine and sparkle of Paris stretching out behind him.

Her gaze drifted to his mouth, that hard, almost cruel mouth that could smile so breathtakingly and could do things to her that made her feel feverish to imagine. She felt her own lips part on a breath, or perhaps it was a sigh, and the world seemed to narrow and brighten all at the same time. She felt the now familiar coiling of tension in her belly, and the corresponding melting in her core. She felt the arch of her back and the matching curve of her toes inside her shoes. She began to *feel* each breath she took, as her heart kicked into a heavy, drugging rhythm that reminded her too well of his mouth upon her own, his hands on her skin.

Suddenly, brutally, the veil lifted. And Jessa realized in a sudden jolt, with an almost nauseating mixture of self-awareness and deep, feminine certainty, that this was exactly why she had come so docilely, so easily. Across borders, onto private planes, with nary a whisper of protest. This was why she had taken such pains in her bath earlier, dabbed scent behind her ears and between her breasts. She had told herself she was putting together her feminine armor. She had told herself she would dress the same way for any person she wished to appear strong in front of, that it was not romantic in the least to want to look her best or pin her hair up into a French twist or wear her most flattering and most lethal shoes. She had lied to herself, even as something within her knew the truth and had cried out for the wicked royal-blue dress that exposed her shoulders, kissed her curves and whispered erotically over her legs.

She had come here for him. For Tariq. For this raging passion that coursed through her veins and intoxicated her, this all-consuming desire that the intervening years and her own sacrifices had failed to douse in any way.

With a muttered oath that even she wasn't sure was a cry of desperation or a simple curse, Jessa rocked forward and to her feet. Restlessly—agitation making her body feel jerky and clumsy—she pushed herself away from the table and blindly headed toward the wrought-iron railing that seemed to frame the Paris street five stories below her feet as much as protect her from falling into it.

The truth seemed as cold as the autumn night, now that she had moved away from the brazier that hovered near the table—and the far more consuming fire that Tariq seemed to light in her.

She wanted him. Arguing with herself did nothing to stop it. She had spent the whole day determined to simply not be at home when he sent his car for her, and yet she had found herself immersed in the bath by half past four. She had ordered herself not to answer the door when the driver rang, but she had had the door open and her wrap around her shoulders before he could press the button a second time.

"Surely this should not distress you," Tariq said from behind her. Too close behind her, and once more she had not heard him move. Jessa closed her eyes. If she pretended, it was almost as if he was the magical, trustworthy lover she had believed him to be so long ago, and she the same starry-eyed, besotted girl. "It is a simple dinner, in a lovely place. What is there to upset you here?"

What, indeed? Only her own betrayal of all she'd thought she believed, all she thought she had gained in the years since his departure. What was that next to a luxurious meal on a Paris rooftop with the man she should avoid above all others?

"Perhaps you do not know me as well as you think," she replied, her voice ragged with all the emotion she fought to keep hidden. Or perhaps she did not know herself.

"Not for lack of trying," Tariq murmured. "But you will keep your mysteries, won't you?"

It was no surprise when his warm, strong hands cupped her shoulders, then stretched wide to test her flesh against his fingers, sending inevitable currents of desire tingling down her arms. She let out a sigh and bowed her head.

Perhaps this was inevitable. Perhaps this had always been meant to happen, somehow. She had never had the chance to say her goodbyes to Tariq, her fantasy lover, had she? She had run away to a friend's flat in Brighton to get her head together. The man she had loved had disappeared, and she learned soon after that he had never existed. But there had been no warning, no opportunity to express her feelings with the knowledge that it was their last time together.

A rebellious, outrageous thought wormed its way through her then, making her catch her breath.

What if she took, instead of lost? What if she claimed, instead of letting herself be deprived? What if she was the one in control, and no longer so passive, so submissive? What if she was the one who needed to get him out of her system, and not the other way around?

She turned in his loose grip, and leaned against the railing, tipping her head back so she could look him in the eye. What if she made this about what *she* wanted?

And what she wanted was the one last night she'd never had. She wanted to say her goodbyes—and it didn't hurt that in giving him one night, in taking it for herself, she was acknowledging that it could never be more than that between them. This was a memory, nothing more.

"I will give you one night," she said, before she lost her nerve. And then it was said, and there was no taking it back.

He froze. His face lost all expression, though his dark eyes glittered with jade fire. She had surprised him. *Good.*

"I beg your pardon?" he asked, enunciating each word very carefully, as if he thought he had misheard her, somehow. It made Jessa feel bolder. "What do you mean?"

"Must I repeat myself?" she asked, taking too much pleasure in tossing his own words back at him. She felt the power of this choice surge through her. She was the one in charge. She was the one who decided whether or not she would burn on this particular fire. And then she would walk away and finally be done with him. It would be like being reborn. "I don't recall you being so slow—"

"You must forgive me," he interrupted her with precious little civility, his teeth bared in something not at all as mild as a smile. "But why would you change your mind so suddenly?"

"Maybe I've considered things in a different light," Jessa said. Did she have to explain this to him, when she could hardly explain it to herself? She raised her brows. "Maybe I'm interested in the same things that you're interested in. Putting the past behind us, once and for all."

"For old time's sake?" he asked. He moved closer, his big body seeming to block out the City of Lights. Tension radiated from every part of him, and she knew she should be afraid of what he could do to her, what he could make her feel. She knew she should feel intimidated, outmatched once again.

But this was the one place where it didn't matter if he was a king and she a commoner. He wanted her with the same unwelcome intensity that she wanted him. In this, at least, they were equals. They matched.

She felt her mouth curve slightly into a smile that was as old as time, and spoke of a knowledge she had never put into words before, never felt so completely, down into her bones.

"What do you care?" she taunted him softly, daring him, challenging him.

His eyes went darker, his mouth almost grim with the passion she could feel surging through her veins.

"You are right," he said, his voice hoarse, and rough against her, though she welcomed it. Exulted in it. "I do not care at all."

His mouth came down on hers in something like fury, though it was much sweeter. Once again, he tasted her and went wild, and yet he merely kissed her, angling his head to better plumb the depths of her mouth, to intoxicate himself with her, with the feel of her soft body pressed against his. Her softness to his hardness. Her moan against his lips.

He had been prepared to seduce her if he had to. He had not been prepared for her to be the aggressor, and the surprise of it had desire raging through him.

"Be certain this is what you want," he growled, lifting his head and scanning her expression with fierce intensity. Her eyes were glazed with passion, her lips swollen from his kisses. Surely this would put an end to all the madness, all the nights he'd woken and reached for the phantom woman who was never there.

"Have I asked you to stop?" she asked, her breath uneven, her tone pure bravado. She tilted her stubborn chin into the air. "If you've changed your mind—"

"I am not the one who required so many games to achieve this goal," he reminded her, passion making his voice harsh. "I made my proposal from the start, hiding nothing."

"It is up to you," she said, her eyes narrowing in a maddening, challenging manner, her words infused with a certain strength he didn't understand. Who did Jessa Heath think she was that she so consistently, so foolishly, stood up to him, all the while refusing to tell him anything about her life, claiming she could only bore him? He could not recall the last person who had defied, much less taunted, him. Only Jessa dared.

A warning bell rang somewhere deep inside of him, but he ignored it.

"You will find that most things are, in fact, up to me," he replied, reminding them both that he, not she, was the one in charge, no matter how conciliatory he might act when it suited him.

He was a king. He might not have been born to the position, and he might have spent the better part of his life as an embarrassment to the man who had been, but he'd spent the past five years of his life atoning. He was in every way the monarch his uncle would have wished him to be, the nephew he should have been while his uncle lived. No imprudent and foolish woman could change that, not even this one, whom he realized he regarded as a kind of specter from his wastrel past. He would never fully put that past behind him until he put her there, too.

Jessa reached out her hand and placed it against his cheek. Tariq's mind went suddenly, scorchingly, blank as electricity surged between them.

"We can talk, if that is what you want," she said, as calmly as if discussing the evening's dinner menu. As unaffected, though he could feel the slight tremor in her delicate palm that belied her tone. "But it is not what I want."

"And what is it you want?"

"I do not want to talk," she said distinctly, purposefully, holding his gaze, her own rich with suggestion and the desire he was certain was written all over him. "And I don't think you want to, either. Do you?"

"Ah, Jessa," he said on a sigh, while a kind of moody triumph pumped through him and pulsed hard and long into his sex. She thought she was a match for him, did she? She would learn. And soon enough he would have her exactly where he wanted her. "You should not challenge me."

She cocked her head to one side, not cowed in the least, with the light of battle in her cinnamon eyes, and smiled.

It went directly to his head, his groin. He reached for her without thought, without anything at all but need, and pulled her into his arms.

CHAPTER SEVEN

IT WAS not enough. Her taste, her scent, her mouth beneath his and her hands tracing beguiling patterns down his chest. He wanted more.

"I want to taste you," he whispered in Arabic, and she shuddered as if she could understand him.

He wanted everything. Her surrender. Her artless, unstudied passion. The past back where it belonged, and left there.

But most of all, he wanted her naked.

Tariq raked his fingers into her hair, never lifting his mouth from hers, sending her hairpins flying and clattering against the heavy stones at their feet. Her heavy mass of copper curls tumbled from the sophisticated twist at the back of her head and fell in a jasmine-scented curtain around her, wild and untamed, just as he wanted her. Just as he would have her.

He lifted his mouth from hers and took a moment to study her face. Why should he spend even an hour obsessing over this woman? She was no great beauty, like some of the women he had been linked with in the past. Her face would never grace the covers of magazines nor appear on twelve-foot-high cinema screens. Yet even so, he found he could not look away. The spray of freckles across her nose, the sooty lashes that framed her spice-colored eyes—combined with her courtesan's mouth, she was something more unsettling than beautiful. She was... viral. She got into the blood and stayed there, changing and growing, and could not be cured using any of the usual methods.

Tariq had no idea where that appallingly fanciful notion had come from. He would not even be near her now were it not for the mornings he had woken in the palace in Nur, overcome by the feverish need to claim this woman once more. He scowled down at her, and then scowled harder when she only smiled that mysterious smile again in return, unfazed by him.

"Come," he ordered her, at his most autocratic, and took her arm. Not roughly, but not brooking any argument, either, he led her across the terrace and ushered her into the quiet house.

His staff had discreetly lit a few lamps indoors. They cast soft beams of light across the marble floors and against the high, graceful ceilings. He led her through the maze of galleries filled with priceless art and reception rooms crowded with extravagant antiques that comprised a large portion of the highest floor of the house, all of them boasting stellar views of nighttime Paris from the soaring windows. He barely noticed.

"Where are we going?" she asked, but there was a lack of curiosity in her voice. As if she was as cool and as unaffected as she claimed to be, which he could not countenance. Surely it shouldn't matter—surely she could pretend anything she wished and he should not care in the slightest—but Tariq fought to keep himself from growling at her. He could not accept that she was so calm while he felt so wild. Even if her calmness was, as he suspected and wanted to believe, an act.

None of this matters, he reminded himself, coldly. *As long as you get her out of your system, once and for all.*

After all, despite his obsessive concentration on a single woman for far too long, the truth was that Tariq did not have time for this. He had a country to run. Nur was poised on the brink of great change, but change did not come easily, especially in his part of the world. There was always a price. There were always those who preferred to stick to the old ways, out of fear or faith or sheer stubbornness. There were those who wanted only to see the old regime, of which Tariq was the last surviving member, crumble and disappear, and no matter that such a thing would cause even more chaos and bloodshed.

There were border disputes to settle, and tribal councils to oversee. Tariq loved his beautiful, harsh, deeply complicated and often conflicted country more than he had ever loved a human being, including himself. It felt like the worst kind of disloyalty to be tangled up with this woman, especially since she was the last one he had been with in his previous incarnation. Perhaps he judged her more severely because she was the other face he saw when he revisited his old disgraceful behavior in his mind.

Tariq led Jessa into the sumptuous master suite that sprawled across the back of the house, and only released her arm when he had closed the door behind them, shutting them in. Would she still be so brave now that the games were quickly coming to an end? Would she dare to continue this foolishness?

She took a few steps into the room ahead of him, her head slightly bent and her hands clasped in front of her as if she was listening for second thoughts or offering up a prayer. *Too late,* he thought with no little satisfaction. He let his gaze follow the soft indentation of her spine down to the flare of her hips, as the royal-blue dress shimmied in the low lights and seemed to grow brighter in the reflection of the gilt-edged opulence that surrounded them. Tariq was no particular fan of French furniture—he found it too fussy, too liable to collapse beneath his large frame—but he could appreciate the way so much Continental splendor seemed to enhance her natural glow. She turned her head then, looking at him over her shoulder.

It was as if the room smoldered. Tariq thought only of flame, of heat, of burying himself so deeply inside of her that the only thing he'd care about would be the way she gasped his name.

She did not speak. She only watched him, her eyes wide but without apprehension as he closed the distance between them with a few short strides. He reached out and used his hands to trace the parts of her body that his eyes had so recently touched: the soft nape of her neck, the sinuous length of her spine, the mesmerizing place where her hips curved gently into her bottom. He reached down and drew the silky dress up over her legs, slowly, letting the fabric caress her. The room was silent, only the sounds of their breathing and the faint, seductive whisper of fabric moving against flesh. He prolonged the moment, enjoying the way the dress felt in his hands, enjoying more the way her flushed skin felt as he touched her in passing, and then he drew the filmy dress over her head and cast it aside.

She turned to face him then, a flush rising in her cheeks, and he saw her arms move as if she wanted to cover herself or hide from him. She stopped herself, her expression betraying nothing more than a quick blink of her eyes, and dropped her arms back down to her sides.

She stood before him, clad only in a black lace bra that

pushed her breasts toward him, the swell of all that creamy flesh calling his name, begging for his tongue, his hands. Below, she wore nothing save a pair of sheer panties and her wickedly high shoes. She looked like something she was not, or had not been when he knew her, when he had claimed her innocence as his right. She looked decadent. Delicious.

Mine.

"It appears I will have my dessert before my dinner," Tariq said, pushing aside the possessive urge that roared through him. He traced the delicate ridge of her collarbone, dipping into the hollow where her pulse beat hard against her throat. She was like his own private banquet. Just because he had ulterior motives it didn't mean he wasn't prepared to thoroughly enjoy himself.

"Perhaps I want dessert as well," Jessa replied, only the slightest tremor in her voice, as if she was not flushed with color and practically naked before him.

She wanted to be tough. Tariq smiled, released her.

"Then by all means, help yourself."

She swayed toward him, rocking slightly on her feet. It could be the precarious shoes in the deep carpet, though Tariq rather thought it was the same strange hunger that gripped him and made him feel curiously close to unsteady himself. Then her hands were on him, sweeping across the hard planes of his chest, testing the hardy muscles he'd built up after five years of intensive training with his royal guard. A king must be prepared to fight the battles he expected his subjects to fight, Tariq's uncle had always believed. And so Tariq had transformed himself from an idle playboy who visited a fancy spa-like gym merely to maintain a certain trouser size that photographed well, to a warrior capable of lethal combat. He shrugged off his jacket and let it drop to the floor. The expertly tailored concoction barely made a sound as it hit the ground. Jessa did not spare it so much as a glance.

Tariq's eyes narrowed against his own pounding hunger as he let Jessa explore this new, fierce body of his, sliding her palms from his shoulders to his waist to yank his shirt-tails free from his trousers. He watched her pull her seductive lower lip between her teeth as she worried the buttons out of their holes one by one and slowly, torturously, exposed his skin to the slightly cooler air of the suite around them. When she had unbuttoned every button and unhooked his cuff links, she pushed the shirt back on his shoulders so it hung there, exposing his chest to her view.

She let out a long hiss of breath. He could feel it tickle across his skin, arrowing straight to his arousal, making him thicken. He made no move to hide it, only continued to wait, to watch, to see what she would do.

She looked up then, and their gazes clashed together in a manner that seemed as intimate and passionate as the kisses they'd shared before. Tariq moved to speak, but no words came.

He did not expect her to move, her expression taking on a look of intense feminine satisfaction. He reached for her, but she shocked him by leaning forward and placing her hot, open mouth, that wicked courtesan's mouth that had featured prominently in his fantasies since he'd tasted it again this morning, in the valley between his pectoral muscles.

When he swore, he swore in Arabic, Jessa discovered in a distant kind of amusement, and he still sounded every inch a king.

Not that she cared. She could not seem to stop tasting him. She trailed kisses across one hard pectoral plane, then moved to the other, worrying the hard male nipple she found with the tip of her tongue, laughing softly when she heard him groan.

Jessa moved even closer and pushed the soft linen shirt from Tariq's broad shoulders, letting it fall to the floor behind him. His strong, muscled arms came around her, crushing her breasts against his chest and drawing her into the cradle of his thighs. Just like that, they were pressed together, bare skin against bare skin, so that the intrusion of her lacy, delectable bra seemed almost criminal. Heat coiled in her groin and shot through her, making her head spin. She fought to breathe, and wasn't sure she much cared if she could not. She felt his bare skin against hers like an exultation, like memory and fantasy come to life.

She had not felt like this in five long years. She had missed his skin, the addictive heat of him that sizzled through her and left her feeling branded and desperate for more. Her head dropped back of its own volition, and she heard him muttering words she could not understand against the soft flesh of her neck. He used his tongue, his lips, his teeth. He surrounded her, held her, his hands finding her curves and testing them against his palms, stroking and teasing and driving her hunger to fever pitch. And all the while his exciting, overwhelming hardness pressed against the juncture of her thighs, driving her ever closer to senseless capitulation.

This was how it had always been, this rush to madness, to pleasure, to the addictive ecstasy that only Tariq could bring her. She could not get close enough. She could not think straight, and she could not imagine why she would want to. This was how she remembered him, so hard, so male, dominating her so easily, so completely—

Careful! a voice in the back of her mind whispered, panicked. Jessa pulled herself back from the brink of total surrender, blinking to clear the haze of passion from her eyes. It was so easy to lose herself in him. It was much too easy to forget. She raised her head and searched Tariq's expression. His features were hard, fierce and uncompromising as he stared back at her. She felt herself tremble deep inside—warning or *wanting*, she wasn't sure. But it didn't matter. She had been the one to make this decision. She was not weak, malleable, *senseless*. She could call the shots. She would.

"Second thoughts?" His voice was a rasp, thick with passion, and her hips moved against his in unconscious response. His eyes glittered dangerously, nearly black now in the center of the opulent gold-and-blue room.

"None whatsoever," she replied. She eased back from him, aware that he let her do it, let her move slightly in the circle of his embrace.

Holding his gaze with all the defiance she could muster—*I am strong, not weak; I am in charge*—she dropped her hands to his trousers. His hard mouth curved, and he shifted his weight, giving her easier access.

Jessa remembered her horror at exactly this image earlier this same day—her fear that she would far too easily find herself doing what she was about to do. But it was different now, because he was not compelling her to do it. She was not begging him for anything—she was taking what she wanted. He was not orchestrating anything. He was hers to experience as she wished, to make up for all those lonely nights when she would have done anything at all for the chance to touch him again.

She pulled his belt free of its buckle and unbuttoned the top button of his whisper-soft trousers, letting the backs of her fingers revel in the blazing heat of his taut abdomen and the scrape of the coarse hair that surrounded his manhood.

She moved the zipper down slowly, careful to ease it over the hard ridge of his jutting sex, and then she freed him entirely, reaching between them to cup him in her hands.

He muttered something too low to catch, though she thought it was her name.

She could not recall him ever allowing her this kind of unhurried exploration before. Their passion back then had always been too explosive, too all-encompassing. She had never thought to ask for anything. She had been too awash in sensation, too overcome and swept off her feet. She had surrendered to him entirely, body and soul.

But that was the past. Here, now, she caressed his impressive length. He let out a sound too fierce to be a moan. He reached for her, his hands diving once again into the thick mass of her hair and holding her loosely, encouraging her, not correcting her. Jessa ignored him, and concentrated on this most male part of him instead. He was softer here than anywhere else on his rugged warrior's form, like the softest satin stretched across steel. And so much hotter, so hot that she felt an answering heat flood her own sex, and an ache begin to build inside her.

She raised her head up to meet his gaze, while his hands moved to frame her face. She frowned slightly when he bent his head toward hers. He paused, his mouth a scant breath away. Jessa felt her heart pound and could feel him stir in her hands.

"No?" he asked softly. He did not quite frown in return. "Is this another game, Jessa?"

"This is my night." She felt his hands flex slightly, but she felt too powerful to allow him to cow her. "My game."

"Is that so?" His eyes mocked her, though his expression otherwise remained the same. He did not believe she could take control, perhaps. Or he knew how close she came to losing herself, her head, when he touched her. Jessa told herself it didn't matter.

"Perhaps you should tell me the rules of this game, before you begin it." His voice and his eyes were more distant, suddenly, but his hands against the delicate skin of her cheekbones were still warm, still exciting.

"There is only one rule," Jessa said evenly. Deliberately, so there could be no misunderstanding. "And it is that I am in charge."

Something ignited in his gaze then, and sent an answering shudder down along her spine to weaken her knees. He pulled himself up without seeming to move, arrogant and imperial, and looked at her as if he could not comprehend what she had said. Jessa held her breath.

"And what does that entail, exactly?" he asked, his voice lower and laced with warning. "Will I wake to find myself bound naked from the chandelier, to be tittered over and eventually cut down by the housekeeper?"

Jessa tested out the image of Tariq so completely at her mercy and smiled slightly, even as a hectic kind of restlessness washed through her, urging her to continue what her hands had already started. She tested his length against her palm once again and watched his arrogant focus shatter.

"If that is what I want, then yes," she said recklessly. "Don't pretend you won't enjoy it."

"And what about what I want?" he asked. Idly, he wrapped a single long, copper curl around his finger and tugged. Jessa did not mistake the sensual menace underlying his tone. She shrugged.

"What about it?" she asked.

"Jessa—"

But he cut himself off, because Jessa sank down in front of him, onto her knees, in a single smooth motion. She heard his breath leave him in a rush. She watched his eyes darken even further, becoming like night.

She did not feel diminished. She did not feel mindless or senseless, or under his power. Quite the opposite.

She felt like a goddess.

"Jessa," he said again, but this time her name was a prayer. A wish.

She smiled. And then she took him deep into her mouth.

CHAPTER EIGHT

JESSA heard him sigh, or maybe he said her name once more, too low to be heard.

It was thrilling. Jessa felt her own sex throb and melt in time to his slow, careful thrusts, and felt him grow harder. He moaned and she felt potent. Alive. Powerful beyond imagining.

"Enough," he said suddenly, abruptly disengaging from her.

Jessa sat back on her heels, stunned.

"I'm the one who will decide when it's enough," she retorted, glaring up at him. "Not you. Or have you already forgotten that I'm to be in charge?"

"I have not forgotten anything," Tariq replied, his voice clipped, rough, impatient with need. "But perhaps you have forgotten that I did not agree."

"But you—"

"Later," Tariq said, interrupting her. He sank to his knees on the carpet in front of her, making her heart stutter in her chest before kicking into a frenetic beat. This close, Jessa could see the wildness in his eyes, and the passion stamped across his features, giving him a certain breathtaking ferocity.

She started to argue, but instead he leaned closer and claimed her mouth with his. He held her head between his hands, held her captive, and she didn't think to fight it. He moved her to the angle that best suited him, plundering her mouth with his, taking control. Claiming her. Proving his mastery, and it made her ache and swell and melt against him. Again. Then again, and again.

Heat like liquid washed over her, through her. She felt hectic, frantic, alive with need, shaky from the inside out. She buried her hands in his thick, black hair, exulting in the way it felt like rough silk against her palms, in such contrast to the punishing, glorious demands of his mouth.

It occurred to Jessa that she should protest, wrench back the control she refused to accept he'd only allowed her, indulged her.

Tariq took one strong, capable hand from her head and slid it down her back, leaving trails of sensation in his wake, causing her to arch against him at the wonder of his touch. Then he moved around to her front and pulled once, twice, against the band of her panties. By the time Jessa registered the fact that he was using both of his hands, and that he seemed to be tugging, there was a rip and he was done. He tossed her torn panties aside, and the look he slanted her way dared her to comment on it.

She didn't say a word. She wasn't sure she could speak. She was having trouble breathing, much less thinking, as they knelt together in the center of the thick Aubusson carpet.

Tariq's long, elegant fingers slipped between her thighs, tracing the contours of her sex, then the honeyed heat within. His green eyes held her still, imprisoned her, even as he tested her tight sheath with one strong finger, then another. Jessa felt herself clench around him, and shuddered.

"Forgive me, but I cannot wait for you to finish playing

your games with me," he said then, but there was absolutely no apology in the way he looked at her. He was all arrogant male, every inch a king, and he did not wait for her to respond. Instead, he slid his hands back up the length of her torso and then picked her up as if she weighed no more than a pound coin. He shifted her across the space between them and settled her astride him.

"Tariq—" But she didn't know what she wanted to say, or how to say it, and he merely twisted his hips and thrust deep inside her.

So deep. So full. Finally.

"Yes," he said, need pulling his face taut, his eyes black and wild for her. "Finally."

Only then did Jessa realize she'd spoken aloud. Her breasts seemed to swell even more against their prison of lace, and she rubbed herself helplessly against the wall of his chest, unable to stop, unable to get enough of the feel of him. Again. *Finally.*

The perfection of it, of him, of their bodies fused together, overwhelmed her. She had no memory of looping her arms around his neck, and yet she held him. Other memories, older ones, of the many times they'd tested the feverish joy of this slick, matchless, breathtaking union, threatened to spill from her eyes.

Now she remembered why she had thrown away her life so heedlessly because of this man. Now she remembered why she had let Tariq twist her into knots and cast her aside like a rag doll—why she hadn't even recognized what was happening until it was done. For the glory of this moment, this connection, this addictive, electrifying link.

And then he moved, one long, sure stroke, and Jessa came apart. He thrust once, twice. She sobbed against him while her body exploded into pieces, as she shook and shook and shook. She panted, her face in the crook of his neck. The world disappeared and there was nothing but the singular scent and taste of Tariq's skin at her mouth, and his hard length still buried deep in her sex.

"Come back to me." His voice was rough, intimate. "Now." It was no less an order for the sensual tone in which it was delivered. Still, it made her shiver.

"I am finished," she managed to say, her eyes still closed, her head still cradled between his throat and his wide shoulder. She meant, *I am dead.* She was not sure she would have minded were that true.

"But I am not." Tariq shifted position, holding her bottom in one large hand and keeping her hips flush with his. "Hold on to me," he demanded, and she was too dazed, too drunk on the sensations still firing through her to do anything but what he asked. She wrapped her arms around his shoulders and then everything whirled around and she was on her back on the plush carpet and he was between her legs and still so deep inside her, so hard and so big, she thought she might weep from the sheer pleasure of it.

Tariq bent his head and took a stiff nipple into his mouth, sucking on it through the lace barrier. Jessa moaned as a new fire seared through her, the slight abrasion of the lace and the hot, wet heat of his mouth together almost too much to bear.

He laughed softly, and began to move his hips, guiding himself in and out of her with consummate, devastating skill. He turned his attention to her other breast, making Jessa arch into him again and raise her hips to meet his every stroke. Their hips moved in perfect harmony. Once again, she ached. Once again, the fire grew and raged and consumed her. Jessa felt the storm growing within her, taking her to fever pitch, though she fought against it.

"Let go," he said, his voice fierce, his gaze intense.

"But you—and I—" But how could she concentrate on what she wanted to say when every slide of his body against hers turned her molten, incandescent?

"I command it," he said.

Her eyes flew wide. Tariq smiled. And then he reached between their bodies and touched her, and she flew over the edge again.

This time, he did not stop. He did not wait. He continued to thrust into her, slow and steady, until her sobs became ragged breaths and her eyes focused once more on his face.

"One more time," he ordered her, his eyes gleaming.

"I cannot possibly!"

"You can." He bent toward her, pulling the lace cup away from one breast to tease the flesh beneath with his lips. His tongue. His teeth. Jessa shuddered in response. Tariq slanted a look at her. "You will."

And when she did, he went with her.

It took a long time for Jessa to return to earth, and when she did, he was still stretched out over her, still pressing her into the floor. She was afraid to think too much about what had just happened. She was afraid to allow herself to face it. She wasn't certain she would like what she might find.

That much pleasure could only be trouble. She could not assign it too much meaning, decide it was something it could never be. She could not allow herself to forget that this was her idea. That she was here to take some of this pleasure for herself and hoard it. This was her long-overdue goodbye, that was all. She didn't know why she felt so fragile, so vulnerable.

Tariq stirred and rolled off her, sitting up as he yanked his trousers back into place. As he fastened them, Jessa struggled to sit up herself. Was this it, then? She hadn't thought much beyond the actual pleasure part of the *one night of pleasure* idea. How was one expected to negotiate such moments? The last time she had been with him, she had been openly and happily in love with him. There had been no awkwardness. Jessa pulled her bra back into position, and swallowed when her eyes fell on the torn scraps of what used to be her panties. She looked down and saw, with some amazement, that she still wore her impractical shoes.

Beside her, Tariq rose to his feet in a single, lithe movement that reminded her that he was a warrior now, in ways she could only pretend to understand. He turned and looked down at her, his expression unreadable.

Jessa was suddenly painfully aware of her surroundings, the majestic grandeur of the well-appointed room, from its carved moldings to the graceful furniture that looked more like works of art than places to sit or to store belongings. It was not even the bedroom, merely the first in what she could see now was a series of rooms. A suite, complete with floor-to-ceiling windows that showed off the lights of Paris shooting off in all directions. Tariq stood before her, half-naked, his thick hair tangled and hanging around his face, making him look untamed and remote but no less regal. He belonged in such a place, surrounded by such things. And here she was, half-naked on a priceless rug, Jessa Heath from Fulford with nothing to show for herself, not even her panties.

It occurred to her that he had only said he wanted to get her out of his system. He had never elaborated what might happen when he had.

The moment stretched between them, long past awkward. Jessa could still feel him between her legs, and yet it was as if a perfect stranger stood before her, carved from stone. Some avenging angel prepared to hand down judgment.

But she had been through worse, she reminded herself,

and no matter what happened, no matter how unpleasant the moment, she had chosen this. That was the key point. She had *chosen* this.

Jessa sat up straighter and pushed her hair back from her face. It hardly mattered if she looked disheveled at this point, after all. He must have had his mouth or his hands on every inch of her body. And what could he possibly do or say to her? Would he leave her cruelly, perhaps? She had already survived that once, relatively unscathed. She met his gaze proudly.

"Thank you," she said in her most polite tone. It was the one she used in fancy restaurants and to bank managers. "That was exactly what I wanted."

"I am delighted to hear it." His tone was sardonic. "I live to serve." Now he openly mocked her. She pretended she could not hear the edge in his voice.

"Yes, well." She got to her feet with rather less grace than he had displayed, and looked around for her dress. She saw it in a crumpled heap a few feet away. "If only that were true. You would be a different man, wouldn't you?" She moved toward the dress.

"Jessa." Her name was another command, and she looked at him even though she knew she should ignore him, pick up her things and walk out. "What are you doing?"

"My dress..." She gestured at it but couldn't seem to turn away from him, not when he was looking at her that way, so brooding and dark and something else, something she might have called possessive on another man.

"You won't need it."

"I won't?"

He didn't move, he only watched her, but his eyes were hot. Jessa was shocked to feel her body respond to him. Anew. Again. Her nipples hardened, her sex pulsed.

It was absurd. She had gotten what she'd wanted, hadn't she? What was the point of drawing it out? No matter how ravenous she seemed to be for him.

"We are not done here," he said quietly. His gaze was hard, yet she softened. "We have hardly begun."

CHAPTER NINE

TARIQ stood at the window that rose high above the bedroom, looking out over the city. Dawn snuck in with long pink fingers, teasing the famous rooftops of Paris before him, yet he barely saw it. Behind him, Jessa slept in the great bed that stood in the center of the ornate room, the heavy white-and-gold-brocade coverlet long since discarded, her naked limbs curled beneath her, rose and pink from the exertions of the long night. He did not need to confirm this with his own eyes again; he would hear it if her breathing altered, if she turned over, if she awoke.

It was as if he could feel her body as an extension of his own. Perhaps this was inevitable after such a night, he told himself, but he knew better. He had lived a life of excess for more years than he cared to recall, and he had had many nights that would qualify as extreme, and yet he had never felt this kind of connection to a woman. He didn't care for it. It reminded him of all the things he had worked so hard to forget.

"You make me feel alive," he had told her once, years ago, recklessly, and she had laughed as she rose above him, naked and beautiful, her face open and filled with light.

"You *are* alive," she had whispered in his ear, holding him close. She had then proceeded to prove it to them both.

Tariq had lost count of the times he had reached for her last night, or her for him. He knew he had slept but little, far more interested in tasting her, teasing her, sinking into her one more time. He had reacquainted himself with every nook and cranny of her body, all of its changes, all of its secrets—the pleasure so intense, so astounding, that he could not bring himself to let it end.

Because he knew that once he stopped, he would have to face the truths he was even now avoiding. And as the night wore on, Tariq had found himself less and less interested in doing so.

"This is a feast," Jessa had said at some point, while they sat in the sitting room and ate some of the rich food they'd ignored earlier, wearing very little in the way of clothes. She had smiled at him, unselfconscious and at ease with her legs folded beneath her and her hair tumbled down around her bare shoulders. She had looked free. Just as she had always been with him.

"Indeed it is," he had replied, but he had not been talking about the meal.

Memories chased through him now, hurtling him back to a time he wanted to forget—had worked to forget, in fact, for years. Touching her, tasting her, breathing in her scent. These things had unlocked something in him that he had worked hard to keep hidden, even from himself.

His parents had died in a car accident when he was too young to remember more than fleeting images of his father's rare smile, his mother's dark curtain of hair. He had been taken into the palace by his only remaining relative, his uncle the king, and raised with his cousins, the princes of Nur. His uncle was the only parent Tariq had ever known, and yet Tariq had always been keenly aware that he was not his uncle's son. Just as he had always known that his cousins were the future rulers of the country, and had been trained from birth as such.

"Your cousins have responsibilities to our people," his uncle had told Tariq when they were all still young.

"And what are my responsibilities?" Tariq had asked guilelessly.

His uncle had only smiled at him and patted him on the head.

Tariq had understood. He was not important, not in the way his cousins were.

And so he did as he pleased. Though his uncle periodically suggested that Tariq had more to offer the world than a life full of expensive cars and equally costly European models, Tariq had never seen the point in discovering what that was. He had played with the stock market because it amused him and he was good at it, but it had been no more to him than another kind of high-stakes poker game like the ones he played in private back rooms in Monte Carlo.

He had long since buried the feelings that had haunted him as a child—that he was an outcast in his own family, tolerated by them yet never of them. He believed they cared for him, but he knew he was their charity case. Their duty. Never simply theirs.

Tariq heard Jessa move in the bed behind him. He turned to see if she had awoken and if it was time at last to have a conversation he had no wish to pursue. But she only settled herself into a different position, letting out a small, contented sigh.

He turned back around to face the window, heedless of the cool air on his bare skin, still caught up in the past. The summer he had met Jessa was the summer his uncle had finally put his foot down. He could not threaten Tariq with the loss of his income or possessions, of course, for Tariq had quadrupled his own personal fortune by that point, and then some. But that did not mean the old man had been without weapons.

"You must change your life," the old king had said, frowning at Tariq across the table set out for them on the balcony high on the cliffs. He had summoned his nephew to the family villa on their private island in the Mediterranean, off the coast of Turkey, for this conversation. Tariq had not expected it to be pleasant, though he had always managed to talk his uncle out of his tempers in the past. He had assumed he would do the same that day.

"Into what?" Tariq had asked, shrugging, watching the waves rise and fall far below them, deep and blue. He had been thirty-four then and so world-weary. So profoundly bored. "My life is the envy of millions."

"Your life is empty," his uncle had retorted. "Meaningless." He waved his hand in disgust, taking in Tariq's polished, too fashionable appearance. "What are you but one more playboy sheikh, looked down upon by the entire world, confirming all their worst suspicions about our people?"

"Until they want my money," Tariq had replied coolly. "At which point it is amazing how quickly they become respectful. Even obsequious."

"And this is enough for you? This is all you aspire to? You, who carry the royal blood of the kingdom of Nur in your veins?"

"What would you have me do, Uncle?" Tariq had asked, impatient though he dared not show it. They had had this conversation, or some version of it, every year since Tariq had gone to university where, to his uncle's dismay, he had not approached his studies with the same level of commitment he had shown when approaching the women in his classes.

"You do nothing," his uncle had said matter-of-factly, in a more serious tone than Tariq had ever heard from him, at least when directed at Tariq personally. "You play games with money and call it a career, but it is a joke. You win, you lose, it is all a game to you. You are an entirely selfish creature. I would tell you to marry, to do your duty to your family and your bloodline as your cousins must do, but what would you have to offer your sons? You are barely a man."

Tariq had gritted his teeth. This was not just his uncle talking, not just the only version of a parent he had ever known—this was his king. He had no choice but to tolerate it.

"Again," he had managed to say eventually, fighting to keep his tone appropriately respectful, "what is it you want me to do?"

"It is not about what I want," his uncle had said, disappointment dripping from every hard word. "It is about who you are. I cannot force you to do anything. You are not my son. You are not my heir."

He could not have known, Tariq had supposed then, how deeply his words cut, how close to the bone. No matter that they were no more than the truth.

"But you will no longer be welcome in my family unless you contribute to it in some way," his uncle had continued. He had stared at Tariq for a moment, his eyes grim. "You have six months to prove this to me. If you have not changed your ways by then, I will wash my hands of you." He had shaken his head. "And I must tell you, nephew, I am not hopeful."

Tariq had left the villa that same night, determined to put distance between himself and his uncle and the words his uncle had said, at last vocalizing Tariq's worst fears.

He was not a son, an heir. He was disposable. He was no more than a duty, dictated by tradition and law. But he was not family in a way that mattered. He shared nothing with them but blood. Whatever that meant.

Tariq had never been so angry, so at sea, in all of his life. He had never felt so alienated and alone, and he was not a man who had ever formed deep attachments, so he had not known how to handle what was, he thought in retrospect, grief.

And then he had met Jessa, and she had loved him.

He knew that she had loved him, instantly and thoroughly. She had charmed him with the force of her adoration and her artlessness—her inability to conceal it, or play sophisticated games. Other women had fallen in love with him before, or so they had claimed, but had they loved Tariq or his bank balance? He had never cared before. He had lied about who he was, angrily attempting to distance himself from his reputation as if that might appease his uncle, but she had not noticed.

"You trust too easily," he had told her one night, when they lay stretched out before the fire, unable to stop touching each other.

"I do not!" she had protested, laughing at him, her face tilted toward him, her eyes warm and soft, like cinnamon sugar. "I am quite savvy!"

"If you say so," he had murmured, playing with her curls, coiling them around his fingers. At first he had waited for her to change, as they all did once they learned who he was. He had waited for those knowing looks, or the clever feminine ways of asking for money, or a new car, or an apartment in a posh neighborhood. But Jessa had never changed. She had simply loved him.

"I trust *you*, Tariq," she had whispered then, still smiling. She had even kissed him, with all the innocence and passion she had in her young body.

When she looked at him with those wide cinnamon eyes that reminded him of the home he wasn't sure he would ever be permitted to see again, he felt like the man he should have been.

But then she had disappeared abruptly and completely, which had bothered him far more than it should have. And before he could make sense of what he felt, his uncle and cousins had died, all at once, and Tariq had been forced to face reality. What was the love of one besotted girl when there were wars to prevent and a country to run and those last, terrible words from his uncle that he could never disprove? He could never show his uncle that he was, in fact, a man. That he, too, could uphold the family honor and do his duty. That he had only ever wanted to be treated as a part of the family in the first place.

He turned then, letting his gaze fall upon the sinuous curves of her body as she lay on her side, facing away from him, the curve of her hip and the dip of her waist even more enticing now, after he had had her in every way he could imagine. He had meant only to slake his desire, to have her and be done with her at last. He had spent years convincing himself that she was no more than an itch that needed to be scratched. He had not expected to feel anything but lust.

He had convinced himself he would *feel* nothing at all.

"You are a fool," he whispered to himself.

But Jessa Heath still managed to cast a spell around him. It was the way she gave herself over with total abandon, he thought, studying her form in the morning light. To her anger, to her passion.

Even now that she knew exactly who he was, she still

wanted nothing from him. If anything, his real identity made her like him less. And yet she still fell to pieces in his arms, shattered at the slightest touch. It was as if she had been made specifically for him. As if she could still make him that man she'd seen in him five years ago, as if he was that man, finally, when he was with her.

Which was why he let her sleep, why he crossed the room and sat beside her, drinking her in, knowing that once she woke, the spell would be broken. Reality would intrude once again and remind him that he needed a queen, and she was the girl who had become the emblem of his disappointing former life.

And this night would become one more fever dream, one more memory, that he would lock away and soon enough, he knew, forget.

Jessa woke slowly.

The morning sun poured in from the tall windows, illuminating the bed and making her feel as if she was lit from within. She tugged the tangled length of her hair out from beneath her, knowing it had to be wild after such a night. Knowing she was wild and raw inside as well, though she couldn't think about it. Not yet. Not quite yet.

Not while he was still so near.

She knew he was there before she saw him, as if she had an internal radar that told her Tariq's specific whereabouts. She turned her head and there he was, just where she had sensed him. He sat on the edge of the bed, still gloriously naked, his body like something that ought to be carved in the finest marble and displayed in museums. He was not looking at her for the moment, so Jessa let herself drink her fill of him.

Something in the way he held himself, the way he stared

broodingly toward the window, made her frown. He looked almost sad. She wanted to reach over and soothe him, to kiss away whatever darkness had come upon him while she slept. She might not know *why* he wanted her as he had told her he did from the first, but she had come to accept that it was true, over and over again in the night. The wonder was, she wanted him too. Still. Even now.

But then he turned his head. His expression was unreadable, his dark green eyes solemn, his dark hair the kind of tousled mess that begged to be touched. Though she did not dare.

It was only to be expected that things should feel strained, Jessa reflected, staring back at him for a moment. One night, they had both said. And now it was morning, and the sun was too bright, and it was best to put all of this behind them.

She would not think about what they had done or the ways they had done it. She would not think about how she had sobbed and cried out for him and screamed his name. Again and again and again. It was only sex, she told herself sternly. Just sex. No need to torture herself about it. No need to give her emotions free rein, no matter how much her heart wanted her to do otherwise. She could be more like a man and compartmentalize. Why not? Sex was simply sex. It had nothing to do with feelings unless one wished otherwise. And she did not wish it. End of story.

Now he could go his way and she hers. Just as they had planned. There was no need to dig any further into their past and haul all of that pain back into the light of day. It could be boxed up and locked away, forever.

She remembered that she was supposed to feel empowered, not suddenly shy, no matter how exposed she felt.

"So," she said, trying to sound matter-of-fact. "It is finally morning."

"So it is." Tariq did not move, he only watched her. It was unnerving. Her heart began to pick up speed, though she was not sure why.

"I can't help but notice that I am in France," Jessa said, looking beyond him to the graceful Paris streets outside the window. She had always meant to visit Paris. She wasn't certain this counted. "Rather farther away from York than I expected to be. I hope you will not mind—"

"Jessa."

She flushed, suddenly furious, or that was what she called the emotion that flashed through her, hot and dangerous. She made a fist and struck the soft bedding beside her.

"I hate it when you do that," she threw at him. "You do not have to interrupt me all the time. I don't care if you're a king. You are not *my* king. It's just rude."

"And, of course, I would not wish to appear rude," Tariq replied, an edge in his voice that made the fine hairs on the back of her neck stand up straight. "I have made you come more times than you can possibly count, and you wish to lecture me on—"

"How do you like it?" she demanded, interrupting him. "It's frustrating, isn't it? Because, obviously, the person interrupting believes that whatever he has to say is of far more importance, that *he* is of far more importance—"

"Or perhaps the person talking is overwrought and hysterical." His voice was cool. Jessa bit her lip and looked away. She became uncomfortably aware of her own nudity, and of the fact that the frustrated heat in her cheeks was no doubt evident all over her exposed body.

She knew what she was doing. She was drawing this out, deliberately avoiding any number of elephants in the room. Another way to do that was simply to leave. The agreed-upon night was over and done. There was no more reason for them to be talking about anything. He had claimed what he wanted, as had she, and her secrets remained safe. It was time instead to return to her life and finally put Tariq where he belonged—in the past.

It was long past time to move on.

She swung her legs to the edge of the bed and stood, not looking at him.

"I think I'll take a bath," she said. She had never sounded so chipper, so polite. "Then I need to return to York."

She felt awkward. Tense. Perhaps that was just how she would continue to feel until she was safely back in her own life. She tried to shake it off. But when she started to move toward the bathroom, a luxurious palace all its own, she had to walk in front of him, and he held up a hand.

"Come here," he said quietly.

She hesitated, but then reminded herself that she had already handled him. She had already made it through the night intact. What could he do now? She had made love to him so many times that she'd forgotten anything existed outside of him, and yet she had still woken up herself. Whole, complete. Not lost in him as she had been before. So why was she this nervous?

She moved toward him, wary. It was something about the look in his eyes, something she couldn't place. Not that dark passion he seemed to fight against as much as she did. Not lust. She was more than familiar with those. He beckoned for her to come closer, inside the vee of his powerful legs. Cautiously, she complied.

He did not look up at her. He raised his hands and placed them on her hips, lightly encircling them. His fingers smoothed against her skin, tracing patterns from her hipbone to her navel, then back. Bemused, and not un-affected by his touch, even now, Jessa blinked down at him.

He looked up then and, as their gazes met, Jessa suddenly knew with searing, gut-wrenching certainty exactly what he was doing.

Her breath deserted her in a rush.

Tariq was not touching her randomly. He was not caressing her. He was tracing the faint white lines that scored her belly—the stretch marks she had tried to rub away with lotions and creams, the lines more visible now in the bright morning light than she remembered them ever being before. They were the unmistakable evidence that she had been pregnant—enormously pregnant.

The world stopped turning. Her heart stopped beating. His eyes bored into her as his hands tightened. She heard only white noise, a rushing in her ears, and everything else went blank as if she had lost consciousness for a moment, though she was not so lucky.

He only waited.

And then, when he had stared at her so long she was convinced he had ripped every last secret from her very soul, his mouth twisted.

She wanted to speak—to yell, to defend herself, to deny everything—but it was as if she were paralyzed. Frozen solid, watching her world end in his dark green gaze, colder now than she had ever seen it. He held her still, his captive, and when he spoke, his voice held so much suspicion, so much accusation, she flinched.

"I have only one question for you," he said, every word like a knife. "Where is the child?"

CHAPTER TEN

EVERY instinct screamed at Jessa to run, to escape, to do anything in her power to put space between herself and the knowledge she saw dawning in his eyes.

But she could not bring herself to move.

"Well?" he asked, his voice like a gunshot. "Have you had a child, Jessa?" His voice dropped to the barest whisper of sound as he searched her face. He actually paled, his eyes widening as he read her expression. "Have you had *my* child?"

Her mind whirled as panic flooded through her, cramping her stomach and making little black spots appear before her eyes. She could feel herself waver as she stood before him. *Think!* she ordered herself. She had never planned to see him again, and once he had appeared, had had no plan to tell him about Jeremy. Why should she? She had expected him to disappear again. What good could come of dredging up a past neither one of them could change?

She hadn't expected to be confronted with that past in so dramatic a manner. She was completely unprepared!

Tariq might suspect that Jeremy existed. But he didn't know who Jeremy was, or *where* he was. Only Jessa could protect Jeremy from Tariq and the devastation that would inevitably rain down on Jeremy's world—because Jessa knew without a shadow of a doubt that if Tariq knew where Jeremy was, Tariq would do everything in his considerable power to take him back. And so she would do what she had to do, no matter what it cost her. She would protect Jeremy, even from Tariq.

"I asked you a question," Tariq said, his harsh tone slicing into her, making her jump again. "Do not make me repeat it."

Jessa sucked in a breath. His fingers were like vises, clamped on to her hips and chaining her in place, though he had not increased the pressure of his hands against her flesh. She didn't know how she managed to keep from collapsing, as her heart galloped inside her chest. *Think of Jeremy,* she told herself. *You must be brave for him.*

"I heard you," she said, fear making her voice sound clipped. It was better than terrified. "I just don't have any idea what you're talking about."

His lips pressed together, and he released her suddenly, surging to his feet. Jessa scrambled away from him, determined to put as much space as she could between them. She moved around the end of the huge bed, pulling the decadently soft top sheet from the mattress and wrapping it around herself. She could not bear to remain naked in front of him, not for one second more. She could have kicked herself for failing to remember that her own body could betray her in this way. But she hadn't paid attention to her stretch marks in ages. They were simply there, a part of her personal landscape she noticed as much as she noticed her knees or her ankles. She was such a fool! But then, she had also thought that she could seduce and control Tariq. What had she been thinking?

He did not have to follow her—he loomed over her

from the other side of the bed, his arms crossed over his powerful chest, his anger making him seem even larger than before. He did not seem to care that he, too, was naked. He was as intimidating now as he was when fully dressed. More, perhaps.

"Is that how you want to play this?" he asked, his eyes dark with outrage. As if he had never whispered her name in passion or cradled her against that hard chest as they each fought for breath. "Do you think it will work?"

"I think you're insane!" she threw at him. She had to get over the shock of this change, this about-face from lover to accuser, and she had to do it immediately, no matter her feelings. Or he would roll right over her and take what he wanted. Of that, she had no doubt.

"Do you think I am a fool?" He shook his head slightly, every muscle in his body tensed. His fury was a palpable thing, another presence in the room, a syrupy cloud between them. "I can see the changes in your body with my own eyes. How do you explain them?"

"It's called *five years!*" she cried, throwing up the hand that did not hold the sheet, letting it show her exasperation, hoping he could not see her terror, her desperation. "I have not pointed out the numerous ways *your* body is not the same as it was when you were five years younger—"

Cold and hard, his gaze slammed into her with the force of a blow, and cut her off that effectively.

"I can tell that you are lying," Tariq said, each word distinct and clear. Like separate bullets fired from the same weapon. "Do you doubt it? Your whole face has changed. You look like a stranger! Where is the child? I saw no sign of one in your home."

Still reeling, Jessa clung to the part that mattered most—he could not know anything about Jeremy specifically. He only knew that Jeremy *could* exist. He had not known about Jeremy before he'd come to York. This was all an accident, her fault.

"You will not even answer the question?" he asked, as if he could not quite believe it. "Your body makes you a liar, Jessa. The time for hiding is over." He was not her lover now. Not the charming, easygoing one she knew now had never been more than a convenient costume for him, and not the intensely sensual one who had taken her to erotic heights last night. His voice was crisp. Relentless. Sure. He was a king with absolute power, and he was not afraid to use it.

"Have you seen me with a child?" she asked coolly, praying he could not see how her hands clenched to white knuckles, or hear the tremor in her voice.

"I will rip your life apart, piece by piece, until I find the truth," Tariq bit out, the supreme monarch handing down his judgment, his eyes blazing. "There is no place you can hide, no part of your life you can keep from me. Is that what you want?"

"Why even ask me what I want?" she said, fear and determination a cold knot in her gut, forcing her to play the part of someone far more brave, far more courageous, than she could ever be. For Jeremy, she could keep from falling apart, falling to pieces, as was no doubt Tariq's goal. For Jeremy, she could fight back. "You did not ask me what I wanted when you abandoned me and ruined my life five years ago. You did not ask me what I wanted when you reappeared in my life. Why pretend you have any interest in what I want now?" She shrugged, meeting his eyes with a brazen courage she did not feel. "If you want to dig around in my life, go right ahead. What could I do to stop you?"

His scowl deepened. "Do you think I am still playing games with you?" he demanded, his voice getting louder, his accent growing more pronounced as his temper grew. "You have no right to keep my child from me! The heir to my kingdom!"

Jessa reminded herself that he did not know. He only suspected. *He did not know.*

"You have no right to speak to me this way!" she retorted.

"Where is the child?" he thundered.

But she couldn't back down, though her knees felt like jelly and her lungs constricted painfully. She wouldn't tell him anything.

The truth was, she hardly knew where to start.

She shook her head, too many emotions fighting for space inside of her, and all of them too messy, too complicated, too heavy.

"Jessa." This time the anger was gone, and something far more like desperation colored his voice. "You must tell me what happened. You must."

But she could not speak another word, and she could not bring herself to look at him. She had the sense that she had finally stopped running a very long, very arduous race, and the wind was knocked out of her.

She didn't have the slightest idea what to do now. She had never so much as considered the possibility that Tariq might discover that he had fathered a child. The time for telling him had long since passed, and she knew that she had tried then, to no avail. She had never anticipated that he might return. She had stopped dreaming such foolish dreams long ago.

And now he stared at her in anguish, which she would give anything to fix and couldn't. It wasn't simply that she couldn't bring herself to tell him what he wanted to know. She physically could not seem to form the words. She could not even think them. She could only lie and avoid and deflect. She could only make it worse.

"I will stop at nothing to locate a child of my blood," Tariq said softly. There was a chilling finality to his words then, as if he was making a vow. He took a step toward her, and it took everything she had to stand her ground before him. "I have believed I am the last of my blood, my family, for five years, Jessa. The very last. If that is not so…"

He didn't finish. But then, he did not have to finish.

Jessa still could not speak. It was as if everything inside her had shut down, turned off.

"You can only remain silent for so long," he said. His voice was like a whip, cracking through the room hard enough to leave welts against her skin. "But do not doubt that there is only one outcome to this situation. I *will* find out. The only question is how much of your life I will destroy in the process."

"Do not bully me!" she cried, surprising herself as well as him, the words ripping from her as if she had torn them from her heart.

"You think I am bullying you?" He was incredulous, pronouncing *bullying* as if he had never heard the term before.

"Threats, intimidation." Jessa pressed one hand against her temple. "Is there another word for it?"

"I am not threatening you, Jessa," he said matter-of-factly, with that ruthlessness underneath. "I am telling you exactly what will happen to you if you continue this. You have no right to keep the truth from me. These are promises."

"What kind of man are you?" she whispered. She wasn't sure why she said it. She wanted to sob, to scream, to somehow release the tension that felt as if it swelled up from inside her.

Their eyes locked across the few feet that separated them. He looked as if he had never seen her before, as if she was a perfect stranger who had wounded him. She realized in that moment that she never wanted to be responsible for his pain. That it hurt her, too. But understanding only made the riot inside swirl faster, swell harder, cause more damage. Jessa made herself hold his gaze, though it cost her.

Tariq looked away from her then, as if he had to collect himself before he did something he would regret.

"I suggest you rethink your position," he said quietly.

Suddenly her tongue was loose. And foolish. "I suggest you—"

"Silence!" He slashed a hand through the air, and said something in what she assumed was Arabic. "I am done listening to you."

He did not look at her again, but strode toward the bedroom door. Jessa could not believe it. Relief flooded through her. He was *leaving?* That was it? Could she really be that lucky?

And what was the part of her that yearned, despite everything, for him to stay?

"Where are you going?" she asked, because she wanted to confirm it.

"Shocking as it might seem to you, I have matters of state to attend to," he growled at her. "Or do you think my kingdom should grind to a halt while you spin your little lies? You can consider this conversation postponed."

"I am not going to sit around and calmly wait for you to come back and be even more horrible to me," she told him fiercely. "I am going home."

He turned when he reached the door to the rest of the suite, his eyes narrow and his mouth hard.

"By all means," he said, his voice as dark as his gaze, and his warning clear, "go wherever you like. See what happens when you do." Then he turned his back on her, seemingly still unconcerned with his nudity, and strode from the room.

His sudden absence left a black hole in the room that Jessa feared might suck her in, for a dizzy, irrational beat or two of her heart. For long moments, Jessa could not move. She told herself she was waiting to see if Tariq would return. She told herself she was merely being cautious. But the truth was that she could not have moved so much as an inch if her life depended upon it.

Eventually, when he did not come back, Jessa moved to the edge of the bed and sat down gingerly, carefully, unable to process what had just occurred. Unable to track the course of the past two days. She remembered going to work in the letting agency that morning, having no idea that her whole world would be turned on its ear. That normal, everyday morning felt as far away to her now as if it belonged to someone else, as if it were a part of some other woman's life. She felt as if she'd just been tipped from a roller coaster at its height and sent tumbling to the earth. She raised a hand to her mouth, surprised to find her hand shook.

She almost let out a sob, but choked it back. She could not break down. She was not safe from Tariq or his questions simply because he had left her alone for the moment. He would be back. She knew that as surely as she knew the earth still turned beneath her feet. He was an implacable force, and she did not know how she had failed to recognize that five years ago. Hadn't she known this would happen? Wasn't this why she'd set upon this course in the first place, to divert his attention?

That is not the only reason… a traitorous voice whispered, but she couldn't allow herself to listen to it. Nor could she savor the heated images of the night before. None of that mattered now.

Jeremy is his child too, the same treacherous voice

whispered, and Jessa felt a wave of old grief rock through her then, nearly knocking her over with all the strength of what might have been. If he had been who he'd said he was. If she had been less infatuated and less silly. If his uncle had not died. If she had been able to care for her newborn child as he deserved to be cared for. *If.*

She balled her hands into fists and stood, ignoring her trembling knees, her shallow breaths, the insistent dampness in her eyes that she refused to let flow free. Tariq would be back, and she did not want to imagine what new ammunition he would bring with him. She was not at all sure she could survive another encounter like this one. In truth, she was not even certain she *had* survived. Not intact, anyway.

But she couldn't think of that, of what more she might have lost. She told herself she had to think of Jeremy. She could take care of herself later.

She had to make certain that whenever Tariq returned, she was long gone.

CHAPTER ELEVEN

IT WAS not until Jessa arrived at the Gare de Lyon railway station with every intention of escaping Tariq—and France—that she realized, with a shock, that she did not have any money with her.

Getting out of Tariq's Parisian home had been, in retrospect, suspiciously easy. She had forced herself into action knowing that the alternative involved the fetal position and a very long cry, neither of which she could allow herself. So after she had taken a shower in the luxurious bathroom suite, scrubbing herself nearly raw in water almost too hot to bear, as if that would remove the feel of him from her skin, Jessa had pulled on one of the seductively comfortable robes set out by the unseen staff and tried to see if she could find something to wear. Her blue sheath dress from the night before had been a crumpled mess, and, in any case, she'd been unable to bring herself to wear it again—she couldn't bear to remember how he had removed it. How she had *wanted* him to remove it.

She'd snuck down to the lower levels of the house, looking for the guest suites that she knew must be somewhere, because how could there fail to be guest rooms in such a house? The house was, as she had only noticed in passing awe the night before, magnificent. Glorious works of art by identifiably famous artists graced the walls, a Vermeer here, a Picasso there, though Jessa had not spared them more than a glance. A sculpture she was almost positive she'd seen a copy of in a London museum occupied an entire atrium all its own.

She'd wondered where Tariq's offices were—purely because she'd wanted to avoid him, she told herself—and had frozen in place each time she'd heard a footfall or a low voice, or had eased open a new door to peer behind it. She'd finally found what she was looking for in a set of rooms hidden away in a closed-off wing on the second floor: a closet filled with women's clothes in a variety of sizes.

She'd pulled on a pair of black wool trousers that were slightly too big, and the softest charcoal-gray linen button-down blouse she had ever worn, that was a bit tighter across the chest than she would have chosen on her own. Then she'd found a pair of black-and-brown ballet-style flats, only the tiniest bit too big for her feet. A black wool jacket completed the outfit and, once she smoothed her hair into some kind of order, had made Jessa look like someone far wealthier and much calmer.

It was remarkable, she'd thought, peering into the standing mirror in the corner of the dressing room, that she could look so pulled-together on the outside when she was still too afraid to look at the raw mess on the inside.

She had felt it, though. The sob that might take her at any moment, might suck her down into the heaving mass of emotion she could feel swirling inside, ready to spill over at the slightest provocation...

But there had been no time to think about such things. She had shaken the feelings off, reminding herself that there was only Jeremy to think about, only his welfare and nothing else. She had to get out of Tariq's house, and as far away from him as possible, before she was tempted to share with him things she had never shared, not in their entirety, with anyone.

Jessa had expected it to be difficult to find her way out of the house—had expected, in fact, to be apprehended by Tariq or his staff or *someone*—and had found herself a curious mixture of disappointed and elated when she'd simply walked down the impressive marble stair and let herself out onto the elegant Paris street beyond.

It had been chillier outside than she'd expected, and wet. She hadn't made it to the first corner before it had started to rain in earnest, and the clothes she'd liberated from the closet were little help. Her mind had raced with every step she took. She couldn't go home to York, could she? It would be the obvious place for Tariq to look, and if he was as serious as she worried he must be about tearing into her life, he was much more likely to stumble upon something there than anywhere else. Jessa had walked until she hit a major boulevard, and then had looked at a map at one of the kiosks. She could hardly take in the fact that she was in Paris, one of the most celebrated cities in the world. She had been much too focused on Tariq and what he might do, and how he might do it.

While she walked, the perfect solution had come to her. Friends of hers from home had gone on a holiday last year, and had taken the train from Paris to Rome. Rome was even farther away from Jeremy. Should Tariq come after her as he'd threatened to do, she would be leading him away from his true quarry. So she'd found the train station on the map, happily located not too far away, and had walked.

She walked and walked, down streets she had only ever seen in photographs, the borrowed shoes rubbing at her cold toes and slapping the pavement beneath her feet. She walked past the soaring glory of the Arc de Triomphe and down the Champs-Elysées, the wide boulevard glistening in the rain, achingly beautiful despite the overcast skies above. She walked in and out of puddles in the Jardin des Tuileries, still crowded with tourists under bright umbrellas, toward the iconic glass pyramid that heralded the entrance to the Louvre. She took shelter from the rain in the famed arcades that stretched beneath the great buildings along the Rue de Rivoli, filled with brightly lit shops and the bustling energy of city life.

And if tears fell from her eyes and rolled down her cheeks as she walked, tears for Tariq and for herself and for all the things she'd lost, they were indistinguishable from the rain.

It was only when she'd finally made her way into the impressive rail station with the huge clock tower that reminded her of Big Ben back home in the UK that the reality of her situation had hit her.

She had no money. And, worse, no access to any money.

She'd tucked her bank card into her evening bag before she'd left her home in York last night, but she hadn't thought to bring it with her when she'd left Tariq's house. She'd been entirely too focused on getting out of there to think about such practicalities.

Once again, she was a fool.

All of the emotions that Jessa had been trying to hold at bay rushed at her then like a tidal wave, forcing her to stop walking in the middle of the crowded station. She thought her knees might give out from under her. She was nearly trampled by the relentless stream of commuters and holidaymakers on all sides as they raced through the building, headed for trains and destinations far away from here. But Jessa was trapped. Stranded. How could she possibly keep Jeremy a secret if she couldn't even take a simple train journey to somewhere, anywhere else? She was soaked through to her skin: cold, wet, miserable, and alone in Paris. She had no money, and the one person she knew in the city was the last person on earth she could go to for help.

What was she going to do?

She felt a hand on her arm and immediately turned, jostled out of the dark spiral she was in.

"Excuse me," she began, apologetically.

But it was Tariq.

He wore another dark suit, expertly fitted to showcase his lean hunter's physique, and a matching scowl. He held her elbow in his large hand much too securely. She did not have to try to jerk away from him to know she would not be able to do so if he didn't allow it. She had no doubt she looked pathetic—like a drowned rat. Meanwhile, he looked like what he was: a very powerful man at the end of his patience.

She hated the way he looked at her, as if she had done something unspeakable to him. When she had only ever acted to protect Jeremy! Hadn't she? She hated that he did not say a word, and only seared her straight through with that dark glare of his. She hated most of all that some part of her was relieved to see him, that that same traitorous part of her wanted him to rescue her, as if he was not the one responsible for her predicament in the first place!

Her eyes burned with tears. He only stared at her, his dark eyes penetrating, implacable. She felt her mouth open, but she could not speak.

What could she say? She didn't know whether to be relieved or appalled that he was beside her, even though he was what she had run from. She only knew there was an ache inside that seemed to intensify with every breath, and it had nothing at all to do with sex. It had to do with the way he looked at her, as if he was disappointed in her. As if she had wounded him in ways words could not express. She couldn't imagine why that should hurt her in return, but it did.

"Come," he said, his voice a powerful rumble yet curiously devoid of anger, which made the dampness at the back of her eyes threaten to spill over again. "The car is waiting."

The damned woman was likely to catch her death of pneumonia, Tariq thought darkly, which would not suit him at all, as she still kept so many secrets from him. As he stepped outside the station, two of his aides leaped to attention, umbrellas in hand, and sheltered them both as Tariq led her to the sleek black car that waited by the curb. Not that an umbrella would do her any good at this point. She might as well have jumped, fully dressed, into the Seine.

His driver opened the back door and Tariq handed Jessa inside, then climbed in after her, sitting so he could look at her beside him. He watched her settle into her seat and told himself he did not notice the way the soaking wet shirt clung to her curves, leaving nothing at all to the imagination. Not that he needed to imagine what he could still taste on his tongue and feel beneath his hands. He wordlessly handed her a bath towel as the car pulled into traffic.

"Thank you."

Her voice was hushed. Almost formal. She looked at the towel on her lap for a moment and then raised her head. Her eyes seemed too wide, too bright, and haunted, somehow. To his surprise, the anger that had consumed him earlier had subsided. Which was not to say he was happy with her, or had forgotten what she'd done to him—the lies she was still telling with her continued silence—but the fury that had seized him and forced him to walk away from her rather than unleash it in her presence had simmered to a low boil and then faded into something far more painful. Anger was easy, in comparison.

He didn't know why. He had been coldly furious all day, and doubly so when she'd left the house. He had had his people monitor her movements as a matter of course, and had seethed about it while he ought to have been concentrating on his official duties. When it became clear where she was headed and he had called for the car, he had felt the crack of his temper, but somehow the sight of her standing in the middle of the busy train station had gotten to him. She had looked so forlorn, so lost. Not at all the warrior woman with more fire and courage than sense who had made love to him all night long. Who had stood up to him consistently since he'd walked back into her life. By the time he'd reached her side, he had been amazed to discover that the angry words on his tongue had dissolved, unsaid.

Yet he still had the echo of what she'd said earlier ricocheting in his head, close as it was to something his uncle had said to him years before: *What kind of man are you?* The kind who terrorized women into risking pneumonia on the streets of Paris, apparently. The kind whose former lover defied him to her own detriment, throwing herself out into a cold autumn rain rather than tell him what had become of their child. What kind of man was he, indeed, to inspire these things?

He watched her towel off her face, then try to tend to the sopping mass of her hair. She shivered.

"You are cold."

"No," she said, but there was no force behind it.

"Your teeth are about to chatter," he said with little patience. Would she rather freeze to death than accept his help? *Obstinate woman.* He leaned forward to press the intercom button, then ordered the heat turned on. "See? Was that so difficult?"

She looked at him, her eyes dark and wary, then away.

"I hope you had a pleasant walk," he continued, his tone sardonic. "My men tell me you nearly drowned in a puddle outside the Louvre."

She looked startled for a moment. "Your men?"

"Of course." His brows rose. "You cannot imagine that a king's residence is left so wide open, can you? That any passerby could stroll in and out on a whim? I told you what would happen if you left."

"I didn't..." She broke off. She swallowed. "You have security. Of course you do." She shrugged slightly. "I never saw them."

Tariq leveled a look at her, lounging back against his seat, taking care not to touch her. Touching her had not led where he had expected it to lead. He had meant to control her and rid himself of this obsession, and instead had risked himself in ways he would have thought impossible. Felt things he was not prepared to examine. *Damn her.*

"If you saw them, they would not be very good at their jobs, would they?" he asked idly.

Silence fell, heavy and deep, between them. She continued to try to dry herself, and he continued to watch her attempts, but something had shifted. He didn't know what it was. Her desperate, doomed escape attempt that had proved her brave, if reckless? Or the fact that she looked not unlike a child as she sat there, as bedraggled as a kitten, her eyes wide and defeated?

"Why did you stop walking in the station?" he asked

without knowing he meant to speak. "You were nearly run down where you stood."

She let out a rueful laugh. "I have no money," she said. She met his gaze as if she expected him to comment, but he only lifted a brow in response.

"And what now?" she asked softly, that defiant tilt to her chin, though her hair was still dark and wet against her face, making her seem pale and small. "Am I your prisoner?"

There was a part of him that wanted to rage at her still. But he had not forgotten, even in his fury, even now, how she had somehow touched him once again, gotten under his skin. He, who had believed himself inviolate in that way. How he had yearned for her all of these years, though he had made up any number of lies to excuse it. How he had waited for her to wake this morning, loath to disturb her. He suspected that a great deal of his anger stemmed from that knowledge, that even as she defied him and lied to him, insulted him and dared him to do his worst, he admired her for it. It had taken him hours, and perhaps the sight of her dogged determination to get away from him in order to keep her secrets no matter what the cost to herself, to understand that truth, however uncomfortable it made him.

What kind of man are you?

And could he truly blame her for what she'd done, whatever she'd done? asked a ruthless inner voice. Given what she knew of him back then—a liar, a wastrel—why would she want to share a child with him? It was as his uncle had told him. He had not been a man. He had had nothing to offer any child.

"I need to know what happened," he said quietly. He did not look at her, watching instead the blurred Parisian buildings and monuments as they sped past.

"So the answer is yes. I am your prisoner." She let out a breath. "For how long?"

He could have said, for as long as he liked. He could have reminded her that he was a king, that he could have absolute power over her if he wished it. Instead, he turned to her and met her troubled gaze.

"Until you tell me what I want to know," he said.

"Forever, then," she said, her voice hollow. "You plan to hold me against my will forever."

"When have you been held against your will?" he asked, though his voice held no heat. "I do not recall your demands to leave last night. And I did not prevent you from leaving this morning."

"With no money," she said bitterly. "Where was I supposed to go?"

"If you are without funds, Jessa," he replied evenly, "you need only ask."

"I have my own money, thank you," she said at once, sharply.

"Then why didn't you use it?" he asked. She sighed and dropped her gaze to her hands. Again, silence stretched between them, seeming to implicate them both.

"Isn't this where you threaten me some more?" she asked softly, her attention directed at her lap. Yet somehow her voice seemed to tug at him. To shame him. "That you'll tear apart my whole life, make it a living hell?"

What kind of man are you?

Tariq expelled a long breath and rubbed at his temples with his fingers. When he spoke, he hardly recognized his own voice.

"You must understand that when I say I am the last of my bloodline, I am not only talking about lines of succession and historical footnotes that will be recorded when I am gone," he said, not knowing what he meant to say. Not recognizing the gruffness in his own voice. "I was orphaned when I was still a child, Jessa. I was not yet three. I don't know if the little I remember of my parents is real or if I have internalized photographs and stories told to me by others."

"Tariq." She said his name on a sigh, almost as if she hurt for him.

"My uncle's family was the only family I ever knew," he said, with an urgency he didn't entirely understand. She bit her lower lip and worried it between her teeth. "I thought I was the only one left. Until today."

"I don't know what you want me to say," she whispered, her voice thick.

"Do I have a child?" he asked her, appalled at the uncertainty he could hear in his own voice. He didn't know what he would do if she threw it back at him as he knew she could. "Is my family more than simply me?"

Her eyes squeezed shut, and she made a sound that was much like a sob, though she covered her mouth with her hand. For a long moment they sat in silence, the only sound the watery swish of traffic outside the car, and her ragged breathing. He thought she would not answer. He felt a new bleakness settle upon him. Would he never know what had happened? Would he be condemned to wonder? Was it no more than he deserved for the way he had behaved in his former life, the way he had treated her, the way he had treated himself and his family, his many squandered gifts?

But she turned her head to look at him, her cinnamon eyes bright with a pain he didn't fully understand.

"I don't know that I can make you feel any better about this," she said, her voice thick and rough. "But I will tell you what I know."

CHAPTER TWELVE

JESSA didn't know why she had said anything, why his obvious pain had moved her so much that she broke her silence so suddenly. She hadn't meant to say a word. And then she'd heard the raw agony in his voice and something inside had snapped. Or loosened. She had thought she might cry. Instead, she had spoken words she'd never meant to speak aloud and certainly not to him.

But the truth was, he hadn't meant to leave her, had he? His uncle had died—his whole family had died. What was he supposed to have done? It had occurred to her, somewhere out in all the cold and wet of the Paris streets, that somewhere along the line it had become important for her to keep blaming him for leaving her because it kept the attention away from what had happened after he left. From the decisions she had made that he had had no part in. Was that what she had been hiding from?

Tariq said nothing. He only looked at her for a long moment, his gaze fathomless, and then nodded once. Definitively. She expected him to demand she tell him everything she could at once, but instead he remained silent for the rest of their short journey to his grand house. Once there, he ushered her back to the suite of rooms on the top floor that she had run from earlier. Was it to be her prison? Jessa felt too raw, too exposed, to give that question the thought she knew she should.

No sign of their long, passionate night remained in the exquisite room. The great bed was returned to its ivory-and-gold splendor, and warm lights glowed from sconces in the wall, setting off the fine moldings and Impressionist art that graced the walls. Jessa stood in the center of the room, deliberately not looking at the bed, deliberately not remembering, and swallowed. Hard.

"You will wish to clean up, I think," Tariq said, an odd politeness in his tone as if they did not know each other. And yet, he anticipated her needs. He gestured toward the spacious dressing room that was adjacent to the palatial bathroom. "I have taken the liberty of having clothes laid out for you that will, I hope, fit."

Jessa looked down at the sodden mess of the clothes she wore, and swallowed again, not sure she could speak. She didn't know how to process his thoughtfulness. Perhaps he was simply tired of looking at her in such a bedraggled state. She was tired of it herself—her shoes so soaked that she could hear her toes squelch into them each time she moved. The room, for all it was large and elegant beyond imagining, seemed too close, too hushed around them. She was afraid to meet his gaze. Afraid she had opened herself up too far, and he would see too much.

Afraid that once she bared herself to him again, he would break her heart as surely and as completely as he had done before.

"There are matters that require my attention," he said after a long moment, still in that stiff way. As if he was as nervous as she was. "I cannot put them off."

"I understand," she managed to say, frowning fiercely at her wet, cold shoes.

"I will return as soon as I can." He sighed slightly and she risked looking at him. "You will wait here?"

Not run away, he meant. Not continue to keep her secrets. Stay and tell him what she'd said she would.

Share with him what should never have been a secret, what should have been theirs. Together.

"I will." It was like a vow.

They stared at each other for a long, fraught moment. Jessa could feel her pulse beat in her ears, her throat.

He nodded to her, so stiff and formal it was like a bow, and strode from the room.

It was already evening when a diffident maid in a pressed black uniform led Jessa through the maze of the house to find Tariq. He waited for her in a cozy, richly appointed room that featured a crackling fire in a stone fireplace, walls of books and deep leather couches. Tariq stood with his back to the door, his stance wide and his hands clasped behind him, staring out the French doors at the wet blue dusk beyond.

Jessa stood in the doorway for a moment, filled with a confusing mix of panic, uncertainty and something else she did not wish to examine—something that felt like a hollow space in her chest as she looked at him, his face remote in profile, his strong back stiff, as if he expected nothing from her but further pain. She shook the thought away, suddenly deeply afraid in a way she had not been before—a way that had nothing to do with Jeremy and everything to do with her traitorous, susceptible heart. She smoothed her palms along the fine wool of the trousers she wore, pretending she was concerned about wrinkles when she knew, deep down, that was not true. And that it was far too late to worry.

Tariq had been as good as his word. When Jessa emerged from her second hot shower of the day, she had found an entire wardrobe laid out for her in the dressing room, complete with more grooming products than she had at her own home in York. All of it, from the clothes to the hair bands and perfumes, had been specifically chosen with her tastes in mind. It was as if Tariq knew her better than she knew herself, a line of thought she preferred not to examine more closely. Not knowing what the night held, and not wanting to send the wrong message or make herself more vulnerable than she felt already, Jessa had dressed for this conversation in tailored chocolate wool trousers and a simple white silk blouse. Over that, she'd wrapped a sky-blue cashmere concoction that was softer than anything she had ever touched before. Now she tightened the wrap around her middle, as if it alone could hold her together. She'd even smoothed her heavy mass of hair back into a high ponytail, hoping it might broadcast a certain calm strength her curls would not.

"I trust everything fits well," Tariq said in a low voice, still staring out through the French doors. Jessa started slightly, not realizing he'd known she was there.

"Perfectly," she said, and then coughed to clear the thickness from her throat.

He turned then, and Jessa was lost suddenly in the bleakness she saw on his face. It made his harsh features seem even more unapproachable and distant. She wanted to go to him, to soothe it away somehow, and then wondered who she'd confused him for, who she thought she was facing. This was still Tariq bin Khaled Al-Nur. He was more dangerous to her now, she thought, than he had ever been before. She would be wise to remember that. Oh, it was not as if she had anything to fear from him—it was her own heart she feared. Perhaps it had always been her own surrender she feared more than anything else.

"Tell me," Tariq said, and she did not mistake his meaning.

She took a deep breath. Stalling for time, she crossed the room and perched on the edge of the buttery-soft leather sofa, but did not allow herself to relax back into it. She could not look at him, so she looked instead into the fire, into the relative safety of the dancing, shimmering flames.

There would be no going back from this conversation. She was honest with herself about that, at least.

"It was a boy," she said, her head spinning, because she could not believe she was telling him this after so long. A sense of unreality gripped her as if she was dreaming all of it—the luxurious clothes, the fire, the impossibly forbidding man who stood close and yet worlds away. "I called him Jeremy."

She could feel Tariq's eyes on her then, though she dared not look at him to see what expression he wore as he digested this news. That he was, biologically, a father. Swallowing carefully, she put her hands into her lap, stared fixedly into the fire and continued.

"I found out I was pregnant when I went to the doctor's that day." She sighed, summoning up those dark days in her memory. "You had been so careful never to mention the future, never to hint—" But she couldn't blame him, not entirely. "I didn't know if it meant I would lose you, or if you would be happy. I didn't know if I was happy!" She shook her head and frowned at the flames dancing before her, heedless of the emotional turmoil just outside the stone fireplace. "That was where I went. I stopped at a friend's flat in Brighton. I...tried to work out what to do."

"Those days you went missing," Tariq said in a quiet

voice. Jessa couldn't look at him. "You hadn't left, then, after all."

"It's so ironic that you thought so," Jessa said with a hollow laugh. "As that was my biggest fear at first—that you would leave. Once you knew." She laughed again in the same flat way. "Only when I returned to London, you had already gone. And when I saw who you really were and what you had to do, I knew that you were never coming back."

Jessa took a deep breath, feeling it saw into her lungs. It would get no easier if she put it off, she thought. It might never get easier at all. She blew the breath out and forced herself to continue.

"I was such a mess," she said. "I was sacked in short order, of course. I tried to get another job in the city, not realizing that I'd been effectively blackballed. My sister wanted me to move back home to York, but that seemed such an admission of failure. I…I so wanted everything to simply go on as if nothing had ever happened. As if *you* had never happened."

She heard a faint sound like an exhalation or a muttered curse, but she couldn't look at him. She couldn't bear to see what he thought of her. She was too afraid she would never tell the story if she didn't tell him now. From the corner of her eye, she saw him move and begin to prowl around the room as if he could not bear to stand still.

"But I was pregnant, and…" How to tell him what that had felt like? The terror mixed in equal part with fierce, incomparable joy? Her hand crept over her abdomen as if she could remember by touch. As if the memory of Jeremy still kicked there, so insistent and demanding.

"You must have been quite upset," Tariq said quietly. Too quietly. Jessa stared down at her lap, threading her hands together.

"At you, perhaps. Or the situation," she said softly. "But not at the baby. I realized quickly that I wanted the baby, no matter what." She sucked in a breath. "And so I had him. He was perfect."

Her emotions were too close to the surface. Too raw, still. Or perhaps it was because she was finally sharing the story with Tariq, who should have been there five years ago. She had almost felt as if he was there in the delivery room. She had sobbed as much for the man who was not her partner and was not with her as she had for the pain she was in as each contraction twisted and ripped through her. Now she pressed her lips together to keep herself from sobbing anew, and breathed through her nose until she was sure she wouldn't cry. This was about the facts. She could give him the facts.

"I had a hard labor," she said. "There were...some complications. I was depressed, scared." She had had postpartum depression on top of her physical ailments, of course, but it had not seemed, at the time, like something she could ever come out of whole. She snuck a look at him then. He had found his way to the couch opposite, but he did not look at her as he sat there, sprawled out before the fire. He aimed his deep frown toward the dark red Persian carpet at his feet.

Jessa wondered what he was thinking. Did this seem unreal to him? Impossible? That they could be sitting in a Parisian room, so many miles and years away from the heartache that they had caused together? It boggled the mind. It made her feel dizzy.

"I had no job, and no idea where I might go to get one," Jessa continued, ignoring the thickness in her voice, the twist in her belly. "I had this perfect baby boy, the son of a king, and I couldn't give him the life that he needed. That he deserved." Her voice cracked, and she sighed, then cleared her throat. "I thought at first that it was just hormonal—just first-time mother fears, but as time went on, the feeling grew stronger."

"Why?" Tariq's voice was barely a whisper, and still so full of anguish. "What was missing in the life you gave him?"

Me, Jessa thought. *You.* But she said neither.

"I was…not myself," she said instead. "I cried all the time. I was so lost." It had been more than she could handle. The baby's constant demands. The lack of sleep. The lack of help, even though her sister had tried. Had she not been so terribly, terribly depressed—near suicidal, perhaps… But she had been. There was no point in wishing. "And how could I be a good parent? The single decision I'd made that led to my being a parent in the first place had been…" Her voice trailed off, and her gaze flew to his.

"To get pregnant accidentally," he finished for her, so matter-of-factly, so coldly. "With my child."

"Yes." Something shimmered between them, a kind of bond, though it was fragile and painful. Jessa forged on, determined to get the rest out at last. "And I had had all this time to read about you in the news, to watch you on the television, to really and truly see that nothing you had ever told me was true. That I'd made up our relationship in my head. That I was a silly girl with foolish dreams, not fit to be someone's *parent*."

He raked his hands through his hair, his expression unreadable. But he did not look away.

"Meanwhile," she continued, her voice barely a thread of sound, "there were people with intact families already. People who had done everything right, made all the right choices, and just couldn't have a baby. Why should Jeremy suffer just because his mother was a mess? How was that fair to him?"

"You gave him up for adoption," Tariq said, sounding almost dazed. "You gave him away to strangers?"

"He deserved to have everything," Jessa said fiercely, hating the emphasis he put on *strangers*—and not wanting to correct him. "Love, two adoring parents, a family. A real chance at a good life! Not...a devastated single mother who could barely take care of herself, much less him."

Tariq did not speak, though Jessa could hear his ragged breathing and see the turmoil in his expression.

"I wanted him to be happy more than I wanted him to be happy with me," she whispered.

"I thought..." Tariq stopped and rubbed his hands over his face. "I believed it was customary in an adoption to seek the permission of both parents."

Jessa bit her lower lip and braced herself. "Jeremy has only one birth parent listed on his birth certificate," she said quietly. "Me."

Tariq simply looked at her, a deep anger that verged on a grief she recognized evident in the dark depths of his troubled gaze. Jessa raised her shoulders and then let them drop. Why should she feel guilty now? And yet she did. Because neither of them had had all the choices they should have had. Neither one of them was blameless.

"I saw no reason to claim a relationship to a king for a baby when I could not claim one myself," she said.

Tariq's gaze seemed to burn, but Jessa did not look away.

"I can almost understand why you did not inform me that you were pregnant," he said after a long, tense moment. "Or I can try to understand this. But to give the child away? To give him to someone else without even allowing me to know that he existed in the first—"

"I tried to find you," she cut in, her voice thick with

emotion. "I went to the firm and begged them to contact you. I had no way to locate you!"

"No way to locate me?" He shook his head. Temper cracked like lightning in his eyes, his voice. "I am not exactly in hiding!"

"You have no idea, do you?" she asked, closing her eyes briefly. "I cannot even imagine how many young, single women must throw themselves at you. How many must tell tales to members of your staff, or your government officials, in a desperate bid for your attention. Why should I be treated any differently?" She shifted in her seat, wanting nothing more than to get up and run, end this uncomfortable conversation. Hadn't she been running from it for ages? "It's not possible to simply look you up in the phone book and give you a ring, Tariq. You must know that."

His expression told her that he didn't wish to know it. He swallowed, and she didn't know how to feel about the fact he was clearly as uncomfortable as she was. As emotional.

"I went to the firm," she said again, remembering that day some months after Jeremy had been born, when she'd been desperate and on the brink of making her decision but wanted to reach Tariq first, if she could. "They laughed at me."

It had been worse than the day they'd sacked her. The speculation in their eyes, the disdain—they had looked at her like she was dirt. Like she was worse than dirt.

"They laughed at you?" As if he didn't understand.

"Of course." She found the courage to meet his eyes. "To them I was nothing more than the slutty intern, still gold digging. One of them offered to take me out to dinner—*wink wink*."

"Wink—?" Tariq began, frowning, and then comprehension dawned and his expression turned glacial.

"Yes," Jessa confirmed. "He was happy to see if he

could sample the goods. After all, I'd been good enough for a king, for a while. But he certainly wasn't going to help me contact you."

"Who?" Tariq asked, his voice like thunder. "Who was the man?"

"It doesn't really matter, does it? I doubt very much he was the only one who thought that way." Jessa shook her head and looked back into the fire, sinking further into the embrace of the cashmere over her shoulders. "I realized that I would have to make the decision on my own. That there was absolutely no way I could talk to you about it. We might as well have never met."

"So you did it." There was no question in his voice. Only that scratchiness and a heavy kind of resignation.

"When he was four months old," Jessa said, surprised to feel herself get choked up. "I kissed him goodbye and I gave him what he could never have if I kept him." She closed her eyes against the pain that never really left her, no matter what she did or what she told herself. "And now he has everything any child could hope for. Two parents who dote on him, who treat him like a miracle—not a mistake. Not something unplanned that had to be dealt with." She could feel the wetness on her cheeks but made no move to wipe it away.

"You don't regret this decision?" His voice seemed to come from far away. Jessa turned to look at him, her heart so raw she thought it might burst from within.

"I regret it *every day*!" she whispered at him fiercely. Unequivocally. "I miss him *every moment*!"

Tariq sat forward, his eyes intent on hers. "Then I do not see why we cannot—"

"He is *happy*!" she interrupted him, emotion making her forceful. But he had to hear her. "He is happy, Tariq.

Content. I know that I did the right thing for him, and that's the only thing that matters. Not what I feel. And not what you feel, either, no matter if you are a king or not. He is a happy, healthy little boy with two parents who are not us." Her voice trembled then, and the tears spilled over and trailed across her cheeks. "Who will never be us."

She buried her face in her hands, not entirely sure why she was crying like this—as desperately as if it had just happened, as if she had just accepted that it was real. It had to do with telling Tariq the truth finally. Or most of the truth, in any case—all the most important parts of the truth. It was as if some part of her she'd scarcely known existed had held on to the fantasy that as long as he did not know, it could not have happened. It could not be true. And now she had lost even that lie to tell herself.

Jessa did not know how long she wept, but she knew when he came to sit beside her, his much heavier body next to hers on the leather making her sag toward him. He did not whisper false words of encouragement. He did not rant or rave or rail against her. He did not plot ways to change this harsh reality, or ask questions she could not answer.

He merely put his arm around her, guided her head to his shoulder and let her cry.

It was late when Tariq got off the phone with his attorneys, having confirmed what he'd suspected but still didn't quite want to accept: British adoptions were relatively rare, and well-nigh irreversible. When the child came of age, he could seek out his parents through a national register if he chose, but not before. And British courts were notoriously unsympathetic to anyone who tried to reverse the adoption process—claiming they acted in the best interests of the child and sought to cause as little disruption as possible.

He left his office and made his way back to the small library where he'd left Jessa when she'd finally succumbed to the stress and emotion of the day and had drifted off to sleep. He found her curled up on the leather sofa, her hands beneath her cheek, looking more like a child than a woman who could have borne one. Much less borne his.

Some part of him still wanted to unleash the temper that rolled and burned inside of him on her, to hurt her because he hurt, but he found he could not. He looked at her and felt only a deep sadness and a growing possessiveness that he wasn't sure he understood. He knew he wanted to blame her because it would be convenient, nothing more.

The truth was that he blamed himself. He was everything his uncle had accused him of being, and while he had known that enough so that he'd altered his life to honor his uncle's passing, he had not understood the true scope of it until now.

He might have spent years haunted by her, but he had not wanted to deal with the young woman who had made his dissipated heart ask questions he hadn't wanted to answer, and so he had excised her when he left England just as he had excised everything that reminded him of his old life. He had transformed himself into the man his uncle wanted him to be, and he'd done it brutally. What would it have cost him to seek her out after the accident, even for something as little as a phone call? What kind of man left a young, obviously infatuated girl in the lurch like that? Had he allowed himself to think about it for even a moment, he would have known that she'd have been devastated first by his disappearance, and then by the shocking truth about who he was. How could he now turn around and blame her for making what she'd thought were the best decisions she could under those circumstances?

After all, she had not known how deeply she had touched him then, and how she had continued to prey on his thoughts for all of those years. Only he had known it, and he had barely allowed the truth of his feelings for her to register. He had buried them with his uncle, buried them with all the remnants of his former life, buried them all and told himself that he preferred his life that way. That Jessa herself was tainted by her association with his former, profligate self, and thus could never be considered a possible consort or queen for the King of Nur. The kind of woman who would fall in love with Tariq the black sheep was by definition unfit for the king. And if he woke in the night and heard her voice, or felt phantom fingers trail along his skin, no one had ever needed to know that but him.

And yet he had still gone to find her, breaking all of his own rules, telling himself any number of lies—anything to be near her once again. Had he known even then that one night could never be enough? Had that been why he had fought against it for so long?

He stooped to shift her from the couch into his arms, lifting her high against his chest and carrying her with him through the house, aware that something in him whispered that she belonged there, that she fit there perfectly. She nestled against him, her body easy with him in sleep in a way she would never be were she awake. He felt a sudden pang of nostalgia for the freely given love of the young girl he'd so callously thrown away. She felt good so close against him. She felt like his.

In his rooms, he deposited her gently on the bed, removing her shoes and pulling the coverlet over her. For a moment he gazed down at her, watching her breathe, and let the strange tenderness he felt wash through him. He did not try to judge it, or deny it. He thought of what it must have been like for her, to be so alone, abandoned and forced into so difficult a position. They were not that different, the two of them, he thought. Each of them thrust, alone, into positions they had never meant to occupy.

Without letting himself think it through, he climbed into the bed behind her, pulling her close, so her back was flush against his chest, her bottom nestled between his thighs. He inhaled deeply, letting her distinct scents wash over him, soothing him, letting him imagine that they could both heal. Jasmine in her hair, and something sweet and warm beneath that he knew was simply Jessa. Vanilla and heat.

She stirred, and he knew when she woke by the sudden tension in her body where before there was only languor. He smoothed a hand down her side, tracing the curves of her body, as if he could erase what she had suffered so easily.

"I did not mean to fall asleep," she whispered into the dark room. She moved under his hands, as if testing her boundaries, as if she thought she was his prisoner.

Tariq did not respond. He only held her and pretended he did not know why he could not let her go.

"In the morning," she continued, her voice much too careful, much too polite, "I will head home. I think it's best." She moved as if to separate from him, and he let his arm fall away from her when he wanted only to hold on, to keep her close, as if she was sunlight and he was an acre of frozen earth, desperate for winter to end.

"Tariq?" She turned toward him. He twisted over onto his back, aware of a different kind of need surging through him. A need for peace, the peace that only holding her close had ever brought him. "Should I find somewhere else to sleep?" she asked, her voice tentative. Scared. Of him. And why shouldn't she be, after the things he had done?

He could not bear it. And he refused to think about why.

And then, from that place inside him that he could not fully admit existed, yet could no longer ignore, he whispered, "I do not want you to go, Jessa. Not yet."

CHAPTER THIRTEEN

ONE week passed, and then another, and the subject of Jessa's departure did not come up again. Jessa had made the necessary calls home to her sister and to her boss, and had taken the long overdue vacation time she was owed that she had never bothered to take before.

"*Where* are you?" her sister Sharon had asked, shocked, when Jessa got her on the phone. "Since when do you run off on a holiday at the drop of a hat?"

"I had an urge to see Paris, that's all," Jessa had lied.

"I wish I could swan off to Paris on a lark!" Sharon had said. And then the time to mention who she was with and why she was with him had passed the moment Sharon put down the phone, so it had remained Jessa's secret.

It wasn't that she was trying to hide the fact that she was with Tariq from her sister, necessarily, but she wasn't planning to trumpet it from the rooftops, either. She told herself that there was nothing unusual in it; she and Tariq were simply giving themselves some space and time to process the loss of Jeremy together rather than apart. Who else could understand how it felt? They were being healthy, she thought, modern; and part of her believed it.

Jessa had all of Paris to explore each day, as Tariq spent

his time closeted in meetings or on the telephone with his advisors, political allies, and business contacts—tending to his kingdom from afar.

"Tell me what you saw today," Tariq asked each evening, and Jessa would relate stories of freshly baked baguettes, lazy afternoons in cafés, or walking tours of famous monuments. Each evening she tried harder to make him smile. Each evening she found herself more and more invested in whether or not she succeeded.

"I have always loved Paris," Tariq told her one night as they lingered over coffee out in one of the city's famous restaurants, where the service was so impeccable that Jessa almost felt compelled to apologize every time she shifted in her chair. "My uncle used this residence as a vacation home, but I prefer to use it as a base for my European business concerns." He leaned back against his chair in an indolent way that called attention to all the power he kept caged in his lean, muscled frame.

"What isn't to love?" Jessa agreed with a happy smile, propping her elbow on the table and resting her chin on her hand. She could look at him for hours. His face alone compelled her—all that harshness and cruelty tempered by the keen intelligence in his eyes. "It mixes magic with practicality."

It was as if she had forgotten they had ever felt like adversaries, though, of course, she had not. This sweet truce between them was far more dangerous than the wars they had already fought and survived. She was so much more at risk when he looked at her the way he did tonight, with something she so desperately wanted to call tenderness.

"Indeed," he agreed now, and their eyes caught, something more potent than the rich brew in their cups surging between them, making Jessa's pulse race.

"Tariq," she said softly, not wishing to break the spell between them but knowing she should speak, knowing she should acknowledge the truth of things, "you know that I—"

"Come," he said, pushing back from the table. "We shall walk home along the Seine and you will tell me which Van Gogh in the Musée d'Orsay you prefer."

"I cannot possibly choose," she said, but she let him pull her to her feet, exulting in the slide of his palm against hers. *Why not dream a little longer?* she asked herself. Who would it hurt?

"Then you must tell me about the Musée Rodin instead," he said, taking a moment too long before releasing her hand and stepping back to pull out her chair. "I have not been in many years."

Jessa had studied every luscious, supple curve of stone in the museum he mentioned, and had marveled at the raw sensual power of marble statues that should have seemed cold and dead yet instead begged to be touched, caressed. As she thought she might do at any moment.

But Tariq only took her arm and ushered her out into the soft Parisian night.

Sharing Jeremy's adoption with him had changed something, Jessa realized as they walked together along the banks of the Seine in a silence that was not quite comfortable—too charged was it with their simmering chemistry and the restraint they had shown in not touching each other in so long. Not since that first night.

Later, back at the grand house, when Tariq had politely excused himself and she was left in the lonely expanse of the bedroom suite, she thought more about the evening's revelation. Jeremy was not her private pain now, to hoard and to hurt herself with. It was theirs to share, and the sharing not only lessened the hurt, it removed all the walls she'd built around it. In place of those walls was something far too delicate and shimmering to name. She did not want to think about when she had felt this way before, and what had become of her.

"You are such a fool," she whispered aloud, her voice swallowed up by the ornate furnishings all around her.

But she also did not want to think about the one crucial bit of information she had withheld from him. The one small yet crucial fact about Jeremy she had not been able to bring herself to share. She could not quite trust him with it, could she? Not when she knew deep down that this was a fantasy she was living in, something that would not, *could not* last. Protecting Jeremy was forever. It had to be.

It was as if, Jessa thought as she changed her clothes for dinner a few nights later, having hurt each other so terribly and so irrevocably they were now both easing their way into enjoying each other's company, as if that might make the pain lessen. As if it could make it bearable somehow.

She twisted her hair into a chignon, gathering her heavy copper curls at the nape of her neck and pinning them into place, then looked at herself in the mirror of the dressing room. She felt like Cinderella. With her hair up in the casually elegant bun, she thought she looked a bit like Cinderella, too. It was so easy to get used to the life she'd been living these past weeks, without a care in the world, wandering Paris by day and exploring the many facets of Tariq's beguiling mind at night. The dressing room contained an array of clothes tailored to her precise measurements, all of which fit perfectly and made her look like someone other than Jessa Heath of Fulford: office manager in a letting agency and all-around nobody.

The Jessa she saw in the mirror was no ordinary Yorkshire lass. Tariq had mentioned the evening would be formal, and so she wore a floor-length satin gown the color of buttercream. It whispered and murmured seductively as she moved, the neckline plunging to hint at her breasts and the perfumed hollow between, then catching her at the waist before falling in lush folds to the ground. Her back was very nearly bare, with only thin angled shoulder straps to hold the gown in place. Though Jessa would have thought her very English paleness would look sickly in a gown so light, the color instead seemed to make her skin glow. Her freckles seemed like bursts of vibrant color rather than an embarrassment.

"You are lovely," a familiar voice said from behind her, causing Jessa to start, though of course she knew who she would see when she looked in the mirror. Her body knew without having to hear the words he spoke. It reacted to the very sound of his voice, the hint of his nearness, with the now familiar rush of wild heat that suffused her.

Tariq stood in the entry to the dressing room, mouth-wateringly debonair in his tuxedo, his long, strong body packaged to breathtaking perfection. His eyes seemed more green than usual, standing out from his dark hair and the black suit like some kind of deep forest beacon. His hard features seemed more handsome than fierce tonight, more approachable. Jessa felt a little stunned herself.

"Am I late?" she asked, feeling unaccountably shy suddenly in the face of so much steely male beauty. It was unfair that any one man could exude as much raw magnetism as he did, and so carelessly. She met his gaze in the mirror and then looked away, heat staining in her cheeks.

"Not at all," he said, and she knew he lied. There was a certain tenderness in his eyes that she could not account for, and could not seem to handle—it made it hard to breathe.

"Where are we going?" she asked.

The room around them seemed to contract and she pretended she was unaffected, that her nipples did not tighten to rigid points, that she could not feel the pull low in her belly. Sometimes he put his hand in the small of her back to guide her, or helped her out of a car, and though she felt even his smallest touch in every part of her being, that had been the extent of it. Though they had spent their first night together in every conceivable position, a vivid and carnal exploration of their passion, they had spent the weeks since merely talking—a curious inversion that was starting to make her shaky with need. He did not sleep with her at night and yet she knew with a deep, feminine certainty that he wanted her as much, if not more, than before.

"I must attend a benefit dinner," Tariq said, and shrugged. "It is of little importance. A dinner, a speech or two, and some dancing. You will be bored beyond reason."

As if that were possible when she was with this man. Jessa forced a smile, determined not to let the deeper emotions she could feel boiling within her spill over. This was a dream, nothing more. Cinderella went to the ball, and she would too, but that was all there was to it. The rest of the story did not apply, had never applied. She had no right to dream any Cinderella dreams, and she knew it.

"I am ready," she said, turning to him, and then stopped, caught by the arrested look on his face. As if he had been waiting for those words, but in a different context. Something unnamed but no less heavy crowded the room, narrowing the distance between them, making her pulse pound.

"Tariq?" Her voice was barely a whisper of sound.

He stood for a moment, his gaze consuming her, his mouth a flat, hard line that against all reason she longed to press her own lips against. Her heart kicked in her chest.

For a moment it seemed as if he might close the distance between them. His eyes dropped to caress her mouth, and Jessa felt it as surely as if he'd used his fingers. Her lips parted slightly, yearning for him.

"Very well then," he said, his voice rough, in his eyes all the things he had not done, all the ways he had not touched her. "Let us go."

Tariq bin Khaled Al-Nur's version of a party of no importance, Jessa found, was in fact a star-studded gala of epic proportions. Dignitaries, politicians and European nobles brushed elbows with cinema stars and international celebrities, in a shower of flashbulbs that overtook one of the famous arcades. The gala took place in a sumptuous hotel near the Place Vendôme and the Jardin des Tuileries, which Tariq confided had less historical significance than the hotel liked to admit. Jessa hardly knew where to look—from the frescoes adorning the ceiling of the reception room to the colossal gilt chandeliers that hung overhead to the rich red of the thick drapes and carpets. She felt as if she were in another world. A dream within a dream.

But this world was one in which Tariq was a king, and treated as such—not merely Tariq, her former lover. Jessa had known he was a powerful man, but she had never seen him in his element before except on television. Tonight, the fact that Tariq was an imperial power was made clear to her in a thousand little ways. It was the near-fawning deference he was shown, the deep bows he was accorded. It was the visible respect of the aides who ran interference for him, tending to his every wish and deflecting those whom he did not wish to interact with. It was the way everyone called him *Your Highness* or

Excellency, when they dared address him at all. Men Jessa only recognized from the news pulled him aside to whisper in his ear.

Once again, Jessa had the odd sensation that the world was shifting beneath her feet. It was one thing to know that Tariq was a king. What did that mean, in the abstract, shut up together in rooms where first and foremost she saw him as a man? It was something else again to really witness what it was for him to be a king, and, she could not help but think, that this was how he was treated in a country not his own. What must it be like when he was at home in Nur? Even among his peers, Tariq stood apart. He was harder, tougher. He was a warrior among bureaucrats.

She had no right to the fantasies that crept in, teasing her when she was less than vigilant. She knew her place in the world. Tariq was meant for a queen, not Jessa. Never Jessa.

"You seem unusually quiet," he said into her ear at one point, as they waited for dinner to be served. She could feel his breath fanning along her skin, teasing her nerve endings. She held back a shiver of delight.

"I am merely basking in Your Excellency's shadow," she replied, smiling at him. His hard mouth kicked up in the corner, surprising her. She snuck a look around the table. Here sat a recognizable head of state, there lounged an internationally acclaimed philanthropist; everyone exuded power of one kind or another.

"I imagine it must go to your head," she said.

He did not pretend to misunderstand her. "It is who I have become," he said simply, his gaze direct. Proud.

Had part of her been resistant to the very idea of his elevation in rank and status, even from a distance? Had she hoped, somewhere deep inside, that the doctor's son she'd loved so totally was the real Tariq and the wildly powerful king only a bad dream? Back then, he had simply been a man, however complicated. And now he was a king, and even more complicated. It was not only his job, his role. It was how he saw the world. It was who he was, every cell and every breath.

"Yes," she said softly. "I see that." She longed to touch him, but she did not dare. She did not know if there were rules of etiquette to follow, boundaries to observe.

"I cannot change the past," he said, and suddenly it was as if no one existed save the two of them. She forgot about rules, or other eyes, and drank him in.

"Neither can I," she replied without looking away.

So much loss. So many years wasted, a whole life created and given away to others. But could she honestly say she would change any part of it? Knowing that it resulted in a happy, thriving Jeremy? Something sharp twisted through her then, reminding her that she had not told him everything—could not tell him everything, even now.

"Perhaps it is time we stop looking back, then, you and I," Tariq said in a hushed voice, no less powerful for its low volume. It made something inside swell with a quiet kind of wonder, pushing all else aside.

"Where should we look?" She was in awe of what loomed between them, that made her fingers tremble and her eyes bright with a wild heat, though she refused to name it. She refused.

Tariq lifted her hand to his mouth and placed a kiss on the back of it, never breaking eye contact, not even when he sucked gently on the knuckle and made her gasp. Heat seared through her, melting her. The fire was never gone when he was near—it was only ever banked. Waiting for a trigger, a spark.

"I am sure we'll think of something," he said huskily.

* * *

Tariq turned to her the moment they crossed the threshold into the house, sweeping her into his arms and fastening his mouth to hers. He could not get enough of her taste, her heat, the soft and warm feel of her pressed against him. Jessa melted against him, her softness inflaming him, looping her arms around the column of his neck and arching into him. He tasted her again and again, exploring her mouth, feeling the kick of her immediate, uninhibited response flood through him.

Once again, he lifted her into his arms and carried her toward the bedroom, up the great stairs and toward their rooms on the top floor. Her fingers toyed with the ends of his hair where it brushed the top of his collar. Her eyes gleamed in the low lights of the quiet house around them while a secret, feminine smile curved her lips.

There were so many things he wanted to say, but he did not know where to start. He only knew that she had become necessary to him. Their tangled history was wrapped around him and growing tighter by the day, making it hard to breathe when she was not within reach. He found his way into the bedroom and set her down, unable to look away. One breath. Another.

She made a soft noise and reached out for him, her small hands framing his face, and pulled his mouth to hers. She tasted like honey and wine and went straight to his head, his heart, his aching hardness.

He set her away from him, turning her so he could look at the expanse of her creamy skin bared by the open back of her gown. He put his mouth, open and hot, on the tender nape of her neck, just to make her moan. He traced her spine with his fingers, making her shiver.

"All night I have wondered how soft your skin would be when I touched it," he told her in a low murmur, continuing to taste and touch. "You are better than crème brûlée, sweet and rich."

She let out a laugh, and the small sound ignited something in him, wild and hot and out of control.

He walked her over to the high bed, bending her forward until she braced herself on her elbows against the mattress. He heard the soft exclamation that she blew out on a sigh, or perhaps her breathing was as ragged as his. She turned her head, peering over her shoulder at him, her cinnamon eyes wide and inviting. Her lips parted, and he was certain he could hear the beat of her heart under his own skin. He held her gaze as he slowly pulled her gown up over her trim ankles, her shapely calves, her knees—

"Tariq, please…" It was a moan.

He knelt down between her open thighs, pushing the soft folds of material out of his way, marveling that her skin was softer than the satin of her gown. He pressed a kiss to the hollow behind her knee, the curve of her thigh, the crease where her thigh ended and her lush round bottom began. He curled his fingers into the soft scrap of material that covered her sex, and pulled her panties down and out of his way, helping her step out of them before he tossed them aside. He could feel her tremble. He ran his hands up her legs, testing her flesh beneath his palms. He leaned in close and inhaled the musky scent of her arousal and, moving forward to lick into her softness, tasted the wet, honeyed heat of her sex.

Tariq heard her cry out his name, but he was too far gone to reply. He knew only that he had to be inside of her, joined with her. So deep it would not matter what he could or could not say. He stood, his hands rough and desperate on the fly of his trousers. He sighed as he released himself, hard and pulsing with need. Stepping closer, he guided himself with one hand while he gripped her hip with the other, and drove into her depths.

It was perfect. She was perfect.

Tariq pressed his mouth against her neck, her shoulder, as he began to move, driving them both slowly insane with each sure thrust. He felt her stiffen, heard her cry out, and then she shook apart beneath him, moaning again and again. He withdrew, flipping her over even while she continued to gasp through the aftershocks, and settled her on the edge of the bed.

Her face was flushed, her hair in a mad tangle over one shoulder. Still she smiled at him and opened her arms, her eyes reflecting the man she saw in him—the man he wanted to be, and could be, when she looked at him that way.

Tariq moved over her, and slid back inside of her, making them both groan. She braced her hands against his chest. Still clad in his coat and dress shirt, he set a fierce, uncompromising pace. She locked her ankles in the small of his back and arched her breasts toward his mouth. He tasted her flesh, like salt and a sweetness he knew was all Jessa. All his.

When he hurtled over the edge, he took her with him. She shook around him, sobbing out his name like a song.

When he could think again, Tariq stood, pulling her to her feet and helping her out of the gown. Sleepy-eyed and deliciously naked, she crawled back into the bed, and curled on her side to watch him as he pulled off his formal clothes and tossed them in the direction of the nearest chair.

She was his. She belonged to him, whether it made sense or not, whether she knew it or not. She had survived their past and still made love to him with her whole self, body and soul. She had seen him in both of his incarnations, the shameful past as well as the present, and wanted him anyway.

There was more to it than possessiveness, a wide swathe of darker, deeper emotion, but Tariq pushed that aside. The possessiveness he understood. He could not give her up. Not again. He could not lose her unrestrained passion, her unstudied abandon when he touched her. He could not lose *her*. He did not want to think about it any further than that. He did not need to. He knew it to be true with a deep, implacable certainty.

"I must return to Nur," he said abruptly. He saw her tense almost imperceptibly and then drop her eyes to the mattress. "I have been putting it off these past weeks."

"Of course," she murmured, her voice even and yet distant, he thought. The hectic color faded from her cheeks as she stared at her hands. "We must all return to real life eventually. I understand."

How could she understand, when he was not sure he did? But he could easily picture her in the royal palace, wearing silks and jewels that enhanced her quiet beauty, while he made love to her on low pillows or feasted on her lush body in some desert oasis. He could see her against the bright blue skies and the shifting white sands, her eyes mysterious like his people's favorite spices, making him long to taste her over and over again. He saw her in his arms and immediately felt better. Safer, somehow, however illogical that seemed.

"I do not think you do," he said slowly, climbing onto the bed, holding her gaze with his as he prowled toward her on his hands and knees. "I want you to come with me, Jessa. I insist upon it."

"You insist…?" she breathed, but the color returned to her face, red and hot. Her eyes glowed.

He would never let her go again. *Never.*

"I am the king," he said, and pulled her to him once more.

CHAPTER FOURTEEN

"I WILL not hold you to what you said last night," Jessa told him the following morning, not quite meeting his eyes as she sat down at the breakfast table. "About going with you to Nur."

The morning was bright and unseasonably warm for Paris in autumn, which seemed to Jessa like a stark, strange contrast to inside the bedroom suite, where Tariq had taken her once again before she had fully come awake, pushing his way into her morning shower with that intense look in his eyes and driving her to ecstatic screams against the tiles. She was still quivering.

Tariq had called for breakfast to be served on the private balcony outside the bedroom, more secluded than the one she had seen that first night. He wore a dark button-down dress shirt over dark trousers, the coarse silk of his hair brushing the collar. She thought he looked like a warrior god pretending to be at rest, masquerading as some kind of businessman. The early morning sun teased the treetops and casement windows that lined the ancient street in front of her, and made her think she could do what she'd decided she must do in the shattering aftermath of his lovemaking. She pulled her robe tighter around her and touched the wet hair she'd piled atop her head. She could act serene and calm and disinterested over rich black coffee and croissants so soft they seemed like clouds and butter. She could prove that she was no longer that infatuated, broken girl he'd left behind once before.

"Will you not?" He did not glance up from the papers he read, and yet the fine hairs on the back of her neck stood up in warning.

"Of course not," she said, feeling her temper engage and roll through her. Surely he should at least pay attention when she was attempting to be noble! She knew that if she went with him to Nur, she would not be able to maintain even a tenuous grip on the realities of their different situations in life. She knew she would be lost. "I have my own life to be getting back to, in any case."

Tariq laid his papers to the side of his plate and leveled a look at her. Jessa kept herself from squirming in her chair by sheer force of will.

"If you do not wish to accompany me to my country, then say you do not wish it," he said evenly. "But do not wrap it up in some attempt to release me from an obligation. If I did not want you to come, I would not have invited you."

"I was not—" she began, stung, though his words resonated more than she would have liked.

"We leave tomorrow morning," he said, rising to his feet. He crooked his brows as he looked down at her. "You must decide."

"Decide?" she echoed, her heart thumping too hard against her ribs. "Decide what?"

"If you will accompany me of your own free will," he said, his eyes gleaming, "or if I will simply take you."

"You cannot *take* me anywhere!" she gasped, but her

body betrayed her, her sex warming and melting as surely as if he'd touched her with his clever, provocative hands.

"If you say so," he said. He reached down and cupped her cheek with one large hand, his mouth unsmiling and his gaze intent, though still showing his amusement. And still it was as if he was branding her with his touch, his eyes. She felt small, safe and threatened at the same time— and more than that, *his*.

Completely and indisputably his.

His thumb dragged across her full lower lip, sending desire shooting through her body, tightening her nipples, wetting her sex further. Tariq smiled then, as if he could see her body's reaction. One dark eyebrow arched as color heated Jessa's cheeks. Point made, he turned away, disappearing inside the house and leaving her to her ragged breathing and her pounding heart.

He wanted to take her to Nur.

Part of her rejoiced for what that must mean, surely. It meant at the very least that he did not want this idyll in Paris to end any more than she did. But, of course, it was not quite that simple. Jessa drew her legs up beneath her on the chair, and stared out over the city she had come to love over the past dreamlike weeks, as if that could give her the answer.

She could not go to Nur. She could not continue to stay with him, ignoring reality while she played pretend. There were hundreds of reasons she should run back to York as quickly as she could.

And only one reason to stay.

Jessa rested her chin on her drawn-up knees and let out a shuddering breath as the shattering truth washed over her like the Paris sunlight, sweet and bright and unequivocal.

I love him.

She was in love with him. With Tariq, who had hurt her and lied to her. Who she was still lying to, if only by omission. Who she had made love to anyway, deliciously and repeatedly. Whose pain upset her, made her want to comfort and heal him, even when she was what caused it, and even when her own pain matched his. Their complicated, messy history should have made him the last man on earth she could ever have feelings for, but instead she felt closer to him because of it. As if no one could ever really understand her or what she'd been through, more than the man who grieved along with her.

Had she always loved him? Had she never fallen *out* of love with him? He had left and she had been forced to carry on, and she had had reason enough to be furious with him in the abstract, but she had still found her way into his bed within days of laying eyes on him again. She had told herself it was for her own purposes, but the reality was, she hadn't leaped into bed with anyone else. She had never wanted anyone else the way she wanted Tariq.

She wondered if on some level she had deliberately left her bag with her bank card behind when she'd set out for the train—because she hadn't really wanted to leave him.

She wanted to go with him wherever he wanted to take her, even though she knew it was highly likely that he would break her heart when he married someone more appropriate, but she couldn't find it in her to be as worried about that eventuality as she ought to be. It was clear to her now that she had been desperately in love with Tariq since the day she'd first seen him all those years ago, and there was no point in pretending otherwise. Just as there was no point attempting to be noble and leave him first— she might as well enjoy what little time with him she had, the better to hold on to in the lonely years to come.

Because Jessa knew that Tariq could never love her, not after what she had done in giving Jeremy away. How could he, when it was obvious to her that he had wanted his own family so desperately for all of his life? The truth was that she knew, deep down, that she had no right to him. She had been given the opportunity for a second chance, and she was not strong enough to resist it, even though it was clear to her that he would leave her once again.

Jessa uncurled from her chair and stood, staring out at the view but seeing instead his hard, proud face. He didn't have to love her. She would love him enough for them both. She was no stranger to hard love, love like stone, all immovable surfaces and impossibilities. She loved Jeremy more than she had ever thought it possible to love another person, and yet she had given him away, and knew with every breath and every regret that it had been the right decision no matter how much it hurt. She was used to love that bit back and left marks and forced her to be strong.

She could be strong for Tariq, too.

Her sister Sharon was a different story.

"Have you gone mad?" Sharon demanded down the telephone line, sounding scandalized—and uncharacteristically shrill.

Jessa had fortified herself with several cups of the hot, rich coffee from the breakfast service, but it seemed to have done nothing but make her agitated. Or perhaps she was already agitated. She had dressed with extra care, as if Sharon might be able to see her through the telephone and perhaps intuit what Jessa had been doing, but she found that the simple silk blouse and A-line skirt made her feel as insane as Sharon accused her of being. Was she dressing up, pretending to be someone else? Someone more sophisticated that Tariq could love? *Foolish,* she scolded herself, and adjusted her position, holding her mobile close to her ear.

"I don't know how to answer that," she told her sister, which was no more than the truth. She'd settled in for this conversation in the sitting room off the master suite, on the prim settee next to the windows, her back to the breathtaking view of Paris and angled away from the stunning Cézanne painting that took up most of the far wall—she wanted no distractions.

"I thought it was strange enough that you'd run off on a holiday with no advance warning," Sharon continued. "But to get mixed up with that man again? Jessa, how could you?"

"You don't know him," Jessa said evenly, feeling called to protect Tariq, even from her sister who could do him no real harm. Quite the opposite, in fact.

"I know quite enough!" Sharon said with a snort. "I know that he lied to you and left you! I know that men like him think they can swan in and out of people's lives as they please, with no thought to the consequences!"

"Tariq is not the same person he was then," Jessa said. She sighed. "And nothing is really as simple as it might have seemed back then."

"You can do whatever you like with your own life, no matter how reckless, but this isn't just about you, is it?" Sharon let out a ragged breath. "Selfish!" she half whispered, but Jessa heard her perfectly. She could even picture what her sister was doing—pacing the kitchen in her cottage with one arm wrapped around her waist, her face set in a terrible frown—as if she was there to see it in person.

Jessa told herself not to snap back at Sharon. Of course her sister was terrified by the prospect of Jessa with Tariq again. How could she not be? Jessa closed her eyes and lay her palm flat against her chest, just above her heart, as if she could massage away the ache that bloomed there. She could love Sharon, too, because she knew full well that beneath her sister's prickly exterior she loved Jessa in return. Sharon had always been there for Jessa. And wasn't that what love was for, in the end? To embrace others when they most needed it, whether they appreciated it or not?

"I would never do anything to hurt you," Jessa said softly, pinching the top of her nose between her fingers, hoping the headache that had bloomed there would fade. "Any of you. As you should know already. But I am going to go with him." She braced herself. "I have to."

"I can't believe this!" Sharon hissed. "What is it about this man that turns you so dense, Jessa? People don't change. He will hurt you all over again. That's a promise."

Jessa felt as if she'd been in suspended animation for years, with nothing but ice water and regret in her veins, until Tariq had roared back into her life and filled her with heat and life and love. How could she ever regret that, no matter what happened? But she couldn't share that with Sharon.

"I only phoned to let you know that I'll be traveling," Jessa said after a moment, fighting to keep her voice steady, and not to give in to the kick of adrenaline and insecurity that made her want to slap back at her sister. "I'm not asking for your permission."

She opened her eyes again and let them fall on the glorious painting on the wall across from her seat. It was a mountain scene, blues and greens and none of it soothing, somehow, with Sharon so angry.

"I cannot believe that you would risk so much on what? Your *hope* that things might be different?" Sharon made a bitter sort of sound. "I *hope* you haven't gone off the deep end!"

"I hope so, too," Jessa murmured, because there was nothing she could say that could make Sharon feel any better.

Sharon hung up the phone. Jessa let hers drop into her lap, and ordered herself to breathe. Her eyes were wide open this time. She had loved him when nothing about him was true, and she loved him now. Still. Did that make her the fool her sister thought her? Did she mind terribly if it did?

"Who were you talking to?" Tariq asked from the doorway, his low voice making Jessa jump in her seat as if scalded. Her eyes flew to his and she felt the blood drain from her face. She felt raw. Exposed. Had she said anything incriminating? Had she mentioned Jeremy?

"How long have you been standing there?" she asked, trying to sound calm, but her voice was far too high-pitched. Her heart pounded as if she'd just run a mile. It was too much—Sharon's frustrated anger and her own realizations about her feelings for Tariq. How could she face him before she had time to pull herself back together?

But it was too late—he was standing right in front of her, and Jessa was suddenly terrified that he could read her like a book.

Guilty. That was the look on her face, he realized after a moment of confusion. Guilty and pale.

"What is the matter?" he asked, searching her expression, all of his senses on red alert. He had finished a meeting more quickly than he'd expected, and had come here hoping to convince her to help him while away the time before the next meeting more pleasurably. He had not expected that he would find her secretive and jumpy. While he watched, she surged to her feet and held her mobile phone behind her, as if hiding it.

"Nothing is the matter," she said, but her voice was too uneven. Tariq felt his instincts kick in, the ones that served him well in politics as well as in combat situations. He moved closer to her.

"Who was that on the phone?" he asked again, this time with less curiosity and more command.

"No one," she said. Then she blinked and smiled, but it was not a real smile. It was far too strained. "It was my sister, Sharon, that's all."

"Did your sister upset you?" he asked. He searched her face. "With your parents gone, you must be close to her and her family."

She flinched, that guilty look stealing across her face again, though this time she tried to hide it. It was an absurd, over-the-top reaction, and he reached out a hand toward her, frowning, worried that something was truly the matter—

And suddenly, somehow, he knew.

The photograph he'd seen in her house flashed before his eyes, the one he'd snatched from the mantel and given only a cursory glance. The sister who looked like Jessa— the same copper-colored hair, the same chin. Her fair-haired, freckled husband.

And their olive-skinned, dark-haired child.

No. He felt himself freeze solid from the inside out, as if he'd been thrown headfirst into a glacier. *She could not have done this and not have told me, not after all of this—*

"Tell me," he said, feeling still, quiet, empty and bleak. "What is the name of your sister's child?"

It was as if he saw her from a great distance then. He saw her face twist into misery. Her hands clenched together in front of her. She was the very picture of distress.

"Tariq," she said, her voice heavy, and he knew it was true. "You don't understand."

All this time he had believed the child lost to him forever, believed that was no more than what he deserved—the reward for his wasted life. And all this time she had smiled so sweetly, made him feel as if she was the family he had longed for—all while knowing exactly where his child, *his son,* was!

"What exactly is it that I do not understand?" he asked her icily, his gaze boring into her. He held himself carefully, afraid that if he moved he would shatter into a rage so hot it would burn him, her, the whole house, the entire damned city. "Were you planning to tell me? Ever?"

"I couldn't," she said, her voice thick, her eyes bright with tears. "It is not my secret to tell."

"That excuse might work, Jessa, were I not the only other person on this earth who has a right to know *at least* as much about the child I never knew I had as you!"

"It is not about you!" she cried, throwing her arms wide. "It's about *him*, Tariq! It's about what *he* needs!"

"You let me think that he was lost to us forever. You *let me* think it!" His whisper was fierce, furious. He could taste the acrid flavor of betrayal in his mouth, feel it corroding him, turning everything he had believed about her—about the two of them—to burned-out husks and charred remains.

"This is exactly the reaction I was trying to prevent!" she cried.

"You have said enough." He silenced her with a slash of his hand through the air, and then he turned and stalked toward the door.

She had never planned to tell him. She had made love to him, comforted him, and had had no intention of telling him that all the while she knew where his son—his heir—was. He stopped walking when he reached the doorway, and stood there for a moment, fighting for control.

"Don't you think I would have noticed the resemblance at some point?" he asked, not turning back to her. "What story did you plan to tell me then?"

"When would you have seen him?" she asked after a moment, sounding genuinely confused. He turned then and stared at her in disbelief.

"Are you ashamed to be seen with me?" he asked acidly. "I think it is too late for these protestations, Jessa. You have been photographed in my company."

"I don't understand what you're talking about!" she cried. "I didn't think you'd ever lay eyes on him. Why would you spend time with my family?"

"I told you I was taking you to my country," he snapped at her. "What do you think that entails?"

"I'm sure you take a thousand women to your country!" she threw back at him, color high in her cheeks, her eyes dark.

"You are incorrect," he said icily, each word cutting. "I would never take a woman to my people unless I planned to keep her. Though that is no longer a subject you need concern yourself with."

She stared at him in shocked silence. He felt something move in him, but stamped it down. *No. Damn her.* Her pain did not, could not, matter—not anymore.

Tariq shook his head and turned back toward the door.

"Please…" she said, though it sounded more like a sob. "Where are you going?"

The look he threw back at her should have burned her alive.

"To see my son," he bit out.

And then he strode from the room before he broke something. Before she broke him any further than she already had.

CHAPTER FIFTEEN

OTHER than informing her that her presence was required only to assure him access to the child, Tariq cut her off completely. He did not speak to her on the plane, he merely sat in a thunderous silence that made Jessa ache in ways she would have thought impossible, though she would not let herself dissolve into tears as she wished. He did not speak to her in the car that took them from Leeds to York and then up the York Road toward the North Yorkshire Moors, and the small village along the way where Sharon had moved almost four years ago. Jessa could hardly stand to look at the cultivated fields that spread out on all sides, that intense British green against the cold gray skies. She could see only the coming heartbreak, the doom, the end of everything she had fought so hard to provide for the son she had loved enough to let go. She knew that no one could emerge from it unscathed, not her sister and Barry, not Tariq, not herself.

And worst of all, not Jeremy.

"I don't know what your plan is," Jessa said in a low voice as the car turned into the village and made its way along the high street. It was not the first time she had attempted to speak to him, but there was a desperation in her voice that had not been there before. "You cannot simply arrive at my sister's house and make demands!"

"Watch me," Tariq said, his voice vibrating with the same fury that had gripped him since Paris. He did not look at Jessa. He kept his brooding gaze fixed on the village that slid by outside the window, one elegant hand tapping out his agitation against the armrest.

"Tariq, this is madness!" Jessa cried. "My sister has adopted him! It is all quite legal, and cannot be undone!"

"You will not tell me what can and cannot be undone," he bit out, turning his head to pierce her with his dark, imperious gaze. He was angrier than she'd ever seen him, and all of it so brutally cold, so bitter. "You, who would lie about something like this? Who would conceal a child from his own father? I have no interest in what *you* think I should or should not do!"

"I understand that you're angry," Jessa said, fighting to keep her voice level. He laughed slightly, in disbelief. She set her jaw and forged ahead anyway. "I understand that you think you've been betrayed."

"That I *think* I have been betrayed?" he echoed, his eyes burning into her. He sat as far away from her as it was possible to sit in the enclosed space of the car, and yet she could feel him invading her space, taking her over, crowding her. "I would hate to see what you consider a real betrayal, Jessa, if this does not qualify."

"This is not about you," Jessa said as firmly as she could when she was trembling. "Don't you see? This has nothing to do with me or you. This is about—"

"We are here," he said dismissively, cutting her off as the car pulled up at Sharon's front gate. Tariq did not wait for the driver to get out of the car, he simply threw open his door and climbed out.

Jessa threw herself out after him, her chest heaving as if she'd run a marathon. Tariq paused for a moment outside the gate, and she knew it was now or never. After everything she had sacrificed—including, though it made her want to weep, Tariq himself—she could not let him wreck it all. She had to try one last time.

She lunged forward and grabbed on to his arm, holding him when he might have walked through the gate.

"Release my arm," he said almost tonelessly, though she did not mistake the menace underneath, nor the way he tensed his strong muscles beneath her hands.

"You have to listen to me!" she gasped. "You have to!"

"I have listened to you, and I have listened to you," Tariq said coldly, his eyes black with his anger. "I have watched you weep and I have heard you talk about how much you regret what you had to do, what you did because of me. I did not realize you were still punishing me!"

"It was not because of you!" Jessa cried as the wind cut into her, chilling her. "It was because of me!" She dragged in a wild breath, all the tears she'd been fighting off surging forth, and she simply let them. "I am the one who was so deficient that you left me in the first place, and I am the one who failed so completely as a mother that I couldn't keep my own baby! *Me.*"

She had his attention then. He stilled, his dark eyes intense on hers.

"But I did one thing right," Jessa continued, fighting to keep the tears from her voice. "I made sure he was with people who loved him—who already loved him—who could give him the world. And he is happy here, Tariq, happier than I ever could have made him."

"A child is happiest with his own parents," Tariq said.

Did she imagine that his voice was a trifle less cold? Was it possible?

Jessa stared at him, her fingers flexing into his arm, demanding that he hear her now if he heard her at all.

"He *is* with his parents," she whispered fiercely.

Tariq made a noise that might have been a roar of anger, checked behind the muscle that worked in his jaw. He shook her hands off his arm. Jessa let them drop to her sides.

"He is my blood," he snarled at her. *"Mine!"*

"His family is here," Jessa continued because she had to. Because it was true. "Right here. And he has no idea that he ever had any parents but these."

"Why am I not surprised that your sister would keep this secret as well?" Tariq demanded. "You are a family of liars!"

"He is a little boy who has only ever known *these* parents and *this* home!" Jessa cried. The wind whipped into her, racing down from the moors, and her hair danced between them like a copper flame. She shoved it back. "There's no lie here! They are his parents by law, and in fact. He loves them, Tariq. He *loves* them!"

His hard mouth was set in an obstinate line. "He is not yet five years old. He will learn—"

"You lost your parents, and so did I," Jessa interrupted, her heart pounding so hard in her head, her throat, that she thought she might faint. But she could not, so she did not. She searched his remote, angry face. "You know what it's like to be ripped away from everything you know. *You know!* How could you do that to your own child?"

The door to the cottage opened, and it was as if time stopped.

"Aunt Jessa!" cried the sweet baby voice. Jessa's heart dropped to her shoes.

"Tariq, you cannot do this!" Jessa hissed at him

urgently, but she did not think he heard her. He had gone pale, and still. Slowly, he turned.

And everything ended, then and there.

My son.

Tariq stared at the boy, unable to process what he was seeing. It had been one thing to rage about a child in the abstract, and quite another to see a small, mischievous-looking little boy, still chubby of cheek and wild of hair from an earlier sleep, toddle out the front door.

Tariq was frozen into place, unable to move, as the boy scampered down the steps. Jessa threw a look over her shoulder as she moved to intercept the child, scooping him up into her arms. She murmured something Tariq couldn't hear, which made the boy laugh and wiggle in her grasp.

The boy. Why could he not bring himself to use the child's name? *Jeremy.*

Another figure appeared at the door. Jessa's sister. She looked at the scene in front of her and blanched, telling Tariq that she knew exactly who he was. For a moment she and Tariq locked eyes, both struck still.

"Jessa," the other woman said, keeping her voice calm for the child's benefit though her eyes remained on Tariq, wary and scared. "What are you doing here? I thought you were on holiday."

Jessa shifted and put the little boy back on the ground. "I was," she said. She shrugged, half apology and half helplessness. "We thought we would stop by."

She looked at Tariq then, her cinnamon eyes swimming with tears. She put out her hand and cupped the top of Jeremy's head in her palm.

Jeremy, Tariq thought. *My son's name is Jeremy.*

"How lovely," the sister said, her voice strained. "You know how much Jeremy loves his aunt."

Jessa stood before him, still touching the little boy, her gaze silently imploring. Tariq felt something rip apart inside of him, and the pain was so intense for a moment that he could not tell if what he felt was emotional or physical.

Jeremy shook off Jessa's hand, his dark eyes fixed on the stranger he only just then seemed to notice standing before him. Tariq's heart stopped in his chest as the little boy moved toward him in his lurching, jerky dance of a walk, stopping when he could peer up from beneath his thick black hair. He was close enough to touch, and yet Tariq could not move.

His eyes were the same dark green as Tariq's. Tariq felt the impact of them like a body blow, but he did not react, he only returned the solemn, wide-eyed stare that was directed at him. Jeremy was as much Jessa's child as his. Tariq could see her in the boy's fairer skin, the shape of his eyes and brows, and that defiant little chin.

"Hello, Jeremy," Tariq said, his voice thick. "I am…"

He paused, and he could feel the tension emanating from both Jessa and her sister. He could almost hear it. He glanced over and saw that Jessa's sister had covered her mouth with her hands, her eyes wide and fearful. And then there was Jessa, who watched him with her heart in her gaze and tears making slow tracks down her cheeks. She stood with her arms at her sides, defeated, waiting for him to destroy everything she had worked so hard to protect.

She mouthed the word, *Please.*

"I am Tariq," he said at last, gazing back down into eyes so like his own, because it was the only thing he could think of that was not threatening to anyone, and was also true.

Jeremy blinked.

Then he let out a giggle and turned back around, to hurtle himself toward the door of the cottage and toward the woman who stood there, still holding her hands over her mouth as if holding back a scream. He buried his face against her leg, his small arms grabbing on to her in a spontaneous hug. Then he tilted back his face, lit from within with the purest, most uncomplicated love that Tariq had ever seen.

"Hi Mommy," Jeremy chirped, oblivious to the drama being played out around him.

Jessa's sister smiled down at him, then looked back at Tariq, her own face stamped with the same love, though hers was fiercer, more protective. But no less pure.

Tariq felt his heart break into a thousand pieces inside his chest, and scatter like dust.

Tariq stood by the gate, his back to the cottage, while Jessa carried on a rushed conversation with her sister. She kept sneaking looks at his strong, proud back, wondering what he must be feeling rather than paying attention to Sharon. When her sister finally went inside and closed the door, she hurried down the path to his side.

He did not look at her. He kept his eyes trained on the fields across the lane, that swept to the horizon.

"Thank you," she said, with all the feeling she'd tried to hide from Jeremy. And even from Sharon.

"I did not do anything that requires thanks," Tariq said stiffly. Bitterly.

"You did not ruin a little boy's life, when you could have and have been well within your rights," Jessa said quietly. "I'll thank you for that for the rest of my life."

"I have no rights, as you have been at great pains to advise me."

"I am sorry," she said. She stepped closer to him, forcing him to look at her. His eyes seemed so sad that it made her want to weep. Without thinking, she reached out and grabbed hold of his hand. "I am so sorry."

"So am I," he said quietly, almost letting the wind snatch it away. He looked down at their joined hands. "More than I can say."

She would not cry for him, not now, not when he held himself so aloof. She knew what that must mean—it was inevitable, really, after what they'd just been through. Jessa took a deep breath and forced herself to smile as she let go of him. She wanted to hold him and kiss him until the remoteness left him and he was once again alive and wild in her arms. She wanted to share the pain of leaving Jeremy behind, and make it easier, somehow, for both of them to bear. Oh, the things she wanted!

But she had always known that she could not have this man. Not for good. And she knew that he had lost something of far greater significance today than her. She could let him go just as she had let Jeremy go. It was the only way she knew how to love them both.

"You should return to Nur as you planned," she said, proud that her voice was even, and showed none of her inner turmoil. She could let him go. She could. "Your country needs you."

So do I! something inside of her screamed, but she bit it back, forced it down. He had never been hers to keep. She had known that from the start.

He seemed to look at her from very far away. He blinked, and some of the darkness receded, letting the green back in. Jessa felt a hard knot ease slightly inside her chest.

"And what about you?" he asked, something she couldn't read passing across his face.

Jessa shrugged, shoving her hands into her pockets so that the fists she'd made could not betray her. "I'll return to York, of course," she said.

The wind surged between them, cold and fierce. Jessa met his gaze and hoped hers was calm. She could do this. And if she broke down later, when she was alone, who would have to know?

"Is this your revenge, then?" he asked, his voice soft though there was a hardness around his eyes. "You wait until I am bleeding and then you turn the knife? Is this what I deserve for what you think I did to you five years ago?"

"No!" she gasped, as stunned as if he'd hit her. Her head reeled. "We are both to blame for what happened five years ago!"

"I am the one who left," Tariq said bitterly.

"You had no choice," Jessa replied. "And I was the one so silly she ran away for days. I left first." She shook her head. "And how can we regret it? We made a beautiful child, a perfect child."

"He is happy here." Tariq said it as if it were fact, a statement, but Jessa could see the pain and uncertainty in the dark sheen of his gaze.

"He is," she whispered fiercely. "I promise you, he is."

She didn't know what to do with the ache inside of her, the agony of feeling so apart from him. She was not the desperate, deeply depressed girl she had been when she had given Jeremy up. She was stronger now, and she knew that the way she loved Tariq was not like the infatuation of her youth. It was tempered with the suffering she'd endured, the way she had come to know him now, as the man she had always imagined him to be.

It might be that she could not bear to make this sacrifice after all.

He is not for you, she told herself fiercely. *Don't make this harder than it already is!*

"Come," Tariq said. He nodded toward the car. "I cannot be here any longer."

Jessa looked back at the cottage, so cozy and inviting against the bleakness of the autumn fields, and yet a place she would always associate with this particular mourning—the kind she imagined might fade and change but would never entirely disappear. She pulled her coat tighter around her. Then she put her arm through Tariq's and let him walk her to the car.

Jessa sat beside him in the plush backseat, feeling his grief as keenly as her own, as sharp as the wind still ripping down from the moors. Tariq did not speak for some time, his attention focused out the window, watching as fields gave way to villages, and villages to towns, as they made their way back through the country toward the city of York. Next to him, Jessa knew that his mind and his heart were still back at her sister's cottage, held tight in Jeremy's sticky little hands. She knew because hers were and, to some extent, always would be.

She had to hope that it would grow easier, as, indeed, in many ways it already had in the past few years. Seeing Jeremy thrive—seeing him happy and so deeply loved—healed parts of herself she had not known were broken. She hoped that someday it would do the same for Tariq.

"I do not know what family means," Tariq said in a low voice. He turned toward her, catching her by surprise, seeming to fill the space between them. "I have never had anyone look at me the way that boy looked at your sister. His mother." His gaze was so fierce then that it made Jessa catch her breath. "Except you. Even now, after everything I have done to you."

Their eyes locked. He reached over and tucked a stray curl behind her ear, then took her face in his hands. The warmth of his touch sped through her veins, heating her from within.

"I have already lost a son," he said, his voice almost too low, as if it hurt him. "I cannot lose you, Jessa. Not you, too."

Joy eased into her then, nudging aside the grief. It was a trickle at first, and then, as he continued to look at her with his face so open, so honest, it widened until it flowed—a hard and complex kind of joy, flavored with all they had lost and all the ways they were tied together.

She reached across the space between them, over her fears and their shared grief, and slid her hand up to hold him as he held her—holding that strong, harsh face, looking deep into the promises in his dark green eyes.

"Then you won't," she whispered as if it were a vow.

She would let the fear go this time, instead of him.

She would love him as long as he let her.

CHAPTER SIXTEEN

HE HEARD her laughter before he saw her.

Tariq strode down the wide palace corridor, past the ancient tapestries and archaeological pieces that told the story of Nur's long history in each successive niche along the way. The floor beneath his feet was tiled, mosaics stretching before him and behind him, all in vibrant colors as befit the royal palace of a king. When he reached the wide, arched doors that opened into the palace's interior courtyard, he paused.

Jessa was so beautiful, she took his breath away. She was a shock of cinnamon and copper against the brilliant blue sky, the white walls, and the palm trees that clanked gently overhead in the afternoon breeze. She seemed brighter to him than the vivid flowering plants that spilled from the balconies on the higher floors, and the sparkle of the fountain in the courtyard's center. She had set aside her novel and was watching the antics of two plump little birds who danced on the fountain's edge. She wore a long linen tunic over loose trousers in the fashion of his people, her feet in thonged sandals. Around her neck she wore a piece of jade suspended from a chain that she had found in one of the city's marketplaces.

She looked as if she belonged exactly where she was. *Mine,* he thought, not for the first time.

He crossed to her, smiling when she seemed to sense him and glanced around—smiling more when her face lit up.

"I thought you would be gone until tomorrow," she said, her delight evident in her voice, in the gleam in her eyes, though she did not throw herself into his arms as she might have in a less public area of the palace.

"My business concluded early," he said. He had made sure of it—he wanted to be away from Jessa less and less. In some sense, she was the only family he had ever known. What they had lost together made him feel more bound to her than he had ever been to another human being. And he could think of only one way to ensure that he never need be apart from her again. The birds chattered at him from their new perch on the higher rim of the fountain. "You have been here nearly a month and still you are fascinated by the birds?" He eyed her. "Perhaps you should get out more."

"Perhaps I should," she agreed. He watched as her gaze shuttered, hiding her feelings from him as she still did from time to time whenever any hint of a discussion of their future appeared. It was time to end it.

"As a matter of fact," he said quietly, "that is what I wanted to talk to you about."

"Getting out?" she asked, frowning slightly.

"In a manner of speaking," he said. He looked down at her, wanting to pull her into his arms and kiss his way into this discussion. That seemed to be the language in which they were both fluent. "I want to talk about the future. You and me."

Jessa went very still. The splash of water in the fountain behind her was all Tariq heard for a long moment, while her eyes went dark.

Then she lifted her chin, defiant and brave to the end. "There is no need," she said with a certain grace, drawing herself up and onto her feet. She picked up her book and tucked it underneath her arm with stiff, jerky movements. "I have always known this day was coming."

"Have you?" he asked mildly.

"Of course," she said briskly. "One of the first things you told me when you walked into my office was that you needed to get married. Naturally, you must do your duty to your country."

She held her head high as she skirted around him. She headed across the courtyard and up the wide steps toward his private quarters. Tariq followed, watching the sway of her hips in the soft linen and admiring the ramrod straightness of her spine. He followed her inside the palace and all the way into the vast bedroom suite, where he leaned against the bed and watched her look wildly around, as if searching for something.

"Never fear," she said in the same false tone, turning to face him. "I have no intention of making this awkward for either of us. I will simply pack a few things and be out of your way in no time."

She looked as if she might change her mind and bolt for the door.

"You are so determined to leave me," he drawled, amused. "It is almost a shame that I have no intention of letting you do so."

She froze in place, her face expressionless while her eyes burned hot.

"What do you mean?" she asked, her voice little more than a whisper.

"What do you think I mean?" he asked.

For a moment she only stared at him.

"I will not be in your *harem!*" she muttered, scandalized. "How could you suggest such a thing?"

"I am not planning to collect a harem." His mouth crooked up in one corner. "Assuming, of course, you behave."

"I don't understand," she whispered, though it was more like a sob.

"You do." He moved closer to her, so he could reach out and hold her by her slender shoulders. "You have simply decided it cannot happen. I do not know why."

Her mouth worked, and she flushed a deep, hot red.

"You must have a queen who is worthy of you," she said after a moment. "One who is your equal in every way."

"I must have *you*," he replied simply, leaning forward to kiss her. Her lips clung to his for a long, sweet moment, and then she pulled back to frown at him.

"No," she said firmly.

"No?"

"I won't marry you," she gritted out, and moved out of his grip. She rubbed at her arms for a moment, her head bent.

Tariq ordered himself to be patient. "Why not?" he asked, in a far easier tone than the possessiveness that clawed at him demanded.

She looked at him. Her lips pressed together, and her hands balled into fists at her side.

"I love you," she blurted out, and then sighed slightly, as if it hurt to say aloud, even as sweet triumph washed through Tariq—making him want to roar out his victory, shout it from the rooftops. When she looked at him again, her eyes were overly bright, but her chin was high. "I cannot marry a man who does not love me," she said. Bravely and definitively. "Not even you."

Tariq closed the distance between them, his expression unreadable. But this was not about sex, explosive as it had always been between them. This was about something bigger.

That must be why she wanted to collapse into sobs.

"Don't!" Jessa whispered, though she did not move—did not make any attempt to avoid him. "This is hard enough, Tariq! Please do not—"

He silenced her with his mouth upon hers, his hand fisting in the mess of her curls. He kissed her until she melted against him, soft and pliant against his hardness despite everything, until her arms crept around his neck and she kissed him back with a matching ferocity. He kissed her until she couldn't tell who moaned, who sighed, while the fire of their connection raged between them, incinerating them both in a delicious blaze.

"I love you," he told her in a low voice when he tore his mouth away from hers, his gaze dark and green and so serious it made Jessa gasp.

She searched his face, not daring to believe she had heard him right. She even shook her head, as if to refute it.

Tariq smiled.

"I have never loved another woman," he said. "I never will. How can you doubt it? I longed for you for five long years. I hunted you to the ends of the earth."

"York is not the ends of the earth," she said, absurdly. He traced a line down her jaw, still smiling.

"That depends where you start." He sighed. "Jessa. What are you so afraid of? Did I not tell you what would happen if I brought you here?"

She remembered he had been angry, but she also remembered what he had said—that he would keep any woman he brought to his palace. But she could not seem to get her head around it. She could not seem to believe.

"That was a long time ago," Jessa whispered.

"I will marry you," he said, as if there had never been any other possibility.

"You cannot!" she cried, hard emotions racking her, fear scraping through her, leaving her trembling in his arms. "I do not deserve you! Not after—" Her eyes swam with tears, blurring the world, but she could still see him, so strong and intent. "I gave him away, Tariq. I gave him up."

"And we will miss him," Tariq replied after a moment, his voice thick with his own emotions. "Together."

Jessa let out a breath and, with it, something tight and frozen seemed to thaw, letting light and hope begin to trickle through her. Letting her wonder, *what if?*

He pressed his lips against her forehead. In a softer tone, yet no less demanding, no less sure, he said, "And we will have another child, Jessa. Not as a replacement. Never as a replacement. As a new beginning. This I promise you."

The tears spilled over now, wetting her cheeks. She touched his face, an echo of that cold day when Tariq had finally understood the magnitude of what she had given up, and why. Jeremy would be an ache they carried with them for the rest of their lives, day in and day out. But for the first time, she dared to hope that they would carry it together across the years, making it easier to bear that way. And someday, only if he wished it, they would tell Jeremy the story of how much he was loved, and how well.

"Yes," she breathed, her heart too full to let her smile. "We will be a family."

"We will," he said gruffly, and something powerful and true swelled between them then, and seemed to spread out around them to fill the room.

The thought of making a child with Tariq—deliberately—in joy and in love, and then raising that child together as she had always wanted to believe they were meant to do… It was almost too overwhelming.

Almost.

"I haven't agreed to any marriage," Jessa told Tariq then, with a small smile, while an intoxicating cocktail of hope and joy surged through her. She could feel it inexorably changing her with every second. Could dreams come true after all, after everything they had been through? After all that they had done? Was it possible?

Looking at him, she dared to believe it for the first time.

She was still twined around him, her legs astride one of his and her sex pressed intimately against his thigh. He moved slightly and made her groan as that sweet, delirious heat rocked through her.

"I suggest you get used to the idea," Tariq said, a smile in his voice, his eyes. "This is my country. I do not require your agreement." He kissed her again, capturing her lower lip between his teeth for a moment before releasing her. He smiled. "Though I would like it."

"Yes," she said softly, wonder rolling through her, making her feel as incandescent as the desert sun. Only with Tariq. Only for him. "Yes, I will marry you."

"You will be happy, Jessa," he vowed, fiercely, sweeping her up off the floor, high against his chest. She wrapped her legs around his waist and gripped tight to his shoulders, looking down at him as he held her. At the jade eyes that so consumed her that she had bought a necklace to match, so she might have something like him to look at when he was away. At this man she had loved for so long, and in so many different ways. Her playboy lover. Her king. *Her husband.*

"You will be happy," he said again, frowning at her as if he dared her to disagree.

"Is that your royal decree?" she asked, laughing as he whirled her around and tipped her backward onto the soft bed behind them. He fell with her, following her down and then bracing himself on his arms before he crashed into her.

"I am the king," he said, leaning over her. "My word is law."

"I am to be the queen," she said, shivering slightly as the idea of it began to truly take hold. She would have this man forever. She would be able to hold him like this, love him like this. She felt her eyes well up as she reached between them to trace his mouth, the hard planes of his face. Harsh, forbidding. *Hers.*

"So my word should also be law, should it not?" she asked.

"If you wish it."

Jessa smiled and lifted her head to kiss him, sweet and more sure than she had ever been of anything.

"Then *we* will be happy," she said and, for the first time, truly believed it, with all of her heart and soul. "Because I say so."

Katrakis's
Last Mistress

CAITLIN CREWS

To Liza, who dreamed of gold-eyed dragons,
Jane, who knew I couldn't pull that punch,
and Jeff, who makes it easy to write
about heroes

CHAPTER ONE

NIKOS KATRAKIS was by far the most dangerous man aboard the sleek luxury yacht. Ordinarily Tristanne Barbery would take one look at a man like him—so dark and powerful her breath caught each time she gazed at him from her place within sight of the elegant marble-topped bar where he stood—and flee for her life in the opposite direction.

Any man who seemed to dim the sparkling blue-green waters of the Mediterranean Sea with his very presence was far too complicated, far too *much* for Tristanne. *This is not about you,* she told herself fiercely, then ordered herself to release the fingers she'd clenched into fists. She willed away her nausea, her shakiness. Her panic. Because this was not, indeed, about Tristanne. It was about her mother and her mother's crippling, impossible debts. And she would do whatever she had to do to save her mother.

There were other rich and powerful men aboard the boat, rubbing expensively clad shoulders together while gazing at the glittering shores of the Côte d'Azure: the olive-clad hills and pastel waterfront facades of Villefranche-sur-Mer to the left, the red-topped villas of Cap Ferrat to the right, and the sparkling sweep of Villefranche Bay spread out around them in the late afternoon sun.

But Nikos Katrakis was different from the rest. It wasn't simply because he owned this particular yacht, though his ownership was as clear as a brand—almost visible, Tristanne thought; almost seeming to emanate from him in waves. It wasn't even the undeniable physical power he seemed to *just* restrain beneath his deceptively calm surface, even dressed as casually as he was, in denim trousers and a white dress shirt left open at the neck to display a swathe of dark olive skin.

It was *him*.

It was the way he stood, commanding and yet so remote, so alone, even in the center of his own party. There was a fierce, unmistakably male energy that hummed from him, attracting notice but keeping all but the most brave away. He would have been devastating enough if he were unattractive—he was that powerful.

But of course, Nikos Katrakis was not, in any sense of the word, unattractive. Tristanne felt a shiver of awareness trace its way down her spine, and she could not bring herself to look away. He was more powerful than her late father had been but not, she thought, as cold. And somehow she could sense that he was no brute, like her brother, Peter—a man so cruel he had refused to pay her mother's medical bills, a man so heartless he had laughed in the face of Tristanne's desperation.

Yet something about Nikos made her think he was different, made her think of dragons—as if he was that magical and that dangerous; as if he was epic. He was too virile. Too masculine. His power seemed to hum around him like an electric current. *Dragon*, she thought again, and her palms suddenly itched to sketch the bold, almost harsh lines of his face—though she knew that was exactly the sort of thing Peter so scorned. There was no explaining creativity to her overbearing brother.

But all of that was precisely why Nikos Katrakis was the only man who would do. She was wasting time simply gazing at him, trying to get up her nerve, when she knew Peter would be searching for her before too long. She knew he did not trust her, no matter that she had agreed to go along with his plan. And she would go along with it, or seem to, but she would do it on her terms, not his. And she would do so with the one man Peter hated above all others—the one man Peter viewed as his chief business rival.

She had moved beyond nervous into something else—something that made her pulse flutter and her knees feel like syrup. She could only hope that it didn't show, that he would see what her brother, Peter, claimed everyone saw when they looked at her: nothing but Barbery ice.

It's about time you used your assets to our advantage, Peter had said in his cold voice. Tristanne shook the memory away, determined not to react to him any further—even in her own mind. Not when so much was at stake. Her mother's survival. The independence she had fought so hard to win. Tristanne sucked in a fortifying breath, sent up a little prayer and forced herself to walk right up to Nikos Katrakis himself before she talked herself out of it.

Nikos looked up from his drink at the polished wood and marble-topped bar and their eyes met. Held. His eyes were the color of long-steeped tea, shades lighter than the thick, dark hair on his head and the dark brows that arched above, making them seem to glow like old gold. They seared into her. Tristanne's breath caught, and a restless heat washed over her, scalding her. The sounds of the high-class partygoers, their clinking glasses and cultured laughter, disappeared. Her anxiety and her purpose fell away as if they had never been. It was as if the whole world—the glittering expanse of the French Riviera, the endless blue-green Mediterranean Sea—faded into his hot, gold gaze. Was consumed by him, enveloped into him—*changed by him*, that fanciful voice whispered in the back of her mind.

"Miss Barbery," he said in greeting, his native Greek coloring his words just slightly, adding a rough caress to his voice. It sounded like a command, though he did not alter his careless position, lounging so indolently against the bar, one hand toying with his glass of amber-colored liquor. He watched her with old, intent eyes. The hairs on the back of Tristanne's neck stood at attention, letting her know that he was not at all what he seemed.

Something wild and unexpected uncoiled inside of her, making her breath stutter. Shocking her with its sudden intensity.

He was not careless. He was in no way relaxed. He was only pretending to be either of those things.

But then, she was banking on that. Surely her brother, who cared only about money and power, would not be as obsessed as he was about this man unless he was a worthy opponent.

"You know my name?" she asked. She managed to keep her composure despite the humming reaction that shimmered through her, surprising and unsettling her. It was the Barbery family trait, she thought with no little despair: she could appear to be perfectly unruffled while inside, she was a quivering mess. She had learned it at her father's emotionless knee—or suffered the consequences. And she wanted only to use this man for her own ends, not succumb to his legendary charisma. She had to be strong!

"Of course." One dark brow rose higher, while his full, firm lips twisted slightly. "I pride myself on knowing the names of all my guests. I am a Greek. Hospitality is not simply a word to me."

There was a rebuke in there somewhere. Tristanne's stomach twisted in response, while he looked at her with eyes that saw too much. Like he was a cat and she a rather dim and doomed mouse.

"I have a favor to ask you," she blurted out, unable to play the game as she ought to—as she'd planned so feverishly once she'd realized where Peter was taking her this afternoon. There was something in the way Nikos regarded her—so calm, so direct, so powerfully amused—that made her feel as if the glass of wine she'd barely tasted earlier had gone straight to her head.

"I'm so sorry," she murmured, surprised to feel a flush heating her cheeks. She, who up until this moment had considered herself unable to blush! "I wanted to work up to that. You must think I am the rudest person alive."

His dark brows rose, and his wicked mouth curved slightly, though his enigmatic eyes did not waver, nor warm. "You have not yet asked this favor. Perhaps I will reserve judgment until you do."

Tristanne had the sudden sense that she was more at risk, somehow, standing in front of Nikos Katrakis in full view of so many strangers than she was from Peter and his schemes. It was an absurd thought. *You must be strong!* she reminded herself, but she couldn't seem to shake that feeling of danger.

Or stop what came next. What had to come next—even though she knew, suddenly, with a deep, feminine wisdom that seemed like a weight in her bones, that this was a mistake of unfathomable proportions. That she was going to regret stirring up this particular hornet's nest. That she, who prided herself on being so capable, so independent, did not have what it took to handle a man like this. One should never rush heedlessly into a dragon's lair. Anyone who had ever read a fairy tale knew better! She bit her lower lip, frowning slightly as she looked at him, feeling as if she fell more and more beneath his dark gold spell by the moment. It was if he was a trap, and she had walked right into it.

The trouble was, that didn't seem to frighten her the way it should. And in any case, she had no choice.

"The favor?" he prompted her, something sardonic moving across his face. Almost as if he knew what she planned to ask him—but that was silly. Of course he could not know. Of all the things that Tristanne knew about Nikos Katrakis—that he was ruthless and magnetic in equal measure, that he had clawed his way from illegitimacy and poverty into near-un-imaginable wealth and influence with the sheer force of his will, that he suffered no fools and tolerated no disloyalty, that he alone drove her cold brother into fits of rage with his every success—she had never heard it mentioned that he was psychic. He could have no idea what she wanted from him.

"Yes," Tristanne said, her tone even. Confident. In direct contrast to the mess of unsettled churning within. "A favor. But just a small favor, and not, I hope, an entirely unpleasant one."

She almost called it off then. She almost heeded the panicked messages her body and her intuition were send-ing her—she almost convinced herself that someone else would do, that she need not pick *this* man, that someone less intimidating would work just as well, could accomplish what she needed.

But she glanced to the side then, to ease the intensity of Nikos Katrakis's gaze and to catch her breath, and saw her brother shoulder his way into the bar area. *Half brother*, she reminded herself, as if that should make some difference. Peter's familiar scowl was firmly in place when he looked at her—and who she was with. Behind him, she saw the clammy-palmed financier Peter had handpicked for her—the man he had decreed would be his ticket out of financial ruin for the modest price of Tristanne's favors.

"You must bolster the family fortune," he had told her matter-of-factly six weeks earlier, as if he was not discussing her future. Her life.

"I don't understand," she had said stiffly, still wearing her black dress from their father's memorial service earlier that day. She had not been in mourning, not even so soon after his death. Not for Gustave Barbery, at any rate—though she would perhaps always grieve for the father Gustave had never been to her. "All I want is access to my trust fund a few years early."

That bloody trust fund. She'd hated that it existed, hated that her father thought it gave him the right to attempt to control her as he saw fit. Hated more that Peter was its executor now that her father was dead—and that, for her mother's sake, she had to play along with him in order to access it. She'd wanted nothing to do with the cursed Barbery fortune nor its attendant obligations and expectations. She'd spent years living proudly off of her own money, the money she'd earned with her own hands—but such pride was no longer a luxury she could afford. Her mother's health had deteriorated rapidly once Gustave fell ill; her debts had mounted at a dizzying rate, especially once Peter had taken control of the Barbery finances eight months ago and had stopped paying Vivienne's bills. It fell to Tristanne to sort it out, which was impossible on the money she made scraping out the life of an artist in Vancouver. She had no choice but to placate Peter in the hope she could use her trust to save her mother from ruin. It made her want to cry but she did not—*could not*—show that kind of weakness in front of Peter.

"You don't have to understand," Peter had hissed at her, triumph and malice alive in his cold gaze. "You need only do as I say. Find an appropriately wealthy man, and bend him to your will. How hard can that be, even for you?"

"I fail to see how that would help you," Tristanne had said. So formal, so polite, as if the conversation were either. As if she did not feel like giving in to her upset stomach, her horror.

"You need not concern yourself with anything save your own contribution," Peter had snapped. "A liaison with a certain caliber of man will make my investors more confident. And believe me, Tristanne, you'll want to ensure their confidence. If this deal does not go through, I will lose everything and the first casualty will be your useless mother."

Tristanne understood all too well. Peter had never made any secret of his disdain for Tristanne's mother. Gustave had put his empire in Peter's hands at the onset of his long illness, having cut off Tristanne for her rebelliousness years before. He had no doubt expected his son to provide for his second wife, and had therefore made no specific provision for her in his will. But Tristanne was well aware that Peter had waited years to make Vivienne Barbery pay for usurping his own late mother's place in what passed for Gustave's affections. He had dismissed her failing, fragile health as *attention-seeking*, and allowed her debts to mount. He was capable of anything.

"What do you want me to do?" Tristanne had asked woodenly. She could do it, whatever it was. She would.

"Sleep with them, marry them, I do not care." Peter had sneered. "Make certain it is public—splashed across every tabloid in Europe. You must do whatever it takes to convince the world that this family has access to serious money, Tristanne, do you understand me?"

On the Katrakis yacht, Tristanne looked away from the financier and back to Peter, whose gaze burned with loathing. And as easily as that, her indecision vanished. Better to burn out on Nikos Katrakis's fire—and annoy Peter in the process by *contributing* using his avowed worst enemy—than suffer a far more clammy and repulsive fate. Tristanne repressed a shudder.

When she returned her attention to Nikos Katrakis, the dragon, his half smile had disappeared. Though he still lounged against the bar, Tristanne sensed that his long, hard-muscled body was on red-alert. She had the sense of his physical might, of tremendous power hidden in casual clothes. It made her throat go dry.

This is a terrible mistake, she thought. She knew it in her bones. She felt it like an ache, a sob. But there was nothing to do but go for it.

"I would like you to kiss me," she said, very distinctly. And then there was no going back. It was done. She cleared her throat. "Here and now. If it is not too much trouble."

Of all the things Nikos Katrakis had expected might happen during the course of the afternoon's party, being solicited in any form by the Barbery heiress had not made the list.

A hard kind of triumph poured through him. He was sure that she could see it—sense it. How could she not?

But she only gazed at him, her eyes the color of the finest Swiss chocolate. A dark satisfaction threatened to get the best of him. He found himself smiling, not pleasantly—and still, she did not look away.

She was a brave little thing. Braver by far than her cowardly, dishonorable relatives.

Not that her bravery would help her much. Not with him.

"Why should I kiss you?" he asked softly, enjoying the flush that heated her skin, making her skin glow red and gold in the late afternoon light. He toyed with his glass, and indicated the throng around them with a careless flick of his wrist. "There are any number of women on this boat who would fight to kiss me. Why should it be you?"

Surprise shone briefly in her gaze, then was replaced by something else. She swallowed, and then, very deliberately, smiled. It was a razor-sharp society smile. Nikos did not mistake it for anything but the weapon it was.

"Surely there are points for asking directly," she said, her distractingly strong chin tilting up, her accent an unidentifiable yet attractive mix of Europe and North America. Her dark lashes swept down, then rose again to reveal her frank gaze. "Rather than lounging about in inappropriate clothing, hoping my décolletage might do the asking for me."

Nikos found himself very nearly amused, despite himself. Despite his urge to crush her—because she was a Barbery and thus tainted, because he had vowed long ago that he would not rest until they were all so much dust beneath his feet, because her spineless worm of a brother watched them, even now. He shifted closer to her, moving his body far nearer to hers than was polite. She held her ground.

He wished he did not like it, but he did. Oh, how he did.

"Some women have no qualms about displaying whatever assets they possess to their best advantage," he said. He placed his drink on the bar. "But I take your point."

He let his gaze travel over her—not for the first time, though she could not know it. But today he had the pleasure of letting her stand there and watch him as he did it. From the gentle waves of her dark blonde hair, to her disarmingly intelligent brown eyes, to the lithe figure she'd poured into a simple shift dress that appreciated her curves almost as much as he did, she was compelling—but more for the ways in which she was not quite beautiful than for the ways she was. The strong chin. The obvious intellect she did nothing to conceal. The faint evidence that she did not spend her free time injecting herself with Botox or collagen or silicone. The signs of tension in her neck and shoulders that she was trying to hide, that hinted at her reasons for such a request. He dragged his attention back to her face, pleased to see a hint of temper crack across her expression before she carefully hid it behind her polished social veneer.

"What can you bring to a kiss that another cannot?" he asked, as if he was unimpressed with what he'd seen.

She did not retreat, or turn bright red with shame, as others might have. She merely crooked one delicate eyebrow, challenging him. Daring him.

"Me," she said. Her expression added, *of course*.

Nikos felt desire flash through him, surprising him. Shocking him. He had not expected it—he should, by rights, despise her by association. But Tristanne Barbery was not at all what he had imagined she would be. He had expected her to be attractive. How could she not be? She had been schooled in the finest finishing schools in Europe, polished to the nth degree. He had looked at her in photographs over the years, and had found her to be natural, unstudied, though it was impossible to tell if that was a trick of the lens. He knew now that photographs could not do this woman justice. She was too alive—too vibrant—as if life danced in her, like a fire.

He wanted to touch it. Her.

And then he wanted to ruin her, just as Althea had been ruined and his father destroyed. Just as he, too, had been ruined, however temporarily. *Never again*, he vowed. Not for the first time.

"You make another good point," he agreed, his voice low as he fought off the dark memories. He reached across the space between them and pulled a long strand of her hair between his fingers. It felt like raw silk, soft and supple, and warm. Her lips parted slightly, as if she could feel his touch. He felt himself harden in response. "But I am not in the habit of kissing strange women in view of so many," he continued, his voice pitched for her ears alone. "It has a nasty habit of ending up in the tabloids, I find."

"I apologize," Tristanne murmured. Her clever eyes met his, daring him. "I was under the impression that you were renowned for your fearlessness. Your ability to scoff in the face of convention. Perhaps I have confused you for another Nikos Katrakis."

"I am devastated," he replied smoothly, his eyes on hers. He moved closer, and something inside him beat like a drum when she still did not step away. "I assumed it was my good looks that drew you to me, begging to be kissed. Instead you are like all the rest. Are you a rich man's groupie, Miss Barbery? Do you travel the world and collect kisses like a young girl collects autographs?"

"Not at all, Mr. Katrakis," she replied at once. She tilted her head back, and raised her brows in that challenging way of hers. "I find rich men are my groupies. They follow me around, making demands. I thought to save you the trouble."

"You are too kind, Miss Barbery." This time he traced the ridge of her collarbone, her taut, soft skin. He felt her tremble, just slightly, beneath his fingers, and almost smiled. "But perhaps I do not share what is mine."

"Says the man on a yacht filled with more guests than he can count."

"I have not kissed the yacht, nor the guests." He inclined his head. "Not all of them, that is."

"You must share your rules with me, then," she replied, her lips twitching slightly as if she bit back laughter. He did not know why he found that mesmerizing. "Though I must confess to you that I am surprised there are so many. So much for the grand stories of Nikos Katrakis, who bows to no tradition, follows no rule and forges his own way in this world. I think I'd like to meet *him*."

"There is only one Nikos Katrakis, Miss Barbery." He was so close now that her perfume filled the space between them, something subtle, with spice and only the faintest hint of flowers. He wondered if she would taste as sweet, with as much kick. "I hope it will not destroy you to learn that it is me."

"I have no way to judge what it will or will not do," she said, her eyes bold on his, "as you have not yet kissed me."

"Ah," he said. "And now it is an inevitability, is it?"

"Of course." She cocked her head to one side, and smiled. It was even more of a challenge, and Nikos had not become the man he was today by backing down from a challenge. "Isn't it?"

This was not what he had planned. Spontaneity was for those with less to lose, and far less to prove. He owed the late Gustave Barbery and his odious son, Peter, payback on the grandest scale, and he had spent the last decade making certain the opportunity would present itself, which it had, again and again. A push here, a whisper there, and the Barbery fortunes had taken a tumble, especially since the old man's illness—but he had not intended to involve the girl. He was not like the Barberys. He was not like Peter Barbery, who had seduced, impregnated and abandoned Althea with so much cold calculation. He refused to be like the Barberys! But then, he could not have predicted that his arch-enemy's sister would approach him in this way.

Or—more intriguing and far more dangerous—that she would tempt him to throw away the iron control he had worked so hard to maintain. He was not averse to using her or any other tool he could find that might lead to her family's destruction. But he could not have anticipated that he might want her—desire her—in spite of it all.

"I believe you may be right," he said quietly. Her bold expression faltered, just for the barest of moments, but Nikos saw it. And something in him roared in triumph. She was not as unaffected as she pretended to be. He did not care to explore why that should please him.

He reached over and slid his palm around to cup her nape. The contact sent electricity surging through him, desire and a deep hunger following like an echo. Her eyes widened, and her hands came up to rest on the hard planes of his chest.

He let the moment draw out, aware of the interested eyes on them from all corners of the yacht's entertainment deck, knowing that no matter what game she thought she was playing, she had no idea who she was dealing with. She had no idea what she'd set in motion by approaching him.

But he knew. He had already won this long, cold battle. She was simply the final straw that would destroy the Barbery empire once and for all, just as they had nearly destroyed him once upon a time.

He had finally done it—and yet instead of reveling in his

hard-won victory, his attention focused solely on the rich, lush curve of her lips.

He pulled her to him and fit his mouth to hers.

CHAPTER TWO

FIRE!

Tristanne would have screamed the word if she could.

Instead she kissed him. If that was the word for the slick, hot meeting of their mouths. If that was why every alarm in her body rang out *danger*, her stomach in knots and her skin ablaze with sensation, as if it was too small or she had grown too big to wear it any longer.

She had not thought too far beyond the simple request— she had not imagined what it would be like to kiss this man. Or, more precisely, to be kissed by him. He was elemental, untamed. He took. He demanded. He possessed.

And she could not seem to get enough of him.

He angled his mouth against hers, exploring her lips, tasting her tongue with his, with an assertive, encompassing mastery that made Tristanne shudder with *want*. With need.

It was so carnal, so naked—and yet she remained fully clothed. His hand on the back of her neck radiated heat, and something far too like ownership. He tasted like expensive liquor and salt, intensely masculine and frighteningly addictive. Tristanne clutched at his shirt, but her hands melted against the steel-packed muscles of his chest rather than push him away.

A million years passed, a thousand ages in that same impossible fire, and then, finally, he raised his head, his dark gold eyes glittering with an edgy need. Tristanne felt the echo of it kick at her, making her legs feel weak beneath her.

She fought the urge to press her fingers to her mouth—to see how completely he had ravaged her, to feel how totally he had claimed her. Her own lips felt as if they no longer belonged to her. As if he had marked her, somehow, as his. Something inside her, low and deep, sang out at the idea.

Idiot.

She should have known better than to play such games with a man like this, a man she knew with a sudden implacable certainty, as his dark eyes bored into hers and she felt herself shiver where he still held her, she could never control. Never. She was not even sure she wanted to.

She was in terrible, terrible trouble.

She had to remember why she was doing this! She had to think of her mother first!

"I trust that was sufficient?" There was an odd light in his eyes—it made her skin draw tight and prickle in warning. He set her back from him, and drew his hand away from her nape, slowly, leaving brushfires in his wake.

She forced herself not to tremble. Not to shiver in reaction. She knew somehow that he would use her responses against her. She knew it.

"I think so," Tristanne managed to say, though her voice sounded packed in cotton wool. Her breasts were taut and full, and she longed to press them against his hard chest. It was as if he had somehow turned her own body against her. She ordered herself to stop, to breathe, to contain the hysteria.

But this was why she had chosen him. This, exactly.

"You do not know?" His full mouth curved slightly, making him look both delicious and amused. "Then I cannot have done it correctly."

Tristanne realized then that she was still touching him. Her head spun and her breath had gone shallow, but her hands still lay against the granite planes of his chest. She could feel the heat of him rise through the cloth of his shirt, and the time had long passed to let go, to step away—and yet she still held on as if he was the only thing keeping her from tilting off the edge of the world.

Get a hold of yourself! she ordered herself, desperately. She thought of Vivienne's pale, too-slender form; thought of her racking cough and sleeplessness. She had to keep her head about her, or all would be lost. *She had no choice.*

She dropped her hands. As she did so, she thought his half smile deepened, grew more darkly amused. Somehow, that made it possible for her to straighten her spine, to remember herself, remember what she must do. And for whom.

"You were perfectly adequate," she told him, trying to sound unaffected. Almost bored, even, while her heart galloped and her stomach twisted.

He did not react to her remark in any way that she could see—yet sensed a certain stillness in him, a certain focused watchfulness, that reminded her of some great predator set to pounce. The dragon, perhaps, a moment before letting loose his fire.

"Was I, indeed?" he asked coolly.

"Certainly." Tristanne shrugged as if she felt nonchalant, as if she could not feel the heat that burned in her cheeks. As if he had not turned her inside out and wrecked her completely with one kiss. One complicated, unexpected, mind-altering kiss.

But it was not the only thing she could feel. And as intoxicating as Nikos Katrakis was—as deliciously unnerving as that kiss had been—now that it was over she could also feel Peter's fury. Her brother had moved closer, and was now standing near enough that he was, no doubt, eavesdropping on her conversation with Nikos. This time, she did not look over. She did not have to—she knew exactly how Peter would be scowling at her, with that anger burning in the eyes that should have looked like hers, but were too cold, too cruel.

"Perhaps it requires further experiment," Nikos suggested, in that velvety caress of a voice that heated her from within. She put Peter out of her mind for the moment. She felt a heavy, sensual fire bloom in her core, and begin to spread outward. "I am happy to extend the favor. I would not wish to disappoint you."

"You are magnanimous indeed," she murmured, dropping her gaze—afraid, somehow, that he could see too much. That he could see exactly how much he had affected her.

"I am many things, Miss Barbery," Nikos murmured, his voice soft though his gaze, when she dared meet it, was hard. "But I am not magnanimous. I have not one generous bone in my body. I suggest you remember that."

She knew what she had to do. She had decided, even before Peter had laid out his disgusting conditions, that she was prepared to do whatever it took to emancipate her mother from Peter's control—to save her. What did she care if the Barbery fortune and financial empire collapsed into dust and ruins? She had turned her back on all of that long ago. But she could not turn her back on her poor mother, especially not now that Gustave—who her mother had loved so blindly, so foolishly—had left her so helpless and so completely under Peter's thumb. She had stayed out of it while her father lived, but she could not abandon her mother now, so frail and at risk even as she grieved for Gustave. She was all her mother had left. She was Vivienne's only hope.

Which meant she had only one course of action.

"That is a pity," Tristanne said, with a calm she did not feel. She felt panic claw at her throat, and rise like heat to her eyes, but she swallowed it. She was determined. She knew her brother was not bluffing, that he had meant every awful word that he'd said to her, that he would not rest until she *earned her keep* in service of filling the family coffers, and that he would think nothing of tossing her mother out into the street if Tristanne defied him. She knew exactly what would happen if she did not do this.

What she did not, could not know was what might become of her if she did.

"Not at all," Nikos said, his golden eyes watchful, intent. "Merely the truth."

Women do this every day, she told herself. *Since the dawn of time. With far lesser men than this.*

"It is a pity," Tristanne forced herself to say, the emotions she would not acknowledge making her voice husky, "because I had heard you were between mistresses at present. I had so hoped to be the next."

His dark eyes flared, then turned to molten gold. She held his gaze as if she were as bold, as daring, as her words suggested. Hoping that she could be. She had to be.

"But, of course," she continued, because this was the crux of it—because she knew Peter was listening, and so she had to push the words out, no matter how they seemed to clog her throat, "as your mistress, I would require your generosity. A great deal of it."

For another endless moment, Nikos only watched her, his gaze still searing through her—reducing her to ash, making her breath desert her—but otherwise his big body remained still, alert. It was almost as if she had not propositioned him. As if she had not offered to prostitute herself to him as casually as she might have ordered a drink from the bartender.

But then, making every hair on her body prickle and her nipples pull to hard, tight points, Nikos smiled.

It had been a long time in coming, this moment, and Nikos could not help but savor it. Revel in it. He had never dared dream that his arch-enemy's sister would offer herself to him, as his mistress, thus ensuring his ultimate victory—his final revenge. But he would take it—and her.

He did not have to look at Peter Barbery to feel the other man's outrage—it poured from him in waves. It felt as sweet as he had always imagined his revenge would, in all these years he'd so carefully plotted and planned, gradually drawing the noose tighter and tighter around the Barberys, forcing them ever closer to ruin.

He only wished he were not the only one left. That his critical, disapproving father, his tempestuous half sister and her unborn child, had lived to see that they had been wrong. That Nikos really would do what he'd sworn to them he would do: take down the Barberys. Make them pay. They had died hating him, blaming him; first the heartbroken Althea by her own hand and then, later, the father he had tried so hard and failed, always, to impress. But he had only used that as further fuel.

Just as he used whatever befell him as fuel. He had not allowed a childhood in the slums of Athens to hold him back, nor his mother's callous abandonment of him. When he had finally wrenched himself from the gutter, using tooth and nail and sheer stubbornness, he had not let anyone keep him from locating the father who had discarded his mother and thus him. And once he'd started to prove himself to his harsh, often cruel father, he had tried to endear himself to Althea, the legitimate, favored and beloved child. He had never resented her for her place in his father's affections, not like she had eventually blamed him, once Peter Barbery was done with her.

He looked at Tristanne, standing before him, her words still echoing in his ears as if they were a song.

He had no idea what game the Barberys were playing here, nor did he care. Did Tristanne Barbery believe she was some kind of Mata Hari? That she could use sex to control him? To influence him in some way? Let her try. There was only one person who called the shots in Nikos's bed, and it would not be her.

It would never be her. He might have felt a wild, unprecedented attraction to her—but he would take her for revenge.

"Come," he said.

He took her bare arm, relishing the feel of the supple smoothness of her bicep beneath his palm. He nodded toward the interior of the yacht, indicating his private quarters. The urge to gloat, to taunt Peter Barbery as the other man had done years ago, was almost overwhelming, but Nikos repressed it. He concentrated on the Barbery he had before him, the one whose scent inflamed him and whose mouth he intended to taste again. Soon.

She looked at him, but did not speak, her eyes dark—again with an emotion he could not name.

"Second thoughts?" He was unable to keep the taunt from his voice.

"You are the one who has yet to answer," Tristanne said, that strong chin tilting up, her shoulders squaring. As if she intended to fight him—as if she were already fighting him. He wanted her naked and beneath him. Now. *For revenge*, he reminded himself, *nothing more.* "Not I."

"Then it appears we have much to discuss," Nikos said.

She swallowed, the movement in the fine column of her throat the only hint she might not be as calm nor as blasé as she pretended to be. Her eyes darkened, but held his.

"You are taking me to your lair, I presume?" she asked.

"If that is what you wish to call it," he replied, amused. And powerfully aroused.

She said no more. And he made sure every eye was on them, every head was turned, her brother's chief among them, so there could be absolutely no mistake whose arm he held with such carnal possession as he led her across the deck.

Toward the master suite. Away from prying eyes—or any recourse.

Straight into his lair.

CHAPTER THREE

SHE had seen him once before.

Tristanne remembered it as if it were moments ago, when in truth it had been some ten years earlier. She walked across the crowded deck next to Nikos with her head high, her spine straight, as if she walked to her own coronation rather than to the bedroom of the man she had just offered to sleep with. For money.

But in her mind, she was seventeen again, and peering across the crowded ballroom of her father's grand house in Salzburg. It had been her first ball, and she had had too many dreams, perhaps, of waltzing beneath all the shimmering lights of the chandeliers and candles in her pretty dress. But Nikos Katrakis had not been a dream. He had strode across her father's ballroom as if it belonged to him. He had been dark and dangerous, and potent, somehow. Tristanne had not understood, then, why she was so mesmerized by the sight of him, even from afar. Why she caught her breath, and could not seem to draw a new one. Why her heart pounded in a kind of panic—and yet she could not bring herself to look away from the darkly handsome stranger who moved through her father's house as if it were his own, or ought to be.

"Who is that man?" she had asked her mother, feeling a strange, new heat move through her, along with an unfamiliar kind of shyness. It terrified her. She did not know if she wanted to run toward this oddly compelling man, or away from him.

"He is Nikos Katrakis," Vivienne had said in a soft tone. Had she also sensed his power, his magnetism? "He has business with your father, my dear. Not with you."

And now, ten years later, Tristanne still did not know whether she wished to run toward the man or away from him. She knew that his kiss was far much *more* than she had ever imagined it might be, ten years ago when she was still a girl. And she knew that his hand felt like a brand against the bare skin of her upper arm. And that she was going with him willingly. She had suggested it, hadn't she?

This was her *choice*.

He led her away from the crowd, away from the shining late afternoon sea, far into the opulent depths of the ship. Tristanne had only the faintest hectic impressions—gleaming wood and lush reception rooms, windows arching high above the dancing waves of the Mediterranean, letting in the golden Côte d'Azur light—because the only thing she could concentrate on was Nikos.

She was aware of every breath he took, every stride, every movement of the powerful body so close to hers. She could feel the hot, bright heat that seemed to burn from inside his very skin, and she knew that the heaviness in her belly, the softening below, was all for him. Her face felt red, then white, then red again, as if she was feverish.

But she knew better.

She had to get herself under control, she thought desperately. She could not lose herself in this man's touch, no matter how formidable and attractive he was. She was only using him, she told herself. He was but a means to an end.

Nikos ushered her into a room, finally, slapping the door shut behind them. Tristanne looked around, but could hardly register a thing. She had only the haziest notion that this was an elegant, spacious stateroom, and that it contained a bed. A large bed. And that she was in it, by her own design, with the most sensually dangerous man she had ever encountered.

"Mr. Katrakis," she began, spinning around to face him. It was not too late to wrest control of this situation. That was what all of this was about, in the end—control. She had only to assert herself, surely. She had only to be strong.

"It is too late for that, don't you think?" he asked, too close already, so close she could have reached out and laid her hand on that swathe of olive skin at his neck, directly in front of her eyes.

Tristanne could not help herself. She backed up a step, then froze, sure that simple reaction would give her away—would show him that she was not the sophisticated mistress sort of person she was pretending to be, that she was just an artist from Canada swept up in events outside her control. But he only smiled.

Tristanne's entire body kicked into red-alert. She felt poised on the brink of some kind of cliff, something steep and deadly, and it was as if he was the harsh, strong wind that might toss her over the side.

Dragon, she thought again. She had known it from the start—she had known it on some level ten years ago, at a distance. And yet here she was, begging to be singed. Or worse—burned to a crisp.

Nikos seemed to take over the room, as if he expanded to fill all the available space, crowding everything else out. He thrust his hands into the pockets of his denim trousers, but that in no way contained the unmistakable sensual menace he exuded like his own, personal cologne. His shoulders seemed broader, his chest wider, his height excessive. Or was it that Tristanne felt so small? So vulnerable, suddenly—completely devoid of the bravado that had carried her this far. She knew what it was now, his particular brand of potent charisma. She knew what it meant.

You must not let him shake you, she cautioned herself. *You must think only of Vivienne.*

And still he watched her with those old coin eyes, as if he was merely waiting for the right moment to pounce.

"Call me Nikos," he invited her after a moment, when the sound of her own breathing threatened to drive Tristanne to the brink.

She knew she should say something. Even, as he'd suggested, his name. But she could not form the word. It was as if she knew that once she said it, there would be no turning back. As if his familiar name was the last boundary between her old life and this new one she had to pretend to live.

And she could not seem to cross it.

His smile grew darker, more sardonic.

He leaned back against the door he'd closed, his eyes hooded. He said nothing. Then—when Tristanne's nerves were stretched to the breaking point, when she was certain she must scream, or sob, or run as her body ordered her to do, anything to break the tension—he raised his hand and crooked his finger, motioning for her to come to him.

Arrogantly. Confidently. Certain of instant obedience.

Like he was no different, after all, than men like her father and her brother.

Like she was a dog.

A sudden wild anger pulsed through her then, but she stamped it down somehow. Was that not what a mistress was, when all was said and done? A woman on command? At a man's whim? Wasn't this precisely what she'd claimed to want?

What did it matter how this arrogant man treated her? She did not, in truth, wish to become his mistress. She wanted only to make Peter think she had done it—she wanted only the appearance of this man's interest, his protection.

A few days, she had thought. What harm could truly come to her in a few short days? They would have a few dinners, perhaps share some more kisses—preferably within sight of the paparazzi who hung about the sorts of places men like Nikos Katrakis frequented. It would all be for show, and Nikos Katrakis himself need never be any the wiser.

And it was all for a good cause, lest she forget herself entirely. For her beloved, incapacitated mother, who could not seem to understand that her stepson was a monster, nor that he had no intention of caring for her as Gustave had intended. Tristanne needed access to her trust fund—which would not come to her until her thirtieth birthday, unless Peter, as executor, allowed it—so she could pay her mother's debts, see to her health and protect her from further harm. She had no choice.

So Tristanne did not laugh at Nikos, or slap him, or storm from the stateroom as she yearned to do. She was not auditioning for the role of this man's partner, much less his wife. A mistress was a mistress—and Tristanne had the feeling that Nikos Katrakis was a man who made very sure that his mistress knew her place. Instead of reacting as she wanted to, as everything in her screamed to do, she moved toward him, her hips swaying as her high heels sank into the plush carpet at her feet.

"Perhaps you should simply whistle," she could not help but say, with a bite to her tone despite the lecture she had given herself. "It will be far less confusing."

"I am not at all confused," Nikos murmured.

He straightened from the door with a lethal grace that might have dizzied her, had she had time to react. But he gave her no such courtesy. Instead he reached over and snagged her wrist with his big, strong hand, then tugged her to him as if she weighed no more than the lightest feather.

He cupped her jaw, lifting her face to meet his. It was a starkly possessive gesture, and yet, somehow, almost tender— making Tristanne gasp in confusion, and something much hotter.

Then his mouth was on hers. He spun her around until her back was against the door, and he kissed her, tasting her again and again, as if he might devour her whole.

And though she knew she shouldn't, though she knew she should think about why she was there and not her girlish fantasies of moments just like this one, she kissed him back as if she might let him—as if she might beg him. Not to let her go. But not to stop.

Never to stop.

He could not seem to get enough of her. Her sweet honeyed taste, the fit of her mouth to his, the little murmurs she made in the back of her throat, as if she could not help but respond to him with such abandon, with such passionate recklessness. Nikos felt a fire rage through him, making him hard and ready, and did not try to stop it. Could not have stopped it, even if he'd wanted to.

She wanted to be his mistress. He wanted her, with an intensity he had not expected, but had no wish to deny. He told himself that he would use it, that was all. It would merely fuel his revenge.

He pressed her back against the door, holding her there with his body while his hands roamed over her curves. One hand fisted in the dark blonde waves of her hair, tilting her head back to give him better access to her mouth, while the other stroked its way along the elegant line of her throat, then down to the sweet perfection of her jutting breasts.

Pulling away from her mouth with reluctance, Nikos turned his full attention to her breasts, tracing the flesh that swelled proudly above the bustline of her dress. He held them in his hands, weighing them against the silken material, testing their shape, running his thumbs across the hard peaks until she groaned.

It was not enough.

His blood pumped in his veins, urging him on. He reached

down and found the hem of her dress, then worked it up toward her waist, exposing her silken thighs, and the heat of her femininity between them. He pulled one long, exquisitely formed leg over his hip, settling himself against her, so his hardness was flush against her center, separated only by his trousers and a single scrap of silk. She moaned. Her hips bucked against him. Her head was thrown back against the door, her eyes closed, as if she felt the heat, the fire, as he did.

He slanted his mouth over hers, tasting her again and again, while his hips moved, rolling against hers, rocking them both toward insanity.

He buried his face in her neck, licking the hollow of her throat, while his hands found her. He cupped her heat with his palm, feeling her molten heat, her softness. She cried out. Was it his name? He found he did not care.

She was a Barbery. She was his enemy. He wanted her for revenge, and he did not yet know what she wanted from him. He only knew, in this moment, that he had to have her.

Nikos pulled her delicate, panties to one side, stroking her with his long fingers. She sobbed out words he could not identify. Then, teasing her, he circled her entrance, before succumbing to the desire he could not seem to control. She was wet, and so soft, so hot, that he had to bite back his urge to throw her to the floor and sink so deep within her that he might forget his own name. Instead he moved his hand, rocking gently against her sex—and then, not so gently.

She made a helpless sound, but then her hips began to move against his hand, riding him, as her hands clutched at his shoulders.

"Look at me," he ordered her.

Her eyes fluttered open. They were wide, and brown, and so wild with desire it made him curse. He felt her stiffen against him. She bit back a cry. Her cheeks flushed hot and red. A purely male satisfaction thrummed through him, along with a deep, primal surge of possession. He ignored it, and focused on the wet heat in his hands, the ecstasy he knew was just within her reach.

"Come for me," he whispered gruffly, pressing kisses against her mouth, her cheek, her neck. "Now."

This is a mistake, Tristanne thought in a desperate, chaotic, panicked rush—but it was too late.

Her body, tuned to his wicked fingers and not her errant thoughts, shattered into pieces at his command.

She was lost.

It took her long, shuddering moments to come back to herself. When she did, he was watching her with those dark, predatory eyes, and she did not know what she was going to do. What she *could* do, with his hand still between her legs and his mouth faintly damp from hers. She felt herself shiver in reaction. Or perhaps it was an aftershock of the explosion that had ripped through her with such strength, such fire.

One dark brow rose.

Good God, she thought with sudden, horrified comprehension, *he was not satisfied.* Of course he was not satisfied. How had she let this happen? How could she have done nothing at all to prevent it—how could she, instead, have encouraged it? She did not understand how she had lost control of the situation so quickly, so completely. She was afraid she might never understand herself again.

And why did some part of her long to simply throw caution to the wind and let him take her wherever he wished to go?

"What are we…" She was appalled to hear herself stammer out her confusion. But she could not control the tremors inside of her, the rush of conflicting emotions that buffeted her. She could not seem to avoid his knowing, faintly mocking gaze. "I did not intend…"

Her hands were braced against the wall of his chest, and she curled them into fists, as if…what? She planned to beat him off? After welcoming him into her body with such un-characteristic enthusiasm? What was *wrong* with her? She wanted to burst into tears, and she could not understand it. Everything felt too large, too unwieldy, too heavy. Her own body felt like a stranger's, humming with sensations she could not identify. She could not seem to catch her breath, and he stood so still, so close, only the barest hint of that sardonic half smile on his mouth.

He let her leg slide to the floor. Tristanne realized that her dress was still around her waist, and, flushed in an agony of shame, jerked it back into place with trembling fingers. How could she have done this? When she should be thinking only of her mother?

"Perhaps I misunderstood you," he said, his voice like velvet, though his eyes were as hard as steel. He did not back away from her. He tucked a strand of her hair behind her ear, making her choke on a breath. "I was under the impression that you wished to be my mistress. Did you not say so? What did you imagine the position entails?"

"I know what it entails," she retorted, without thinking.

"Apparently not." His mouth crooked in one corner. "Or perhaps your experience of such things differs from mine. I prefer my partners to be—"

"I am merely astounded at the speed at which you wished to consummate the relationship," she interrupted him tartly. "I do not know how things are done where you come from, Mr. Katrakis—"

"Nikos, please," he said silkily. "I know how you taste. *Mr. Katrakis* seems a bit absurd now, does it not?"

"—but I prefer a little more…" Her voice trailed away. Exactly what *did* she expect? This was…a business proposition. She had absolutely no experience to draw from, save what information she had gleaned from novels. Hardly help-ful, under the circumstances.

"Wining and dining?" he finished for her. "Artifice and

pretense? I think that perhaps you do not understand the requirements here. I make the rules and demands. You do not." His head cocked slightly to the side as he regarded her with those unfathomable eyes. "Tell me, Tristanne. How many men have you been mistress to, in your glorious career?"

"What?" She was horrified, even as she shivered at the sound of her name in his wicked, talented mouth. "None!"

She should not have said that. She could have kicked herself. She might have, had he not been in the way.

"Ah, I see." That dangerous satisfaction gleamed in his gaze again. "Then why am I so lucky? What brings the heiress to the Barbery fortune to my bed, offering herself to me? I cannot make sense of such a thing."

Tristanne felt cold, suddenly; her sense of danger heightened. It was the tone in his voice, perhaps, or the way he watched her. *Remember why you are doing this,* she cautioned herself. *Remember what is at stake!*

"These are difficult times," she said with a careless sort of shrug, though she felt anything but careless. She eased away from him, moving further into the room. She was all too aware that he let her go. She did not mention that her brother was on the brink of losing the family fortune or that Peter was obsessed with Nikos and considered him his main rival and enemy. She knew, somehow, it would not be wise.

"And you are, as you know very well, a highly desirable man," she managed to say after a moment. It was no more than the truth, though perhaps the least interesting truth.

"I do not think you have the slightest idea what it means to be a man's mistress," he said from behind her, his voice soft, but with that dark current beneath.

Tristanne could not bear to look at him. She could not understand the wild tumult of emotion that seized her, that filled her eyes with tears she would rather die on the spot than shed, but she knew with perfect clarity that she could not look at him now. She could not.

"I am a quick study," she heard herself say, because she had to say something.

She heard a soft sound that could have been a low laugh, though she could not be sure.

"Turn around, Tristanne."

She did not want to. She did not know what he might see on her face—and she was certain it would only expose her further.

But this was not about her. This was about being a good daughter, for once. This was about protecting Vivienne. If she had not run off to Vancouver when her father revoked her university tuition... If she had not abandoned her mother to the tender mercies of both Gustave and Peter... But then, she had always been stronger than her mother. And now she would prove it.

She turned. He was dark and dangerous, and still as breathtaking as when she'd been seventeen. He watched her with eyes that seemed to know things about her she did not know herself, and that ever-present hint of a smile. As if she amused him. She lifted her chin, and waited.

She could do this. She would.

"This boat sails in the morning for the island of Kefallonia, my home," he told her, his velvet and whiskey voice a rough caress. His eyes gleamed with challenge. "If you wish to be my mistress, you will be on board."

CHAPTER FOUR

HE SAT at a small table on one of the yacht's decks, news-papers in three languages spread out before him and thick, rich Greek coffee within reach, basking in the morning sun-shine. The golden light poured over him, calling attention to his haughty cheekbones and the fathomless dark eyes he'd neglected to cover with sunglasses, before seeming to caress his full, wicked mouth. His long legs, encased in comfort-able tan trousers, stretched out in front of him, and he wore a linen shirt in a soft white that drew the eye, unerringly, to the hard planes of his chest and the shadow between his pectoral muscles. His feet, disarmingly, were bare.

He did not look up when Tristanne approached. She was not so foolish as to imagine, however, that he did not know she was there. She knew that he did. That he had tracked her from the moment she stepped onto this deck—perhaps even from the moment she'd climbed aboard the boat itself.

She stopped walking when she was only a few feet away, and tried to regulate her choppy, panicked breathing. She stood straight, her spine stiff and her head high. She hated herself—and him, she thought with a flash of despair, as she continued to stand there, like some supplicant before him. But she would not bow, or scrape, or whatever else she imagined a man like this must require. She would play her role—tough, sophisticated, focused entirely on what he could provide for her. She would think of her poor mother, whose cough was worsening and whose bills were staggering. It didn't matter, at the end of the day, what Nikos Katrakis thought of her. Much less what she thought of herself.

Whoring yourself out to the highest bidder, are you? Like mother, like daughter after all, Peter had sneered—but she would not think of Peter. The temptation to dissolve into misery was far too great, and far too dangerous now. She resisted the urge to check her smooth chignon, to run her hands along her clothes as if her crisp white trousers and long-sleeved, sky-blue cotton blouse might somehow have become unkempt in the time it had taken her to board the yacht. She could not show nervousness. She could not show… anything, she thought, or she would crumble beneath the pressure of what she must do.

Still, he did not glance up at her, and there was nothing to do but stand there. She knew what he was doing—knew that this was a casual and deliberate display of his power, that he could and would ignore her until he saw fit to acknowledge her presence. Whenever that might be. Her role was to take this treatment. To ignore it, as if she often stood on the deck of luxury yachts, listening to the sounds of surf and water and the distant tolling of church bells, waiting for powerful men to condescend to notice her. The events of the previous day washed over her then and she could feel a scarlet fire roll along the length of her body, making her stomach clench and her breath catch. Had that really been her? That wanton creature, so easily commanded to passion by a man she had once dreamed might one day dance with her? Desire mixed with shame and twisted through her stomach, but she gritted her teeth against both.

It didn't matter what she felt. It didn't matter what had happened, or would happen. She was here. She had put these events into motion, and she had no choice but to see them through. She had to think of her mother—of her mother's future.

"How long will you stand there?" Nikos asked casually, without looking up from his paper. His voice was like a touch, a rough caress that made her shiver. "Why do you loom about with that serious look on your face, as if you are attending your own execution? This cannot be how you think mistresses act, Tristanne, can it?"

Hateful man.

"I am calculating your net worth," she replied coolly. She arched her eyebrows when his old gold eyes met hers, and ruthlessly tamped down her urge to squirm, to look away, to submit to the command in even his gaze. "I imagine that is the favorite pastime of most mistresses, in fact."

His full lips twitched slightly, though he did not quite smile, as if he could not decide whether to laugh or cut her into pieces. Time seemed to fall away, as if he commanded that, too, with the power and heat in his gaze. Tristanne was aware of too many things at once, all conspiring to keep her under the spell of this dark, hard man. The golden sunshine. The lapping waves against the hull of the yacht as it moved beneath them, cutting through the swell and heading away from the French mainland. From all safety, however relative. The way his gaze touched her, heated her, for all that it was proprietary and, on some level, insulting.

"You are overlooking the primary purpose of keeping a mistress," he said softly, breaking the spell, even as he cast another with his whiskey and velvet tone. He laid his paper flat on the tabletop and leaned back against his chair, every inch of him seemingly indolent and careless. She knew better than to believe it.

"By all means," she replied evenly. She forced a smile, and reminded herself that it had been her *choice* to play this game, and there was no use being surly about it now. Vivienne was depending upon her. "Enlighten me."

He nodded at the chair next to his, a hard sort of amusement flaring in his gaze. Once again, there was no denying the command in even so small a gesture. Nor the fact that he expected instant obedience. She longed to throw it in his face with her whole heart, with every cell of her being—even as she walked slowly, casually, to the spot he had indicated and sat. Like a good, docile, well-trained girl. Like a mistress.

He was too close. He was too overwhelming. She imagined, hysterically, that she could feel the intense heat of him caressing her—even though she knew it must be the summer sun high above them. She could not seem to look away from his hands, so strong and too clever, that rested on the small table between them.

He watched as she settled herself, his lips curved into something far too cynically amused for Tristanne's comfort. His hot gaze tracked the way she folded her hands so politely in her lap, the way she sat straight in her chair, the way she crossed her legs just so—as if she was that proper, and there was no wild mess hidden beneath her surface.

As if he had not held the heat of her in his hands, and made her sob.

"Fantasy," Nikos said quietly.

Tristanne stiffened, and fought the pulsing heat that bloomed inside of her and then washed over her skin, scorching her.

"I'm sorry?" At least she did not stammer or gasp. Though she could feel a warmth behind her eyes, threatening her with complete exposure.

"A mistress's primary occupation is the spinning of fantasy," Nikos said patiently—too patiently, though Tristanne could feel the dark edge beneath. "A mistress is always ready to entertain, to soothe. She is always dressed in clothes that invite, seduce. She does not complain. She does not argue. She thinks only of pleasure." His dark eyes met hers. Burned. "Mine."

"That sounds delightful," Tristanne murmured politely. She meant to sound sultry, alluring—but just like the day before, her words somehow came out prim. Tart. "Something to aspire to, surely. With so many days at sea ahead of us, I am certain that you will find me an avid pupil of all things mistress-related."

"This is not meant to be an apprenticeship, Tristanne. I am no teacher, and I do not require a student." His dark gaze made her feel heated, restless. She thought again of mythical creatures, fairy tales. Larger than life and twice as terrifying, that was Nikos Katrakis. Just as she had dreamed long ago.

And now she was entirely within his power.

"My apologies," she said, her voice huskier than she intended. "What would you like me to do?"

"First things first," he said, his voice and gaze mocking her—daring her. "Why don't you greet me properly?" He indicated his lap with the faintest hint of a smile. "Come here."

She looked terrified—or appalled—for the barest moment, but then schooled her features with the same ruthlessness that he had seen her employ several times already. Nikos nearly laughed out loud.

Tristanne Barbery, he was certain, had about as much interest in becoming his mistress as she did in swimming across the width of the Ionian Sea with an anchor tied around her neck. And yet she rose from her seat with that quiet grace that he found uncomfortably captivating, and moved to settle herself in his lap. Somehow, she managed to do it gracefully, politely, as if seating herself on a man's lap was as decorous an activity as, say, needlepoint.

But that didn't change his body's immediate reaction, and his body was under no illusions—no matter how distant and polite she might wish to act, Nikos wanted her in every indecorous manner he could imagine. And his imagination was extraordinarily vivid.

He put his arms around her, holding her close, letting himself feel the suppleness of her skin beneath his hands and the soft cotton blouse she wore, that covered far too much of her body. He felt himself harden, instantly aroused and ready for her. It did not help that he knew exactly how soft, how hot, she would be for him. How uninhibited in passion. He let his head drop close to hers, and took a deep breath to keep himself from taking her where they sat.

It was not time. Not yet. This was about revenge, not merely sex. He did not understand why he had to keep reminding himself of that.

She wore the same sweet and spicy scent as the day before, inflaming his senses, just as she had yesterday. Her hair smelled of apples and musk, and something far more intoxicating that he suspected was all Tristanne. He dug his fingers into the sleek knot of her chignon, destroying it and its appearance of refinement, and sent her heavy mass of hair cascading down her back, enveloping them both in the scent and warmth of the dark blonde waves.

She did not say a word. She only gazed at him, her chocolate eyes shuttered; wary. She shifted against his thighs, as if nervous, moving against his arousal and then away from it, though she had little room to maneuver. She let her palms rest gingerly on the width of his shoulders, as if she was afraid to touch him.

"Much better," he said. Their faces were so close together. He could lean forward and press his mouth to the elegant column of her throat, taste that strong, determined chin. "No man likes to see his mistress looking so civilized. It borders on insult."

"I will endeavor in future to look as disreputable as possible," she said crisply. But he could feel her against him, not so restrained, her thighs restless against his. "Shall I make certain to keep my hair in a great tangle? Is that what you require?"

"That would be a good start," he said, keeping his voice serious, though he wanted to laugh. He could see the color, high and hectic, that stained her marvelous cheekbones and added a frantic sheen to her eyes, though she still held herself so rigidly against him. "But you must also do something about your clothes."

"My clothes?" she asked, stung. Her gaze narrowed on his. "What is the matter with my clothes?"

"You are dressed to meet someone's mother," he replied easily. "It is entirely too conventional and inoffensive."

"You prefer...offensive garments?" Her jaw tensed, that strong little chin lifting. "I wish you had mentioned that yesterday. I'm afraid I packed clothes more in keeping with your reputation for exquisite taste." Those challenging brows rose again. "My mistake."

"I prefer as few garments as possible," Nikos said silkily. "Exquisite or otherwise." He let one hand trail along her spine, tracing the contour of it, the shallow valley below and the ridge of it above. "Skin, Tristanne," he whispered, close to the tempting hollow of her ear, and smiled when she shivered in helpless response. "I want to see skin."

Her lips parted, though no sound emerged. Nikos smiled. She might be here for any number of reasons—and he would find her out, of that he was certain. But in the meantime, there was this chemistry between them, so surprising and electrifying. He had no intention of ignoring it. He would use it, he told himself, to make his revenge upon her—and her family—all the more devastating. It was a tool, that was all.

"When you enter a room, you must always come to me," he continued, his voice a low murmur. One hand tangled in her hair, while the other continued its lazy exploration of her back, flirting with the hem of her blouse, teasing the band of flesh exposed between the top of her trousers and the shirt's tail. "You should assume that you will sit on my lap, not your own chair, unless I tell you otherwise." He pressed his lips to the curve of her ear, then traced a pattern with his lips and tongue along the length of her fine cheekbone. She shuddered.

"I understand," she said, but her voice was the faintest whisper of sound. Her dark lashes covered her eyes, and her face was flushed. He could feel the electric current that moved through her body, making her tense and vibrate against him.

"And you should greet me, always, with a kiss," he whispered, and then took her mouth with his.

Once again, that treacherous fire swept through Tristanne, reducing her to ruins.

She was nothing but need and yearning, gasping against his mouth yet held deliciously immobile in his strong arms. She nearly forgot herself as his lips claimed hers, tangled and teased and beguiled. She *wanted* to forget herself.

But that was the one thing she must never, ever do.

Tristanne leaned back, breaking off the kiss and daring to look down at Nikos, to meet his gaze full-on. His eyes were molten gold, dark with a passionate heat that made her sex pulse in response. His mouth, so wicked and masterful, curled into the slightest of smiles.

"Thank you for the lesson," Tristanne said. Her voice was the breathiest thread of sound—completely insubstantial—and told them both far more about her frenzied state than she would ever have wished to share. How could he do this to her so easily? Some part of her had thought—hoped—that yesterday's explosive passion had been an accident of some kind—an anomaly. But this was not the time to agonize over it. There was nothing to do but brazen her way through such an unexpected obstacle.

She must not succumb to passion. Hadn't that been how her mother had thrown herself into her father's power in the first place? Tristanne would not be so stupid.

"Has it ended?" His gaze dropped from hers to trace her mouth, and his fingers spread against the exposed skin of her lower back. She fought off a shudder of reaction, but couldn't keep the heat from her face.

"Of course," she said, pretending that she could not feel the heat between them—or in any case, did not care. She leaned back slightly. *Barbery ice*, she reminded herself, with some desperation. "We already have an idea of how well we suit in this area. There are so many other areas yet to explore."

"Again, Tristanne, I believe you miss the point of the entire exercise." His voice was low, rich, amused. His midnight brows arched up, while his dark gold eyes saw far too much.

It would be so easy, Tristanne thought as she fell into that dark, honeyed gaze—too easy—to simply bend into his will. He was so powerful, so commanding, and it would be the simplest thing in the world to let herself go, and let him take control as he was, clearly, so used to doing. Hadn't yesterday showed her exactly how easy that would be? It would be like diving into the sea—the decision to dive would be the only difficult part, and everything after that would be gravity.

But who would she be then, when she had fought so hard to make a life for herself—a name for herself that borrowed nothing from her family, had nothing to do with any of them? And more important—what would become of her mother?

She thought of her mother's tears at Gustave's grave. She thought of Vivienne's forced, determined cheer in the following weeks. She thought of the fine bones on the back of her mother's delicate hand, far too visible now.

Tristanne could not acquiesce to this man, however easy it might be. *Especially* because it would be so easy to do so, and such a mistake. She had to maintain control of this situation—tenuous though it might be—or she would lose everything she had worked for over the past years, and everything she hoped for her own future and her mother's life. She had to stand up to this man, somehow—when she had chosen him precisely because he was the kind of man that no one stood up to, because no one would dare.

"Not at all," she said now, gathering her courage as best she could. She tossed her hair back from her face, and made herself smile down at him, still perched on his lap like she was sitting on a hot, iron stove. She could do this. She could hide everything she felt, and show him only what she wanted him to see. Hadn't Peter accused her of being frigid and cold a thousand times? She could pull it off. Couldn't she?

"Oh?" he asked, still so amused. Still so unmanageable, so impossible.

"While I appreciate your list of rules and regulations, and will make every effort to follow them, being a mistress is much more than the ability to follow orders." She traced the strong line of his jaw, the proud jut of his chin, with a lazy fingertip—though she felt as far from lazy as it was possible to feel. She kept on. "A good mistress must anticipate her partner's needs. She must adapt to his moods, and follow his lead. It is like a complicated dance, is it not?"

"It is not like a dance at all," Nikos replied, his eyes glittering. "Not if you are doing it correctly. Euphemism cannot change the facts, only the way they are relayed, Tristanne."

"The man is not supposed to see the steps of this dance, of course," Tristanne continued airily, as if she had such conversations regularly and they affected her not at all. "That is my job. And I do not wish to be protected from anything, I assure you. Least of all you." She lied easily, because she had no choice, and then met his gaze, hoping her own was clear, guileless. Unclouded by her own fears and indecision. "But I will confess that I am something of a perfectionist."

She shifted her weight then, leaning back so that he would

have to choose between letting her stand up or grabbing her close to his chest and making a deliberate show of his superior strength. He chose the former—though not without the faintest hint of a smirk. But Tristanne would take whatever small victories she could with this man. She knew without having to be told directly that they would be far and few between.

"By all means," he murmured, lounging back against his seat, his eyes trained on her, burning into her, "tell me more about this *job* you plan to perform with your perfectionist tendencies."

"Sex is so reductive," Tristanne said briskly. Rather than take her seat, she moved over to the nearby rail and gazed out at the sea, the passing red and gold French countryside. Her palms were damp. She could still feel the heat of him, stamped into her skin. She turned to face him, hoping she looked nonchalant.

His brows arched as he regarded her, his gaze steady. "I would imagine that depends entirely on the quality of the sex," he replied. "And with whom you are having it, yes?"

Tristanne waved a hand in the air, with a breeziness she did not feel, as if discussing sex with him was nothing to her. As if her heart did not pound heavily in her ears, her neck, her softening core. As if she could not feel a faint sheen of heat along her skin, making her too hot, too aware. *Think of your purpose here!* she ordered herself.

"There is so much more to an artful, sustained seduction," Tristanne continued, as if she had spent a significant amount of time puzzling over the issue, instead of merely last night, while she stared desperately at the ceiling in lieu of sleep and tried to come up with a plan to handle this man. She leaned back against the rail. "And that is what a mistress must do, is it not? Produce the fantasy on command. Seduce on call."

"I am glad we agree on the command and the call," Nikos

said, rubbing a finger over his chin. "It is the most important part of the equation."

"Is it?" Tristanne let out a trill of laughter, and immediately regretted it. The laughter was too much—too absurdly blasé. It gave her away, surely. But he only watched her, much the way large and deadly predators watched their prey before making a quick meal of them. *He is a dragon*, she reminded herself, and she already felt as if she had the burn marks to prove it. Blisters everywhere he'd touched her. She could almost feel them on her skin.

"It is to me," Nikos said after a moment. "This conversation is missing the crucial point, I think. I am delighted that you wish to perform well as my mistress. But if you think that there is some debate, some contention, over who is in charge of the relationship, I must disabuse you of the notion at once."

He did not need to deepen his tone, or strengthen the force of his dark gaze when he said such things and, indeed, he did not. He actually relaxed. He lounged in his chair, and stretched out his long legs. He spoke casually, almost as if what he said was an afterthought.

But his undisputable power hummed in the air between them, making the fine hairs on the back of Tristanne's neck stand at attention.

"You are misunderstanding me," Tristanne said in the soothing, conciliatory tone she used primarily with her mother when Vivienne was inconsolable, from her ailments or her grief. When that maddening half smile of his deepened, she knew he recognized exactly what sort of tone it was. That it was meant to handle him, appease him.

"I doubt that very much," he said. "But, of course, I did not have the benefit of your expensive education. Perhaps you must explain things to me in very small and simple words, so that I will understand you."

Tristanne did not address the idiocy of that remark, though

the hard gleam of something like bitterness in his eyes was momentarily disconcerting. She shook it away. In a week's time, she would be on her way back to Vancouver with her trust fund and her mother, and whatever bitterness he carried within him would remain his and his alone. It was no concern of hers.

"I am trying to point out to you that we must concentrate on things other than sex," she said matter-of-factly, pushing away the odd urge to ask him what he meant about his education, or hers. "Sex is easy, but seduction requires more flair, does it not? If I am to serve you well, I must access your brain as well as your body. All good seductions begin with the brain, and only use the body as something secondary. A dessert, if you will."

"My brain," he repeated. He shook his head. "*My brain* is not the part of me that invited you on to this yacht, Tristanne."

"It should have been," she replied. She met his gaze again, and then there was nothing left but to go for it. "Because we cannot have sex, Nikos. Not so soon. Certainly not on this boat."

CHAPTER FIVE

HE LAUGHED.

It was a bold, bright sound. It took Tristanne by surprise, and seemed to ring inside of her like some kind of bell. She had to remind herself to breathe, to keep herself from laughing with him—it was that compelling.

"Why am I not surprised by this turn?" he asked. Rhetorically, obviously. Still laughing slightly, his teeth gleaming white and his eyes like rich honey, he met her gaze. "Explain to me, please, why I would consent to such a thing?"

"I've just explained it to you," Tristanne replied, trying to maintain the air of insouciance she had managed to use like a shield so far.

"So you have." He shook his head slightly. Then shrugged. "If that is what you want, then what is it to me?" His tone was light, his eyes anything but.

She was so consumed by that hard, hot gaze that she almost didn't hear him. Then, when his words penetrated, she thought for a long moment that she had misheard him. Had he…agreed?

"What does that mean?" she asked when he did not speak again.

"You may set whatever limits you like," he said easily. Again, that careless shrug that only called attention to the muscles that moved, lithe and dangerous, beneath his skin. "You need only mention that they have been reached, and I will not argue."

For a moment, she watched him, caught by his potent masculinity in ways she was afraid to examine. Far above, a gull called, then dropped in a graceful arc toward the beckoning sea.

"That is not quite the same thing as agreeing, I cannot help but notice," she said, when the odd hush around them made her too restless to remain silent any longer.

"No." His half smile appeared again, mocked her. "It is not."

"I really feel that we must come to some kind of—"

"We will not come to an agreement," he interrupted her smoothly, unapologetically. He rose then, in a show of graceful, careless strength, and moved toward her, blocking out her view of the Mediterranean, the sun, the world. He reached across the scant space between them, and tugged on a stray strand of her hair. It was an oddly affectionate gesture, for all that it was also a naked display of possession.

"I will not promise you such a thing. I will only promise you that if you do not wish it, you need only say so. Isn't that enough?"

It would be enough if he were any other man alive, Tristanne thought with no little bitterness. She had never had any trouble at all before, because she had never combusted before at a man's slightest touch. She had never had to *remind herself* of all the reasons why she could not simply surrender herself to a man's fire; she had instead had to come up with reasons why she should bother to go on a second date or return a telephone call.

"It is a start," she said eventually, feeling mutinous as she looked at him.

"If it helps," he said softly, still far too close, his hands coming to rest on either side of her, caging her against the boat's rail, "I believe in a more holistic approach. Mind and body as one. You might wish to incorporate that into your seduction plans."

"A good seduction does not simply *happen*," Tristanne retorted, aware that her voice sounded cross, when, once again, she'd wanted to appear effortless. Easy. "It requires a certain amount of research, of mystery, of planning—"

"Of this," he said. He bent and nipped gently at her chin, then pressed his lips to hers. It was not the consuming kiss of before, but it was no less demanding. It was like a brand. A stamp of ownership. Of intent.

He pulled back, and laughed again, more softly this time. Then he let his hand drop down, tracing a path from her neck, across her collarbone toward her shoulder, and then squeezed the bicep that he had held yesterday.

She tried to control her immediate wince of pain, but knew she failed when his dark eyes narrowed. He released her immediately.

"That hurt you?" He frowned.

"No," she lied, shame twisting through her, cramping her stomach. "It was a sudden chill, I think…"

But he ignored her, and drew the billowing sleeve of her shirt up along the length of her arm. Tristanne did not know why she simply stood there and let him do it, as if he had somehow mesmerized her into compliance. But she did.

He muttered something harsh in Greek, and stared at her upper arm. Tristanne knew what he would see—she had seen the livid marks after her shower this morning, red and blue and black. One for each of Peter's fingers.

She felt a rush of that toxic cocktail of shame, rage and fear that always flooded her when Peter's aggression came out—and when it was noticed. When she was forced to explain that this was how her only sibling treated her. She felt that blackness roll through her, tears much too close—

"It is nothing," she said in a low voice, and then, finally, jerked away from him, pushing her sleeve back down. She tilted her chin up, not sure what she would do now. What she would do if she saw even the faintest hint of pity in those dark gold eyes where there had been so much heat—

But his gaze was unreadable. He only watched her for a long moment, and then stepped away from her in one of those impossibly graceful movements that took her breath away and in the same instant reminded her of how dangerous he was.

"I must tend to some business affairs," he told her, towering over her. She told herself that it was the simple fact of his height that made her feel so small, so vulnerable—not what he had just seen. Not what he now knew, that she had never meant to share. "I suggest that you slip into something significantly more revealing and enjoy your indolence. We will dock this evening in Portofino."

He sent her another long, intense, unreadable look, and paused for a moment. A shadow moved across his face, and she thought he might speak, but it passed as quickly as it had come. He turned and walked away without another word, leaving her to the tumult of her own thoughts.

A proper mistress would have availed herself of the opportunity to flaunt her wares, Nikos thought later that afternoon as he concluded another in a long series of tedious phone conferences with business associates in Athens who could not, apparently, follow simple instructions. A malady that was going around.

An enterprising mistress might have indulged in topless sunbathing, perhaps. Or in the lengthy and comprehensive application of unnecessary lotion while in deliberately provocative poses, having known full well that he was watching. A mistress would have known that a day on a yacht was meant to be spent securing her position, and the best way to achieve that was to make certain her every word and deed served to arouse her protector.

Tristanne Barbery, yet again, proved that she had no concept at all of what made a decent mistress. She had spent the entire day with her face pressed into a novel. A large, heavy paperback, with exceedingly dense and small print. The sort of novel that announced its reader *had thoughts.* Deep and complex thoughts, no doubt, which no man sought in his mistress—as she might look to share those deep and complex thoughts with him when he wished only to be soothed and eased and pampered. Still, the book might have been marginally acceptable had she been wearing something appropriate to her station. A miniscule bikini, perhaps, to soak in the Mediterranean sun. One of those gauzy so-called coverups that clung to each curve and begged to be removed. But Tristanne, despite what he had told her earlier, quite clearly, he'd thought, had not changed her clothes.

He would assume she was defying him, deliberately, had he not had the lowering suspicion that she was genuinely caught up in her reading and had forgotten him entirely.

He had no earthly idea why he found her so entertaining, when she was meant to be no more than the key to his revenge. The means to a long overdue end.

"Arketa," he said into the telephone now. *"Teliosame etho."*

He did not need to give the conversation more than a shred of his attention to know that it should end, and now. After some back and forth regarding the details of a particular contract he had expected to have signed weeks before, he finished the call. He rubbed his hands over his face, leaning back in the great leather chair that sat behind the highly polished wood of his desk. He knew that if he turned around and looked out the window, he would see Tristanne as she had been for hours now—curled up on one of the bright white loungers beneath an umbrella out on the deck, her attention entirely focused on the book in her hands.

But he did not need to turn, because the image was already

seared into his brain. Why should he find her so arousing? So amusing? Why did he feel a smile on his own lips, even now, when he was alone?

His reaction to her was unusual. He had never experienced anything like it—it was intriguing as much as it was unwelcome. He had had women who fulfilled every last "requirement" he had laid out for Tristanne this morning. Many of them. And none of them had interested him half as much as this one, who was, if today was any indication, shaping up to be, quite possibly, the worst mistress of all time.

He turned without meaning to do so, and sure enough, she was still in the same position on the plush lounge chair. Her knees were pulled up, and she frowned as she read, oblivious to the world around her—and to his gaze from the window above. Her dark blonde hair was back in another forbidden twist, though strands flew free in the breeze from the ocean, and she nibbled gently on one finger with that lush mouth of hers that he was not nearly done with, not yet. He felt desire pulse in his sex, low and insistent.

He wondered what game she thought she was playing, still. Did she think she would win it? Did she imagine that Nikos Katrakis was the posturing, toothless dog that her brother was? She would learn soon enough that he could not be leashed.

His mood darkened immediately at the thought of Peter Barbery—but not, for once, with thoughts of the damage Peter had wrought so long ago on what had passed for Nikos's family. Instead he thought only of those bruises on Tristanne's otherwise flawless flesh—bruises he had no doubt whatsoever Peter had put there.

He was surprised at the smoldering rage that rolled through his gut, and the possessive edge to it that fanned it on. It was no more than any man must feel when faced with evidence that another of his sex was no better than an animal, he told himself resolutely. He did not prey upon the weak and innocent like Peter Barbery.

Except for Tristanne—

But he did not allow himself to finish the thought, because it was impossible. Tristanne Barbery, sister of his sworn enemy, had not walked up to him and demanded he kiss her in front of some seventy witnesses by divine accident. She had had an agenda from the first—one that was very obvious to Nikos, for all that she tried to weave her desperate webs to conceal it. She had no interest in the role she'd claimed to want, and no talent for it, either. Nikos didn't know yet what she did want, but he did know that the fact she was not what she claimed to be meant she could not possibly be an innocent in all of this. She could not.

She was a Barbery. How could anything else matter? She was a Barbery—and that was all Nikos needed to know. That was all there was to know.

She might entertain him in a way he had not imagined a woman could, but that was of no matter. He might want her in a way he had not expected, but then, he had never been one to deny his appetites, no matter how inconvenient. He could use all of that for his own ends.

It would in no way prevent him from taking his revenge.

"Tell me," Nikos said that evening, his low voice making the fine hairs all over Tristanne's body stand at attention. "Does your brother often leave his mark upon your skin?"

It was the first time he had spoken since they'd left the yacht, and his voice seemed to echo off of the cobblestone street around them, ricocheting off of the famous yellow and pink pastel buildings of Portofino that clustered in a sparkling curve around the pretty, tiny harbor, and stood out against the green hills of pine, cypress and olive that rose steeply behind them. Or perhaps she only thought so, as she flexed her bruised arm slightly in response and felt that twist of shame roll through her again. That deep, black despair.

Tristanne took a quick breath to dispel it, and snuck a glance at the striking man who walked so quietly, so deliberately, at her side. His mood had changed considerably over the course of the day. Gone was the mockery and the sly insinuations; the man who met her for dinner after the sun had set in a red and orange inferno above the turquoise sea was quiet and watchful now. Brooding. He walked beside her with his hands thrust into the pockets of his dark trousers, a crisp white shirt beneath his expertly tailored jacket, which hugged the contours of his broad, muscled shoulders intimately.

"Of course not," Tristanne said. She was surprised to hear her own voice sounded so hushed, as if she expected to hear it tossed back from the hills, her lie repeated into every passing ear. She frowned at her feet, telling herself that she was concentrating on walking in her high, wedged sandals over such tricky, ancient ground. That was all. That was the only reason she felt so unsettled, so unbalanced.

She wished she had not dressed for him. She wished even more that she did not know perfectly well that she had done so. At first she did not understand how she had found herself in this particular dress, an enticing column of gold that reminded her of his eyes. It poured over her curves from two delicate wisps of spaghetti straps at her shoulders and swished enticingly around her calves as she moved. She did not know why she had left her hair down, so that it swirled around her upper arms and her naked back, nor why she had dabbed scent behind her ears and between her breasts, so that it breathed with her as she moved. Why she had so carefully outlined her eyes with a soft pencil, or why she had darkened her lashes with a sooty mascara. It was as if someone else, some other Tristanne, had done those things, made those choices.

Until she had walked out onto the deck, and seen him, and then she'd known exactly what she'd been doing, and why. That knowledge poured into her, filling her and washing through her, nearly making her stumble as she walked. Her motivations were suddenly as clear to her as if she'd written them out in a bullet-point list. As if they were glass. It had been all for that quicksilver gleam in his eyes when he looked around from his position at the railing and saw her. That sudden flare of heat in his old coin eyes, quickly shuttered.

And what did that make her, already far too susceptible to the one man to whom she could never, ever surrender herself? What in the world did she think she was doing with him— when she should have thought of nothing but her necessary goal? Her poor mother? She should have dressed in sackcloth and ashes—anything to repel him.

But she did not wish to repel him, a traitorous voice whispered. Not really. Perhaps not at all. She pulled her wrap closer around her shoulders, and frowned intently at the cobblestones beneath her feet as they made their way along the harborside quay toward the bustling center of the small village.

"That is all you have to say?" Nikos asked, a certain tenseness in his voice. Tristanne looked at him then, no less imposing in the soft, Italian night than he was in the stark light of morning.

"Must I defend my family?" she asked, with a casual sort of shrug that she did not feel. She had perfected it over the years, to deflect exactly this kind of attention. "All families have their little skirmishes, do they not? Their bad behavior and regrettable scenes?"

"I am no expert on families," he said, with a derisive snort. "But I am fairly certain most restrain themselves from physical displays of violence. Or should."

"I bruise very easily," Tristanne murmured dismissively. Better Peter should take out his rage on her than on Vivienne,

Tristanne thought, as she always had. She did not want to think about the way Peter's fingers had dug into her flesh, nor the words he had thrown at her, his face contorted in fury. And she did not want to talk about this. Not with Nikos. Not ever. She felt the punch of something edgy and heavy in her gut, but she struggled to repress it.

Not now, she ordered herself fiercely, blinking back the heat behind her eyes. *Not with him. It does not matter what I dreamed of when I was seventeen—he can be nothing to me!*

Nikos stopped walking, and she did, too, turning toward him warily. He stood with his back to the famous Piazzetta, the faint breeze from the water playing through his thick, black hair. His gaze was dark, troubled.

"What kind of man is your brother, that he would put his hands on you in this way?" he asked, condemnation ringing in his voice. "Surely your father would not have countenanced such behavior, were he still alive."

It was the *certainty* in his voice that did it, somehow. It was all...too much. Tristanne flushed hot with that toxic mixture of shame and fury, and it was all directed at the man who stood there before her, beautiful and disapproving in the lights that spilled from the restaurants that lined the Piazzetta.

It was all his fault! He was beguiling when he should have disgusted her, and she hated that he knew what Peter had done. That he knew exactly how little her own brother thought of her. What did that say about her? About how worthless her own brother found her?

And what did it say about her that she cared what this man thought about it? About her? When his thoughts should not matter to her at all?

"What kind of man is Peter?" she asked, her temper kicking in again, harder, and scalding her from within. At least it was better than tears. Anything was better than tears. "I don't know how to answer that. A typical man? A normal man? They are all more or less the same, are they not?" She felt wild, as if she careened down a narrow mountain pass, out of control and reckless.

The elegant arch of his dark brows did nothing to stop her. "Careful, Tristanne," he said softly, but she did not wish to be careful.

"They control. They demand. They issue orders and care not at all for the feelings or wishes of anyone around them." She threw her words at him like blows, for all the good it did her. He did not move. He did not flinch. He only stared at her with eyes that grew darker by the second. And still she continued. "They crush and flatten and maim as they see fit. What is a little bruise next to everything else a man is capable of? Next to what *you* are capable of, for that matter?"

It seemed as if the world stopped turning. As if nothing existed save her labored breathing and the sounds of *la dolce vita* all around, spilling out of the cafés and trattorias and somehow failing to penetrate the tense, tight bubble that surrounded them.

She did not want to feel this way. She wanted to play her part the way she'd planned—bright and easy and seductive—and instead she kept tripping herself up on her own jagged emotions. Was it him? Was he the reason she could not control herself the way she wanted to—the way she had prided herself on doing the whole of her adult life? Her control had saved her in tense interactions with her family—why couldn't she summon it now?

Nikos did not move, and yet he seemed to loom over her, around her, filling her senses and her vision. Filling the whole universe with his smooth muscles, his dangerous mouth, his molten gold eyes with that hard edge within. Just as she feared he would do. Just as she knew he would.

He reached over and brushed her hair back from her face with a gentleness that belied the tension she could feel shimmering between them, then followed a long strand down toward her neck, pulling it between his fingers as if he could not quite bear to let it drop. His mouth moved as his hand returned to his side, but then he shook his head slightly, as if thinking better of whatever he had been about to say.

A couple strolled too close to them on the narrow quay, almost jostling into Tristanne. But Nikos shot out a hand again and moved her out of the way, his touch shocking against her skin for all that it was protective, even kind. He did not speak, but he did not drop his hand from her forearm, either. Tristanne imagined she could see the force of his touch, the feel of it, dancing over her like light, illuminating all of her hidden places, her shadows.

She could not do this. Any of this. She could not *feel*. Neither temper nor despair nor...this softer, scarier thing she dared not name. Emotion had no place here, between them. She could not allow it.

She cleared her throat. "I am speaking rhetorically, of course," she said, her voice husky with the things she could not show, not even to herself.

"Of course."

His mouth flirted with that half smile of his that she was appalled to realize she wanted to see, even *yearned* to see, while his eyes gleamed almost silver in the dark. She shivered, though she was not cold.

"Come," he said quietly. "It is time for food, not fighting."

CHAPTER SIX

NIKOS did not understand how he could possibly have rowed in a public street. With a woman he had yet to take to his bed, no less. It defied all reason. It went against nearly forty years of habit and precedent, for that matter, and disturbed him deeply.

He was not in the habit of suffering through emotional scenes, his own or anyone else's. He did not soothe hurt feelings or tactfully contain angry explosions. He had never before entertained the faintest urge to do either. He did not allow emotion into his life, in any form. Not anymore. It had been long years since he'd backed down from a challenge or left accusations unanswered—in fact, he preferred to respond as forcefully as possible, decimating his accusers, grinding them into dust beneath his feet, ensuring neither they nor anyone in their vicinity would dare to test him again.

Until tonight.

He sat across from Tristanne in his favorite waterfront trattoria, the light from a hundred flickering candles playing over her lovely features, wondering what spell she had cast upon him to make him behave so unlike himself. He paid no attention to the fine, fresh food before them—airy foccacia with a tangy olive tapenade, hand-crafted pasta flavored with *pesto corto*, grilled peppers and anchovies, and the freshest fish imaginable tossed with garlic and olive oil. How could he concentrate on food? He was galled by his own uncharacteristic display of something very close to weakness. The worst kind of weakness—and to a Barbery, no less!

Was that her game? To make him betray his own vows to himself? If so, he was appalled to see how well it was working. What was next? Would he break into sobs in the center of the village piazza? Weep for his wounded inner child? He would more readily saw off his own head with the butter knife that rested on the crisp white linen tablecloth before him.

"You are by far the most mysterious member of your family," he said, because that was the point, after all, of this charade, was it not? To destroy the Barberys by whatever means necessary, to gather the information he needed to do so? More than this, he needed to break the silence. Quiet between them seemed too dangerous now; too fraught with undercurrents and meanings he refused to explore. Sexual tension he understood, even encouraged. Anything beyond that was anathema to him. He was here to seduce her, to wreak his revenge on her very skin—not to *comfort* her.

"Mysterious?" He noticed the way she tensed in her chair. Did she expect an attack? Perhaps she should. Her eyes met his briefly. "Hardly."

It made it worse, somehow, that she looked so beautiful. Still not the obvious, provocative beauty of a proper mistress, but rather her own potent brand of bewitching femininity that seemed to go straight to his head—and his groin. She looked too good for a sewer rat like him, far too pedigreed and finished and perfected. She was all gold and class and melted chocolate eyes—the kind of woman he would have yearned for heedlessly in his desperate youth, knowing his hands would only dirty her, ruin her, destroy her in the very act of worshipping her. He almost hated her for reminding him of those terrible days, when he'd still operated blindly from his rage, his agonized determination to escape, rather than the cool analytical mind and sharp business acumen he relied on as an adult.

But he was no longer that child. He had exorcised that particular demon, and any outward expression of his darkest rage, many years ago.

"Your father and brother and even your mother have been seen in all the halls of Europe over the past decade," he said simply, ignoring the unacceptable mix of chaos and desire that surged within him, focusing on his purpose. "You have not. One began to imagine you were merely a legend. A fairy story of the lost Barbery heiress."

She gazed at him for a moment, then returned her attention to her plate. "I was not lost." She smiled then, that excessively polite curve of her mouth that put him instantly on alert. "My father and I had a difference of opinion regarding my course of study at university. I chose to follow my own path."

"What does that mean?" he asked. He was caught by the way the candlelight made her skin glow like rich, sweet cream above the warm golden caress of her gown. He blinked. She did not appear to notice his fascination.

"It means that I chose to pursue a Fine Arts degree, even though my father felt that was a waste of time. He thought Art History would be more appropriate—better suited to cocktail party conversation with potential husbands." Tristanne toyed with her fork—nervously, he thought, and then finally set it down against her plate. "I wanted to draw, you see. To paint."

That simply, she reminded him of who they were, and why they were here. Nikos had never had the luxury of indulging the creative impulse—he had been far too busy fighting for survival. And then, when survival was assured, making certain that he would never again even approach destitution, or anything like it. Drawing? Painting? That was someone else's life. Not his.

"That is not very practical," Nikos said, unable to keep

the bite from his tone. "Is that not the point of university? Practicality? An education in service of your future?"

"You would have gotten on well with my father," Tristanne said dryly. She shifted in her seat, the candlelight caressing her cheeks, her neck, the hint of velvety shadows between her breasts. "When I opted to ignore his advice, he retracted my funding. I decided to move to Vancouver, which, apparently, sent him into apoplexy, as my father did not care to be defied." She smiled slightly. "None of this made for pleasant family reunions, so you will understand why the halls of Europe were without me for so long."

There was a subtle mockery in her tone. He ignored it.

"I trust you do not cast yourself as the victim in this scenario," he said, his voice like a blade. "Those who accept financial support cannot whine about their loss of independence. About feeling *crushed* or *flattened*. Everything comes at a price."

He expected a storm of emotion—tears, perhaps; a repeat of what had occurred in the piazza. But Tristanne only held his gaze, her own surprisingly clear, if narrowed.

"I do not disagree," she said after a moment. "I am not, I think, the hypocrite you would prefer me to be. I chose not to accept any financial support whatsoever from my father once I moved to Canada."

Something he could not identify moved through him. He called it anger. Distaste. And yet he knew it was not that simple—or, perhaps, it was not directed across the table.

"You *chose*?" he echoed. "Or were you disowned?"

"Who can say who disowned who?" Tristanne replied in a light tone he did not quite believe. "Either way, I never took another cent from him." Her chin tilted up; with pride, he thought. He felt a stab of recognition, and ruthlessly suppressed it. "I may have to wait tables or tend a bar, but it's honest work. I don't have much in Vancouver, but everything I do have is mine."

He could not have said what he felt then, staring at her, but he told himself it was a simmering rage. They were not at all similar, despite her words. Her pride. For what was she really but one more spoiled heiress who made the usual noises about her independence, but only so far as it suited her? She had come running back to Europe quickly enough after Gustave had died, hadn't she? Did she hope to get into her brother's good graces now that he controlled the purse strings? What did she know about real struggle, about truly fighting for something, anything, to call one's own because the alternative was unthinkable?

Not a damn thing.

"How noble of you to abandon your considerable fortune and fight for your preferred existence by choice rather than necessity," Nikos drawled, and had the satisfaction of watching her pale. His smile could have drawn blood. He wished it did. "The desperate residents of the slums where I grew up salute you, I am sure. Or would, if they could afford to have your exalted standards."

He had the pleasure of watching her flush red, though she did not otherwise change expression. She met his gaze steadily, as if she was not afraid of him, when he knew better. He had seen to it that she was. Or should be. And he knew that she should be.

"And, of course, those standards no longer apply," he said smoothly, daring her to continue defying him. "Since you are here. My brand-new mistress, who has such high hopes for my *generosity*. Did the charms of honest work pale, Tristanne? Did you remember that you need not work for your money after all?"

"Something like that," she bit off.

Her gaze dropped then, and her hands trembled slightly, and he told himself he was glad. Because this was how it had to be between them, no matter how much he desired her, and how he planned to indulge that desire. She was payback, nothing more.

He was certain of it.

Tristanne was still smarting from that conversation and the unpleasant emotions it had stirred up within her the following afternoon, some two hundred kilometers to the south and east in Florence.

Their strained evening in Portofino had led to a long, sleepless night aboard the yacht. For her, in any event. Tristanne had tossed from side to side in her stateroom's large, unfamiliar bed as the hours ticked by, growing increasingly more frustrated as the night wore on into morning. Had part of her been waiting, wondering if Nikos would come to her as she'd thought he might—to assert whatever "rights" he believed he had over her? She was supposed to be his mistress, after all, and he had made it clear he intended that relationship to be sexual upon his command—which, she told herself firmly, made her despise him. *That*, clearly, was the source of the burning restlessness that had her nerves stretched thin, her skin too sensitive to the touch.

Or had she simply been too agitated from all that he had said to her—and, worse, all that she had felt? Why should she feel anything at all, she had asked herself again and again throughout the night? Why should she care what he thought, especially about her, when he was nothing but smoke and mirrors, a trick, to make Peter do as she wished?

Not that any of it had mattered, in the end. She had fallen into a dreamless sleep just as the night sky began to bleed into blue through her porthole. She had not wanted to wake for the breakfast Nikos had told her, curtly, would be at half past nine—but she had. She had taken a very long, very hot shower in an attempt to conceal her exhaustion, and yet when she'd found him in the boat's lavish receiving room, Nikos had barely spared her a glance.

"Be ready in thirty minutes," he had said without looking up from his high-tech PDA, Greek coffee steaming at his elbow. "We must go to Florence."

"Florence, *Italy*?" Tristanne had asked. She'd shaken her head in confusion or exhaustion, or some combination thereof. "I thought we were going to Greece." She had stared at the plentiful breakfast buffet spread out before her on the rich wood table, bright and colorful fruits, fluffy egg dishes, flaky, perfect pastries—and, for some reason, all of it had seemed completely unappealing.

He had looked at her then, his dark eyes hard and that full mouth unsmiling. She had had to order herself not to react, not to shiver, not to give in to the command in that searing gaze.

"Be ready," he said again, his voice low, his tone ruthless, "in thirty minutes."

She had taken forty minutes—her own quiet protest— which he had assiduously ignored. He had continued to ignore her. He had taken several calls as they walked into the village of Portofino again, barking out orders in emphatic Greek as they climbed the hill away from the piazza where, she had been ashamed to remember, she had so betrayed herself the night before.

He had handed her into the gleaming black, low-slung Italian sports car that awaited them at a private garage, and had not bothered to make conversation with her as he drove. Tristanne told herself she did not care what he did; it did not matter. Nikos drove as he did everything else—with ruthless command and a complete disregard for others. She had stared out the window as the powerful car hugged the craggy coast-line, her eyes drinking in the Italian sea spread out below her, sparkling in the morning light. It was mesmerizing, turquoise and inviting, and she'd wanted to be out of that car and as far away from the dark, grim driver beside her as the sea could take her. She must have drifted off to sleep at some point, for when she woke, it was to find herself deep in the heart of Florence.

The city was a hectic blur of russet-topped stone buildings and narrow, medieval streets; the Tuscan hills rising serene and green in the distance, the gleaming waters of the wide River Arno welcoming and yet mysterious as it cut through the city. Yet the city seemed strangely distant for all that it was right there on the other side of the car window. It was the man beside her, she realized as she came fully awake. He was like some kind of electrical source, emanating heat and power with such force that even the jewel of the Italian Renaissance seemed to fade when he was near.

You must still be dreaming, she told herself sharply now, as the car purred around a tight corner, low and muscular. *Wake up!*

"How long was I asleep?" she asked, her voice sounding much too loud in the close confines of the car. Had she really fallen asleep in this man's presence? She could only blame her sleepless night—surely, only exhaustion could possibly have allowed her to lower her walls so completely. Her hands moved to her hair involuntarily, as if smoothing it back into place might ease her sudden acute embarrassment that he had seen her in so defenseless a state.

"I stopped counting your snores some time ago," Nikos responded dryly. "Musical as they were."

She shot him a look, and saw that half smile of his playing over his mouth. She could not imagine what it might mean— or why she interpreted it as softer, somehow. She knew better. She knew any softness from this man was momentary at best, like a trick of the light.

"I do not snore," she said, her voice sharper than she meant it to be. She cleared her throat, and forced herself to relax, at least outwardly. "How rude!"

"If you say so," he replied. His dark gaze swept over her for a brief, electric moment, then returned to the road in front of him. "But I think it is far ruder to fall asleep in someone else's presence. I am wounded that you find me so profoundly boring, Tristanne."

Intuition—and the suicidal urge to poke at him—made her smile like a cat with a bowl of cream. Perhaps she thought she was dreaming, and that he could not harm her. Awake, she should have known better.

"Poor Nikos," she said with bright, false sincerity. "This must have been a new experience for you. I am sure the women of your acquaintance normally go to great lengths to pretend that you are so captivating, so *interesting*, that they can scarcely breathe without your express permission. Much less sleep." She made a show of yawning, and stretched her feet out in front of her, as if she was not in the least bit captivated, interested, or even aware of his brooding presence beside her.

She was dimly aware that the car stopped moving, but she could hardly concentrate on something so minor when he was turning toward her, his big body dwarfing the sleek confines of the car's leather interior, his dark eyes glittering with something edgy and wild that she could not identify.

Though her body knew exactly what it was, and hummed in sensual response, her breasts growing heavy and her nipples hardening beneath the simple green knit sheath she wore.

"Once again," he said, his voice smooth and dangerous, "I am astonished at how little you seem to know about being a man's mistress, Tristanne. Do you truly believe that my former mistresses taunted me? *Mocked* me?"

Some demon took her over, perhaps, or it was that restlessness inside of her that made her ache and burn and *need*. But she did not—could not—cower or apologize or back down at all, despite the clear sensual menace in his voice, his gaze, the way his arm slid along the back of her seat and hemmed her in, caged her, *reminded* her of the role she was supposed to be playing.

Whatever it was, she met his gaze. Boldly. Unapologetically. As if this was all part of her plan. She raised her brows, challenging him.

"And how quickly did you tire of them, I wonder?" she asked softly, directly. "So accommodating, so spineless. Do you even remember their names?"

Something too primal to be a smile flashed across his face then. His eyes turned to liquid gold, like a sunset across water, and Tristanne forgot how to breathe.

"I will remember yours," he promised her. "God help you." He let out a sound too harsh to be laughter, and nodded toward her window, and through it toward the covered archway that led to the imposingly large door of the ancient-looking building before them. "But there is no time for this now. We have arrived."

She could not say if she was relieved or disappointed when he left her scant moments after he ushered her into the sumptuous foyer of the sprawling flat. It commanded the whole of the top floor of an old building tucked away on an ancient side street in the city center. Tristanne did not realize how central it was, in fact, until the door closed behind Nikos and she turned to gaze out the floor-to-ceiling windows that comprised the far wall. She was staring directly at the famous red and marble dome of the cathedral of Santa Maria del Fiore itself. Brunelleschi's world-renowned Duomo was the whole of the view—filling the wall of windows and so close she felt as if she could very nearly reach out and touch it.

Naturally this would be where Nikos Katrakis kept an extraordinarily sumptuous flat he could not possibly use very often. It was an architectural feat—high, graceful ceilings and a loft's sense of space inside a historical building dating back to the Middle Ages. *Of course* he simply kept such a place as his Florentine pied-à-terre.

Tristanne had grown up with wealth; had been surrounded by it for all but the last few years of her life. And still, the cold calculation necessary to make and maintain such wealth remained breathtaking to her, even shocking—the reduction of everything, anything, *anyone* to little more than currency, items to be bought, hoarded, sold, or bartered. Tristanne's father had been that kind of man. Cold. Assessing. Moved by money alone, and sentiment? Emotion? Never.

Nikos had not even glanced at the stunning view that would no doubt transport the sea of tourists who swarmed the city daily into raptures. The Duomo was one of the foremost sights in Italy, in the world. It was internationally, historically significant. And yet he had given a few curt orders to his staff, informed Tristanne he had meetings he expected to return from no later than six in the evening, and had then left. Had he bought this flat because he loved this view and wished to gaze at it whenever he happened to be in Florence? Or had he acquired it simply because it made good business sense as an investment property—because it had one of the most desirable and thus most expensive views in the whole city?

"You are leaving?" she had asked, surprised, when he'd turned to go. "And what am I to do for all of these hours?"

He had looked almost affronted by the question. "What mistresses always do, I would imagine," he had replied in that silken tone. He'd crooked his brow. "Wait. Prettily."

Wait. Prettily. Like a seldom-used property. Had that not been what Tristanne's mother had done her entire life?

She moved closer to the windows now, something like sadness seeming to suffuse her, to swallow her whole, though she could not have said why. She did not know how long she remained in that same position, staring unseeing at the glorious marble and distinctive red tiles before her. She felt a sudden, sharp pang of homesickness stab at her. She wanted to be back in her cheerful little apartment in the Kitsilano neighborhood of Vancouver, free again. She wanted none of the past few days to have happened. Or, for that matter, the previous month. Outside, the light changed; dark gray clouds rolled in, and slowly, quietly, it began to rain.

Tristanne pulled out her mobile and called her mother, who was, after all, the reason she was standing in Florence in the first place instead of in her own living room, which she'd set up as a makeshift artist's studio and from where she had a view of nothing more remarkable than the backyard she shared with her neighbor. She loved that yard, Tristanne reminded herself as the phone rang. She liked to sit out in it with a glass of wine when the evenings were fine. She did not know why she felt as if she needed to defend it to herself now, much less the rest of her life—as if it was all slipping out of her reach with every breath.

"Oh, darling!" Vivienne cried into the phone when she answered. No sign in her voice of her illness, her persistent cough or her unexplained fevers. Tristanne wondered what it cost her—though she knew her mother would never complain. "Are you having a lovely holiday?"

Which was, Tristanne thought when she ended the call a few moments later, really the most she could expect from her mother. Her flighty, fragile, unendingly sweet mother, who had spent her life being looked after by one man or another. Her father, her husband, her stepson. She was anachronistic, Tristanne often thought, with varying degrees of frustration— a throwback to another time, a different world. And yet she had always been the single bright light in Tristanne's life—the only thing that had made her childhood bearable. Vivienne had been a flash of bright colors and boundless enthusiasm in the midst of so much grim, cold darkness. And now she was unwell, and needed her daughter. Tristanne would do anything for her. Anything at all.

Even this.

"You must take pictures," Vivienne had said, nearly bubbling over with her excitement—which was at least an improvement over her grief, or her weakness. "You must record your adventures for posterity!" Because a lady did not discuss the reasons for a trip like Tristanne's, just as a lady did not discuss her debts, or her failing health.

"I'm not sure this is the sort of trip I'll want to remember," Tristanne had said dryly, but her mother had only laughed gaily and changed the subject.

What pictures should she take to capture the moment? Tristanne wondered now, her mind reeling. She pressed a hand against her temple. What would best express the Nikos Katrakis experience? What single image would conjure up the dizzy madness of the last two days?

She did not—*would not*—think of his wicked mouth on hers, his hands smoothing fire and need into her skin until she'd shaken with it. She could not think of his devastating quiet on that darkened street, the way he had held her captive with only that dark, too-perceptive gaze. His cutting mockery, that beguiling almost-smile… She wanted none of those images in her mind. She had to remember why she was here—why she was doing this.

She let her head fall forward until it touched the cool glass of the great window, and sighed. It seemed to take over her whole body.

She would do what she must, but that did not mean she had to sit here like this apartment, empty and discarded until Nikos condescended to return and begin their little dance anew. A whole city waited just outside, brimming with art and history in the summer rain, the perfect balm for the heart she told herself did not ache within her chest, the tears she would not allow herself to cry; for the life she suddenly feared would never fit her again as well as it used to, as well as it should.

CHAPTER SEVEN

HE WAS waiting for her when she rounded the corner.

At first she thought he was some kind of hallucination—the same one she had been having to some degree or another all afternoon, to her great irritation. She'd seen the side of his head in the crowded rooms of the Uffizi Gallery, startling her as she gazed at Botticelli's famous painting of Venus rising from the water, all lush curves and flowing hair. But it had only been a dark-haired father bending to whisper to his two wriggling children, not Nikos at all. She'd glimpsed his unmistakable saunter from a distance on the Ponte Vecchio, the ancient bridge crowded full of shops and arches and tourists that stretched across the Arno—but then she had blinked and seen the figure approaching her was nothing so special after all, just a local man crossing a bridge.

So Tristanne did not immediately react when she saw him this time, expecting the figure lounging in the archway that led into Nikos's old building to turn to vapor, fade into shadow, or step forward and reveal himself to be an ordinary resident of the city, simply going about his business in the wet summer evening.

But as she drew closer, her footsteps echoing off the ancient cobblestones, the image before her only intensified. The jet-black hair. The dark, tea-steeped eyes, swimming with gold and fire. The dragon in him infused his very skin, making him seem almost to glow with all the power he held carefully leashed in that lean, muscled torso, so wide through the shoulders and narrow at his hips. He leaned against the stone wall, protected from the rain, his long arms crossed and his gaze intent upon her as she approached.

"Where have you been?"

The question seemed to echo even louder than her shoes against the stones, and her heart beat like a drum in her chest. Tristanne told herself that it was simply a trick of the fading light and the effect of the rain, as the old city settled into evening all around her. This section, hidden in a series of twisted age-old streets that seemed to double back and forth on top of each other, was so very quiet in comparison to the high traffic areas she'd walked earlier. He only sounded dangerous and on edge because there were not seas of tourists to dull the sound of his voice.

And even if he was on edge, for some no doubt inscrutable reason he would not bother to share with her, why should she act as if that cowed her? She did not understand why this man made her forget herself so easily, but she could not let it continue. It did not matter how she *felt*, she reminded herself—a key point she had returned to again and again as she wandered through centuries of art all afternoon—it only mattered how she *acted*.

"My apologies," she said, curving her mouth into an approximation of meek smile. "I had so hoped to beat you here, so that I might arrange myself on your sofa like a still-life painting. *Prettily*, of course. As directed."

He only watched her as she closed the distance between them and stepped under the archway with him. She knew she was soaked through, but she could not bring herself to care as she no doubt should. The rain was warm, and had seemed to her like some kind of necessary cleansing as she'd walked through Florence's famous piazzas. As if she had needed to bathe in all the sights and centuries arrayed before her, and if the price of that was her bedraggled appearance now, well, so be it.

"You look half-drowned," he said after a long moment. His eyes were too hot on hers, too unsettling. "What could possibly be so important that it lured you out in this weather without so much as an umbrella?"

"I cannot imagine," she said dryly, pushing her damp hair back from her face. "Surely there is nothing in the whole of the city of Florence that could possibly interest an artist."

"Art?" He pronounced the word as if it was an epithet in some foreign language he did not know. His head tilted to the side as he looked down at her, arrogant and imperious. "Are you certain it was *art* that drew you into the streets, Tristanne? And not something significantly more prosaic?"

"Perhaps a man of your stature does not notice art until you purchase it to grace your walls, or to appear as a coveted view outside your windows," Tristanne said tartly, before she could think better of it. "But there are people in the world— and I realize this may surprise you—who find art just as moving when it is displayed in a public square as when it is hidden away in private collections for the amusement of the very rich."

"You will have to forgive me if I cannot live up to your rarified expectations," Nikos said coolly, though his eyes narrowed. "There were not many opportunities for art appreciation classes in my childhood, in public or private. I was more concerned with living through the week. But do not let me keep you from feeling superior because you can tell the difference between medieval sculptors at a glance. I am sure that is but one among many useful skills you possess."

"You will not make me feel badly about something that has nothing to do with me!" Tristanne threw at him, her cheeks hot with sudden embarrassment and a sinking sensation in the pit of her stomach that she refused to acknowledge. "You loom here, *oozing* your power from every pore, *dripping* luxury items like yachts and cars and sprawling flats, and yet *I* am supposed to feel badly because of your past? When you have obviously overcome it in every conceivable way and now flaunt it across Europe?"

His dark eyes glittered, and his mouth pulled to one side. Tristanne knew beyond a shadow of a doubt that she did not want to hear whatever cutting thing he was about to say—that he would shred her without a second thought, just to assuage whatever mood this was that had him in its grip.

"I am not the one with expectations," she hissed, hoping to stave him off. "You are."

"You expect me to believe you wandered around looking at art in the rain?" he asked after a long, brooding moment. There was an urgency in his tone, a certain intensity, that she didn't understand. That she didn't *want* to understand, because she didn't *want* to feel the urge to comfort him, to soothe him, however unlikely it was that he might let her do such a thing. She wanted only to complete this task, to gain her trust fund. That was the only thing she could allow herself to want.

"I do not care if you believe it or not," she said instead, confused by the direction of her thoughts. She raised her shoulders only to let them fall again. "It is what I did."

"And why would you do this?" His dark gaze moved over her face, and she was afraid, suddenly, of the things he might see, the urges he might notice and use against her. She looked away, back toward the street, letting her gaze follow the shadows and graze the cobblestones. She crossed her arms over her chest, half to appear defiant, but half to hold herself still as well.

"I suppose you will tell me a mistress does not do such a thing," she said softly, shaking her head slightly at the water coursing down the street. "I imagine the perfect mistress...

what? Shops for outfits she does not need? Sits in a room and contemplates the state of her hair?"

He almost smiled. She could sense it more than see it, in the closeness of that archway, hidden away together from the falling rain and coming dark.

"Something like that," Nikos said. "She certainly does not roam the streets in a wild state, dripping wet and looking primitive."

She looked at him then, and something flashed between them, hot and intimate. Dangerous. Uncontrollable. Tristanne felt her breath catch, and released it, deliberately. *Count to ten*, she cautioned herself. *Do not fan this fire—it will burn you alive. It will ruin everything.*

"I only said I wanted to be your mistress," she said slowly, her voice lower and huskier than she'd intended, as if it had plans of its own. "I never said anything about being perfect."

Something about her undid him. Her wide brown eyes, perhaps, so clever and yet so wary. The tilt of that chin, so pugilistic, as if she wanted to fight him, hold him off, defy him at all costs when her very presence here as his supposed mistress should have ensured the opposite. That lush, wide mouth that he wanted to taste again, every time he looked at it. And the way that green dress clung, wet and heavy, to curves that he was beginning to believe might haunt him for the rest of his days.

It did not matter that he had deep suspicions about her activities this afternoon. Had she met with her pig of a brother? Had she received further orders, whatever those might be? He could not seem to get a hold of the searing anger he felt when he thought about such a meeting—and he had been unable to think of anything else since he'd arrived back at the flat to find her out, whereabouts unknown. He knew it made no sense. It was not logical, or rational. She had never pretended to owe him any allegiance, and he had known she must have ulterior motives the moment she'd walked up to him on his yacht. He knew why he was using her—why should he think she was not using him equally?

"No," he said slowly, pushing away from the wall. "We cannot call you perfect, certainly."

She blinked. "That sounds significantly more insulting when you say it."

He wanted to demand that she tell him what her game was, that she admit whatever nefarious scheme she'd cooked up with her vile brother. As if it would mean something, such a confession. As if it would somehow excuse the need for her that itched in him, that he was beginning to worry was not, as it ought to be, purely physical.

The urge to take her, to lose himself in her lush body, to drown in her sweet and spicy scent, in her soft skin, in her scalding heat—all of that was completely understandable. Expected, even. Part and parcel of his ultimate revenge. It was...this other thing that was driving him insane. The odd and novel urge to leave her untouched at the door to her stateroom the night before, with only a gruff demand that she meet him for breakfast. Why had he done that? That had not been the way he'd planned the night at all.

But he had lost his purpose, somehow, between the oddly quiet moment after her outburst on the streets of Portofino and the stunned, hurt look in her eyes after he had ripped into her about her *exalted standards*. If he was someone else, he might have wondered if he'd been loathe to hurt her feelings—which was impossible as well as ridiculous, for how did he expect to enact a fitting revenge on her family without doing exactly that? In spades? It was as if she bewitched him somehow, with her frowns and her challenges, her sharp tongue and her unexpected naps—all things that should have made him dismiss her entirely.

And would have, he told himself fiercely, if she was anyone else.

"And now you are scowling at me," Tristanne said, her eyes scanning his face as she frowned back at him. "I don't know what it is you think I did—"

"What haven't you done?" he asked, almost as an aside. Almost as if he asked himself, not her. Perhaps he did, though he had little hope of an answer.

"I haven't done anything at all!" she protested.

"That, too," he said, and sighed. And then gave up.

He reached over and hooked his hand around her crossed arms, tugging her toward him with very little effort. She came without a fight, her expressive face registering a series of emotions—confusion, worry, and what he wanted to see most of all. Desire.

He pulled her off balance, deliberately, so that she sprawled across the wall of his chest and he could feel, finally, her soft breasts pressed into him, her body sodden and warm against his. Her head tipped back so she could look at him, her brown eyes wide and grave but with that heat within.

"Nikos," she began, that slight frown appearing again between her brows.

He did not know what he meant to do until he did it. He leaned down and pressed his lips to that serious wrinkle, smoothing it away, hearing her gasp even as he felt it against the skin at his neck.

"I think—" she started again.

"You think too much," he muttered, and then he kissed her.

He wanted lust, fire, passion, and those things were there, underneath. She tasted of the rain, and something else. Something sweet. He could not seem to get enough of it. Of her. He cradled her face between his hands, and kissed her again and again, until they were both gasping for breath.

He pulled away, and, giving in to an urge he didn't

understand and didn't care to examine, tucked her beneath his chin. Her arms were folded still, her fists against his chest, and he held her there, listening to their hearts pound out their need together.

Mine, he thought, and knew he should thrust her away immediately. Put distance between himself and whatever spell this was, that made him feel things he could not allow himself to feel. It wasn't simply that he should only want her for a very specific reason—he knew better. Hadn't he paid this price already? Hadn't he vowed that he would never put himself in a position like this again? That he would not want what he could not have? He did not believe in the things that would make such moments as this possible. Redemption. Forgiveness. Those were for other men. Never for him. *He knew better.*

But he did not move.

"I don't understand you at all," she whispered. Her hands uncurled against him, and spread open, as if to hold him. As if she could heal him with her touch. As if she knew he was broken in the first place.

He did not believe in any of that, either. He knew exactly who she was and why she was here. What he must do, and would. Still, he did not push her away.

"Neither do I," he said.

And then stood there, holding her, much longer than he should.

Any leftover feelings Tristanne might have had from their interaction in the rain—and his devastatingly tender kisses—were obliterated the moment she saw herself in the dress.

"I brought you something to wear tonight," he had said when they entered the flat. His distance and cool tone should have alerted her, but did not. "I will leave it for you when you are finished with your shower."

"Tonight?" she had asked, her emotions still in a near-painful jumble. She'd told herself that was why his suddenly brusque tone seemed to rub her the wrong way, after those unexpected moments in the archway. Or perhaps it was just her impatience with herself, for being so emotional when she could so little afford it.

"It is a small business function," he had said with a dismissive shrug, and she had thought no more about it until it came time to pull the dress from the hanger where he had left it, suspended from the door inside the guest suite he had indicated she should use to get ready.

Now, her hair dried and blown out to hang in a straight, gleaming curtain, cosmetics carefully applied to accent and emphasize her eyes, she stared at herself in the full-length mirror that stood at an angle in the corner of the richly furnished room. But she could not see the royal blue and gold accents that graced the walls and brocaded the commanding, four-poster bed. She could hardly catch her breath. She could only stare at her reflection, literally struck dumb.

She felt herself flush, deep and red and panicked, so red she nearly matched the scarlet fabric that *barely* made up the dress she wore. He could not mean that he wanted her to wear what little there was of *this* dress, could he? She could not go out in public dressed like this! She could not leave the *room* dressed like this!

She tried to take a deep breath, and made a sound like a sob instead. She squeezed her eyes shut, and her hands into fists. Then, slowly, she opened her eyes and forced her hands to open, too.

The dress was obscene. There was no other word for it.

It clung to her body like paint, leaving nothing to the imagination. There was not a single curve that was not outlined by the tight, clinging garment that slicked its way from tiny capped sleeves to her midthighs. If she tried to cover a decent amount of her breasts, the hem rose to a scandalous height, and if she tugged the hem lower, she risked having her breasts fall out of the tiny bodice. There was no happy medium. It required that she remove her undergarments entirely, or risk calling more attention to them, so clearly outlined were they by the tight, too-tight, material.

There was only one kind of woman who wore a dress like this, Tristanne thought, humiliation thick in the back of her throat, and she was pretending to be one of them. Was this Nikos's goal? Did he *want* her to feel this way? Did he take pleasure in imagining Tristanne walking into a public event like this? So scandalously, tackily, *barely* attired?

Or, she thought, fighting back the angry tears that flooded her eyes, that she refused to shed, perhaps she was missing the point entirely. Perhaps he was not trying to embarrass her, necessarily—perhaps this was how he preferred to see his women dressed. Perhaps he liked to make his mistress's position perfectly clear to everyone he encountered. It need not be personal at all. It should not have felt like such a slap.

She glanced at the clock and saw that she had wasted far too much time, and was once again late. She bit at her lower lip as she looked at herself again, but she knew she had no choice but to brazen it out. She had to do what he wanted for just a little bit longer. Her mother had made it sound as if Peter was already in a much better frame of mind, which made Tristanne hopeful that her plan was working and this mad scheme of hers could end. Because she was not at all sure that she could take too much more of this…exposure, in all senses of the term.

But whatever might happen in the days to come, she still had to walk out of this room in this scandalous, appalling dress. She closed her eyes for a brief moment, a breath, and then turned on her heel and forced herself to leave the room before she could think better of it.

She found him in the living room, swirling whiskey in a crystal tumbler and staring out at the glorious Dome before him. He turned slowly, and Tristanne came to a stop in the center of the room to let him look his fill. Surely that was his intention—the point of this whole exercise?

"Is this what you had in mind?" she asked, her voice throatier than she would have liked, from all the emotions she was fighting to keep to herself, to keep inside. To pretend she did not feel at all.

His face was in shadow, yet she could still feel the searing heat of his dark gaze. She could feel it traveling over her exposed skin, making her nipples contract and goose bumps shiver across her shoulders. It was as if some unseen cord connected them, forcing her to react to him, however little she might wish to do so.

"Do I please you?" she asked, an edge in her voice that she could not control. "Is that not what mistresses ask?"

"If they do not, they should," he replied in that lethally quiet voice that made her knees weaken beneath her. She wanted to hate him. She did. "And I must congratulate you, Tristanne."

His mouth moved into that mocking curve, and she braced herself. But he moved closer, and there was no mistaking the hot, possessive gleam in his burnished dark gold eyes. Nor the answering throb that bloomed in her sex and made her mouth go dry.

What she would do to hate him! Or, at the very least, not to want him.

He reached over and took her hand, enveloping it in the heat of his own. Never taking his eyes from hers, pinning her to the spot and making her pulse flutter wildly in her temples, her throat, he raised her hand to his warm, full lips.

"You have finally met, if not exceeded, all my expectations," he murmured.

But what she heard was the sound of her own doom, the clang of a cage door slamming shut, as something in her she did not want to acknowledge whispered words she could not bring herself to accept. And it had nothing to do with her mother, with her reasons for being here. *You will never escape this man*, the voice told her, wise and deep, as something like truth twisted in her gut. *You will never be free of him*.

CHAPTER EIGHT

THE party Nikos took her to was neither small nor a stuffy business affair—it was a star-studded gala event held at the Palazzo Pitti, a vast Renaissance palace that had once been home to the Medicis, not far from the Ponte Vecchio on the south side of the Arno. The building was a cold and severe stone edifice that hovered imposingly over her, Tristanne thought, glancing up at the forbidding facade as Nikos helped her out of his car into the sudden blaze of flashbulbs.

Though in truth, the same could be said of Nikos.

Tristanne had no choice but to walk at his side as if she did not notice the second-looks, the ripple of whispers in her wake. She had no choice but to smile for the photographers who formed a scrum at the entrance to the palace, and pretend she was delighted to be seen out with Nikos, thrilled to be displayed like the spoils of war in a bimbo's dress. There was nothing she could do except attempt to handle the whole thing gracefully. She kept her head held high, her smile in place, and hoped that all the years of pretending to be made of Barbery ice would pay off now, when needed.

And after all, she reminded herself, the publicity was the point—not what she happened to be wearing.

Nikos led her into a courtyard open beneath the clear night sky. The rain had finally ended and the evening was warm and close, making the lights seem denser and more intriguing as they shone on the fountain up above and the white marble statues that stood frozen still in their giant stone alcoves. Aristocrats and matinee idols wore the finest Italian couture and dripped priceless gems, murmuring to each other over cocktails at small white-topped tables.

"What business is this, exactly?" Tristanne asked, glancing around. To her left she saw businessmen whose names were always mentioned in awed tones in newspaper editorials, to her right, a philanthropic rock star stood in deep conversation with a British socialite.

Nikos slanted a look down at her. "Mine," he said, with a certain amused finality.

"Meaning you own it?" Tristanne asked with asperity. "Or that you would like me to mind my own? A man in possession of as many things as you are really must be more clear."

Their eyes met, and once again, she felt a melting that shook her to her bones. Could it not leave her for even a moment? she wondered, in something like despair. Not even for tonight, when he had deliberately dressed her like a tart and dragged her here to make certain she—and half of Europe—knew her place? But none of that seemed to matter. He looked at her as if he knew things about her that she did not, yet, and she felt her chest constrict, her pulse race in helpless reaction, as if there was no greater purpose to her being with him than that. As if she was his mistress.

"Would you like a drink, Tristanne?" he asked softly.

"That would be lovely," she managed to say. "Thank you."

She watched him cut through the crowd on his way to the bar, his lean form expertly displayed in a dark Italian suit that made love to his wide shoulders and long legs. As he had on the yacht—had that been only days ago?—Nikos stood out from the rest. It was the simmering energy that he exuded as some men did cologne. It was the way he moved, restless and aware, ready for anything. His history showed in his body, she thought, if nowhere else. He was ready to fight, and his well-honed physique was his first weapon. It was why some avoided him, why others were drawn to him. He was a man, in the most traditional, physical sense of the term. She had no doubt that he knew what every single one of his muscles was for, and how best to use each one to get the better of an opponent. It was almost unfair that such a formidable physical presence was not the sum total of who he was—that it should merely be the packaging for a mind such as his, incisive and quick. He was like no one she had ever met. It was one more thing about him she wished she did not admire.

Not that it mattered, she reminded herself forcefully. She could admire him all she liked—it did not change what she must do, did it? She had known when she'd first approached him that this would be a terrible mistake. It had not stopped her then. And now it was much too late.

"Ah, Tristanne."

The sneering, hateful voice announced his identity, making her stiffen in surprise and dismay, before she turned to confirm it. *Peter.*

"I see you have finally embraced your true heritage," he continued.

She turned to face him fully, taking her time as if that might lessen her shock. Her brother stood before her, his dark eyes alive with malevolence. Could no one else see it? she wondered—and not for the first time. A well-cut suit could not hide the darkness in him, the bully he truly was. She had always seen it. She suspected he'd wanted her to see it, to fear it, from the start.

"Peter," she said with a great and abiding calm she did not feel. She forced herself not to look down at her arm, where the bruises he'd left were almost completely faded now—only a smudge or two of yellow remained as testament to his violence, his utter disregard for her. "What a delightful surprise."

"I asked myself what sort of trollop would parade through the Palazzo Pitti dressed like a two-dollar whore," he said in his most snide voice, just loud enough to insinuate itself into Tristanne's ear and make her feel dirty by association. "I should have known at once that it was you."

"Do you not like my dress?" she asked. She raised her brows, allowing herself no other expression, no outward sign of how her stomach heaved, how her pulse raced in panic. "Of course, Nikos picked it out. Would you prefer I fight with him over something so small as a dress?"

Peter only glared at her for a moment, his gaze cold. Tristanne ordered herself to gaze back with every appearance of unruffled tranquility.

"You have outdone yourself, my dear sister," he said after an uncomfortable moment, his lips curled. "I assumed Katrakis would use what you so blatantly offered him and cast you aside." His gaze raked over her, and she knew, with a scorching sense of shame, exactly what he could see, and in what detail. It made her wish she could disappear into the stones beneath her feet. Instead she stood straighter. "And yet here you are with him, tarted up at his command. How enterprising and inventive you have turned out to be."

She should feel triumphant, she realized as she looked at her brother. He believed she was Nikos's mistress. Her plan was working, just as she'd anticipated. So why did she feel so hollow instead?

"I want my trust fund," she told him flatly. She smiled then. "Wasn't this what you wanted? Surely Nikos Katrakis is *visible* enough to suit you? I believe our picture was taken at least fifty times as we walked in."

That had been his claim the night before she had boarded Nikos's boat—that her liaison must be with someone *visible*. He had wanted to choose the man, of course, for reasons

Tristanne would prefer not to investigate too closely. It was clear, he had shouted that awful night, that she would only make a fool of herself with a man like Nikos and then be ruined for his purposes. She'd suspected he'd simply wanted an excuse to put his hand on her and shake her. Hard. And so he had.

"Careful you do not overplay your hand," Peter retorted now, his eyes cold. "What is his angle? Have you figured it out?" When she did not respond, he laughed in a way that made her skin crawl. "Surely you don't believe that a man like Katrakis would find *you* quite so captivating, Tristanne. Perhaps he wishes to trade on the Barbery name himself." He shook his head, his lips thinning. "A man can climb out of the sewer, one supposes, but he still walks around with the stench of it."

Tristanne wanted to haul off and slap him for that, but she did not dare. *Think of your mother!* she warned herself. There was too much at stake. And Nikos did not need her to defend him to Peter, of all people. So why did she want to? She was not even sure where the urge to defend him had come from, nor why it lingered, making her stomach tense.

"He has not shared his ulterior motives with me," she said icily. "Just as I have neglected to share yours with him."

"You will need to keep him happy for the next few weeks, at least," Peter said offhandedly, his attention on the crowd around them, as if he was searching for more important people. "Perhaps a month."

"A month?" Tristanne clamped down on her panic, her anger. "Don't be absurd, Peter. That is far too long. The pictures taken tonight should be all you need."

"I will decide what I need, Tristanne, thank you," he snapped. His gaze narrowed, and an insinuating smile played on his thin lips. "What's the matter? Afraid you don't have what it takes to keep Katrakis's interest? I have heard his tastes are…earthy."

"I want my trust find," she said again, more succinctly. She did not know what Peter meant by that comment, nor wish to know. Though her imagination could not help but supply vivid images to suit the word earthy, each more devastating than the last. Nikos's hot, tender mouth upon her flesh, his strong, capable hands lifting her, his whipcord strength all around her, above her—

"It will take a month," Peter said, snapping Tristanne back into the courtyard with a jolt. Peter's cold eyes bored into her. "But if it makes you feel any better, I think it is clear that you have found your life's work." He laughed, unpleasantly.

He thinks I am nothing but a whore, Tristanne thought dully. Yet she could not seem to summon up any outrage on her own behalf. After all, he always had. The only difference was that now, if she peeled away the shocking heat that consumed her whenever she thought of Nikos, she feared that Peter might be right. And worse, that she might like it where Nikos was concerned—but she could not allow herself such incendiary thoughts!

"I want to see the paperwork regarding the transfer of my funds by next week." She gazed at him coldly, determined to look unafraid. Unaffected. "Is that clear enough? Do we understand each other?"

"I understand you better than you think, *sister,*" Peter hissed at her, the word *sister* sounding like a vicious insult, like the hard slap he no doubt wished to give her. But Tristanne did not recoil. Not even when he smiled that horrible smile. "All the years you spent spouting off about your *principles* and your *honor,* and all the while you were no better than a whore, just waiting for the right price." He waited, letting that sink in, and then his nasty smile deepened. "Exactly like your mother."

Each word, she knew, was carefully calculated to maim, to wound. To prey on her feelings for Vivienne and force her to reveal herself. But she would rather die than give him the satisfaction of knowing he'd been successful. She would keep what she felt locked down, hidden away. She would not react. *She would not.*

"Next week, Peter," she said through her teeth. "Or you can forget the whole thing."

His eyes narrowed, that malevolent gleam flaring to sickening life, and she braced herself for whatever he might say next.

But instead she felt her body thrill to a sudden heat beside her, and knew without looking that Nikos had returned. Was it absurd that she felt as if he'd saved her, simply by standing beside her? *It is certainly foolish,* she admonished herself. Nonetheless, relief—thick and sweet—flooded through her. She had the insane urge to move closer to him, to burrow against his hard chest as if they were truly lovers, as if he would care for her in that way, protect her, but she shook it off.

"Katrakis." Peter nodded in greeting, looking at Nikos with ill-concealed distaste.

Nikos smiled. It was that wolf's smile, far too dangerous, and Tristanne knew that Peter was out of his depth even if he seemed to be unaware of that fact. She took a deep breath, feeling her spine ease its erect posture just a bit.

"Barbery," Nikos said, his arrogant brows raised and his expression faintly amused. Tristanne could see how little Peter liked it. His gaze darkened.

"When my sister announced that she was spending a few days sailing to Greece, I could not imagine she meant with you," Peter said.

As if there was some other Nikos Katrakis? What game was he playing now? Not for the first time, Tristanne wondered *why* Peter hated Nikos so much, when surely Nikos was exactly the sort of man Peter normally attempted to cultivate. All she had ever known was that Peter hated even the mention of his name, and always had.

"What, I wondered, could a Katrakis want with a Barbery?" Peter asked.

"It cannot be a mystery to you, surely," Nikos drawled. Tristanne felt her skin prickle with heat. Nikos's smile deepened, turned more mocking. "Buy me a drink sometime and I will clear it up for you."

"My sister is usually not quite so charming as you seem to find her," Peter said darkly, as if he was discussing a fractious mare or a disobedient hound. "I am amazed you have found her so…congenial."

"No doubt your amazement is what caused you to lose your head and put your hands upon her," Nikos said then, his voice smooth and deadly, like a whip. His eyes flashed dark gold fire. To Tristanne's shock—and shame—he reached over and sketched the back of his fingers across the fading bruises on her upper arm, though he never looked away from Peter. "For surely you must know that I prefer that what is mine bear no mark but my own."

She did not care for that, Nikos could tell. He was learning to read her now, and though her facial expression remained remote, almost bored, he could feel her tense beneath his hand. She did not look up at him, though that defiant chin inched upward. She kept her eyes trained on the snake before her, her brother, who could not keep the vicious glee from his own gaze.

Nikos had expected Peter's presence—it was why they had come to Florence in the first place—but he had not anticipated the hard kick of anger that had spiked through his gut when he'd seen the vicious look on Peter's face, and Tristanne's carefully blank expression. It had taken him by surprise. He told himself it was because Barbery believed that he'd won, that he'd planted Tristanne with Nikos and Nikos was none the wiser. He told himself that it had nothing to do with his protective urges toward this woman, urges he could not permit himself to indulge unless they aided him in his revenge against the swine of a man before him.

"But you have spent time with her now," Peter said, with a shrug. "I do not need to tell you how difficult it is to keep her in line, do I?"

Nikos wanted to destroy Peter. He told himself that was the way he would feel no matter what the man had said, simply because of who he was, but he knew better. He knew exactly why he wanted to wrap his hands around Peter Barbery's throat.

It made an alarm sound deep within him. But, defying all logic, he ignored it.

"I do not find it difficult at all," he said quietly.

"Then you must have abilities that I do not," Peter said, in a sneering voice that Nikos did not much care for. "I confess that our father found her so tiresome that he washed his hands of her years ago."

"I am, in fact, standing right here," Tristanne said crisply, her brown eyes snapping with temper—and something far darker. "I can hear you."

Peter smirked, but continued to gaze at Nikos. "Or perhaps your definition of *keeping her in line* and mine differ," he said with a sniff. "She is too insolent by half. A trait she gets, no doubt, from her mother."

"My mother is many things," Tristanne said with marked calm. Nikos admired her smile, so pointed and bright, and her seeming ease. He believed neither. "But insolent is not one of them. Come now, Peter. Must we air our family laundry in public? I am certain Nikos must be bored to tears."

"And by all means," Peter said in that oily voice, "you must keep Katrakis happy."

Nikos felt her tense again next to him, as if she was contemplating hurling herself at her brother and pummeling him into a pulp with her fists. Or perhaps that was only his own desire, projected upon her. Either way, the conversation had served its purpose. Nikos wanted to waste no more time on Peter Barbery than strictly necessary.

"You will excuse us," he said abruptly to Peter, dismissing him with an offhanded arrogance he knew would enrage the other man. "I must circulate."

"Of course," Peter said, with an icy nod. He turned his gaze on his sister. She smiled at him, if something that frigid could pass for a smile. And then Peter moved off into the crowd without a backward glance.

Giving into an urge he could not name, and did not want to admit, Nikos slid his arm around her bare shoulders, pulling her closer to the expanse of his chest.

Tristanne looked up at him then, her eyes dark and stormy. He could not sort through the emotion he saw there. But he could see that same fire banked in her that he knew was in him, even now. She was too responsive. Too aware of his every move. How was he to resist that? Why was he bothering to try?

This is all part of your revenge, he reminded himself. *Even this. Especially this.* But he was not certain, suddenly, if he believed it.

Nikos handed her the drink he had procured for her, having foregone his own when he'd seen her brother approach her, and noted that her hand was trembling slightly as she took the wineglass from him. It was the only outward sign he could see that her brother had affected her.

"You and your brother do not get along," he observed in a low voice. It was an absurd understatement, and her mouth curved into something near a smile.

"In our family, emotions were viewed as the enemy," she said. "Woe betide the person who showed them, no matter the circumstances. We were expected to be perfect little automatons, smiling on command, and attending to my father's wishes without so much as an altered expression." She shrugged, and stepped away, out from under his arm. He let her go, reluctantly. "So you see, I am not certain Peter gets along with anyone. But he would never show it either way." She did not look at him, and Nikos could not understand why he wanted her to. Badly. She took a careful sip from her glass instead.

Nikos could not make sense of his own urges. Everything was proceeding exactly as he'd planned it, aside from today's strange interlude in the rain. He was squiring the Barbery heiress in front of cameras, at an event filled with business associates and gossipmongers. To say nothing of her despicable brother. The fact that they were an item would be assumed—and there would be few who would not speculate about any relationship between Nikos Katrakis and a Barbery. Nikos was not the only one with a long memory. When it came time to spurn her as Althea had been spurned years ago, it would be all the more devastating, all the more embarrassingly public. He was sure of it. It was just as he wanted it.

But all he could really concentrate on was that damned dress.

It licked over her curves, plastered itself to them and dared any man in the vicinity to notice another woman in all of Florence. Nikos could not tear his eyes away from her. She stood out like a ripe, hot flame, begging to be touched. She did not look trashy, as he had intended, thinking it some kind of punishment for her obstinacy. In truth, he had expected her to refuse to wear the dress at all.

But instead, she had beaten him at his own game. The dress was pure sex, a wicked invitation to her lush, tight body. And yet she looked almost aristocratic, as if the tight dress were the perfect accessory for her beauty, her position. It was the scene smile she wore, as if she had never been more comfortable in her life that she was in that scant dress, standing on the arm of a man who made no attempt to hide the fact that he would much prefer to be deep inside her than attending this function. Surely everyone could see his desires, written across his face. He hardly cared.

He could not remember ever wanting another woman more.

"You are staring at me," she said after a long moment. The tension spun out between them, shimmering and unmistakable, and Nikos knew that he was finished waiting. He had to have her, and to hell with his reasons *why*. It felt as if it had been years. Decades. A lifetime.

"You are mesmerizing," he said, his voice low. "But surely you know it."

"You are the one who found this dress," she said. Finally she looked at him. Her eyes were melted chocolate, rich and dark, a temptation he could no longer resist. "I am merely wearing it."

"It is the way you wear it," he told her, standing too close, not daring to touch her as every cell in his body demanded. Not here. Not in public. Not where he would have to stop. "I want to take it off you. With my teeth."

CHAPTER NINE

THE ride back to the flat passed in a liquid kind of silence, heavy and weighted, yet shimmering with unmistakable heat.

She had not agreed to anything, Tristanne reminded herself. She had only gazed at him and that addicting fire in his dark eyes, and he had not said another word. He had led her from the courtyard, fetched the car from the valet and handed her into it with a quiet chivalry completely at odds with the frank sensual hunger in his gaze.

Before she knew it they were back in that vast loft of a living room high above the ancient streets. She was caught between the epic grandeur of the Duomo on the other side of the window behind her and the heavy front door to the flat that Nikos shut tight and bolted, locking them in.

Locking *her* in.

Suddenly the enormous space seemed to contract, until there was nothing but that hot, hard gleam in his dark eyes. Tristanne felt her heart beat, wild and loud, in her throat, her temples, her chest, her sex. She wanted to run, then—run through the old streets and over the cobblestones, run and run and run as if that might make this feeling disappear, as if she could leave it behind somehow. That same thought that had troubled her earlier in the evening returned, with force. She could not escape him. She would never be free of him.

But not, she thought now with devastating insight, because he would chase her—but because for all her panic and her pounding heart, she did not move. Could not move. Did not *want* to move.

Dragon, she thought almost helplessly, and she knew with a deep certainty that she was about to see his real fire—the flames she had been dancing around since the moment she'd met him. The powerful conflagration that had always been there, waiting in his dark gaze, his mocking smile, while she'd tried to talk her way out of exactly this moment. The fire that she knew would consume her, immolate her, turn her into nothing more than ash.

Still, she did not turn away from him. She did not scream, or run for her room, or for the streets, or do anything except hold his gaze. She did not understand how she could be so fascinated with him even when she knew he was the reason for her panic. She did not know how now, when it mattered the most, she could be so heedless of her own self-preservation. He stood opposite her, that half smile carved into the sculpted leanness of his hard jaw, his dark eyes making the kind of sensual promises that made her feel shaky, intoxicated.

"Come here," he said, his voice a ribbon of sound across the elegant room, seductive and stirring. Tristanne felt it against her skin like a caress. Like another one of his promises, the ones her body ached for—the ones she knew she had to fight off at all costs.

"I don't think so," she said. She hadn't meant to say it—had she? She only knew that she could not let this happen. She could not surrender to this man. *She could not.* And not only because of her ulterior motives. She coughed slightly. "I think, in fact, that I will stay over here instead."

His smile deepened, turned dangerous in ways that made her nipples peak and her belly tauten, further signs that she was in so far over her head, she might as well consider herself half-drowned.

"Of course not." But he did not seem angry, or even particularly tense. Instead his gaze moved over her, sending heat flashing across every place on her overtly displayed body that his eyes touched. When his eyes met hers again, he seemed almost relaxed. Almost. "Why am I not surprised?"

"You promised..." she began, but she lost track of the sentence because he moved, that long, rangy body eating up the distance between them with sure strides. He shrugged out of his jacket and tossed it aside, in the general direction of the grand sofa that commanded one wall. Never taking his eyes from hers, he removed his cuff links in a few quick jerks and dropped them on the wide, wooden coffee table.

He stalked toward her, and she knew he was doing it deliberately. Openly. She could not seem to summon breath to fill her lungs, much less the will to step back, to avoid him.

"No," he said, as he came to a stop a scant few inches in front of her. His voice was soft, his gaze so hot, so terribly, impossibly hot, and she felt an echo of that dangerous fire flash through her. "No, I did not promise you a thing, Tristanne."

"Of course you did," she contradicted him desperately, that thrumming, tightening panic making her scowl at him. "And even if you did not, what does it matter? Surely the great Nikos Katrakis does not have to take unwilling women to his bed!"

"Do you see such a creature in this flat?" he asked, his eyes molten gold and impossible to look away from. "Perhaps you see unicorns, too?"

"You cannot imagine that anyone could turn you down, can you?" she threw at him, her head spinning, her chest tight, as if she had in fact been running all this time, putting all of Florence between her and this man.

Instead of what she was actually doing, which was simply standing there, hoping her legs would hold her up, hoping the bravado that had gotten her through every other complicated interaction with this man would keep her going just a little bit longer. Just this one night more.

He smiled then, a real smile, for all that it was stamped with a deeply male satisfaction that seared through her, making her eyes heat and her sex pulse in want, in need. In that instinctive, insane response to him that she could not seem to control, nor reason away.

"I cannot imagine that *you* can turn me down, Tristanne," he said quietly, that undercurrent of certainty, of command, somehow more shattering than anything he might have said. "But by all means, prove me wrong."

He began to unbutton his shirt as he stood there, looking down at her like some kind of ancient god, all arrogant male confidence and power. Tristanne swallowed convulsively as her eyes, of their own accord, dropped to follow the widening swathe of smooth, olive-toned skin, brushed with a dusting of jet-black hair.

She could not remember her arguments, her strategies. It was as if the entire world had disappeared—all she was, all she had been, all she had planned to do—and all she wanted was to touch the hard male flesh he was unveiling so close in front of her. Taunting her, she was sure. Torturing her.

"I don't know what you're doing," she managed to say, somehow. "This display is highly unlikely to make me change my mind. I told you on the boat—"

"We are not on the boat," he said, amusement and fierce, unmistakable intent in his gaze, in his voice.

He peeled his shirt back from the hard planes of his chest and let it drop from his arms, and then there was no more hiding from his stark male beauty, rough and compelling, hard-worn steel covered in satin. He was the most glorious man she had ever seen, and she was trembling with the effort it took to keep her hands away from the expanse of smooth, muscled *male* that stood so tantalizingly close. *So close.* She curled her hands into tight balls, her fingernails digging into the soft flesh of her palms.

"Nikos…" she whispered, and she knew then that she was lost. All she had was her bravado, her reckless, hopeless willingness to fight the inevitable against all odds. To throw words at him in desperation, because she had nothing else. And if she could not deflect him, if she could not keep him at arm's length…

"I told you," he said in that velvet and whiskey voice that thrilled her deep in her feminine core, in ways she did not dare admit to herself. "You need only tell me that you have reached your limits. You need only say the word."

There was a moment then, shimmering and tense, when she wavered. When she thought in a brief burst of something darker than mere bluster that she could do it, that she could say the one small word that would end this. As she should. As she knew she should. She opened her mouth to say what she knew she ought to say, what she knew she must say if she was to survive this encounter with this tempting, impossible man.

"Nikos…" she breathed.

The fire in his dark gold eyes flared to a blaze, and his mouth moved into a hard, triumphant curve.

"That is not the word," he said, satisfaction coloring his low, knowing tone.

But she still did not, could not, say it.

He reached over, and traced the shape of her cheek with one large, confident hand. His palm was too hot, his fingers too clever. Her skin was too sensitive, too raw. But, unaccountably, she felt herself sway toward his hand, not away from it.

"Tell me to stop," he urged her, his eyes nearly black now with a passion she could not help but feel, humming through her like electricity, making her yearn for things she knew on some deep, primitive level would destroy her.

Giving in to an urge that was so intense it nearly felt like pain, Tristanne reached over and placed her palms against the wall of his chest. Heat exploded through her hands and ricocheted up her arms, searing a path that led directly to her swollen breasts, her aching sex. He hissed in a breath, then let it out in a sound that was too harsh to be a laugh.

"Tell me to stop," he said again, a taunt, and then he pulled her toward him and fitted his mouth to hers.

The dark sorcery of his mouth, his taste, overwhelmed her. Tristanne forgot everything. He kissed her like they would both perish if he stopped, and she kissed him back as if she believed him. She tasted the warm, tanned skin of his strong neck, let her hands trace the magnificent male architecture of his ridged abdomen, so much heat and power, all of it like warm, hard rock beneath her hands.

His hands dove into her hair, anchoring her head in place so he could tease her lips with his, tasting her again and again, pausing only to whisper words in Greek she could not understand, hot and dark words that inflamed her, made her try to move closer to him, to press against his wicked body with her own.

She felt the room tilt and whirl around her, and realized only as her back met the softest suede, that he had picked her up and laid her down on the sofa. He stretched out above her.

Finally, she thought, as his body came up hard against hers. It was too much and it was not enough, and she could not stop touching him.

"Tell me," he said roughly, as his hard chest crushed her breasts with a delicious pressure, as her hips cradled his maleness, hard and hot, as she gasped in delight and a kind of sensual terror. "Tell me, Tristanne."

Some part of her objected, in some dim corner of her mind—how could he still have the presence of mind to taunt her when she was very nearly in pieces? And yet the same deep, feminine part of her that had warned her away from this man knew, now, that her power lay not in words, but in an age-old knowledge that seemed to flood into her as she stared up at his face, so dark and determined above her.

She did not speak. She merely moved her hips in a lazy circle, and had the instant satisfaction of making him groan and grow, if possible, harder against her. He muttered something incoherent, and took her mouth again, his own insistent, demanding.

She met his demands, gloried in them. His hands slicked down the sides of that scandalous dress, tracing the curves he had displayed so unapologetically for all of Florence to see. He moved from her mouth, tracing a searing path down to her breasts, tasting them through the material. Hot, wet heat. Tristanne arched against the delicate torture of his mouth, gasping, as a tremor snaked through her, lighting her up from her sex to the tips of her toes.

His dark eyes caught hers, then, as he reached between them, his movements sure, his gaze like some kind of heat lightning. He pulled the stretchy fabric up around her waist, and then released his own trousers. As if they had done this a thousand times before, as if she knew his moves as well as her own, she wrapped her legs around his hips.

Tristanne felt that mad fever break over her, making her flush with want, with heat, with hunger. She moved against him mindlessly, helplessly. He angled his hips, held her thigh in his strong, commanding grasp, and in one, sure stroke, sheathed himself deep inside her.

She might have screamed. She thought she did—she could hear the echo of it, the force of it, ricocheting through her, the pleasure almost too much, almost too great to bear.

"Tell me to stop, Tristanne." It was a hoarse whisper. A taunt, or perhaps a dare. She was too far gone to care which.

"Stop!" she threw at him, fiercely, surprising them both.

He froze at once. *"Talking,"* she hissed. Her hands fisted against his broad, hard back. "Stop talking!"

A breathless, impossible moment. His hard length so deep inside of her she could not tell where she ended and he began, the pleasure emanating in waves from every place their bodies touched, the dress plastered to her, trapping her—and his dark, addictive gaze, seeing so far inside of her she knew she should be afraid of what he would know.

But instead, he moved.

She fit him like a glove. Like a benediction.

She was wrapped around him, her spicy-sweet scent and her soft moans almost too much for him to bear. Almost. He pulled himself back from the edge with iron control, and angled himself back so he could look down at her.

She was wild with passion beneath him, her eyes dark with need, her lips parted. Her hair was tangled from his fingers, her mouth slightly reddened from his kisses. A rosy glow brightened her skin, made her look even warmer, even hotter, than she felt against him. The scarlet dress wrapped around her lushness like a candy wrapper. She looked edible. Her hips moved beneath his, demanding and hungry, as if she could not get enough of him.

Mine, he thought again, from a dark place inside of him he did not care to explore, yet still rang through him with the force of a vow. He ignored it, and concentrated instead on those tiny noises she made in the back of her throat. On her long, shapely calves that were pressed against his hips, urging him on, deeper, closer.

He thrust into her slowly, deliberately, setting a lazy, un-hurried pace that soon had her panting in a mixture of need and frustration. Her hips rose to meet his. Her back arched as she fought to get closer, to speed him on. He ignored his own hunger, her wordless demands, even the pounding of his own blood, and kept it slow. Easy.

Devastating.

He felt the fire build in her, the tremors that began to make her quiver. Her eyes fluttered shut, and her breath came faster and faster, as her moans turned to helpless pleading. Still, he waited, maintaining that same measured pace, that same iron mastery, turning her incandescent beneath him.

She was so alive. So vivid. *His.*

When her head began to toss against the cushions, he bent to the tempting swells of her breasts, and began to lick the sweet flesh he found there, spilling out from her bodice. She tasted like cream with the faintest hint of peach, and her own feminine musk. She went straight to his head like the finest whiskey, making him surge against her like an untried boy. He peeled back the bodice of the dress and let her plump, round breast free. Then, never breaking his rhythm, he began to learn each breasts with his lips, his tongue, the faintest hint of his teeth.

She cried out his name, a broken sound of uninhibited passion. Of mindless pleasure. And that was when he found her nipple, sucking the peak into his mouth with a gentle insistence.

This time, she screamed his name. And when she hurtled over the edge, he followed.

CHAPTER TEN

THERE were things he should think about, he knew; strategies he should put into place and advantages he should press, even while his heart thudded out a jagged beat. There would never be a better time to start the slow and steady process of destroying her family. Her. But she lay there beneath him so soft and warm, her eyes closed and her breath still coming hard, and Nikos could think of none of those things.

He was still inside of her, and he wanted her again. Immediately. He could not make sense of it. Hunger moved through him, making up his mind for him. There would be time enough to think, to plot. Now was the time to slake his unshakeable thirst for this most maddening, most inconvenient of women.

He moved, pulling himself away, and was pleased to see her stir as if reluctant to let him go. Her brown eyes opened, wary and still dazed with passion. She blinked at him as if she was not sure whether or not she had dreamed him. He stood up, kicking off his trousers. Her eyes darkened, and she propped herself up on her elbows, watching him carefully. Cautiously.

Did she know the wanton, disheveled picture she made? She sprawled across the sofa, a scarlet band of bunched-up dress clinging to her waist, her breasts free and her long legs splayed before her. He should, he knew, point out that she looked more like a mistress ought to in this moment than ever before. Compliant. Alluring. Thoroughly debauched. He knew saying such things would put them back on to the solid ground he had the strangest feeling he had lost somewhere while losing himself in the delirium of her body.

But he did not say a word, and he could not have told himself why not.

Instead he reached down and picked her up as if she weighed nothing, as if she were insubstantial. She gasped as he lifted her, holding her high against his chest, but she did not speak. Instead she let her head drop onto his shoulder, her hair falling to cover her—almost as if she was hiding.

He should call her on that weakness. He should force her to face him. He should make sure they both had nowhere to hide. Because hiding places suggested intimacy, and that was impossible. This was sex. Long overdue sex, that was all.

That had to be all.

He set her down on her feet in the lushly appointed bath that sprawled next to his master suite. He did not meet her gaze, though he could feel her looking at him, searching his expression. He preferred to look at her body, he told himself. It was a work of art. Skin of cream and pink and gold, up-turned breasts, and that band of tight scarlet wrapped around her middle, emphasizing the perfection of her figure, the swell of her hips and her long, silken legs.

Silently he reached down and took hold of the red dress, tugging it up and over her breasts and then helping her move the heavy mass of her hair through it. He cast it aside, and only then did he look at her.

She moistened her lower lip with her delicate tongue, making a new hunger uncoil within him. He leaned down and tasted the shape of her lips, that full, sweet bow, and then tested that delicate tongue with his own. He meant only to maintain this quiet between them, as if it was a sacred thing, though he refused to think of it that way—but her taste went to his head again, making him hard and ready. Unwilling to wait. Unable to think. As desperate to have her as if he had not just done so.

He pulled her flush against him, pressing his maleness against the soft skin of her belly. She gasped, and then shivered, bracing her small hands on his chest. He saw the tiny goose bumps rise along the curve of her arms.

"Nikos," she began, in a shaky kind of whisper.

"Hush," he murmured. He kissed her neck, and ran his hands along the seductive line of her spine, following it to the breathtaking swell of her hips. He tested the weight of her pert, round bottom in his hands, and then slipped his fingers lower, curving around into her furrow, finding her soft and hot.

Just as ready for him as he was for her. A flash of possessiveness roared through him.

"Do not tell me—" she started, in that same breathy voice, and he could not allow it. If she started playing her little games again, he would have to think about the many reasons he should be handling this moment differently, and then he would have to do so.

"Hush," he said again, and he took her hips between his hands and lifted her high into the air, sliding her breasts against the wall of his chest.

She gasped again, but threw her arms around him, clutching fast to his shoulders. He slid his hands down to her delectable behind and then, propping her up with his hands and holding her in place, he thrust into her, hard. She stiffened, then let out a long, low moan and let her head fall forward against the crook of his neck. He could feel her mouth there, open against his skin, her sudden, labored breathing electrifying his own, making his heart beat faster, harder.

"Put your legs around my waist," he ordered her, widening his stance. She obeyed him at once, locking her ankles in the small of his back. It was as if she had been made for him, carefully engineered for this slick, impossibly perfect fit. He lifted her slowly, then let her sink back down, making them both shudder as his hard length filled her completely.

He did it again. Then again. Then one more long, slow stroke of her body against his, his shaft deep inside her, and she began to shake against him, sobbing out her pleasure against his neck. He waited for her to stop shaking, still hard within her, and then sank down to his knees into the thick, soft carpet beneath their feet. Never releasing her from that most intimate contact between them, he settled her on to her back beneath him, nestling himself between her soft thighs.

She was still breathing heavily, and her chocolate eyes were dazed when she finally opened them. It took her a long moment to focus on him.

When she did, he smiled. He could not seem to help himself. But he could not bring himself to worry about that as he knew he should.

"My turn," he said.

She was lost.

Tristanne clung to Nikos's sinfully hard body, and, impossibly, felt herself start to quicken once again with every long, slow stroke. He loomed over her, his dark gold eyes serious, his face drawn with passion.

It should not be like this. She should not have been capable of the feelings he invoked in her. She should not have felt as if his slightest touch might send her spinning into ecstasy. Or at the very least, she should fight it. But with every thrust of his powerful body, she found she could not think of anything save him, as if nothing existed except the two of them and the sensations that threatened to overcome her entirely.

Too soon, too quickly, she felt her breath catch. It should not have been possible. It should not have felt more electric, more overwhelming, with every slick movement of his hips.

He murmured encouragement in dark, rich words she could not understand, pressing his mouth against her neck, and into her hair.

He reached between them, and pressed against her hidden nub, making her writhe against him and then, at his soft command, explode into pieces. She heard his hoarse shout, and then, for a time, knew nothing.

He did not let her rest too long. Instead he pulled her into the wide, luxurious expanse of his shower. Multiple jets of water created steam and heat, and washed away everything outside of their hot, wet cocoon. Nikos washed her carefully, thoroughly, as if she were something indescribably precious.

Not precious, she reminded herself. *Merely a possession. He is a man who takes good care of his possessions.*

He did not speak as he washed her, and he did not speak when he pulled her from the shower's warmth and dried her, still so carefully, with towels as soft as clouds. He pulled the fluffy cotton around her, and their eyes caught. His gaze was serious, more brown than gold. She had never felt more naked, more vulnerable. More exposed.

She had known from the moment she set eyes on him on the yacht that she should not—must not—allow this night to happen. And she had even known why. She had known that he would tear her into pieces, rip her open and leave her helpless. She could not handle this. Him. She had known all of that, and she had done it anyway.

The worst part was, even now, even knowing that she was in deeper trouble than she had ever been in before, she could not bring herself to regret it. Not a moment of it. Not even *this* moment. Biting her lip, she pulled the towel tighter across her breasts.

His eyes searched hers, then dropped to her mouth as if he, too, felt the pull of this impossible, incandescent attraction. But he did not act upon it. He merely ushered Tristanne into the other room, and into the vast bed that sat raised upon a dark marble platform.

Tristanne lay with her head nestled into his shoulder and wondered how she could ever, possibly, survive this. Survive him.

His hands stroked through her damp hair, as if learning the raw silk of its texture with his fingers. He sighed slightly, as if the same words bubbled up in him that she knew fought to escape her own mouth, though she bit them back, preserving the silence between them—knowing what would happen once the silence between them ended. What had to happen.

Words were the only weapon she had, and she had abandoned them entirely tonight. She could not understand why she had done so. Was it Peter? Had his nastiness finally proved too much for her? Had she been desperate for Nikos's touch because she wanted to prove, to herself at the least, that everything Peter said was a twisted lie? Or was it that Nikos was the only person who had ever made her feel safe in Peter's presence? Did she want all of this heat, all of this fire, to mean something more than she knew it could?

Tristanne was almost afraid to take the necessary steps back, to try to navigate their relationship now that it had gone so physical, so atomic. How would she handle what had happened between them, when she could still hardly manage to take a deep breath? How could it still be happening, even now?

She should have been exhausted, but instead she felt herself soften and grow restless as she lay against him, breathing in the dizzying, seductive scent of his warm skin. She felt that now familiar, but no less irresistible, fire move through her, making her limbs feel heavy, and her mouth go dry.

How could she want him, when she had already had him, and more than once? Something like anguish moved through her, mingling with the ever-present burn of desire, making her wonder what kind of sorcery this was—and how she would ever escape him. She knew, now, what it meant to be burned alive by this man. Before, she had only considered how he would ruin her. She had not imagined that she would crave the very thing that would destroy her, slowly and surely, with every touch of his hands and every tantalizing kiss.

She knew that he would haunt her for the rest of her days.

Perhaps that was why she turned her head, and pressed desperate kisses against his hard, wide chest, hardly understanding her own urges. Perhaps that was why the way his hand closed around the back of her neck was like gasoline against a flame, and his mouth against hers a bright new inferno. She could not help but surrender herself to the now-familiar, still-devastating whirl, the kick and the fire. She moved against him helplessly, wantonly, and then somehow she was astride him.

For a moment she looked down at him, and all she could see was the gold gleam of those eyes, and the wicked curve of his mouth as she took him deep inside of her.

She was irrevocably, irretrievably lost. In more ways than she could possibly count.

She had known it would be this way from the start. She had dreamed this when she was still just a girl, and had only imagined him from afar. *She had known.*

And so she moved against him, losing what was left of her in the glory of the fire that raged between them, not caring, in the dark of the night, that it left her little more than ash. Just as she had expected. Just as she had worried.

Exactly as she had feared.

CHAPTER ELEVEN

HIGH on the green and gray cliffs of Kefalonia, Tristanne sat out on the wide stone patio that encircled the sumptuous villa and let the wild, rugged coastline of the Greek island sink into her bones, as if the shining Ionian Sea could soothe her, somehow, as it crashed against the dark rocks far below. Olive groves, bursts of pine and columns of cypress trees lined the narrow isthmus that stretched out before her in the late morning light. The tiny fishing village of Assos straddled the small spit of land, cheerful orange roofs turned toward the sun, while the ruins of a sixteenth century Venetian palace stood sentry above. This was not the smooth, white and blue beauty of the better-known Greek islands that Tristanne had explored in her youth. This was tenacious, resilient Greece, beautiful for its craggy cliffs as well as its unexpected and often hidden golden-sand beaches.

It did not surprise her that this remote and isolated stretch of land, torn between the cliffs and the sea, was the place Nikos Katrakis called home.

Tristanne shifted in her seat, and deliberately did not look over her shoulder to where Nikos sat closer to the wide-open patio doors that led inside, taking one of his innumerable business calls on his mobile phone in clipped, impatient Greek. She did not have to look at him to know where he was and what he was doing. It was as if she had been tuned to him, on some kind of radio frequency that only she could hear. She knew when he was near. Her breasts tightened and her sex warmed, readying her body for him, no matter what.

It was only one among many reasons to despair, she knew. Only one among many reasons to accept that she had lost any measure of control she might have had over this odd interlude in her life. If there was any way she could have been further complicit in her own destruction, Tristanne could not imagine what that might be.

He had taken her over, body and soul. He made love to her so fiercely, so comprehensively, so well and so often, that she wondered how she would ever be the same again. She worried that she had completely lost touch with whoever she might have been before that night in Florence. And the most frightening part was that she was not at all certain she cared as she should, as she knew she had back in Florence, standing in that flat with the Duomo looming behind her, trying to stop the inevitable. The days turned to weeks, and she could do nothing but burn for him. Again and again and again.

They had sailed from Italy to Greece, stopping wherever the mood took them. Sorrento. Palermo. The sights blurred in her memory, narrowing to a singular focus. Nikos. She remembered his slow, hot smile on a sun-baked street in Sorrento. She remembered the possessive weight of his hand in the small of her back as they explored the old seawall in the ancient city of Valletta in Malta. Then they had sailed on to the famed island of Ithaka, before mooring in Assos, the small village on neighboring Kefalonia that Nikos called his home.

"The villa was originally my grandfather's," he'd said that first afternoon, when they'd left the yacht in the tiny harbor and were in the back of an exquisitely maintained Mercedes as it navigated the twisting, turning road toward the hills. "It came to me following my father's death."

"So you never came here as a child?" she had asked. She had been staring out the window of the car at the pebbled beach in the village center, where children played beneath white umbrellas, and the pastel facades of the houses seemed to beg to be photographed, all of it beneath the impossible blue of the Greek sky.

His look had been dark, and far too cynical to be amused.

"I did not holiday on the island, if that is what you mean. I grew up in Athens, and stayed there," he'd said, matter-of-factly, and she'd remembered, then, his talk of slums and poverty, and had flushed. It had already started then, she knew, the need she felt to protect him—even from his own past. She had not yet allowed herself to think about what that must mean—what it could not mean. What she refused to permit it to mean.

"Since you call it home, I assumed that meant you had some childhood connection to it," she had said stiffly. She was terrified that he could sense that she had softened considerably, that she *cared* in ways she knew perfectly well would appall him. It appalled her. His dark gaze had been cool, assessing, and she'd frozen next to him in the backseat of the old Mercedes that his servant drove carefully up the snaking, hilly road, hoping her expression would remain calm, removed.

"It is the only one of my father's properties that he never visited as long as I knew him," he'd said in that detached, cold way that did not encourage further discussion. "I suppose I find his absence soothing."

She had not asked any further questions about his father. Not then. He had swept her into the villa, and then into the wide bed in his stark white room that took its only color from the sea beyond, the stretch of water and the gleaming bowl of the endless sky. And she had been so hungry for him, so desperate to feel that heady rush and that exquisite fall into ecstasy, that she had not minded such diversions.

If only we could stay in bed forever, she thought now, her eyes on the horizon.

But once they were in Greece, where Nikos seemed to be as much a part of the island landscape as the olive trees and the rugged hills, it seemed almost inevitable that the old tycoon should come up in conversation. His father, she'd learned, had been raised on this island by Nikos's grandfather, then sent out into the world to help run the old man's business concerns. It was difficult to say which of those two men had been the harder, the more driven. She told herself she wanted to know about his family because it made sense to learn all she could about the man who had so entranced her, however brief this liaison must be, but she was afraid she knew perfectly well that was not the reason she asked.

"Did you know your grandfather?" she had asked one afternoon, as they sat in a bustling taverna in the village square lunching on goat *stifada* and fresh-grilled sea bass in a delectable lemon sauce. Tristanne sipped at a dry white wine while Nikos drank from a large glass of Mythos beer.

"You are obsessed with a man who has been dead for decades," Nikos had said in quelling tones. His brows had arched high, mocking her. "Are you looking for ghosts, Tristanne? The island is full of them, I am sure. There are plenty of saints and martyrs here to occupy your thoughts. There is no need to go digging in my history."

"I am hardly obsessed," she had replied in the calm voice that she wielded as her only remaining weapon. Her only armor, however weak. She'd taken a sip of her wine and had pretended to be unmoved. "I am interested, however. He built an amazingly artistic home for a man you refer to in such harsh terms." The villa was an artist's dream—every room carefully designed to captivate the senses, and to gracefully frame the stunning views.

"My grandfather was not a particularly nice man, Tristanne," Nikos had said, a gleam in his dark eyes that had made the fine hairs on the back of her neck prickle in warning. "And the only artistic impulse he possessed involved buying things that others told him were sought-after." He'd shrugged, though his gaze had been hard. "But what man who builds an empire is *nice*? He raised his son to be even worse. His own image, magnified." His mouth had twisted. "This is my heritage, of which I am deeply proud."

She'd let his sardonic tone wash over her, and schooled herself not to react. He would not respond well to any show of emotion, she knew—any hint of compassion, or identification. She'd sometimes thought he deliberately tested her to see if there was any hint of softness in her demeanor. It was her duty to behave as if all that was between them was sex and the promise of money. Perhaps, for him, that was even true.

"Whether you are proud of it or not," she had said then, "it is still where you come from. It is worth knowing."

"I know exactly where I come from," he had retorted in that quiet, dangerous tone that Tristanne remembered only too well from Portofino. Did it mean she had struck a nerve? Or only that he wished to slap her down, put her in her place? She'd felt her chin rise in automatic defense. His mocking half smile had seemed extra bitter then, as if he'd been able to read her as well as she was learning to read him.

"Then there is no need to get so upset about it, is there?" she had asked lightly.

His eyes had seemed to catch fire and his smile had deepened to a razor's point.

"Why should I be upset?" he had asked, in that cutting tone, though whether he'd wished to slice into her or himself, she'd been unable to tell. "In retrospect, I should thank my father for casting my mother aside when her charms as a mistress grew stale. After all, she was merely a dancer in a club. What did he owe her? That he chose to favor her at all was more than she could have dreamed. No doubt that is why she succumbed to the usual narcotics, and abandoned me. But then, as he told me himself many years later, long after I proved myself to him through DNA and hard work—the streets hardened me. Made me a more formidable opponent." His shrug then had struck her as almost painful to watch. "Truly, I should have thanked him while I had the chance."

"He sounds deeply unpleasant," Tristanne had said quietly.

"He was Demetrios Katrakis," Nikos had said coldly. "What softer feelings he had, and he did not have many, he reserved for his late wife and their daughter. Not his gutter trash bastard son." His expression had been so fierce then, almost savage. Tristanne had known, somehow, that were she to show even a hint of sympathy, he would never find it in himself to forgive her.

So, instead, she had settled back in her seat, sipped at her wine and gazed out at the picturesque little village, quite as if her heart were not breaking into pieces inside her chest, for the discarded little boy she knew he would never acknowledge had existed.

He never spoke of these conversations. He only made love to her with an intensity that she worried, sometimes, in the dark of night, might destroy them both. How could anyone live with so much stark, impossible pleasure? How could they handle so much fire so often, and not turn themselves into cinders?

So rather than voice the thoughts and feelings that she was afraid to entertain even in the sanctity of her own head, Tristanne drew. She drew Nikos in a hundred poses, in a hundred ways. She told herself he was no more and no less than an example of a particular kind of hard male beauty, and she owed it to her artistic growth to master his form with pencils and a pad of paper.

That was why she traced the line of his nose a thousand times, the high thrust of his cheekbones, the proud set of his chin. That was why she agonized over the fullness of his lips, so wicked and seductive even at his most mocking, his most cutting. She spent whole afternoons learning the sweep of his magnificent torso; spent endless hours studying the strength and cleverness of his hands. It was to improve her craft, she told herself—to become a better artist.

"Surely you have drawn me more than enough," Nikos said now, coming to stand behind her. His fingers moved through her hair, pulling at the dark blonde waves almost absently. "Why not sketch the rocks? The cliffs? The cypress trees?"

Tristanne had not heard him end his call, but she had known the moment he moved across the wide patio to join her. She sat on one of the comfortable chairs that was placed to take advantage of the sweeping views of the Assos peninsula and the Ionian Sea beyond. But on the pad propped up on her knees in front of her was another drawing of Nikos. This time, she had drawn him in profile, his brow furrowed in thought, his mouth curled down at the corners. This was the Nikos she knew all too well, she thought now, looking at the drawing with a practiced eye. Resolute. Commanding. In control.

"I prefer to draw people—it's far more challenging. And you are the only person I see regularly," she said airily. "I could ask one of the tourists in the village to pose for me, but I do not believe you would care for it if I did."

"Indeed, I would not." There was an undercurrent of amusement in his rich voice, and she knew if she looked that he would be biting back that almost-smile.

"So, you see, I must use you," she said. "It is an artistic imperative."

She put down her pencil, and twisted to look up at him. As ever, her breath caught in her throat as she gazed at him. As ever, he seemed larger-than-life, blocking out the enormous azure sky. She could not see the gold in his eyes with his face in shadow, but she felt it anyway, as if another kind of gold hummed within her, and turned into an electric current when he touched her.

"I must go into Athens this afternoon," he said in a low voice. His hand moved from her hair to her cheek. His thumb traced a firm line along her jaw.

"Do I accompany you?" she asked softly. She could not pretend that she was not his mistress now, in word and in deed. Not when she knew what to ask and how to ask it, with no expectation or recrimination. Only availability. She was endlessly, terrifyingly available. She told herself that she was only ensuring Peter's continued compliance, and thus her mother's future, as they came ever closer to the month her brother had demanded at the party in Florence. Peter had even sent the papers that indicated she would have access to her trust, should she continue as she was. She was not doing this on a whim, she reminded herself firmly. Her plan was working just as she'd hoped. She had not meant to sleep with Nikos, it was true, nor had she anticipated spending more than a few days with him, but the fact that those things had changed did not alter the rest of her plans in any respect. She was not like her mother in her earlier, healthier days, kept for a man's pleasure like an inanimate object; a toy. She was not. She told herself so every day.

"I will only be gone a few hours," he said. He meant he would take the helicopter, which made the trip to his office in Athens merely a long, if rather flamboyant commute. "I will return tonight."

"I will miss you, then," she said, in that casual tone that she knew would not set off his alarms. She was so calm, so blasé. She worked so hard to appear that way. "Luckily I have my drawings of you. In case I begin to forget what you look like."

He pulled her to her feet, sliding a hand around to the small of her back and holding her against his wide chest. He looked down into her face. She felt the heat of his hand seep into her skin, warming her, even as she felt the usual quickening within. She did not know what his expression meant—only that he searched her own, and that his eyes burned into hers.

Did he know? she wondered in a sudden panic. *Had she somehow given herself away?*

"Perhaps you can help me pack," he murmured suggestively.

Because that was the only fire they acknowledged, the only way they could.

She hid the rest of it. Sometimes even from herself.

"Of course," she said, like the perfect mistress she was more and more these days. Just as she'd always feared. Just as Peter had predicted. She smiled at him. "I can think of nothing I would rather do."

Because she knew beyond the slightest doubt that she could not tell him that she loved him. She could not. She could never tell him that she loved him—she could not even think the words, for fear they would bleed onto her tongue without her knowledge.

She could only love him with her body, and the soft strokes and broad lines of her pencils, and pray with all she had that he never, ever knew.

Nikos strode through the villa, his temper igniting with every step.

She was nowhere to be found. She was not lounging suggestively in his bed, wearing something appropriately saucy. She was not taking a coincidentally perfectly timed shower, the better to lure him in. She was not in any number of places

she could have been in—should have been in—and the fact
that he had rushed home from Athens to see her made him
more furious about her deficiencies as a mistress than he
might have been otherwise.

A man should not have to hunt down his mistress. A man
should simply cross the threshold and find her waiting there,
beautiful and sweet-smelling, with a soft smile on her lips
and a cold drink in her hand.

Nikos stopped on the patio, and scowled at the sun as it
sank toward the horizon, spilling red and pink fingers over
the gleaming sea. It infuriated him how often he seemed to
forget the fact that Tristanne was not, in point of fact, his mistress. He was no better than a boy, letting his head get turned
by scaldingly hot sex. It had taken today's meeting with his
team in his office to reacquaint himself with his goals. Peter
Barbery, as expected, was trading on Nikos's good name
with all manner of investors, Nikos's people had confirmed.
Apparently the man's personal loathing of Nikos would not
prevent Peter from acting as if the two of them were thick as
thieves. Which meant that everything was in place. All that
Nikos needed to do now was up the stakes. Raise the bar just
that little bit higher, so when he sent it all crashing down, it
would really, truly hurt. Leave scars, even.

And he knew just how to do it.

He had rushed back to the island, telling himself that he
was not *excited* to do this thing so much as finally recommit-
ted to his original vision of how this entire operation would
proceed. He had lost his focus slightly, he had admitted to
himself on the helicopter ride from Athens. Tristanne was a
beautiful woman, and he was a man who greatly appreciated
beauty, especially when he found it wrapped around him
every morning like a vine. More than that, she grew more
mysterious by the day, and he found he was more and more
intrigued by his sense that she was hiding more than she
shared. But this, he had concluded today, was simply because

he wondered what the Barberys' end game was; what they thought they could gain from him.

He would accept no other reason for his uncharacteristic obsession with this woman. There was no room for anything but his revenge, surely.

He heard a scuffing sound then, and turned to see Tristanne emerge from the bushes that marked the edge of the cliff. She held her drawing pad in one hand, and looked at the ground as she walked. Her hair was twisted back into one of those smooth, efficient knots he hated, and she wore rolled up denim trousers, thronged-sandals, and an oversize shirt. She looked like a local painter, not a beguiling mistress—and she did not seem to notice that he was standing there, watching her approach.

Of course. Why had he expected anything different?

He told himself that what he felt was annoyance. Irritation that she should be so desperately inept. He told himself that he was simply shocked that she was so ill equipped to play her own game of deception.

"Look at you," he said coolly, his low voice rolling through the falling dark and wrenching her head up. "Have you been climbing up and down the cliffs? You look bedraggled enough to have attempted it."

"Not at all," she said as she closed the distance between them. Her chin, as ever, firmed and rose. The frown that had dented the space between her brows disappeared as her eyebrows arched. "Did you not indicate earlier that you preferred me to draw inanimate objects? I was merely obeying you. Rocks. Trees. As ordered."

The sarcastic inflection to her voice infuriated him. The defiant gleam in her brown eyes, reflecting the last red streaks of the sunset, provoked him. She should have been begging, pleading, *insinuating* herself. Wasn't that why she was here in the first place? Instead she had challenged him from the start. She did it even now. He was not even sure she did it deliberately.

She was *naturally* provoking.

"You," he said coldly, "are very possibly the worst mistress in the history of the world."

CHAPTER TWELVE

His words seemed to hang there in the dusk, swirling around them both like the sea air and the sound of the waves against the base of the cliffs far below. He did not know why he felt his heart pound so hard against his chest, much less why he felt himself harden.

"I beg your pardon," Tristanne said, her eyes throwing daggers at him. He watched her shoulders tense and then square. "I had no idea I was so deficient."

"Now you do." He swept his gaze over her. "What do you call this ensemble, Tristanne?"

She stiffened, and her free hand curled over into a fist before she shoved it into her pocket. "I believe the word I would choose is *comfortable*," she said, very precisely.

"*Comfortable* is not a word in a mistress's vocabulary." He shook his head at her. "Unless you are referring to my comfort. I expected to enter this villa and find you arrayed in front of me, like a banquet for my eyes."

"Are you sure you are discussing a mistress?" Tristanne asked in the same irritatingly cool, calm tone. "Because it sounds to me as if you are referring to a pack mule. Or the family hound."

"You are argumentative," Nikos said, as if he were checking off a list. "Independent." She blinked, and then averted her gaze, and he hated it. "Unacceptably mysterious," he gritted out.

"You will find, I think, that those are characteristics of most adults," Tristanne said. She moved to the nearby table and set her pad down upon it. "Perhaps you do not encounter such creatures in your daily attempts to rule the world, but I assure you, they are out there."

"And you are too clever by half," he replied in a silky tone. "And do not mistake me, Tristanne. That is not a compliment."

She turned toward him then, something he could not understand moving quickly across her face, gone in an instant. Was it…a kind of grief? But that made no sense.

"You will have to excuse my ignorance," she said, a storm brewing in her gaze, though no hint of it touched her voice. "I thought that your initial objections to my concept of my role as your mistress centered entirely on whether or not we would fall into bed. Having answered that question, in a way that I am quite certain is to your satisfaction, I fail to see how anything else matters."

"You fight with me at the slightest provocation," he said as if she hadn't spoken. As if he did not want to explore the satisfaction to which she had just referred, despite his body's instant and enthusiastic reaction. He crossed his arms over his chest as he looked down at her, enjoying himself. "How is this proper behavior? How is this enticing?"

At that, she actually laughed. "You are claiming that you do not find it enticing?" she asked. "My mistake. I thought your preferred method for conflict resolution proved otherwise."

Just yesterday she had argued with him about something absurd—some take on an article in the local paper—and he had had her there in the infinity pool while the sun beat down on them and birds called to each other from above, rendering them both happily wordless. *Conflict resolution*, indeed.

He could not help but smile.

"My point is that you do not suit as a mistress," he said. "How could you? I should have known when you asked for the position that it could never work."

"And why is that?" she asked, a hint of pink high on her cheeks.

"Because women do not *ask* to become my mistress," he said softly. "Why should they? They either are, or are not. It is always quite clear." He was fascinated by the ruthless way she kept her expression under control. Only a twitch near her eyes, and the faintest tremble of her lips betrayed her. "And I am the one to do the asking."

"I believe I get your point," she said crisply. "There is no need to belabor it. What is next, Nikos? A play-by-play breakdown of every time we—"

"You do not get my point." He interrupted her, his gaze hard on her face. "I am only stating a fact, which should in no way surprise you. Do you think I did not know perfectly well that you had no interest at all in becoming my mistress?"

She seemed to freeze then.

"I don't know what you mean," she said after a moment. He suspected that if she were another kind of woman, she might have stammered.

"You do." He arched a brow. "But you need not concern yourself, Tristanne. I know what you wanted."

She swallowed. "You do?" Her chin rose. "You must enlighten me. I thought I was perfectly clear about what I wanted. And perfectly satisfied with the result."

He let the moment drag out, enjoying himself far too much. He loved the panic that flashed in her gaze before she shuttered it, the nervousness she betrayed by the smallest of gestures—*almost* shifting her weight from foot to foot, *almost* biting her lower lip.

"I cannot have you as my mistress any longer, Tristanne," he said quietly. "You are terrible at it."

"Very well," she said, her voice even, her eyes carefully

blank. He wondered what that cost her. "I am devastated, of course."

He almost laughed at the insulting blandness she managed to inject into that last line—a fighter until the end, this woman. She would go down swinging, or die trying. He could not help but admire the sheer force of her bravado. It reminded him of his own bullheadedness, back in his angry youth.

"You are an idiot," he said then. He shook his head at her. "I am not casting you aside."

"Are you certain of that?" she asked dryly. Something flashed in her eyes. Relief? Irritation? "The recitation of my many flaws and the myriad ways I have disappointed you seems to suggest otherwise. Or perhaps this is the Nikos Katrakis brand of affection? How delightful."

"You cannot help yourself, can you?" he asked, his voice almost mild. He moved closer to her, then reached over to trace the mouth that spat such foolishness at him, the mouth that poked at him and exasperated him—the mouth that he found himself fantasizing about when she was not in the room. "You will keep going until you drop, no matter the cost to you."

She did not jerk her head back from his touch, nor shiver beneath his hand, but he had the sense that she fought off both. Her gaze searched his.

"I don't understand this conversation," she said quietly.

And then, he could put it off no longer. He felt something powerful move through him. *Revenge*, he told himself. Finally he would have his revenge. But it felt much more like a necessity than a tactic or a strategy—though he refused to consider why that might be.

"Marry me," he said.

"Oh," she managed to say somehow, her mind reeling, while her heart galloped wildly in her chest. Did she fall back a few steps? Had she fainted? But no, she was still standing there on the patio, too warm from her hike back up the side of the cliff—and from Nikos's unexpected, scowling appearance.

Or perhaps the heat that washed over her had more to do with what he had just said.

"I will not get on my knees, Tristanne," he told her in his infuriatingly arrogant way. He looked almost amused at the thought. "Nor will I spontaneously burst into poetry."

She could not think. She could not *think*, and that was the danger, because if she could not think, she could only feel… and she did not want to feel the things she felt. She could not allow herself to feel the emotions that coursed through her, buffeting her, as if she were no more substantial than a leaf in high winds.

A fierce, overwhelming joy suffused her, pulsing through her veins, blocking out the world for a moment—blocking out reality. The tantalizing idea, as painful as it was inviting, that she could have this man—really have him, when she knew she could not—called to a deep well of hope she had not known she held inside. But oh, the joy of imagining, even for a second, that she was not deceiving him! That he was proposing to a woman who actually existed—instead of this fake mistress person she had tried so hard to put on, like a second skin. He thought she was a failure at it, but then, he had no idea how far from herself she'd had to go to get here.

He had no idea.

"If I were someone else," he drawled then, his dark eyes a harder version of amused, "I might be rendered insecure by your continued silence."

But her mind was still racing, her heart still pounding—and she was frozen solid. Peter, she knew, would exult in this opportunity. Marrying Tristanne off to a rich man he could then lean on for financial support was an abiding fantasy of his; their father had shared it. It would solve all of her problems. Nikos would help her help her mother, of course, and Vivienne would finally be debt-free and on the way to recovery. Tristanne would be free of Peter, finally, for she could not imagine that her brother would bother with her any longer if he could approach Nikos directly. If he dared.

If only she did not love him.

"I can see your brain working overtime," Nikos said, tilting his head slightly as he gazed down at her. "What can there be to think about, Tristanne? We both know there can be only one answer."

If only she did not love him.

But she did love him, every arrogant, demanding, exasperating inch of him. She loved the way he moved through the world, using that powerful body and his far more impressive mind to cut a swathe before him. She loved the way he held her so tenderly sometimes, though she knew he would deny any and all softer emotions—or any emotions at all—were she to say such a thing aloud. She loved the defiant way he spoke of his past, as if it did not hurt him, as if it had not shaped him. *She loved.* She loved with every breath, with every caress of pencil against paper, with every touch of skin to skin. She loved him more than she had ever loved another person in her life, more than she could ever say, and she knew that she could not marry him. Not when almost everything she'd said to him, more or less, was a lie.

He had not spoken of love, she knew, nor would he. But did that matter? She knew the truths between them that only their bodies could speak. He did not have to feel as she did. She was not certain that he could, even if he'd wanted to do something so anathema to him.

Which only made it more clear what she must do, though every part of her rebelled. Every cell rose up in revolt, almost choking her to keep her from saying what she resolved she must say. She felt a sharp heat behind her eyes, but she would not cry. She would not.

"I cannot marry you," she said at last, the words ripped from her, seeming to tear at her throat, her tongue, her lips. She was not sure how she managed to do it. But she could not lie to the man she loved, not any longer. She simply could not. She would find some other way to save her mother, somehow, but she could not do this anymore. The fact that she had done it at all was something she would regret for the rest of her days.

"No?" He did not seem particularly taken aback by her declaration. "Are you certain? I feel sure that you can."

"I mean that I *will not* marry you," she amended, with every last drop of bravado she possessed. As if it did not kill her to say it. As if it were not a supreme act of sacrifice to say such a thing to him when she knew, she just *knew*, that she could love enough for both of them. She could feel the force of it, thudding heavy and hard against the walls of her chest.

"Ah." He studied her. "Have you gone over all romantic, Tristanne? Has talk of marriage led you to fantasize about notions of forever and matching rings?" He laughed, shortly. "I assure you, I will have my lawyers bury us both in prenuptial contracts. I imagine that will prove a cure for any lingering romantic fantasies."

"That would be a relief, I am sure," Tristanne somehow brought herself to say, even managing a certain level of dryness. As if she could be as cynically detached as he was—as he expected her to be.

"Then what is your objection to my proposal?" He shrugged with the supreme confidence of a man who knew himself to be one of the world's greatest catches, wanted by untold numbers of women on innumerable continents. "You cannot say we do not suit."

"You just spent some time detailing the ways in which we do not suit," Tristanne said, almost testily. She did not know why she continued to spar with him. She should simply leave him, she knew. She should do it now, while she still felt virtuous for refusing him. Before the pain caught up with her and laid her out, flat, as she suspected it would. As she feared it would.

She had always known he would haunt her—and that was before she'd been foolish enough to fall head over heels in love with her.

"A man does not expect to argue with his mistress," Nikos said, his mocking half smile appearing again. "But that is the province of a wife, is it not?"

"I do not think you believe half of the things that come out of your mouth," Tristanne threw at him, fighting the swell of her own emotions. She wanted, too badly, to be the woman she'd pretended to be. The woman he'd actually proposed to, instead of the woman she was. "I think you simply say these things for effect!"

"Marry me, and see for yourself," he suggested, completely unperturbed. Daring her, in fact, to marry him!

Tristanne felt something break inside of her, and had to bite back a gasp that she feared would come out more of a sob. She could not cry. She *would not* cry, not now, not in front of him. But she felt all of her fight, all of the bravado she'd clung to as her only defense against this man, go out of her in a great rush.

What was she fighting for? Why was she being so noble? The truth was that she was selfish, not sacrificing, because she wanted to say yes more than she could remember wanting anything else, ever. She wanted to disappear completely into the life that Nikos offered her, and bury herself in the sizzling heat of his embrace. The truth was that she loved Nikos, and while it was something Peter could never possibly understand, she knew in her heart that her mother would. And how could she walk away from him without even trying to tell him the truth about herself? How would she ever manage to live with herself if she did such a thing?

She loved him, for all she knew that such a thing was neither wise nor rational, and she had to believe that somewhere inside of him, buried beneath all those layers of masculine pride and years of neglect and solitude, he felt something for her. Surely she had to trust him enough to tell him the truth, if she had any hope at all of trusting him with her heart—or, at the very least, of surviving this relationship with him with any part of herself intact.

She let her fists clench at her sides. She stood straight. She raised her head high, and she looked him straight in the eye. She let his old gold gaze warm her, and she refused to let herself give in to the heat that prickled behind her eyes.

"I cannot marry you," she said quietly, with as much dignity as she could muster, "because I am lying to you. I have been lying to you from the start."

CHAPTER THIRTEEN

"Have you?" Nikos sounded almost offhand, very nearly bored, as if people confessed to deceiving him several times a day. Perhaps they did, Tristanne thought ruefully. Or, much more likely, this show of nonchalance was carefully calibrated to disarm the unwary so he might strike when they least expected it.

"I have," she said. She studied his dark face. The haughty cheekbones, the full mouth pulled into its characteristic smirk. She wanted to press herself against the heat of him; lose herself in the heady passion that only he had ever aroused in her. But she had already lost too much of herself in this terrible game, so she merely waited.

"Come," Nikos drawled after a long moment. "We will have some wine and sit, like civilized people, and you will tell me how you have lied to me for all of this time."

Bemused, Tristanne could do nothing but follow Nikos inside. He poured himself a glass of wine from the bar in the corner of the living room, and merely shrugged when Tristanne refused one for herself. The tasteful room was all done in whites and neutral colors that inexorably led the eye to the spectacular view, visible through the floor-to-ceiling glass on three sides. He settled himself into one of the low-slung armchairs and raised a brow, inviting her to continue.

Tristanne laced her fingers together before her, and

frowned down at her clasped hands. She could not bring herself to sit down, as if they were having cocktails and everything was perfectly normal. She did not feel civilized in any respect. Her heart beat too fast, and she felt too hot, too restless. Dizzy. She wished she could go back in time and keep herself from speaking at all. She should have either accepted his proposal, or simply said no and left it at that. Why was she exposing herself like this? What was there to gain? He was so remote, so cold now—sitting there as if they hardly knew each other. And she was making it worse by dithering over it, dragging the uncomfortable silence out…

"I remembered you," she said, not knowing what she planned to say until it was out there, hanging in the air of the elegant room while the Greek night pressed against the windows, dark and rich. "I saw you at a ball in my father's home when I was still a girl. I mention this because it was the first lie, that I saw you for the first time on your yacht that day."

He took a sip of his wine, then lounged back against his chair. His eyes were so dark, yet still shone of gold. She took that as a good sign—or, at least, not a negative one. Not yet.

And so she told him. She stood like a penitent before a king, and she confessed every part of it. Peter's mismanagement of the family finances and her mother's frailty and ill health. Her need for her trust fund in order to settle her mother's debts and take her somewhere safer and better, which Tristanne felt she owed her. Peter's revolting ultimatums, and his obsessive hatred of Nikos, which had been one of the reasons she'd picked him. The things Peter had said about Nikos, and about Tristanne, and what she knew Peter hoped to gain from her liaison with Nikos. What she had expected to gain from her association with Nikos, and how surprised she had been by the passion that had flared between them.

She talked and she talked, a ball of dread growing larger

and heavier in her gut with each word. As she spoke, Nikos hardly moved. He drank from his wineglass from time to time, but otherwise merely listened, stretched out in his chair with his hard face completely unreadable, propped up against one hand.

She realized that she had no idea what he would do. He was a ruthless, dangerous man—she had known that from the start, hadn't she? It was why she'd chosen him. She had no doubt that he dealt with betrayal harshly. Like the dragon he was. What would he do to her?

When she was finished, she found herself staring down at her hands once more. She willed herself not to shake. Not to weep. Not to beg or plead with him. And not, under any circumstances, to let it slip that she was in love with him. She nearly shuddered then, at the very thought. She did not have to know what would happen next to know *that* would be like throwing gasoline on an open flame.

"And this is why you say you will not marry me?"

Her head shot up at the sound of his low, firm voice. She searched his face, but could see nothing save that same fire in his gaze. She could only nod, no longer trusting herself to speak.

Nikos leaned forward, and set his wine down on the wide glass coffee table. As Tristanne watched, panic and hope and fear surged through her in equal measure, making her feel light-headed. He stood up with that masculine grace that, even now, made her throat go dry.

"I do not care," he said quietly, fiercely, closing the distance between them. He reached over and cupped her cheek in his hand, his eyes dark and intense. "I do not care about any of it."

"What?" She could barely speak. Her voice was a thread of sound, and she knew she was trembling, shaking—finally breaking down in front of him, as she had vowed she would never do. *Must* never do! "How can you say such a thing? Of course you must care!"

"I care that you have been put in a position to do such things by your pig of a brother," he growled at her, his voice low and rough, as if he, too, did not entirely trust himself to speak. "I care that had I refused your proposition, you might have made it to someone else." His hand, hot against her skin, tightened a fraction. "I care that you are standing before me trying your hardest not to weep."

"I am not!" she snapped at him, but it was too late. She felt all of her fear, all of her anger and pain and isolation and love, so much desperate, impossible love, coalesce into that searing heat in her eyes and then spill over, tracking wet, hot tears down her face.

She disgraced herself, and yet she could not seem to stop.

He murmured something in Greek, something tender, and it made it all the worse. Tristanne jabbed at her eyes with the back of one hand, furious at herself. What was next? Would she start to cling to the hem of his trousers as he made for the door? How soon would she become her mother, in every aspect?

It was a chilling thought. Her very worst nightmare made real—but then Nikos took her face in both of his hands, and she could think only of him.

"Listen to me," he said, in that supremely arrogant way of his—that tone that demanded instant obedience. "You will marry me. I will handle your brother, and your mother will be protected. You will not worry about any of this again. Do you understand me?"

"You cannot order me to marry you," she said, pricked into remembering her own spine by the sheer conceit of him, by his overwhelming confidence that her very tears would dry up on the spot at his command.

His hands tightened slightly, and his mouth curved into a very male smile.

"I just did," he said. "And you will."

And then he kissed her, as if it was all a foregone conclusion; as if she had already agreed.

She could have been putting on an elaborate act, but he did not think so, Nikos thought much later as he stood out on the balcony that hung high over the cliffs, far above the crashing waves. He did not believe that her body could deceive him on that level, even if she wished it to do so.

He turned to look at her, stretched out across the rumpled bed inside the master suite, her eyes closed and her mouth slightly open as she slept. Her hair was a satisfying tangle around her shoulders, and her curves seemed to gleam in the moonlight—beckoning him with a siren's call he could not seem to escape. He felt himself stir, always ready for her, always desperate to lose himself inside her once again. He felt something squeeze tight inside of his chest, and turned his back on her again, ruthlessly.

The night was cool, with a brisk breeze coming in off the sea, smelling of salt and pine. Nikos stared out at the dark swell of the water and the twinkling lights of the village below, and could not understand why he did not feel that kick of adrenaline, that hum in his veins of victory firmly within his grasp. He had felt it when he'd weakened the various Barbery assets enough that, following the old man's death, it had taken the merest whisper to send them tumbling. He had celebrated that victory—remembering too well what it had been like when the situations were reversed and it had been the Katrakis fortune on the line. He remembered Peter's gloating laughter when he'd called to announce the deal was off, the Katrakis money lost, Althea discarded, and all of it according to the Barberys' plan. Nikos imagined the Barberys had celebrated that, too, all those years ago. He had made himself coldly furious over the years, imagining that very celebration in minute detail, reliving Peter's vile words.

So why did he not now feel as he should? He had reeled her in, completely. He had been astonished when she'd made her confession to him, though he could not allow himself to speculate too much on what might have led her to unburden herself. He could only think of a handful of motivations, none of them coming from places he wished to think about. What was important, he told himself, was that she'd told him everything there was to tell about her brother's plans. About her own part in those plans. And then she had made love to him like a wild thing, untamed and ravenous, moving over him in the dark of the bedroom as if she were made of fire and need, bringing them both to writhing ecstasy.

But Nikos did not feel that cool beat of triumph—he felt something else, something elemental and dark. Something wholly unfamiliar. Some deep-seated streak of possessiveness rose in him, roaring through him, making him question the scheme he had committed himself to so long ago.

You never meant to involve the girl, he reminded himself now, as if he still had a conscience. As if he had not rid himself of that encumbrance long since, as his actions with Tristanne made perfectly clear. *You never meant to do what Peter did.*

He thought of Althea then. Beautiful, impetuous, foolish Althea. His half sister by blood, though she claimed no particular family relationship to him unless it suited her purposes. He had been something like her bodyguard and her convenient escort, when she did not wish to be seen on the arm of their grizzled old father. And he, damn him, had been so desperate for her favor, for her approval. He had wanted to protect her, to make her smile, to prove to her that he deserved to call himself her brother even while their father treated him like the unwelcome hired help.

But she had not been interested in her feral half brother.

She had not cared if he stayed to ingratiate himself with their father or if he disappeared back into the ghetto from whence he came. If anything, she had resented the fact that she was no longer the sole focus of their father's attention—and even if what attention Demetrios Katrakis gave to his bastard son was negative, it was attention. She had not minded that Nikos was there, necessarily, but nor would she have cared particularly if he was not. Her indifference had only made him that much more determined to win her over.

But then she had fallen madly in love with Peter Barbery, and had sealed all of their fates.

Nikos let his hands rest on the rail in front of him, and forced himself to breathe. What was done was done, and there could be no undoing it. Peter had tossed Althea aside the moment Gustave Barbery had succeeded in cheating Demetrios out of a major deal. The entire Katrakis legacy had faltered. Althea had killed herself, and when it was found that she had been pregnant, Demetrios had blamed Nikos even more. For failing to protect her and the child? For surviving? Nikos had never known. A year later, Demetrios, too, had died, leaving Nikos to pick up the pieces of the Katrakis shipping empire.

It had all happened so fast. He had only just found his family, and the Barberys had ripped them away from him, one by one.

What was done was done, he repeated to himself. And what would be, would be. He had vowed it over his father's grave, and he was a man who kept his promises. Always.

But still, he did not feel that surge of cold certainty that had led him here. That focus and intensity that had allowed him to plot and plan from afar, across years. Was it because, as a little voice in the back of his head insisted, doing what he planned to do to Tristanne made him exactly like Peter Barbery? Worse, even—for Barbery had promised Althea nothing, while Nikos had every intention of abandoning Tristanne at the altar.

He could see it play out in his mind's eye, shot for shot, like he watched it in the cinema. Tristanne would walk down the aisle, dressed in something white and gauzy and ineffably lovely, and he would not be there. He would never be there. She would not cry, not in front of so many. He knew that the fact she'd cried in front of him tonight meant things he was unwilling to look at closely. But she would not cry in her moment of greatest humiliation. He could see, as if she stood before him, that strong chin rise into the air, and the tremor across her lips that she suppressed in an instant. He saw the smooth, calm expression she turned toward the crowd, toward the cameras, toward the gossip and the speculation.

And he saw the great bleakness in her chocolate eyes, that he feared she would never be rid of again.

He hissed out a harsh curse and let the night wind toss it toward the rocks far below, battering it into a million pieces.

This was different, he told himself fiercely. He had never intended to use Tristanne; she had approached him. How was he to refuse to use the perfect tool when it fell into his lap? After all this time? He thought of that odd, tender moment in the rain in Florence. He had been trying to forget it ever since it had happened. He was not like Peter Barbery, he told himself, even though he had the strangest feeling that when he did this thing to Tristanne, when he wounded her so deeply, so irrevocably—it might even wound him, too.

He, who had shut off that part of himself so long ago now that it was almost shocking to recall how much he had loved his spoiled, careless half sister, and how much it had hurt when she'd thrown that in his face. He had never thought anything could hurt him again.

"You are nothing to me!" she'd screamed at him when he'd attempted to console her after Peter's vicious termination of their relationship. He had not known, then, that she was pregnant. That Peter Barbery had scoffed at her and called her a whore—then claimed his own child could have been anyone's. All Nikos had known was that Althea had been in a lump on the floor of her room in their father's elegant mansion in Kifissia, her face streaked with tears. Still, her eyes, as they focused on him, were narrow and mean. Like their father's.

"Althea," he had said, his hands in the air, trying to soothe her. He had thought he had shown her that he was trustworthy—the older brother she had never had. Someone she could love and lean on. That was what he'd wanted.

"I wish you had never been born!" she had thrown at him, cutting him as surely as if she'd thrown a knife. "This is your fault! You were the one who was too cocky, too sure—"

"I will make this right," he had promised her. "I will. I swear it on my honor."

"Your honor? What is that to me?" She had been scornful then, her pretty face twisted, spiteful. "You may have climbed out of the sewer, Nikos, but you still walk around with the stench of it clinging to you, don't you? And you always will!"

Nikos shook the unpleasant memory away, gritting his teeth. Only a week later, she had been gone, her pregnancy uncovered. So much lost. So much wasted.

The Barberys deserved whatever they got, even Tristanne, the innocent one. He would not feel guilty for it.

He would not.

She was still half-asleep when he pulled her into his arms. Tristanne came awake as his body moved over hers, her own already responding to him, already softening for him, before she was fully aware of what was happening.

"You have yet to answer me," he said softly, moving his

mouth along the column of her neck. "I presume this is merely an oversight."

"What if my answer remains no?" she said, her voice husky from sleep, and, she thought, the fact that no secrets remained between them. Not any longer. She felt…naked unto her soul. New.

Vulnerable.

A faint memory stirred then, of Peter in Florence, asking snidely after Nikos's angle in all of this. She shook it away, concentrating instead on the feel of Nikos's hard muscles beneath her hands, his hot mouth against her skin, her breast. What could she do? She had told him everything. She could only hope that he would do her the same courtesy—but even if he did not, it was not as if she could simply decide to stop loving him in the meantime.

Her body would not allow her to stop wanting him, not even for the barest moment.

"Yes," she said, as he twisted his hips slightly and thrust deep into her, making her sigh with wonder at the perfect, slick fit.

"Yes, what?" he taunted her as, slowly, he began to move, stroking in and out of her, sending shivers of delight all through her limbs.

"You are a bully," she said, gasping.

"I am merely emphatic," he growled against her throat, nipping at her. "And very, very focused."

And because she could do nothing else, because ripples of pleasure fogged her brain and coursed through her veins, she wrapped her legs around him and held on tight.

His eyes were dark, threaded through with gold, and yet seemed almost conflicted as they met hers. He dropped his gaze, and kissed her, taking her mouth with an intensity she might have called desperate in another man. He began to thrust faster, harder, holding her bottom in his strong hands to please them both with the deeper angle.

"Yes," she said, because she could not remember, now, why she had denied him. She wanted to soothe him, to ease the darkness in his gaze. She *wanted*. "I will marry you."

He did not speak again. He merely lowered his head, and then he took them both over the edge.

CHAPTER FOURTEEN

"WE MUST marry quickly," Nikos said the following evening as they sat in the fading light, startling Tristanne as she feasted on tangy kalamata olives and sharp feta drenched in locally grown olive oil and spices. The sun had only just ducked below the horizon, and Nikos had only just returned from another day in Athens.

Part of her, she realized now, had wondered if the events of the previous night were real—of if she'd dreamed them. His words sent a thrill of anticipation through her.

"Why must we do anything of the kind?" she asked. "Surely we can have the usual engagement period. We would not want to suggest that there is any reason to rush, would we?"

"Will this turn into another battle, Tristanne?" he asked, his mouth curving into that familiar half smile, though there was a hardness to it tonight. "Will you explain to me what will and will not happen, at great length, only to acquiesce to my wishes in the end? Is that not the pattern?"

She wished there was not that edge to his voice, as if he meant his words on several levels she could not quite understand. She wished she did not feel slapped down, somehow. But she reminded herself that everything between them was different now. She had come clean and even so, he wanted to marry her.

Or so she kept telling herself, as if it were a mantra.

"Why do you wish to marry quickly?" she asked calmly, as if she had not noticed any edge, or even his usual sardonic inflection.

His dark eyes touched on hers, then dropped to caress her lips, then her breasts beneath the light cotton shift she wore. She ordered herself not to squirm in her seat; not to respond. Her body, as ever, reacted only to Nikos and ignored her entirely.

"Must you ask?" His voice was low. "Can you not tell?"

"I do not believe in divorce," she said quietly, holding his gaze when he looked at her again. She did not know why she felt compelled to say such a thing, even while her heart fluttered wildly in her chest. "I realize it is unfashionable to say so, but I have never understood the point of getting married at all if one does so with an escape clause."

"I assure you, divorce exists." He shook his head, and reached for one of the spicy olives. He popped it into his mouth. "My grandfather divorced three wives in his time."

"Especially not if there are children," she continued, ignoring him. She shrugged. "I have seen too many children destroyed in their parents' petty little wars. I could not do that to my own."

Something in his gaze went electric then, making her breath catch.

"If there are children," he said quietly, fiercely, "they will be born with my name and live under my protection. Always."

He did not speak for a long while then, looking out to sea instead. Something about the remoteness of his expression made her heart ache for him, for the abandoned child he had been, though she dared not express her sympathy. She was too worried he would read into it what should not be there—her unreasonable empathy, her compassion, the love she felt for him that scared her, on some level, with its absoluteness. Its certainty. It was a hard rock of conviction inside of her, for all that so much about him remained a mystery—as out of reach as the stars that shone ever brighter above her in the darkening sky.

Was it love? she wondered. Or was she deluding herself in a different way now? First she had thought she could maneuver around this man, use him for her own ends. That had proved laughable. Now she thought she could love him and make a marriage between them work based on only her love, and their breathtaking, consuming chemistry? Was she as foolish as the waves in the sea far below her, thinking they would remain intact as they threw themselves upon the rocks?

Did she really want to know?

"We will marry in two weeks," he said at last. His head turned toward her, his expression almost grim. "Here. If that suits you."

"Are you asking my opinion?" she asked dryly, as if things were as they'd used to be between them. As if he was not so stern, suddenly—so unapproachable. "How novel."

"If you have another preference, you need only make it known." His brows rose a fraction. "I have already notified the local paper. The announcement will be made in tomorrow's edition. Everything else can be expedited."

"Two weeks," she repeated, wishing she could see behind the distant expression he wore like a mask tonight. Her intuition hummed, whispering that something was not as it ought to be, but she dismissed it. *Nerves*, she thought. His as well as hers, perhaps. And well she should be nervous, marrying such a man. He would bulldoze right over her, if she showed the slightest weakness. He might do it anyway. He was doing it now.

And yet some primitive part of her thrilled to the challenge of it. To the challenge of *him*. Even this somber version of him. What did that say about her?

"Two weeks," he said, as if confirming a deal. He settled back against his chair, and picked up his ever-present mobile. "Perhaps you should take the helicopter into Athens and find yourself something to wear."

"Perhaps I will," she agreed, and picked up another crumbled-off piece of the feta, letting the sharp bite of it explode on her tongue. No matter how spicy, or sharp, she always went back for more. She could not fail to make the obvious connection. Perhaps, she thought with some mixture of despair and humor, that was simply who she was.

She did not notice, until much later, that he had not told her *why* he wanted to marry so quickly. That he had talked around it entirely.

Everything seemed to speed up then, making Tristanne feel almost dizzy. Soon they would be married, she told herself, and they would have the rest of their lives to sort through whatever lay beneath his sudden remoteness. She told herself that this was simply the male version of jitters—and at least her focus on what Nikos was or was not feeling, or how he was behaving, allowed her to avoid focusing on the things *she* did not want to think about.

He was busy all the time, he claimed. He was always on his mobile, talking fiercely in Greek. When he found time to speak to her, it was to confirm that she was tending to the wedding details he had given over to her. She found a simple dress in a boutique in Athens, as directed. She met with a woman in the capitol city of Argostoli on the island who bubbled over with joy at finding the perfect flowers for Nikos's bride.

She contacted her family. Vivienne, predictably, was overjoyed—her enthusiasm not quite hiding the tremor in her voice, though she tried.

"That is how it was for your father and me," she said with

a happy sigh. "We took one look at each other and everything else was inevitable."

Tristanne could not reconcile the cold parent Gustave had been with the stories her mother told of him, but she did not argue. Once her mother arrived, she would be safe. And soon, Tristanne had no doubt, well. It was all as she'd planned, back when she'd believed she could manipulate Nikos to her will.

"You must come to Greece," she said softly. "We cannot marry without you."

Peter, of course, was more difficult, even after she had the pleasure of telling him she no longer required his help in any respect—that he could keep her trust fund for the next three years, with her compliments.

"You've upped the ante, haven't you?" He sneered into the phone. "How proud you must be of yourself. I had no idea you could make a man like Katrakis turn his thoughts to matrimony. What a perfect little actress you are!"

"You are, in point of fact, my only sibling," Tristanne said coldly. "That is the only reason I am extending an invitation."

"That and the fact it would look powerfully odd if I did not attend," Peter shot back. "Never fear, Tristanne. I will be there."

She rather thought that sounded like a threat.

But there was no time to worry about Peter and whatever new atrocity he might be planning. Tristanne was infinitely more concerned about her husband-to-be, whose demeanor seemed to grow colder and more unapproachable by the hour as the clock ticked down to their wedding day.

If it were not for the nights, she would have panicked. But he came to her in the darkness, without fail. She would lie awake until his dark form appeared, crawling over her on the wide bed. Silent and commanding, he made love to her with a fierce urgency that she felt sear her all the way to her soul.

He held her in the aftermath, close to his chest, his hands tangled in her hair, and he never said a word.

She should talk to him, she reasoned in the light of day. She should interrupt one of his interminable business calls and ask him what was bothering him. She would have, she told herself, were she not able to perfectly envision the kind of mocking set-down he might deliver. He was not the kind of man who could be asked about his feelings. She was not even certain if he was aware that he had any.

The truth was, she missed him. She missed his teasing, their sparring—that half smile of his and the gleam of old coin gold in his dark eyes—but the sudden stiffness between them felt precarious, like something fragile stretched across a great morass of darkness. Tristanne was afraid to poke at it.

That was the real reason, of course, she admitted to herself only when she was standing alone with the Greek sunlight drenching her in its shine. She was terrified that if she mentioned anything—anything at all—he would think better about all the ways she had deceived him and change his mind. And she could not bear to think of losing him.

It was as simple—as wretchedly, starkly simple—as that.

She could not imagine a day without his touch, without looking at that hard, beautiful face. Without seeing those deep gold eyes, those haughty cheekbones. Without feeling the heat of that steely chest. She did not want to imagine it.

She knew that she should loathe herself for falling so hard, so heedlessly—for risking so much. For being, as Peter had always told her, so very like her poor mother. But try as she might, she could not seem to gain the necessary distance. It was as she'd sensed it would be from the start. Perhaps as she'd imagined when he'd left her breathless at that ball so long ago. The moment she'd let her defenses down, and let him in, she had been forever altered. She wanted him more, it seemed, than she wanted to keep herself safe.

She could only hope she would not have to choose between the two.

It was like déjà vu.

Nikos stood on the deck of his yacht and watched the well-dressed and well-preserved guests mingle with each other in front of him. He, too, was dressed exquisitely in a beautifully tailored Italian suit, as befitted the host and the bridegroom on the night before his wedding was supposed to take place. But he could not seem to pay the proper amount of attention to his business associates or the expected luminaries who milled about, drinking his wine and laughing too loudly into the coming evening. He could not even pay his respects to the coast of his beloved Kefallonia as the boat slowly moved past this stunning cliff, that hidden gem of a beach and yet another picturesque village. It was all a blur to him.

He only had eyes for Tristanne.

She wore something blue tonight that seemed spun from clouds, so effortlessly did it dance over her curves, calling attention to the bright spark in her warm eyes, the golden glow of her skin. Her hair swept over her shoulders in dark blonde waves, calling to mind the golden Kefallonian sands as they basked beneath the Greek sky. She was too alive, too vibrant. Too beautiful.

And he was keenly aware that this was the last night she would seem so. That he would crush the very thing he found so intoxicating about her from her as surely as if he planned to do it with his own foot.

He could not make sense of the churning in his gut, or his own inability to carry through with his plan with all the comfort of the righteousness that had been his only companion these many years. Why should he regret that she must feel the consequences of her family's actions? That she must pay for the loss of three lives? Why should he regret anything?

As if she could feel his gaze upon her, she turned away from the guests she was talking to and smiled at him. He watched her excuse herself with a word and her perfect social smile, and then he allowed himself to sink into the vision of her as she crossed the deck to him.

He let himself pretend, for just one moment, that she would truly become his bride in the morning. *His wife.*

He could not deny the sense of rightness that spread through him then, spiraling out from the part of him that had told him she was his since the start and taking him over in a heady kind of rush. But it did not matter what he *felt*, he reminded himself grimly, forcing himself back under control. It only mattered what he did. What he had vowed he would see through to the bitter end.

"You look forbidding," she said, her voice light, though her eyes searched his. He caught the faintest hint of her perfume, something fresh and enticing, that made him want to put his mouth on her. He did not know how he refrained.

"I find I am less interested in parties than I was once," he said. He tugged at the collar of his shirt, wishing they were hidden away in the villa, where he would already be naked and she would already be astride him. Why could it all not be as simple, as elemental as that?

She smiled, as if she could read his mind. "This party is in your honor," she pointed out, angling her body toward his. "You could smile. Or at least stop frowning. I don't think it would ruin your mystique."

He smiled without meaning to, and then wondered how he could be so susceptible to her. How he could let his control slip so easily. He had ignored the way she had watched him over the past weeks, her brown eyes grave and thoughtful. He had ignored the way he had gone to her, then held on to her as if he could hold back the night, keep reality at bay. He had ignored everything.

But tonight, his resolve seemed to have been left behind when the boat left the shore in Assos. He looked at her, her face so open and trusting, and wanted more than anything to be the man she thought he was. The man he ought to be.

But that man did not exist—and what possibility there might have been of his becoming that man had been snuffed out by the Barberys ten years ago. Why was that so hard to remember when she was near?

"And that is important to you?" he asked idly. He wished that it was done. He wished that he had finished with this act of revenge already, and that it was behind him. He told himself it was the drawing out that was killing him, the waiting even now, at the eleventh hour. "You feel I should pretend to be friendly and approachable for the benefit of wedding guests who, presumably, already know perfectly well I am neither?"

She laughed, and it hurt him, though he refused to acknowledge it. Her eyes were so warm, so happy as she looked up at him.

"Oh, Nikos," she said, as if she was still laughing, as if the words bubbled up from within her like a mountain spring, fresh and clean and pure. "I do love you."

He felt himself turn to stone.

He knew who he was. He knew what he must do.

And he did not believe in love.

Even hers.

Tristanne felt him freeze solid beneath her hands. Her words hung there between them, taking over the night, seeming to gather significance—seeming to echo back from the cliffs.

"I did not mean to say that!" she whispered, stricken. Appalled at herself and her carelessness.

He looked like a stranger suddenly—so faraway, so

alien—though he had hardly moved a muscle. Panic and dread exploded inside of her, making her feel almost drugged—heavy and close to tears, where seconds before she had felt like air.

"I'm so sorry," she said hurriedly. "I did not know I was going to say it!"

"Did you not?" His voice was so cold. So distant. Condemning. "Perhaps you meant it in the casual way. The way one loves a car. Or a shoe."

He sounded almost uninterested. Almost as if he was poking at her as he'd used to. But Tristanne could see something that looked like anguish in his eyes, turning them very nearly black.

She sucked in a breath, skimmed her hands over his wide shoulders. Took another breath, and met his gaze. For a moment she did not know if she could do this. She, who had stood up to him when her very knees threatened to give out. She, who had argued with him when she would have been better-served trying to protect herself.

But if she could not keep herself safe, she could pretend to be brave.

"I did not mean to say it, but it's true," she said, her voice soft, but sincere. "I do, Nikos. I love you."

He only stared at her, as the party seemed to dim and disappear around them. His eyes were so dark as he looked down at her, with no hint at all of gold. No trace of something like tenderness she'd thought she'd seen there on occasion. It was almost as if he could not make sense of her words.

Something passed between them, heavy and unspoken, thick. Tristanne felt her eyes well up, though she did not cry, and saw a muscle twitch in his jaw—though she sensed he was not angry. He was nothing so simple as *angry*.

"This wedding has addled your brain," he said, hoarsely, after moments—or years—had passed. "How can you love me, Tristanne? You hardly know me. You have no idea what I am capable of!"

She remembered the words she had thrown at him on the cobblestones in Portofino, and shivered involuntarily. Had that been foreboding? A premonition? Had she been waiting, since then, for the other shoe to fall?

"I know you," she said softly. She squared her shoulders, and met his gaze straight on. "Better than you think."

"Very well then," he said then, biting the words out. So cold, so far away suddenly. "I hope that knowledge brings you great comfort in the days to come."

"You mean when we are married?" she asked, not quite following him, but feeling somehow that they were poised on the edge of a great disaster.

"Yes," he said, his mouth twisting, bitterness thick in the air between them, though she could not understand it. "When we are married."

CHAPTER FIFTEEN

TRISTANNE stood before the floor-length mirror in the villa's master suite, staring at the vision before her. Her hair was caught back in a clasp at her crown, then tumbled about her bare shoulders in a cascade of dark blonde waves. The ivory dress clasped her tight around the bodice, then skimmed to the ground, light and airy, simple and elegant. Her makeup was flawless, calling attention to her eyes, her lips, and making her complexion seem to be a deep cream, with a glow within. She wore her mother's pearls and behind her, near to the chair where Vivienne sat clasping her hands to her chest in delight, a bouquet bursting with fragrant white flowers graced a low table.

Tristanne was the perfect vision of the perfect bride. And yet she could not seem to shake the terrible sense of foreboding that had gripped her ever since Nikos had left her side the night before. Ever since she had told him she loved him and he had stared at her as if he'd never laid eyes on her before. She trembled again, now, thinking of it.

"You are a beautiful bride!" Vivienne cried from behind her, as if she were neither fragile nor upsettlingly pale.

"Am I?" Tristanne was hardly aware of having spoken. She felt as if she was in a dream. How could this be her wedding day? How could she be dressed to marry a man that she did not quite trust, who did not love her, who might never care for her as she did for him? How could it all have come to this? Surely, on this day of all days, she should feel some kind of certainty about the man she was about to vow to spend the rest of her life with. Instead all she could see was that odd, cold look in Nikos's dark eyes last night. All she could feel was a low-level panic, making her faintly nauseous, slightly dizzy. And she could not seem to do anything but stare at herself, as if her reflection held the answers, were she only to look hard enough.

The logical part of her mind knew exactly what she should do. It had spent the long night drawing up exit strategies and outlining escape plans. She could not possibly marry a man who had reacted to her declaration of love in such a way. A man whom she did not trust, who, as he had said himself, she barely knew. What was she thinking? She was the result of a hasty marriage, had grown up watching her mother beg for the scraps of her father's attention—and she had vowed she would never put herself in that position. How could she possibly sentence herself to the very same fate?

But the logical part of her mind was not the part that had dressed in this gown, allowed her hair to be teased into place or her makeup to be applied with such care by her attendants. The logical part of her had nothing to do with the serene bridal vision she saw reflected in her mirror. And the truth was that Tristanne had no idea what she should do—what she *wanted* to do.

Except…that was not the truth, was it?

Tristanne felt something click into place inside of her then, as realization finally dawned, the fog that had invaded her brain seeming, finally, to clear.

A woman who was appropriately appalled by the fact that Nikos had, very clearly, wanted nothing to do with her declaration would have done something about it. She might have left, called off the wedding, or found Nikos to demand that he explain himself. A woman who was not afraid to push the issue would…have pushed. But Tristanne was afraid. She was afraid that if pushed, Nikos would disappear. Hadn't she been afraid of this very thing since the evening he had proposed? So instead, she had allowed herself to be carried along by the age-old rituals of the bride's toilette. She had chosen what she wanted by pretending not to choose.

"You must come and see," Vivienne said then, her thin, breathy voice breaking in to Tristanne's reverie. "Look at this fine sight, Tristanne!"

Tristanne blinked, feeling as if she was waking from some kind of drugged sleep. She turned to find that her mother had moved across the room to peer out of one of the windows that looked out over the villa's sculpted gardens where the civil ceremony was supposed to take place. Tristanne walked over to join her there, feeling the caress of her gown against her legs, the brush of her curls against her shoulders. Her skin felt too sensitive, as if Nikos was in front of her, that half smile on his dark face and molten gold in his eyes. Her body knew what it wanted. What it always wanted and, she feared, always would. No matter what.

She stood at her mother's side and looked down into the sun-kissed garden. Guests were already taking their seats in the rows of chairs set to face the gleaming blue sea. White flowers flowed from baskets, and birds sang from above. It was a beautiful scene—as if ripped from the pages of some glossy wedding magazine and brought to life.

All that was missing was the groom.

"No, I am sure he will come," Tristanne said at first, when the appointed time had come and gone. The guests' murmurs had turned to open, speculative conversation that Tristanne could hear all too well from the windows above.

But he did not come. Fifteen minutes became thirty. Then forty-five minutes, then an hour, and still Nikos did not appear.

"He would not do this," Tristanne said, her voice wooden. She had said it several times already—to her mother's drawn and anxious face, to her increasingly furious brother—both before and after the necessary announcement had been made to the assembled guests.

She had shut herself down. Her stomach might heave, her head might spin, and she might be fighting back tears that seemed to come from her very soul—tears she was afraid to give into because she did not think she would ever stop—but she would not show it. *She could not show it!*

"Would he not?" Peter spat this time, whirling to face her. "He has no doubt lived for this moment for the past ten years!"

"You do not know what you're talking about," Tristanne said, automatically jumping to Nikos's defense, even as she heard the desperate edge in her voice. How could this be happening? How could he have done this?

Please... she cried inside her mind. But she remembered that bitter undercurrent to his words. That bleak look in his eyes.

"It had to be Nikos Katrakis, didn't it?" Peter sneered. His pacing had rendered him red-faced and slightly shiny, and his cold eyes slammed into her. Ordinarily she would heed these warning signs and try to maintain a safe distance from Peter's rage—but she could not seem to move from the chair she had sunk into when the clock had struck an hour past the time she had been meant to walk down the aisle. She could only stare at him, willing herself not to break down.

Not in front of Peter. She had never broken down in front of Peter. Not even when he used his hands.

"I don't know what you mean," she said, with admirable calm. From a distance, she thought, she might even look calm, while inside she thought she might already have died.

"You had to pick out the one man alive who could make our situation worse! We will be the laughingstock of Europe!"

Peter hissed. "I knew this would happen—I *told* you this would happen! You selfish, irresponsible—"

"That's rich, coming from you," Tristanne heard herself saying, with fight and spirit that felt completely foreign to her. As if she cared about Peter, or, perhaps, it was that she no longer cared at all, about anything. "I am not the one who lost the family fortune."

She heard her mother gasp in horror, but she could not tend to Vivienne just then. She could not even tend to herself. She could only sit there, her hands clenched in her lap, her dress stiff and uncomfortable all around her, trying to make sense of what was happening. *What could not be happening.* What was, it became clear with every passing second, really and truly happening after all.

He would not do this! something inside of her howled. Not after she had told him everything. Not after all that had passed between them. She thought of that archway in Florence—the way that he had held her then. The fierce, consuming way he had made love to her. So raw, so desperate. How could none of that be real?

Peter laughed, unpleasantly. "I hope you enjoyed your low-class love affair while it lasted, Tristanne. I hope it was worth the humiliation we will now face in front of the entire world! Our father must be turning over in his grave!"

"Something must have happened to him," Tristanne said, but even she could not believe it at this point. Two hours and thirty-six minutes, and Nikos was not here. He was not coming. *He was not coming.* Though, in truth, she was still hoping. That he had been in a car accident, perhaps. His broken body in a hospital bed, and wouldn't they all be so ashamed of their revolting speculation—

But then there was a commotion near the door, and one of his servants stood there, looking embarrassed. And she knew before he said a single word.

"I am so sorry, miss," he said, not making eye contact,

wringing his hands in front of him. "But Mr. Katrakis left this morning. He took the helicopter into Athens, and he has no plans to return."

Tristanne got up then. It was that or simply collapse into herself. She launched herself to her feet, and moved away from the chair, looking desperately around the stark, white room as if something in it might calm her, or make this nightmare better somehow. *He has no plans to return.*

"What a surprise," Peter snapped, advancing on her. His face was screwed up with rage, and that black hatred that had always emanated from him in waves. "He remembered that he is a Katrakis and you are a Barbery! Of course he could not marry you! Of course he chose instead to humiliate you! I should have expected this from the start!"

"I have no idea what you're talking about," she told Peter, through lips that felt numb. She wanted to scream, to run, to hide…but where on earth could she possibly go? Her old life in Vancouver? How could it possibly fit her now? How could she ever pretend she had not felt what she had felt, nor loved as she still loved, even now, in the darkest of moments? It was choking her. Killing her. And she had the strangest feeling that even should she survive the horror of this moment, what she felt would not diminish at all. She knew it in the exact same, bone-deep way that she had known that Nikos Katrakis would ruin her. *She knew it.*

"Did you think he wanted *you*, Tristanne?" Peter hissed. "Did you imagine he was sufficiently enamored of your charms? The only thing you had that Katrakis wanted was your name."

"My name?" She felt as thick, as stupid, as Peter had always told her she was. "Why would he care about my name?"

"Because he loathes us all," Peter threw at her. "He swore he would have his revenge on us ten years ago, and congratulations, Tristanne—you have handed it to him on a silver platter!"

"Peter, please," Vivienne murmured then. "This is not the time!"

But Tristanne was watching her brother's expression, and a prickle of something cold washed over her.

"What did you do?" she asked. Her fists clenched, as if she wanted to protect Nikos from Peter—but no, that could not be what she felt. She wanted to make sense of what was happening, that was all. There had to be a reason he had abandoned her—there had to be! "What did you do to him?"

"Katrakis is nothing but trash," Peter snapped. "Ten years ago he had ideas above his station. He got in over his head in a business deal, and could not handle himself. He lost some money, made some threats." He shrugged. "I was astounded he ever made anything of himself. I expected him to disappear back into the slime from which he came."

"Then let me ask you another way," Tristanne said coldly, Nikos's words spinning through her head, their whole history flashing past her as if on a cinema screen. "What does he think that you did?"

"I believe he blames me for any number of things," Peter said dismissively. "He had a rather emotional sister, I believe, who fancied herself in love and then claimed she was pregnant." He scoffed, and made a face. "He blamed me when she overdosed on sleeping pills, but his own mother was a known drug user. I rather think blood tells, in the end." His lip curled. "Look at yours."

Vivienne made a soft sound, and something ignited inside of Tristanne. She waited to feel the usual wave of shame, of anger, that someone who should love her should find her so disgusting, so worthless. But it never came. All she could think was that this was how her brother chose to speak to her just after she had been left at the altar. This was how he chose to behave. And the worst part was that it was in no way a departure from his usual behavior. He had treated her this way for years—and she had allowed it, because better her than her mother. But why would he stop, now that Gustave was gone? Soon, she had no doubt, he would turn it on her mother directly, and she could not have that.

She had not gone through this, all of this, to watch Peter destroy Vivienne as she knew he wished to do—as he had already tried to do. She did not know how she would survive the next moment, or the next breath, with the vast, impossible pain that ate her from the inside out. She wondered who she was now that it was over, now that Nikos had left her, and how she might ever put the pieces of herself back together. She had no idea what might become of her.

But she was still standing, and maybe that was all that mattered. For as long as she could stand, she could protect her mother. Which was why she was here in the first place.

"You are a monster," she said softly, but distinctly, to Peter. "I do not think there is a shred of humanity within you. Not one shred."

Peter moved closer, his face set into a scowl. Yet Tristanne did not step away. Or shrink back. After all, what could he do to her that Nikos had not already done? Threaten her? Bruise her? Why should she care? The worst had already happened. She was a fool in the eyes of the world, and worse, she was in love with the man who had abandoned her. She had no idea how she would ever get past this. She had no idea where she would start. How could Peter possibly compete?

"You had better watch yourself, *sister*," he hissed, his voice menacing.

It was the word *sister* that rang in her, then. That ricocheted inside of her and made her realize that he had never honored that term, not even when they were children. At least her father, for all that he had been cold and dismissive, had performed his fatherly duties. He had fed her, clothed her, paid for her schooling until he no longer felt he could support her choices. And perhaps Nikos had been right to make her question the appropriateness of those choices. It had hurt her at the time that Gustave could not be more supportive of her—but then, that was not at all who Gustave Barbery had been. He might not have been the best father she could have hoped for, but at least he had been a father.

What had Peter ever done? Tristanne, who had never asked him for anything, had asked him for access to her trust fund a few years early and what was his response? To whore her out at his command, for his purposes. And now, in the worst moment of her life, abandoned at the altar on her wedding day—still wearing her wedding dress—he behaved liked this. If she could have felt something beyond the agony of Nikos's betrayal, she might have felt sick.

"I am not your sister," she told him, feeling more free in that moment than ever before. "I don't know why I ever cared to honor the relationship when you, clearly, do not. Consider it ended."

"How dare you—" he began.

She turned her back on him, and looked wildly around, her gaze landing on her mother. Beautiful, vibrant Vivienne, so diminished now. So delicate. She was the only family Tristanne had ever had. The only thing worth protecting. And she was worth this, Tristanne told herself fiercely. Her mother was worth any price, no matter how heavy.

"Mother," she said, her voice rough enough to be a stranger's. But then, she felt like a stranger to herself, almost as if she inhabited someone else's body. A body Nikos would never love again, never taste again; a body that would never melt into his—she shook the thoughts away, and bit back the sob that threatened to spill out. "I must change out of these clothes, and then we are leaving this place."

"Where will we go?" Vivienne asked, like a child, her voice soft. Weak. It only hardened Tristanne's resolve.

"You will go directly to Salzburg," Peter ground out behind

her. "Or I will cut you both out like the parasites you are. Do you hear me?"

"Do what you must," Tristanne said offhandedly—only to gasp when he reached over and grabbed her arm, hauling her toward him as he had many times before, his fingers digging into the flesh of her arm.

"Where do you think you're going?" he demanded. "Your pathetic life in Canada? You are useless and *she* makes you look industrious! Do you imagine you can *both* work on your backs?"

Tristanne heard Vivienne's shocked exclamation, but she focused on Peter's hard, cold eyes, and let all of her pain and rage build inside of her.

"I doubt my imagination is half so vivid as yours," she spat at him. She jerked her arm out of his grasp, shoving back from him with a force that surprised them both. He was stronger than her—and a true bully—but he did not expect her to push back. He dropped his hand. She moved around him, heading for the dressing room door.

"This is all very impressive, but we both know you'll come crawling back to me within the month," he snarled. "Don't think I will be as generous with you as I was this time."

"Believe me," she threw over her shoulder, her sarcasm practically burning her tongue. "I am well aware of the limits of your generosity."

He laughed at her. "And what exactly do you think will become of you, Tristanne?" he taunted her.

She looked back then. For the last time. She knew in that moment that she would never see Peter again. And in the midst of all the rest of the pain, the horror, that she was not certain she would ever sort out, it ignited one small flare of hope.

"I will survive," she told him, and she knew, somehow, that she would. "No thanks to you."

All she had to do was keep standing.

CHAPTER SIXTEEN

NIKOS sat in his favorite small bar in Athens, drinking the most expensive liquor available, and told himself he was celebrating.

He had been celebrating in this manner for weeks now. He had so much to celebrate, after all. He should be overjoyed. The pictures of his aborted, abandoned wedding were in all the papers, the humiliation for the Barberys as extreme as he'd anticipated. He had it on excellent authority that Peter Barbery's investors had abandoned him, and the Barbery fortunes were in free fall. Peter was expected to declare bankruptcy before the year was out, whether he had faced this truth or not.

At first, Nikos told himself that the odd feeling that claimed him was no more than the usual letdown after a particularly long campaign. One should expect to feel the absence of focus after living with such a specific goal for so long. It was natural—logical, even. And that was all that it was. There could be no other explanation.

So he told himself while he closed other deals, racing through them like a madman. A chain of hotels in the Far East. A thoroughbred race horse considered highly likely to win the Triple Crown. A boutique inn on the French Riviera that catered to a very elite, very private few. All deals that should have made him feel that his position—his global dominance—was cemented. Unassailable and assured. All deals that would have had him truly celebrating not so long ago. With the prettiest women, the most expensive wine, in the most glamorous places he could find.

Instead he found himself on the same bar stool in this same hidden-away bar that he had once worked in, in another lifetime, bussing tables for the actors and actresses who frequented the place. Tonight he swirled a fine whiskey in his glass and stared at nothing, unable to avoid the truth any further.

He had achieved his ultimate revenge—made all of his dreams come true—and he simply did not care. He had stood at his father's grave, laid flowers for Althea and her lost child and he had not felt a thing. *What a pointless exercise*, he had thought, staring down at a stone marker that commemorated the man who had never cared overmuch for him, the girl who had hated him and the baby who had never had a chance. He had become the man his father would be proud of, finally. He knew this was true the moment he realized he simply could not bring himself to care about the family name he had taken all this time to avenge. It was as if he had turned to stone himself.

He motioned the bartender toward his glass, and stared down at the amber liquid. That emptiness had been the first feeling, and he had denied it, but he had never expected what came behind it. He had never imagined that he, Nikos Katrakis, could *hurt*.

Because he knew that was the only word to describe the agony in his chest, the heat of it, the impossible weight of all that he had lost. He was not ill, as he had first assumed. He simply ached. He could not sleep. He was irritable by day and his head was a vivid mess—and she was the only thing he saw. He imagined what she must have done that day, how she must have felt. He imagined how she had received the news, and how soon she had accepted what, he knew, she could not have wanted to believe could be true. How long had it taken? What had she felt? He tortured himself with images of her tears—or, worse, her bravery. Then, even more insidious, he imagined different endings to the same day. What if he had not left her there? What if he had chosen to marry her despite everything? What if he could lay beside her tonight, smelling the sweet scent of her hair, the faint musk of her skin?

What if he had let himself believe her when she'd claimed to love him?

Nikos growled under his breath, cursing himself in every language he knew. Now that he had done what he set out to do, he could not see how it had consumed him for so long. What had he won? What had he achieved? Why did it all feel like so much wasted breath and misery, for absolutely no reason?

How could he have prized a loyalty to people who had disdained him over what he should have owed to Tristanne—the only person in all his life who had looked at him with joy in her eyes, however briefly? She had told him that she loved him, and he had responded by abandoning her at the altar. He was no better than an animal. He was exactly the kind of scum he had spent his life attempting to distance himself from. He, who had always vowed that he would never be Peter Barbery, had become something far worse. At least Peter had ended things with Althea himself—he had not allowed his absence to speak for him.

What kind of man was he, that he could have done what he had done?

"She is not worth it, my friend," the bartender said, shaking Nikos out of his brooding contemplation of his whiskey.

Nikos focused on him, surprised that the man dared to speak to him after weeks of careful silence.

"Is she not?" he asked lightly. "How do you know?"

"She never is," the man said. He shrugged. "What do they

say? You can't live with them and you can't live without them, yes? It is always the same old story."

He moved down the bar to answer another patron's demands, but Nikos felt frozen into place. It was as if a light had gone off inside of him, and he finally, finally understood.

He was not a man who wallowed—nor one who ever backed down from a challenge, even if the challenge was of his own making. He had more money than he could ever spend. He had homes in every city that had ever caught his eye. He had come from nothing, and now he had everything. And none of it meant anything to him without Tristanne. He could not live without her scowl, her defiant chin, her thoughtful brown eyes. He did not *want* to live without her, no matter what her last name was, no matter who her family were, no matter what.

He could not feel this way. It could not continue. He could not live without her. It was as simple as that.

Everything else was negotiable.

Tristanne was not surprised, necessarily, when the sleek black car pulled to a stop beside her as she walked back along the avenue toward the little house she and Vivienne had rented when they'd first arrived back in Vancouver. She was not *surprised* when Nikos unfolded himself from the back of the car, his long, hard frame as lethally graceful as she remembered.

But that did not mean she was happy about it, either— to look up from her life and see him. To feel him steal all the light from the world and the breath from her body. She stopped dead in her tracks, a carrier bag swinging from her arm, and stared.

He had commanded all the light in the sunlit glory of the Mediterranean; on a street in a Vancouver neighborhood, gray with the start of the fall rains, he was magnificent—like a supernova, for all that he was dressed in black. Dark black sweater, charcoal-colored trousers and that sleek black hair that very nearly tousled at the ends. Tristanne ignored the wild tumult of her heart, her nerves, her stomach as he moved toward her. He looked graver than she remembered—more grim. No hint of that half smile on his full lips, no gleam at all in his tea-steeped eyes.

She told herself she was glad. That it made him a stranger to her. And there was no need at all for her to talk to a stranger.

"I imagine you hate me," he said, coming to a stop in front of her.

For a moment she could only blink. Then Tristanne felt a wave of something deep and messy wash over her, through her. Rage? Grief? She could not distinguish between the two.

"No preamble?" she threw at him. "No greeting, even? Do I deserve so little from you, Nikos? Not even the sort of courtesy you would extend to a stranger?"

She started moving then, jerky and rough, but she could not stay there. She could not look at him. She needed to barricade herself in her new bedroom, cry into her pillow and tell herself that she did not still yearn for a man who could treat her like this. *She could not.*

"Did you mean what you said?" he asked. He kept pace with her with no apparent effort, which made her even more furious.

"We said a great many things, you and I," she muttered, scowling at the ground. "One of us meant what was said and the other was nothing but a very practiced liar—so you will have to be more specific."

She could not seem to keep her composure any longer. She had cried more in the past weeks than she had in the previous long years of her life. She hardly recognized herself anymore. She was what he had made her—this smashed, ruined, broken thing.

"You are crying," he said, as if he was horrified. She stopped walking and whirled on him, wishing she was stronger, bigger. Wishing she could make him feel what she felt. Wishing she could hurt him.

"I do that often," she snapped. "Congratulations, Nikos. You undid almost thirty years of self-control in one day."

"And yet this is the man you claimed to love," he said, his voice darker and rougher than she remembered. Almost as if he hurt, too, though she knew that must be impossible. "This monster, who would do this terrible, unforgivable thing!"

"I know what you did," she gritted out. "You did it to me. But why are you here? What could you possibly want?" She laughed then, the kind of laugh that was torn from inside of her, hollow and broken. "I have to tell you, Nikos—I do not think there is anything left."

"I am not a man worth loving," he told her. "You were a fool to say such a thing to me, to admit to such a weakness. You should count yourself lucky that I did not believe you— that I did not hold you to such an insane pledge."

She opened her mouth to scream at him, to demand he leave her before she broke into even tinier fragments, but something stopped her. His eyes were too dark. His mouth was too hard. If he was another man, she would have said he looked almost…desperate.

"Is that why you came all the way to Vancouver?" she asked him, her voice uneven. "To explain to me why I should not have fallen in love with you?"

"There is nothing in me worth loving," he said, his gaze intent. "You need only look at my history. My mother. My father. My sister. All these people abandoned me, hated me. All of them. One family member, perhaps, could be excused away as an anomaly, but all of them? One must look to the common denominator, Tristanne. One must be logical."

"Logical," she managed to say. She shook her head, as if

that could make what he said make sense. "You think this is logical? You truly do, don't you?"

She searched his face, that dark face she had never thought she'd see again, though in the dark of night, when she could no longer hide painful truths from herself, she'd *hoped*. She saw the truth in it—that he believed what he said. That he had not believed her when she'd said she loved him. That he did not—could not—know what love was. It made her ache. For him, in ways she knew she should not.

"It is as if you have some hold on me," he said, his voice almost accusing. "I spent years dreaming of revenge, and now I dream only of you. I destroy everyone I touch." He shook his head. "I am a curse."

Hadn't she said the same thing herself? Hadn't she screamed it into her pillow to muffle the noise, so as not to disturb her mother? So why, now, did she feel herself frowning up at him, as if she wished to contradict him? As if she wanted to argue with him—make him treat himself better than he had ever treated her?

What was the matter with her?

She looked around as if she might find help, or answers, on the sidewalk. But the day was chilly and wet. Everything was gray, except for Nikos, and that hard look in his eyes that made her want to cry and not, for once, for herself.

She could not pretend to herself—when he stood in front of her, when he was within reach, when her palms itched to touch him and her body ached to press against him—that her feelings had changed at all. She wanted it all to have disappeared, or for the anger and betrayal to have bleached away what she'd felt for him.

"I can't blame you for hating me," he said quietly. He shoved his hands into the pockets of his trousers, and she had the distinct impression that he was uncomfortable. He, who had never seemed to show the slightest bit of uneasiness. It sent an arrow spearing through her, piercing through her anger, making it wither away, leaving the maelstrom beneath.

"I want to hate you," she said, with more honesty than he deserved. "But I don't."

"You should," he bit out. "If you had any sense of self-preservation at all, you would."

"You are the expert," she retorted. "Aren't you? Hate, revenge, deceit. I believe that is your forte, not mine. I merely wanted to marry you. More fool, me."

"I do not care about revenge!" he burst out. "I wish I had never heard the word!"

"How can that be true?" she asked, dashing the wetness from her eyes with the backs of her hand. "Peter told me. What he did to you. To your family. To your sister—"

"My sister took her own life, with her own hand. Nothing Peter did can match what I did to you," Nikos said, in that low, painful voice. "I promise you."

"You promise me," she echoed. She laughed again, another hollow sound. "Please, Nikos. Do not make me any more promises. I do not think I can survive them!"

He looked at her for a long moment, those dark eyes seeing into her, through her. Seeing far more than they should.

"I cannot pretend I did not deceive you, because I did. I do not deserve you, Tristanne, but…" His eyes when they met hers were so dark. Tortured. His hands reached out, but did not touch her. "Please believe me," he whispered. "I cannot let you go."

She felt the truth of things well up in her, then, despite everything. She felt that fierce, uncompromising love for him soar through her, making her feel both impossibly dizzy and firmly grounded at the same time. It moved through her like the blood in her veins. Like the air in her lungs. An irrevocable biological necessity without which she could not walk, talk, *live*. And so she knew why she could not run away. Why she could not bring herself to leave him here on the street, as she should. Why she would not abandon him, even when he all but told her to do so.

My dragon, she thought, and it felt like a promise. A vow.

She could not remember who she had been before him, or who she had tried to be during these past weeks. She could not imagine a future without him in it. She had…simply kept standing, because there was nothing else to do. But now that he was here, she could feel the difference singing through her, lighting her up from within, even though it hurt—even though none of this was easy, and all of it was far more painful than she could ever have imagined she could bear.

"Tristanne," he said, as if her name was a plea. His eyes were agonized, as dark and stormy as she felt. "I tried to let you go, but I cannot do it."

She reached over and took his hand, exulting in the feeling of his skin against hers, the heat of him, the sense of *rightness* that flooded through her. What else could she do? She had already lost everything, and survived it. He had already done his worst. And even so, she loved him. She could not hide from that inconvenient truth. It might not be wise. It might not make sense. But the inescapable truth of it felt like heat, like dragonfire, and burned its way through her, marking her forever. As his.

"Then do not let me go," she said over the lump in her throat, looking at him with all she felt bright and hot in her gaze. Because she had already chosen, long ago, to be brave if she could not be safe. She had already decided. "If you dare."

CHAPTER SEVENTEEN

"WHAT am I to do with you?" he asked her much later, his voice rough. He sat next to her in the luxurious depths of his private jet's leather seats. Far below them, North America was spread out like a patchwork quilt, and above them was nothing but blue sky and sun. He reached over and pulled a blonde wave into his hand, wrapping it around one finger. He tugged on it slightly.

"Marry me, apparently," she said. She did not shiver away from his dark golden gaze. She leaned closer. She had wanted him when she was just a girl. She had chosen him on his yacht, so long ago now. Then in the villa. And again, just yesterday, on a street in Vancouver. She had chosen *him*. "That is why we are flying across the world, isn't it?"

"And what makes you think you can handle such a thing?" he asked, searching her face with a deep frown marring his. "I warn you, Tristanne, I do not improve upon a longer acquaintance. Familiarity breeds—"

"Contempt?" she finished for him. She wanted to kiss him, though she did not dare, not when he was in so dark a mood. "Surely not. You are Nikos Katrakis. Who alive could be more fascinating?"

"I am not joking." His voice was stark, and she understood, suddenly, that he was terrified. This strong, harsh, ruthless man. She had this power over him. She reached over and put a hand on his muscled thigh.

You must love who you love, Vivienne had said with a shrug when Tristanne had haltingly explained that, indeed, she planned to marry Nikos after all, despite everything. *And it is only cowards who do not follow their hearts, Tristanne. Remember that.*

"I am not from your world, much as I pretend to be," Nikos said, almost more to himself than to Tristanne. He drummed his fingers against the polished armrest. "People enjoy my money, my power, but do not mistake it—they never forget where I came from."

"Nor should they," she shot back at once. His head snapped around in surprise. "You say that as if it is something shameful. There is no shame in your past, Nikos. You overcame near-insurmountable obstacles, and you did it with absolutely no help from anyone. Not even your own father." She shook her head. "You should be proud."

"You do not understand," he began.

"And who, may I ask, finds it so impossible to overlook your origins?" she asked, cutting him off. "People like my brother? Pampered and spoiled, handed vast fortunes made by others? Why should you care what they think?"

He stared at her then, his gaze hotter and more flinty than she had ever seen it. There was no hint of gold there, only dark like the night. Possessive. Implacable. A deep fire that she knew, low in her bones, was for her alone.

"You cannot take it back," he told her, his voice flat. If she did not know him better, she might have thought him unemotional. "If you marry me, Tristanne, that is the end of it."

"As usual," she said, slipping her arm through his and tilting her head back to look at him, so strong and grim against the bright light all around them, flooding into the cabin, "you have it all wrong. This is only the beginning."

And then, finally, she leaned over and pressed her mouth to his.

He knew the moment she woke.

He turned away from the full moon that shone above the dark sea, and watched as the light skimmed into the room and illuminated her. *His wife.*

He had married her in a private ceremony in the very spot he had abandoned her before; the symmetry healing, somehow. And now she was his, forever.

Nikos could not seem to get his head around the concept.

"What are you doing?" she asked, her voice a mere thread of sound. He moved across the moonlit room to the bed, and lowered himself down to sit beside her. He wanted to take her into his arms again, to lose himself in her body as he had done so many times before—as he had done this very night—but there were too many questions swirling around them and he could not ignore them any longer.

Though part of him wanted to ignore them forever.

"I do not understand," he said quietly.

Next to him, she sat up, pulling the coverlet with her to drape it around her naked shoulders. Her hair tumbled wild and free around her, emphasizing the delicate arch of her collarbone, the creamy softness of her skin. She was exquisite. And she was *his*. She had chosen him, after everything.

"What is there to understand?" she asked, that warm humor lacing her tone, making him nearly forget himself. "It is the middle of the night. Surely understanding can wait until dawn."

"Why would you do this?" he asked, the question ripped from him as if by unseen hands. He did not want to know the answer. Yet he had to know. "After all that I did to you? Why would you not run as fast and as far as you could?"

Her eyes seemed to melt in the darkness, and she reached over to run her fingers along his shoulder, then down to his bicep before dropping her hand back to the bed.

"You already know why."

"Love," he said, harshly. Almost angrily. "Is that what you mean? Love does not exist, Tristanne. It is a lie people tell themselves. A way to hide, to make excuses."

"Here, now, it is real," she said softly, leaning toward him to press her lips against his shoulder. "It is not conditional. You have nothing to prove. It is a fact."

He felt disarmed by that. His heart beat too fast. He felt drunk when he knew he had not touched any spirits in hours. He could not bring himself to look at her, to see whatever lurked in her expression then. Or, perhaps, he was afraid to let her see what was in his own.

"Tomorrow we will leave for our honeymoon," he said instead, his voice too loud in the dark. "The Maldives. Fiji. Whatever you prefer."

"We are already on an island, Nikos," she said in a dry voice, the one that made his heart feel lighter in his chest. "Must we travel great distances to find ourselves on a different one?"

"It is what people do. Or so I am informed."

"Must we worry about what people do?" she asked. "Or shall we worry instead about what we will do?"

He shook his head, unable to answer. Responding to an urge he could not make any sense of, yet could not deny, he slid from the bed and found himself on his knees before her. He ran his palms along her warm thighs, and then gazed up at her. She was heat, warmth. She had melted away all of his defenses.

"I love you," she said. Her tough chin tilted into the air, daring him to argue with her. Daring him not to love her, just as she had dared him not to leave her. She was the bravest woman he had ever known.

"I do not know what love is," he said, the words coming to him as if in a new language. He picked through them carefully. "No one has ever loved me, I do not think. All those who should have—whose obligation it might have been—abandoned me. Hated me."

"I know," she whispered. Her full mouth trembled—for him. She reached for him, ran her fingers through his hair.

"You are the only person who has ever known the truth about me," he managed to say, from that darkness inside of him that he had denied for so long, and that new, strange wellspring of hope that had appeared with her on a Canadian street, so shining and bright and impossible. "The only one who has seen the worst of me, and stayed with me anyway."

She made a soft noise of distress, and then leaned forward to press a kiss against his brow, his cheek.

"I love you," she said simply. "Your darkness as well as your light. How could I do anything but marry you?"

"I told you that you should hate me," he said. "I meant it."

"But it is too late," she whispered. "I have been in love with you since I met you. Perhaps even before. I am the incapable of hating you, I think, despite your best efforts."

"Tristanne…" But he did not know what he could say, except the prayer of hope that was her name. It was like a song in him. He felt that cracking inside of him again, as if he had been buried deep in ice but the long, bitter winter in him had finally ended. And he was starting, at last, to thaw.

"I do not know what love is, or how to go about it," he whispered, looking into the chocolate-colored eyes that were all the world to him now. All that mattered. "But I will spend my life trying to love you as you deserve, Tristanne. I swear it.

Even if you have to teach me, even if it is remedial, I promise I will learn."

She smiled then, a real smile, bright and true. He felt something in him ease, even as he began to burn for her anew. Again. Always.

"I think I can meet that challenge," she said, that strong, sure love in her gaze, changing him as she looked at him. "But first things first, Nikos."

He remembered his own words, long ago, and found himself smiling.

"First things first?" he echoed.

"Why don't you greet me properly?" she dared him. "I am your wife."

"Indeed you are," he said in a low voice. "And I am your husband."

"And this is the first night of our married life. Of the future."

"Our future," he said, and part of him dared to believe in it.

She opened her arms wide, offering him everything he'd ever wanted, and long since ceased hoping for, until she burned her way into his life. Home. Family. Love.

For her, he would dare. For her.

"Then come here," she whispered, her eyes full. "We have a lot of ground to cover."

Princess From the Past

CAITLIN CREWS

This one is for Jeff.

CHAPTER ONE

BETHANY Vassal did not have to turn around. She knew exactly who had just entered the exclusive art-gallery in Toronto's glamorous Yorkville neighborhood. Even if she had not heard the increased buzz from the well-clad, cocktail-sipping crowd, or felt the sudden spike in energy roll through the long, bright space like an earthquake, she would have known. Her body knew and reacted immediately. The back of her neck prickled in warning. Her stomach tensed. Her muscles clenched tight in automatic response. She stopped pretending to gaze at the bold colors and twisted shapes of the painting before her and let her eyes drift closed to ward off the memories. And the pain—so much pain.

He was here. After all this time, after all her agonizing, planning and years of isolation, he was in the same room. She told herself she was ready.

She had to be.

Bethany turned slowly. She had deliberately situated herself in the furthest corner of the upscale gallery so she could see down the gleaming wood and white corridor to the door, so she could prepare herself when he arrived. But the truth, she was forced to admit to herself as she finally twisted all the way around to face the inevitable commotion near the great glass doors, was that there was really no way to prepare. Not for Prince Leopoldo Di Marco.

Her husband.

Soon to be ex-husband, she told herself fiercely. If she told herself the same thing long enough, it had to become true, didn't it? It had nearly killed her to leave him three years ago, but this was different. She was different.

She had been so broken when she'd met him—still reeling from the death of the bed-ridden father she'd cared for through his last years; still spinning wildly in the knowledge that suddenly, at twenty-three, she could have any life she wanted instead of being a sick man's care-giver. Except she hadn't known what to want. The only world she'd ever known had been so small. She had been grieving—and then there had been Leo, like a sudden bright sunrise after years of rain.

She'd believed he was perfect, the perfect prince out of a story book. And she'd believed that with him she was some kind of fairy-tale princess who could escape into the perfect dream come true. Bethany's mouth twisted. She'd certainly learned better, hadn't she? He'd smashed that belief into pieces by abandoning her in every way that mattered once they'd reached his home in Italy. By shutting her out, leaving her more alone than she had ever been before, overwhelmed and lonely half a world away from all she'd ever known.

And then he'd decided he wanted to bring a child into all of that despair. It had been impossible, the final straw. Bethany's hands clenched at her sides as if she could strike out at her memories. She forced herself to take a deep breath. Anger would not help her now— only focus. She had very specific goals tonight. She wanted her freedom, and she could not allow herself to get sidetracked by the past.

Then she looked up and saw him. The world seemed to contract and then expand around her. Time seemed to stop—or perhaps that was simply her ability to draw breath.

He strode through the gallery, flanked by two stone-faced members of his security detail. He was, as he had always been, a heartbreaking study of dark-haired, gleaming-eyed Italian male beauty. He wore, with nonchalant ease, an elegantly tailored dark suit that somehow made him seem even more ruggedly handsome than he naturally was. It clung to his broad shoulders and showcased his mouth-watering physique.

But Bethany could not allow herself to focus on his physicality; it was too dangerous. She had forgotten, somehow, that he was so…vivid. Her memory had made him smaller, duller. It had muted the sheer force of him, making her forget how commanding he was, how his uncompromising masculinity and irrefutable power seemed to radiate from him, making everyone in his vicinity both step back and stare.

It also made her profoundly sad. She swallowed and tried to shake the melancholy away. It could not possibly help her here.

His long, tall, exquisitely hewn body, was all rangy muscle and sensual male grace, moving through the crowd with a kind of liquid ease. His cheekbones were high and pronounced—noticeable from across a large room. He carried himself as if he were a king or a god. His mouth, even in its current flat, disapproving line, hinted at the shattering sensuality she knew far too well he could and would use as his most devastating weapon against her. His rich, thick, dark-brown hair was cut to suit perfectly the ruthless, focused magnate she knew him to be—whatever else he might be.

Everything he wore, even the way he held himself, broadcasted his wealth, his power, and that dark, sexual magnetism that was uniquely his. It was as much a part of him as his olive skin, his corded muscles and his earthy, woodsy scent—which she must be remembering, she told herself, frowning, for she was certainly not close enough to him to smell his skin. Nor would she be ever again, she vowed.

For he was no fairy tale prince, as she had once so innocently imagined. Bethany had to bite back a hollow laugh. There were no swelling, happy songs, no happily-ever-afters—not with Leo Di Marco, *Principe di Felici*. Bethany had learned that the hardest, most painful way possible. His was an ancient and revered title, with ancient responsibilities and immutable duties, and Leo was its steward. First, foremost, always, he was the title.

She watched his dark eyes flick through the crowd with ruthless impatience. He looked annoyed. Already. She sucked in a shaky breath. Then, inevitably, he found her. She felt the kick of his gaze like a punch to her gut and had to breathe through the sudden light-headedness. She had wanted this, she reminded herself. She had to see this through now, finally, or she did not know what might become of her.

Bethany had to force herself to stand up straight, to simply wait there as he bore down on her. She crossed her arms, held on tight to her elbows and tried to look unmoved by his approach even as she quaked with that inevitable, unfair reaction to his presence that had always ruined her attempts to stand up to him before. Meanwhile memories she refused to delve into haunted her still, flickering across her mind too quickly, leaving the same old scars behind.

Leo dismissed his bodyguards with the barest flick of a finger, his dark gaze fused to hers, his long legs eating up the distance between them. He looked overpowering and overwhelming, as he always had, as he always would—as if he alone could block out the rest of the world. Worst of all, she knew he could. And would. And did.

Bethany's throat was too dry. She had the overwhelming urge to turn away, to run, but she knew he would only follow. More than that, it would defeat her purpose. She had chosen this particular meeting-place deliberately: a bright and crowded art-opening filled with the sort of people who would recognize a man of Leo's stature at a glance. Protection, she had thought, as much from Leo's inevitable fury as from her own ungovernable response to this man.

This would not be like the last time. He had been so angry and she had foolishly thought that maybe they might work something out—if he'd actually spoken to her for once, instead of putting her off. Three years had passed since that night, and still, thinking of the things he had said and the way it had all exploded into that devastating, unwanted and uncontainable passion, that still shamed her to remember—

She shoved the memories aside and squared her shoulders.

Then he was right there in front of her, his gaze taut on hers. She could not breathe.

Leo.

Already, after mere seconds, that heady, potent masculinity that was his and his alone pulled her in, tugging at parts of her she'd thought long dead. Already she felt that terrible, familiar yearning swell within her, urging her to move closer, to bury herself in the heat of him, to lose herself in him as she nearly had before.

But she was different now. She'd had to be to survive him. She was no longer the naïve, weak little girl he had handled so carelessly throughout the eighteen harrowing months of their marriage. The girl with no boundaries and no ability to stand up for herself.

She would never be that girl again. She had worked too hard three years ago to leave her behind. To grow into the woman she should have been all along.

Leo merely stared at her, his dark, coffee-colored eyes narrowing slightly, as bitter and black as she remembered. He would have looked indolent, almost bored, were it not for the faintest hint of grim tension in his lean jaw and the sense of carefully leashed power that hummed just beneath his skin.

"Hello, Bethany," he said, his sardonic voice richer, deeper than she'd remembered.

Her name in his cruel mouth felt…intimate. It mocked her with the memories she refused to acknowledge, yet still seemed to affect her breathing, her skin, her heartbeat.

"What game are you playing tonight?" he asked softly, his eyes dark and unreadable, his voice controlled. "I am touched that you thought to include me after all this time."

She could not let him cow her; she could not let him shake her. Bethany knew it was now or never. She clenched her hands tighter around her elbows, digging her fingers deep into her own flesh.

"I want a divorce," she said, tilting back her head to look at him directly.

She had planned and practiced those words for so

long in her mirror, in her head, in every spare moment, that she knew she sounded just as she wished to sound: calm, cool, resolute. There was no hint at all of the turmoil that rolled inside of her.

The words seemed to hang there in the space between their bodies. Bethany kept her gaze trained on Leo's, ignoring the hectic color she could feel scratching at her neck and pretending she was not at all affected by the way he seemed to go very still as he looked at her with narrowed eyes. As if he was gathering himself to pounce. Bethany's heart pounded as if she'd screamed that single sentence loud enough to shatter glass, shred clothing and perhaps even rebound off the top of the iconic CN Tower to deafen the entire city.

It was the man standing much too close to her. Leo was next to her, so close she could nearly feel the waves of heat and arrogance emanate from him. Leo, watching her with those intense, unreadable eyes. It made something deep inside of her flex and coil. Leo was the husband she had once loved so destructively, so desperately, when she did not know enough to love herself. It made her want to weep as that same old sadness washed through her, reminding her of all the ways they had failed each other. But no more. No more.

Her stomach was a tense, clenched ball. Her palms were damp. She had to fight to keep her vision clear, her eyes bland. She had to order herself repeatedly not to heed her body's urgent demand that she wrench her gaze away and flee.

Indifference, she reminded herself. She must show him nothing but indifference, however feigned it might be. Anything but that, and all would be lost. She would be lost.

"It is a great pleasure to see you too," Leo said finally

with an unmistakable edge in his voice. His English had a distinctly British intonation that spoke of his years of education, with the sensual caress of his native Italian beneath. His dark eyes gleamed with cold censure as they flicked over her, taking in the careful chignon that tamed her dark-brown curls, her minimal cosmetics, the severe black suit. She had worn it to convince them both that this was nothing more than a bit of unpleasant business—and because it helped conceal her figure from his appraisal. She was a far cry from the girl he had once memorably brought to climax with no more than his hot, demanding gaze, and still he made her want to squirm. Still, she felt brushfires blaze to life in every place his dark gaze touched her.

She hated what he could do to her even now, after everything. As if three years later her body still had not received the message that they were finished.

Leo continued, his voice dangerously even, his gaze like steel. "I do not know why it should surprise me in the least that a woman who would behave as you have done should greet your husband in such a fashion."

She could not let him see that he rattled her still, when she had thought—prayed—that she'd put all that behind her. But she told herself she could worry about what that might mean later, at her leisure, when she had the years ahead of her to process all the things she felt about this man. When she was free of him.

And she had to be free of him. It was finally time to live her own life on her own terms. It was time to give up that doomed, pathetic hope she was embarrassed to admit she harbored that he would keep his angry promise to come after her and drag her back home if she dared leave him. He had come that one terrible night and then left again, telling her in no uncertain terms of her importance to him. It was three years past time to accord him the same courtesy.

"You will forgive me if I did not think the social niceties had any place here," she said instead as calmly as she could, as if she could not feel that sharp gaze of his leaving marks on her skin. "Given our circumstances."

Bethany had to move then, or explode. She walked toward the next bright, jumbled canvas on the stark-white wall and sensed instead of saw Leo keep pace with her. When she stopped moving, he was beside her once again, close enough that she could almost feel his heat, the corded strength in his arm. Close enough that she was tempted to lean into him.

At least now she could control her destructive impulses, she thought bitterly, even if she could not quite rid herself of those urges as she'd like.

"Our 'circumstances,'" he echoed after a tense, simmering moment, his voice dark and sinful, at odds with the razor's edge beneath. "Is that what you call it? Is that how you rationalize your actions?" A quick sideways glance confirmed that one dark brow was raised, mocking and cruel, matching his tone perfectly. Bethany knew that expression all too well. A chill moved through her.

She was aware of her own pulse drumming wildly in her veins and had to stop herself from fidgeting with the force of will that, three years ago, she had not known she possessed. But it had been forged day by day in the bright fire of his cold indifference. At least she knew it existed now, and that she could use it.

"It does not matter what you wish to call it," she said, fighting to remain cool. She turned toward him and wished at once that she had not. He was too big, too male, too much. "It is obviously time that both of us moved on."

She did not care for the way that Leo watched her then, his eyes hooded, predatory. They reminded her exactly how dangerous this man was and exactly why she had left him in the first place.

"This is why you deigned to contact me tonight?" he asked in a deceptively soft voice that sent a chill spiraling down her spine. "To discuss a divorce?"

"Why else would I contact you?" she asked, wanting her voice to sound careless, light, but hearing all too well that it was tight with anxiety.

"I can think of no other reason, of course," he said, his eyes fixed on her in a way that made her deeply uncomfortable down into her very bones. She set her jaw and refused to look away. "Certainly I knew better than to imagine that you might finally be ready to resume your duties or keep your promises. And yet here I am."

She did not know how long she could keep this up. He was too overwhelming, too impossible. She had been unable to handle him when he had been as lost in the volcanic passion between them as she was. But his anger, his lacerating coldness, was much, much worse. She was not certain she was equal to it. She was not at all sure she could pretend not to be wounded by it.

"I do not want anything from you except this divorce," Bethany forced herself to say.

Her body was staging a civil war. One part wanted to run for the door and disappear into the chilly fall evening. What was truly distressing and shocking was that part of her did not. Part of her instead ached for his hands that she knew could wield such dark sorcery against her flesh. She did not want to think about that. To remember. Touching Leo Di Marco was like leaping head-first into the sun. She would not survive it a second time. She would feel too much, he would feel too little and she would be the one to pay the price. She knew it as well as she knew her own name.

She straightened her shoulders, and made herself look at him directly, as if she were truly brave instead of desperate. Did it really matter which? "I want to be done with this farce, Leo."

"And to what farce, exactly, do you refer?" he asked silkily, thrusting his hands into the pockets of his trousers, his gaze fixed on her face in a way that made her want to fidget. It made her feel scorched from the inside out. "When you ran away from me, from our marriage and our home, and relocated halfway across the globe?"

"That was not a farce," she dared to say. There was no longer anything to lose, and she could not give in to her own desolation. "It was a fact."

"It is a disgrace," he said, his voice deceptively quiet, though she did not mistake the cold ferocity and hard lash of it. "But why speak of such things? You prove with your every breath that you have no interest at all in the shame you bring upon my family, my name."

"Which is why we must divorce," Bethany said, fighting to keep the edge from her voice and failing. "Problem solved."

"Tell me something," he said. With a peremptory jerk of his chin, he dismissed a hovering gallery-worker bearing a tray of champagne flutes then returned his gaze to Bethany's. "Why this particular step? And why now? It has been three years since you abandoned me."

"Since I escaped, you mean," she retorted without thinking, and knew as soon as the words had passed her lips that she had made a grave error.

His dark eyes flared with heat and she felt an answering fire rage through her. It was as potent as the sense of being nothing more to him than prey, but she could not allow herself to look away.

She could not allow him to railroad her into another bargain with the devil made out of desperation and, cruelest of all, that tiny flicker of hope that nothing had ever managed to stamp out—not even his disinterest. She had to be out from under his thumb.

For good.

Prince Leo Di Marco told himself he was coldly, deeply furious. But it was no more than anger, no more than righteous indignation, he assured himself; it went no deeper than that. This woman's uncanny ability to sneak around his lifelong armor and wound him was a thing of the past. It had to be.

He had spent the whole of his day in meetings on Bay Street, Toronto's financial center. There was not a banker or businessman there who dared challenge the ancient Di Marco name—much less the near-limitless funds that went with it. Bethany was the only woman who had ever defied him, who had ever hurt him. The only person that he could remember doing so.

Three years on and she was doing it still. He had to fight himself to maintain his controlled exterior. He could feel the anger that only she inspired in him opening up that great, black cavern within him that he had long preferred to ignore. He knew exactly why she had demanded they meet in a public place—as if he was some kind of wild animal. As if he needed to be contained. Handled. He was not certain why this insult, atop all the others, should bite at him so deeply.

It infuriated him that he was not immune to her fresh-faced beauty that had so captivated and deceived him in the first place. She was still far too much of a temptation. Her angelic blue eyes were such an intriguing contrast to her dark-brown curls, all of it tempered with the faintest spray of freckles across her pert nose. He did not allow himself to concentrate on the delicate fullness of her mouth. It did not seem to matter that he knew her appearance of wide-eyed innocence was nothing more than an act.

It never seemed to matter.

He wanted his hands on her skin, his mouth on her breast. Those tight, ripe nipples against his tongue. He told himself it was all he wanted, all he chose to allow himself to want.

"Escaped?" he queried, icily. "The last I checked, you were living quite comfortably. In a house I own."

"Because you demanded it!" she hissed, that fascinating splash of color rising from her graceful neck toward her soft cheeks. He knew other ways to raise that color upon her delicate skin and very nearly smiled, remembering. She darted a glance around at the crowd which surrounded them, as if for strength, then faced him again. "I wanted nothing to do with that house."

He was a man who commanded empires. He had done so since his father's death when he was only twenty-eight, maintaining his family's ancient wealth while expanding it into the new era. How could this one woman continue to defy him? How was it possible? What weakness in him kept him from simply crushing her beneath his foot?

But he already knew the weakness intimately. It had already ruined him. He felt it in the heaviness in his groin, the edgy need that spiraled through him and demanded he get his hands beneath the heavy black suit he knew she was wearing to hide from him. Because she could never deny what she felt when he touched her, that he knew full well. Whatever else she chose to deny, or he preferred to ignore.

"I am fascinated by your uncharacteristic acquiescence," he said through his teeth, furious with himself and with their entire tangled history, her trail of broken promises. "I recall making any number of demands that you chose to ignore: that you remained in Italy, as tradition required. That you refrained from casting shame on my family's name with your behavior. That you honored your vows."

"I will not fight with you," she told him, her blue eyes flashing and her chin rising. She made a dismissive gesture with one hand, the one that should have worn his ring yet was offensively bare. He clamped down on the surge of temper. "You can choose to revise history however you like, but I am finished arguing about it."

"Then we are in perfect agreement," he bit out, keeping his voice low and for her ears alone despite the fierce kick of his temper—and that hollow place beneath it that he refused to acknowledge. "I have not gained an appreciation for public scenes since we last met, Bethany. If it is your plan to embarrass me further tonight, I suggest you rethink it. I do not think this will end the way you wish it to end."

"There is no need for a scene," she said at once. "Public or otherwise." She shrugged, drawing attention to her delicate neck, and reminding him of the kisses he'd once pressed there and the sweet, addictive taste of her skin. But it was as if that was from another life. "I only want to be divorced from you. Finally."

"Because it has been such a hardship for you to

stay married to me?" he asked, his voice cutting and sarcastic. "How you must struggle."

He was not a man who believed in impassioned displays—particularly in public, where he was forever being held up against the example of his family's long legacy—but this woman had always provoked him like no other. Tonight her eyes were too blue, her mouth set in too firm a line. It clawed at him.

"I understand how it must cut at you," he continued coldly. "To live in such unearned luxury. To have all the benefits of my name and protection with none of the attendant responsibilities."

"You will be pleased to learn that I no longer want them, then," she said. She raised her brows at him in direct challenge, but he was caught by the flash of vulnerability he saw move across her face. Bethany— vulnerable? That was not a word he'd ever use to describe her. Wild. Uncontrollable. Rebellious. But never defenseless, wounded. Never.

Impatiently, Leo shoved the odd turn of thought aside. The last thing in the world he needed now was to become intrigued anew by his wife. He had yet to recover from the initial disaster that had been his first, ruinous fascination with this woman. Look where it had led them both.

"Do you not?" he asked, his voice harsh, directed as much at his errant thoughts as at her. "How can you be certain when you have treated both with such disrespect?"

"I want a divorce," she said again with a quiet strength. "This is the end, Leo. I'm moving on with my life."

"Are you?" he asked, his tone dangerous. She either did not hear it or did not care. "How so?"

"I am moving out of that house," she said at once, a wild fire he could not entirely comprehend raging in her sky-blue eyes. "I hate it. I never wanted to live there in the first place."

"You are my wife." His voice cracked like a whip, though he knew the words had long held no meaning for her, no matter that they still moved through him like blood, like need. "Whether you choose to acknowledge it or not. Just because you have turned your back on the vows you made, does not mean that I have. I told you I would protect you and I meant it, even if it is from your own folly and stubborn recklessness."

"I'm sure you think that makes you some kind of hero," she threw at him in a falsely polite tone that he knew was for the benefit of the crowd around them. Yet he could see the real Bethany burn bright in her eyes and the flush on her neck. "But I never thought anyone was likely to kidnap me in the first place." She let out a short, hollow laugh. "Believe me, I do not advertise our connection."

"And yet it exists." His voice brooked no argument; it could have melted steel. "And because of it, you are a target."

"I won't be for much longer," she said, her foolhardy determination showing in that stubborn set to her jaw and the fire in her eyes. He almost admired it. Almost. "And you'll find that I've never touched any of the money in that account of yours, either. I'm going to walk out of this marriage exactly as I walked into it."

"And where do you intend to go?" he asked quietly, softly, not daring himself to move closer. He knew, somehow, that putting his hands on her would ruin them both and expose too much.

"Not that it's any of your business," she said, her gaze direct and challenging, searing into him. "But I've met someone else."

CHAPTER TWO

THE room seemed to drop away. All Bethany could see was the arrested look in his eyes that narrowed as he gazed at her. He did not move, yet she felt clenched in a kind of tight fist that held only the two of them, and that simmering tension that sparked and surged between them.

Had she really said that? Had she truly dared to say something like that to this man? To her husband?

How much worse would it be, she wondered in a panic, if it was actually true? She found she was holding her breath.

For a long, impossible moment Leo only stared at her, but she could feel the beat of his fury—and her own heart—like a wild drum. He looked almost murderous for a moment—or perhaps she was succumbing to hysteria. Then he shifted, and Bethany could breathe again.

"And who is the lucky man?" Leo asked in a lethally soft voice. When she only stared at him, afraid that her slightest movement might act as a red flag before a bull, his head tilted slightly to the left, though he did not lift his dark eyes from hers. "Your lover?"

Bethany somehow kept herself from shivering. It was the way he'd said that word. It seemed to skate over her skin, dangerous and deadly. She already regretted the lie. She knew she had only said it to hit at him, to hurt him in some small way—to get inside that iron control of his and make him as uncertain and unsettled as she always felt in his presence. To show him that she was deadly serious about divorcing him. Why had she sunk to his level?

But then she remembered who she was dealing with. Leo would say anything—do anything—to get what he wanted. She must be as ruthless as he was; if he had taught her nothing else, he had taught her that.

"We met at university while I finished my degree," she said carefully, searching his hard features for some sign of what might happen next, or some hint of the anger she suspected lurked just out of sight beneath those cold eyes.

She reminded herself that the point was to end this tragedy of a marriage once and for all. Why should she feel as if she should go easy, as if she should protect Leo in some way? When had he ever protected her—from anything?

"He is everything I want in a man," she said boldly. Surely some day she would meet someone who fit that bill? Surely she deserved that much? "He is considerate. Communicative. As interested in my life as in his own."

Unlike Leo, who had abandoned his young wife entirely the moment they'd reached Italy, claiming his business concerns were far more pressing. Unlike Leo, who had closed himself off completely and had been coldly dismissive, when Bethany had not been able to understand why the man who had once adored her in every possible way had disappeared. Unlike Leo, who had thrown around words like 'responsibility' and 'duty' but had only meant that Bethany should follow his orders without question.

Unlike Leo, who had used the powerful sexual chemistry between them like a weapon, keeping her addicted, desperate and yet so very lonely for far longer than she should have been.

Something flared in the depths of his dark gaze then, something that shimmered through her, arrowing straight to her core, coiling tight and hot inside of her. It was as if he knew exactly what she was remembering and was remembering it too. Their bodies twined together, their skin slick and warm, their mouths fused— and Leo thrusting deep inside her again and again.

She took a ragged breath, jerked her gaze away from his and tried to calm her thudding heart. Those memories had no place here, now. There was no point to them. Leo had not destroyed her, as he'd seemed so bent on doing. She had survived. She had left him, and all that remained was this small legal matter. She would have spoken only to his staff about it and avoided this meeting, had they not insisted that the principe would wish to deal with this, with her, personally.

"He sounds like quite the paragon," Leo replied after a long moment, much too calmly. He raised his dark brows slightly when she frowned at him.

"He is," Bethany said firmly, wondering why she felt so unbalanced, as if she was being childish somehow— instead of using the only weapon she could think of that might actually do more than bounce off of him. Perhaps it was simply that being near Leo now made her feel as she had felt when she'd been with him: so very young and silly. Naïve and foolish.

"Far be it from me to stand in the way of such a perfect union," Leo murmured, running his hand along the front of his exquisite suit jacket as if it required smoothing. As if anything he wore would dare defy him and wrinkle!

Bethany's frown deepened. That was too blatant, surely? "There is no need for sarcasm."

"I must contact my attorneys," Leo said, his dark eyes hard on hers. Bethany felt slightly dizzy as that familiar old fire licked through her, making her legs tremble beneath her and her breath tangle in her throat.

How unfair that he could still affect her so after everything that had happened! Yet there was a part of her that knew that it was safer to acknowledge the attraction than the grief that lurked beneath it.

"Your attorneys?" she echoed, knowing she had to say something. She knew she could not simply stare at him with that impossible yearning welling up within her for the man he could never be, the man he was not.

She wished suddenly that she had more experience. That she had not been so sheltered and out of her depth when she'd met Leo. As if she'd spent her youth hermetically sealed away, which of course, in many ways, she had. But how could she have done anything else? There had been no one but Bethany to nurse her father through his long, extended illness; no one but Bethany to administer what care she could until his eventual death.

But she had had to drop out of her second year of university to do it when she was barely nineteen. She had been twenty-three when she'd met Leo on that fateful trip to her father's favorite place in the world, Hawaii. She had dutifully traveled with the small inheritance he'd left behind to spread his ashes in the sea, as he'd wished. How could she have been prepared for an honest-to-goodness prince?

She had hardly imagined such creatures existed outside of fiction. She had been utterly off-balance from the moment he'd looked at her with those deep, dark eyes that had seemed to brand her from the inside out. Maybe if she'd been more like other girls her age, if she'd been more mature, if she'd ventured out from the tiny little world her father's needs had dictated she make her own...

But there was no use trying to change the past—and, anyway, Bethany could not begrudge the years she'd spent caring for her father. She could only move forward now, armed with the strength she had not possessed at twenty-three. She had been artless and unformed then, and Leo had flattened her. That would never happen again.

"Yes," he said now, his gaze moving over her face as if he could see the very things she so desperately wished to keep hidden: her lies. Her bravado. That deep despair at what they'd made of their marriage. That tiny spark of hope she would give anything to extinguish, once and for all. "My attorneys must handle any divorce proceedings, of course. They will let me know what is involved in such a matter." His smile was thin, yet still polite. Barely. "I have no experience with such things."

Bethany was confused and wary. Was this really happening? Was he simply caving? Agreeing? She had not imagined such a thing could be possible. She had imagined he would fight, and fight dirty. Not because he wanted her, of course, but because he was not a man who had ever been left, and his pride would demand he fight. She was not certain what the hollow feeling that washed through her meant.

"Is this a trick?" she asked after a moment.

Leo's brows lifted with pure, male arrogance. He

looked every inch the scion of a noble bloodline that he was.

"A trick?" he repeated, as if he was unfamiliar with the term yet found it vaguely distasteful.

"You were opposed to my leaving you in the first place," she pointed out stiffly. That was a vast understatement. "And you did not seem any more resigned to the idea of it tonight. How can I trust that you will really do this?"

He did not speak for a long moment, yet that simmering awareness between them seemed to reach boiling point. Once again, Bethany felt heat and a deep, encompassing panic wash over her. She thought he almost smiled then.

Instead, he reached over and took her hand in his impossibly warm, hard grasp.

Flames raced up her arm, and she felt her whole body tighten in reaction. She felt the ache of it, both physical and, worse, emotional. She wanted to yank her hand from his more than she wanted to draw her next breath, but she forced herself to stand still, to let him touch her, to pretend she was unmoved by the feel of his skin against hers.

Leo watched her for a moment then dropped his brooding gaze to her hand. His thumb moved back and forth over the backs of her fingers, sending sensation streaking through her. She felt herself melt for him, as she always had at even his slightest touch. She ached—and she hated him for it.

"What are you doing?" she managed to say through lips that hardly moved. How could she still be so helpless? How could he have this power over her?

"You seem to have misplaced your wedding ring," he said quietly, still looking at her hand, the chill in his voice in direct contrast to the bright, hot flame of his touch.

"I did not misplace it," she gritted out. "I removed it a long time ago. Deliberately."

"Of course you did," he murmured, and then murmured something else in Italian that she was delighted not to understand.

"I thought about pawning it," she continued, knowing that would bring his gaze back to hers. She raised her brows. "But that would be petty."

"And you are many things, Bethany, are you not?" His mouth was so grim, his eyes a dark blaze. He let her hand go and she pulled it back too quickly, too obviously. His mouth twisted, mocking her. "But never petty."

Leo stared out the floor-to-ceiling window of the penthouse condominium that had been secured for his use. But he did not see the towers of Bay Street, nor the muted lights of downtown Toronto still glittering at his feet despite the late hour.

He could not sleep. He told himself it was because he hated the inevitable rain, the cold and the wet that swept in from Lake Ontario that chilled to the bone and yet passed for autumn in this remote, northern place. He told himself he needed nothing but another drink—perhaps that might ease the tension that still ravaged through him.

But he could not seem to get Bethany's bright blue eyes, clear and challenging, out of his head. And then that flash of vulnerability, as if she'd hurt—and deeply.

She was like some kind of witch.

He had thought so when they had collided in the

warm, silky surf off of Waikiki Beach. He had caught her in his arms to keep her from tumbling with the breakers toward the sand, and it had been those eyes that had first drawn him in: so wide, so blue, like the sea all around them and the vast Hawaiian sky above. And she had looked up at him with her wet hair plastered to her head and her sensual lips parted, as if he were all the world. He had felt the same.

How times changed.

It was not enough that he had lost his life-long, renowned control with her then. That he had betrayed his family's wishes and his own expectations and married a nobody from a place about as far away from his beloved northern Italy as it was possible to get. He had been supposed to choose an appropriately titled bride, a woman of endless pedigree and celebrated blood—a fate that he had accepted as simply one more aspect of the many duties that comprised his title. He was the *Principe di Felici*. His family's roots extended back into thirteenth-century Florence. He had expected his future wife to have a heritage no less impressive.

Yet he had eloped with Bethany instead. He had married her because, for the first and only time in his life, he had felt wild and reckless. Passionate. Alive. He had not been able to imagine returning to his life without her.

And he had paid for his folly ever since.

Leo turned from the window, and set his empty tumbler down on the wide glass table before him. He raked his fingers through his hair and refused to speculate as to the meaning of the heaviness in his chest. He did not spare a glance for the sumptuous leather couches, nor the intricate statuary that accented the great room.

He thought only of Bethany, saw only Bethany, a

haunting he had come to regard as commonplace over the years. She was his one regret, his one mistake. His wife.

He had already compromised more than he could have ever imagined possible, against all advice and all instinct. He had assumed her increasing sullenness in their first year of marriage was merely a phase she had been going through—a necessary shift from her quiet life into his far more colorful one—and had therefore allowed her more leeway than he should have.

He had suffered her temper, her baffling resistance to performing her official duties, even her horror that he had wanted to start a family so quickly. He had foolishly believed that she needed time to grow into her role as his wife, when retrospect made it clear that what she'd truly needed was a firmer hand.

He had let her leave him, shocked and hurt in ways he'd refused to acknowledge that she would attempt it in the first place. He had assumed she would come to her senses while they were apart, that she needed time to adjust to the idea of her new responsibilities and the pressures of her new role and title. Neither was something a common, simple girl from Toronto could have been prepared for, he had come to understand.

After all, he had spent his whole life coming to terms with the weight and heft of the Di Marco heritage and its many demands upon him. He had reluctantly let her have her freedom—after all, she had been so young when they had married. So unformed. So unsophisticated.

And this was how she repaid him. Lies about a lover, when she should have known that he had her every movement tracked and would certainly have allowed no lover to further sully his name. Claims that she wished to divorce him, unforgivably uttered in public where anyone might hear. Aspersions cast without trepidation upon his character, his honor.

He took a kind of solace in the anger that surged through him. It was far, far easier to be angry than to confront what he knew lay beneath. And he had vowed that he would never show her his vulnerabilities—never again.

Revenge would be sweet, he decided, and he would have no qualms whatsoever in extracting it. He thought then of that confusing vulnerability he'd thought he'd seen but dismissed it.

Di Marcos did not divorce. Ever.

The Princess Di Marco, Principessa di Felici, had two duties: to support her husband in all he did, and to bear him heirs to secure the title. Leo sank down onto the nearest couch and blew out a breath.

It was about time that Bethany started living up to her responsibilities.

And, if those responsibilities forced her to return to him as she should have done years before, all the better.

Bethany should not have been surprised when she looked up from packing a box the next morning to see Leo looming in the doorway of her bedroom. But she could not contain the gasp that escaped her.

She jerked back and pressed her hand against her wildly thumping heart. It was surprise, she told herself; no more than surprise. Certainly not that wild, desperate hope she refused to acknowledge within her.

"What are you doing here?" she asked, appalled at the breathiness of her voice. And, in any case, she knew what he was doing: this was his house, wasn't it? Three stories of stately brick and pedigreed old-money in Rosedale, Toronto's wealthiest neighborhood. It was exactly where Prince Leopoldo Di Marco, *Principe di Felici*, ought to reside.

Bethany hated it—she hated everything the house stood for. Her occupying such a monied, ancestrally predetermined sort of space seemed like a contradiction in terms—like one more lie. Yet Leo had insisted that she live in this house, or in Italy with him, and three years ago she had not had the strength to choose her own third option.

As long as she lived under this roof, she was essentially consenting to her sham of a marriage—and Leo's control. Yet she had stayed here anyway, until she could no longer pretend that she was not on some level waiting for him to come and claim her.

Once she had accepted that depressing truth, she had known she had no choice but to act.

"Surely my presence cannot be quite so shocking?" Leo asked in that way of his that felt like a slap, as if she was too foolish, too naïve. It set her teeth on edge.

"Are you so grand that you cannot ring the doorbell like anyone else?" she asked more fiercely than she'd intended.

It did not help that she had not slept well, her mind racing and her skin buzzing as if she'd been wildly over-caffeinated. Nor did it help that she had dressed to pack boxes today, in a pair of faded blue jeans and a simple, blue long-sleeved T-shirt, with her curls tied up in a haphazard knot on the back of her head. Not exactly the height of elegance.

Leo, of course, looked exquisite and impeccable in a charcoal-colored buttoned-down shirt that clung to his flat, hard chest and a pair of dark, wool trousers that only emphasized the strong lines of his body.

He leaned against the doorjamb and watched her for a simmering moment, his mouth unsmiling, those coffee eyes hooded.

"Is your lot in life truly so egregious, Bethany?" he asked softly. "Do I deserve quite this level of hostility?"

Something thicker than regret—and much too close to shame—turned over in her stomach. But Bethany forced herself not to do what every instinct screamed at her to do: she would not apologize, cajole or soothe. She knew from painful experience that there was only one way such things would end. Leo took and took until there was nothing in her left to give.

So she did not cross to him. She did not even shrug an apology. She only brushed a fallen strand of hair away from her face, ignored the spreading hollowness within and concentrated on the box in front of her on the wide bed.

"I realize this is your house," she said stiffly into the uncomfortable silence. "But I would appreciate it if you would do me the courtesy of announcing your arrival, rather than appearing in doorways. It seems only polite."

There were so many land mines littered about the floor and so many memories cluttering the air between them—too many. Her chest felt tight, yet all she could think of was her first night in Italy and Leo's patient instructions about how she would be expected to behave—delivered between kisses in his grand bed. He had grown less patient and much less affectionate over time, when it had become clear to all involved that he had made a dreadful mistake in marrying someone like Bethany. Her mouth tightened at the memory.

"Of course," Leo murmured. His dark gaze tracked

her movements. "You are already packing your belongings?"

"Don't worry," she said, shooting him a look. "I won't take anything that isn't mine."

That muscle in his jaw jumped and his eyes narrowed.

"I am relieved to hear it," he said after a thick, simmering moment.

When she had folded the same white cotton sweater four times, and still failed to do it correctly, Bethany gave up. She turned from the bed and faced him, swallowing back any fear, anxiety or any of the softer, deeper things she pretended not to feel—because none would do her any good.

"Leo, really." She shoved her hands into her hip pockets so he could not see that they were curling into fists. "Why are you here?"

"I have not visited this place in a long time," he said, and she hated him for it.

"No," she agreed, her voice a rasp in the sudden tense air of the room.

How dared he refer to that night—that awful, shameful night? How could she have behaved that way, so out of control and crazed with her heartbreak, her desperate resolve to really, truly leave him? And how could all of that fury and fire have twisted around and around and left her so wanton, so shameless, that she could have... *mated* with him like that? With such ferocity it still made her shiver years later.

She'd had no idea of the depths to which she could sink. Not until he'd taken her there and then left her behind to stew in it.

"I have news," he said, his gaze moving over her face, once again making her wonder exactly what he could read there. "But I do not think you will be pleased." He straightened from the door and suddenly seemed much closer than he should. She fought to stand still, to keep from backing away.

"Well?" she asked.

But he did not answer her immediately. Instead, he moved into the room, seeming to take it over, somehow, seeming to diminish it with the force of his presence.

Bethany felt the way his eyes raked over the white linen piled high on the unmade bed even as her memory played back too-vivid recollections of the night she most wanted to forget. The crash and splintering of a vase against the wall. Her fists against his chest. His fierce, mocking laughter. His shirt torn from him with her own desperate hands. His mouth fused to hers. His hands like fire, punishment and glory all over her, lifting her, spurring her on, damning them both.

She shook it off and found him watching her, a gleam in his dark gaze, as if he too remembered the very same scenes. He stood at the foot of the bed, too close to her. He could too easily reach over and tip her onto the mattress, and Bethany was not at all certain what might happen then.

She froze, appalled at the direction of her thoughts. A familiar despair washed through her, all the more bitter because she knew it so well. Still she wanted him. Still. She did not understand how that could be true. She did not want to understand; she only wanted it—and him—to go away. She wanted to be free of the heavy weight of him, of his loss. She simply wanted to be free.

It was as if he could read her mind. The silence between them seemed charged, alive. His gaze dropped from hers to flick over her mouth then lower, to test her curves, and she could feel it as clearly as if he'd put his hands upon her.

"You said you had something to tell me," she managed to grate out as if her thighs did not feel loose, ready, despite her feelings of hopelessness. As if her core did not pulse for him. As if she did not feel that electricity skate over her skin, letting her know he was near, stirring up that excitement she would give anything to deny.

"I do," Leo murmured, dark and tall, too big and too powerful to be in this room. This house. Her life. "The divorce. There is a complication."

"What complication?" she asked, suspicious, though her traitorous body did not seem to care. It throbbed for him, hot and needy.

"I am afraid that it cannot be done remotely." He shrugged in that supremely Italian way, as if to say that the vagaries of such things were beyond anyone's control, even his.

"You cannot mean...?" she began. His gaze found hers then, so very dark and commanding, and she felt goosebumps rise along her arms and neck. It was as though someone walked across her grave, she thought distantly.

"There is no getting around it," he said, but his voice was not apologetic. His gaze was direct. And Bethany went completely cold. "I am afraid that you must return to Italy."

CHAPTER THREE

"I AM not going back to Italy," Bethany blurted out, shocked that he would suggest such an outlandish thing.

Had he lost his mind? He had managed to ruin the entire country for her. She couldn't imagine what would ever induce her to return to it. In her mind, any return to Italy meant a return to the spineless creature she had been when she lived there; she could not—would not—be that person ever again.

But Leo merely watched her with those knowing, mocking eyes as if he knew something she did not.

"Don't be ridiculous!" she tossed at him to offset the panic skipping through her nerves.

Leo's dark brows rose in a haughty sort of amazement, and she remembered belatedly that the *Principe di Felici* was not often called things like 'ridiculous.' He was no doubt more used to being showered in honorifics. 'Your Excellency.' 'My Prince.' She bit her lower lip but did not retract her words.

"I am afraid there is no other way, if you wish to divorce me," he said. If he were another man, she might have thought that tone apologetic. But this was Leo, and his eyes were too unreadable, so she could only be suspicious. "If you wish to remain merely separated, of course, you can continue to do as you please."

"I am not the idiot you seem to think," she said, her mind reeling. "I am a Canadian citizen. I do not need to go all the way to Italy to divorce you—I can do it right here."

"That would be true, had you not signed all the papers," Leo said calmly. His gaze was disconcertingly direct, seeming to push inside of her and render her transparent. Yet she could not seem to look away. His head tilted slightly to one side. "When you first arrived at the castello. Perhaps you do not recall."

"Of course I remember." Bethany let out a short laugh even as her stomach twisted anxiously. "How could anyone forget three days of legal documents?"

She remembered all too well the intimidating sheaves of paper that had been thrust at her by an unsmiling phalanx of attorneys, her signature required again and again. Sign here, principessa.

Most of the documents had been in Italian, affixed with serious and official seals and covered with intimidatingly dense prose. She had not understood a single thing that had been put in front of her, but she had been so desperately in love with her brand-new husband that she had signed everything anyway.

That great cavern of sorrow she carried within her yawned open, but she ignored it. She could not collapse in that way. Not now.

"Then you perhaps have forgotten what, exactly, it is that you signed," Leo continued, his cool, faintly mocking voice kindling fear and fury in equal measure and sending both shooting along Bethany's limbs like a hot wind.

"I have no idea what I signed," she was forced to

admit. It pained her that she could ever have been so blindly trusting, even five years ago at the start of her marriage when she had thought Leo Di Marco was the whole of the cosmos.

He inclined his head toward her, as if that statement said all that need be said.

"I signed it because you told me to sign it," Bethany said quietly. "I assumed you were concerned with my best interests as well as your own." She eyed him and gathered her courage around her like a shield. "Not a mistake I intend to repeat."

"Of course not," Leo said in that smooth, sardonic tone, crossing his arms over his hard chest.

He looked around the room, pointedly taking in the elegance of the furnishings, the pale blue walls beneath delicate moldings and the thick, rich carpeting beneath their feet.

"Because," he continued in that same tone, "as we have established, you have lived as if in a nightmare ever since the day you agreed to marry me."

"Are you going to tell me what rights I signed away, or would you prefer to stand there making sarcastic remarks?" Bethany snapped at him, exasperated at her own distressing softening as well as his patronizing tone. She hated the way he looked at her then, his arrogant gaze growing somehow more intimidating, burning into her.

"My apologies," he said, his tone scathing. "I was unaware that my preferences were of any interest to you."

He almost smiled then, a hard, edgy crook of his sensual mouth. Bethany wanted to look away but found she couldn't—she was as trapped, as if he held her in his hands, which she knew would be the end of her.

"But that is neither here nor there, is it?" he asked in that deadly, soft tone that sent shivers down Bethany's spine and twisted through her stomach. "The salient point is that you agreed that any divorce proceedings, should they ever become necessary, would be held in an Italian court under Italian law."

"And, naturally, I have only your word for that," Bethany pointed out, horrified that her voice sounded so insubstantial. She cleared her throat and jerked her gaze from his as if she might turn to stone were she to lose herself any further in that bittersweet darkness. "I could have agreed to anything and I would have no way of knowing, would I?"

"If you wish to hire a translator and have the documents examined, I will instruct my secretaries to begin compiling copies for your review immediately," Leo said in a mild way, yet with that sardonic current beneath.

"And how long will that take?" Bethany asked, her bitterness swelling, hinting at the great wealth of tears beneath. She blinked them back. "Years? This is all just a game to you, isn't it?"

His gaze seemed to ignite then, hard, hot and furious. The room constricted around them, narrowing, until there was nothing but Leo—the real Leo, she thought wildly—too dark, too angry and too close. Bethany felt panic race through her; a surge of adrenaline and something far more dangerous kicked up her pulse, hardened her nipples and pooled between her legs. She hated herself for that betrayal above all else.

And she suddenly realized how close together they were standing, with only the corner of the platform bed between them. She could reach out her hand and lay it against his hard pectoral muscles, or the fascinating valley between them. She could inhale his scent.

She could completely ruin herself and all she'd fought so hard to achieve!

"You must return to Italy if you wish to divorce me," he said, his voice low and furious, like a dark electrical current that set her alight. "There is no other option available to you."

"How convenient for you," she managed to say somehow, not fighting the faint trembling that shook her—not certain she could have hid it if she'd tried. "I wonder how the foreign wife of an Italian prince can expect to be treated in Italy?"

"It is not your foreign birth that should worry you, Bethany," Leo said, his noble features so arrogant, so coldly and impossibly beautiful, even now—his low voice like a dark melody. "The abandonment of your husband and subsequent taking of a lover? That, I am afraid, may force the courts to find you at fault for the dissolution of the marriage." He shrugged, seemingly nonchalant, though his eyes were far too dark, far too hard. "But you are quite proud of both those things, are you not? Why should it distress you?"

Bethany felt as if something huge and heavy was crushing her, making it impossible to breathe, making tears prick at the backs of her eyes when she had no desire to weep. It was the way he said 'abandonment' and 'lover,' perhaps. It tore at her. It made her nearly confess the truth to him, confess her lie, simply to see his gaze warm. It made her wish she could still believe in dreams she had been forced to grow out of years ago.

But she knew better than to give him ammunition. Better he should hate her and release her than think well of her and keep her tied to him in this half-life, no matter how much it hurt her.

"There must be another way," she said after a moment or two, battling to keep her voice even.

Leo merely shook his head, his features carefully blank once again, just that polite exterior masking all the anger and arrogance she knew filled him from within. She could feel it all around them, tightening like a vice. Too much emotion. Too much history.

"I don't accept that," Bethany said, frowning at him.

"There are many things that you do not accept, it seems," Leo said silkily. "But that does not make them any less true."

He wanted her. He always wanted her. He had stopped asking himself why that should be.

He did not care about her lies, her insults—or he did not care enough, now, having been without her for so long. He only wanted to be deep inside of her, her legs wrapped around his waist, where there could be only the truth of that hot, silken connection. The only truth that had ever mattered, no matter what she chose to believe. No matter what he felt.

She should know better than to row with him so close to a bed. She should remember that all her posturing, all her demands, rages and pouts, disappeared the moment he touched her. His hands itched to prove that to her.

She pushed her curls back from her face and looked unutterably tired for a flashing moment. "I would ask you what you mean, and I am certain you would love to tell me, but I am tired of your games, Leo," she said in that quiet yet matter-of-fact voice that he was growing to dislike intensely. "I will not go back to Italy. Ever."

He thought of the vulnerability he had sensed in her, that undercurrent of pain. He could see hints of it in the way she looked at him now, the careful way she held herself. Sex and temper, he understood; both could be solved in the same way. But this was something else.

A game, he assured himself. This is just another game.

"You make such grand proclamations, luce mio," he said softly, never taking his eyes from hers. "How can you keep them all straight? Today you will not go to Italy. Three years ago you would not remain my wife. So many threats, Bethany, all of which end in nothing."

"Those are not threats," she threw at him, her eyes dark in that way that made things shift uncomfortably in him, her soft mouth trembling. "They are the unvarnished truth. I'm sorry if you are not used to hearing such a thing, but then you surround yourself with sycophants, don't you? You have only yourself to blame."

Leo moved toward her, his gaze tight on hers. "There were so many sweeping threats, as I recall," he said softly, mockingly, as if she had not spoken. As if there were no shifts, no darkness, no depths he could not comprehend. "You would not speak to me again once you left Italy. You would not remain in this house even twenty-four hours after I left you here. They begin to run together, do they not?"

She only stared at him, her blue eyes wide, furious and something else, something deeper. But her very presence before him, in the house she had vowed to leave, was all the answer that was needed.

"And we cannot forget my favorite threat of all, can we?" He closed the space between them then, though he did not reach over and touch her as he longed to do. He was so close she was forced to tilt her face up toward his if she wanted to look at him. Her lips parted slightly, her eyes widening as heat bloomed on her cheeks.

"Is this supposed to terrify me?" she asked, but it was hardly a whisper, barely a thread of sound. "Am I expected to cower away from you in fear and awe?"

"You promised me you would never go near me again, that I disgusted you," he said softly, looking down into her eyes, reading one emotion after another—none of them disgust. "Is that why you shake, Bethany? Is this disgust?"

"It is nothing so deep as disgust," she said, her voice a thread of sound, her eyes too bright. She cleared her throat. "It is simply acute boredom with this situation."

"You are a liar, then and now," he said, reluctantly intrigued by the shadows that chased through her bright blue eyes. He was not surprised when she moved away from him, putting more space between their bodies as if that might dampen the heat they generated between them. As if anything ever could.

"That is almost funny, Leo," she said in a quiet voice, her gaze dark. "Coming from you."

"Tell me, Bethany, how have I deceived you?" he asked softly, watching her school her expressive face into the smooth blandness he hated. "What are my crimes?"

"I refuse to discuss this with you, as if you do not already know," she said, squaring her shoulders. "As if we have not gone over it again and again to the point of nausea."

"Very well, then," he said, hearing that harsh edge in his voice, unable to control it. "Then let us discuss your crimes. We can start with your lover."

His words seemed to hang there, accusation and curse wrapping around her like a vise. She wanted to scream, to rage, to shove at him. To collapse to the floor and sob out her anguish.

But she could not bring herself to move. She felt pinned as much by the heat in his dark gaze as her own eternal folly. Why had she told him such an absurd lie? Why had she put herself in a position where he could claim the moral high-ground over her?

"You do not wish to discuss my lover," she told him stiffly, hating herself, her own voice sounding like a stranger's. But she had to make it believable, didn't she? "You do not compare well in any department."

"How will you tell him that you cannot ever do more than commit adultery so long as you remain married to me?" he murmured in that way of his that seemed to channel directly along her spine, making her feel shivery and weak. "What man would tolerate such a thing, when all you need do is fly to Italy to take care of that one, small detail?"

"He is enormously tolerant," Bethany said through her teeth. The word 'adultery' seemed to ricochet through her, chipping off pieces of her heart until they fell like stones into the pit of her stomach.

"As it happens," Leo said in that quiet, lethal tone, "I am flying to Italy tomorrow morning. We could finish with this unpleasantness in no time at all."

It paralyzed her. For a moment, she simply stared at him, lost, as if he'd reached over and torn her heart from her chest. It was as if she could no longer feel it beating. She could not begin to imagine the damage his capitulation caused her. She did not want to imagine it.

"If there is no other way," she said slowly, feeling as if she was teetering on the edge of a vast, deep abyss, as if her voice was something she'd dug up somewhere, rusty and unused, not hers at all. "Then I suppose I will have to go to Italy."

Leo's eyes darkened with that pure male fire she knew too well. It called to that twisted part of her, the part she most wanted to deny.

Because despite the pain, the grief and the loneliness, she still wanted him. She still ached for him, that wave of longing and lust that made everything else the very lies he accused her of telling. His body. His presence. The light of his smile, the brush of his hand, the very fact of his nearness. She ached.

Time seemed to stand still. There was only that fierce, knowing gleam in his eyes, as there had always been. One touch, his gaze promised her, hot, gleaming and sure. Only one small touch and she would be his. Only that, and she would betray herself completely.

And she knew some part of her wanted him to do it—wanted him to tumble her to the bed and take her with all the easy command and consummate skill that had always shaken her so completely, melted her so fully, made her his in every way. She no longer even bothered to despair of herself.

"My plane awaits," he said softly, and she could hear the intense satisfaction behind his words. As if he had known they would end up in exactly this place. As if he had made it so. As if he could read her mind.

"I will not travel with you," she told him, holding her head high even as she surrendered, because she could not think of anything else to do, any way to escape this. Escape him. Their past. She would go to Italy and fight it there, where it had gone so wrong in the first place.

She glared at him. "I will find my own way there."

And Leo, damn him, smiled.

CHAPTER FOUR

THE small, achingly picturesque village of Felici—ancestral seat of the Di Marco family and the very last place Bethany ever wanted to visit again—clung to the hillside in the late-afternoon sun, red-roofed and white-walled.

The local church thrust its proud white steeple high into the air, bells tolling out the turn of the hour. Carefully cultivated vineyards stretched out across the tidy Felici Valley, reaching toward the alpine foothills rising in the distance. And at the highest point in the village loomed the ancient Castello di Felici itself, defining the very hill it clung to, announcing the might and power of the Di Marco family to all who ventured near.

Yet all Bethany could see was ghosts.

She drove the hired car along the main road that wound up into the village, so renowned for its narrow medieval streets and prosperous, cheerful architecture. She pulled into the small parking area near the pensione located at the hill's midway point. But she still couldn't seem to draw a full breath, or calm the nervous fluttering in her belly.

It had been that way since her plane had taken off from Toronto two nights before. She had only managed a fitful, restless kind of doze for most of the long overnight flight. When she had managed to sleep, her dreams had been filled with dread, loss and panic and Leo's bitter-sweet, chocolate gaze like a laser cutting through her. Hardly rejuvenating.

"My men will meet you at the airport," he had told her, in that peremptory manner that made it clear there was to be no discussion before taking his leave from the house in Rosedale.

It had been like a flashback into the very heart of their married life, and not a pleasant one. Bethany had not been able to stand the thought of doing what he'd decreed she should do, and not simply because he'd decreed it. She'd felt claustrophobic imagining how it would go: she would be marched from the plane, deposited into one of the endless fleet of gleaming black cars he had at his disposal and spirited away to his castello like…property.

She shuddered anew, just thinking of it. That was exactly why she had opted to fly into Rome instead of the much-closer Milan.

She'd fought off her exhaustion throughout the long drive up the middle of the country, arriving in the outskirts of Milan early the previous evening. She'd fallen gratefully into a clean bed in a cheap hotel outside the city limits and had finally slept. It had been nearly noon when she'd pulled herself out of bed, cotton-headed and reeling, her thudding heart telling her the anxiety dreams had continued even if she hadn't quite remembered them once awake.

She'd remembered other things, however, no matter how she'd tried to keep the memories at bay.

"Ah, luce mio, how I love you," he had whispered as he had held her close, high on a balcony that overlooked the Felici Valley as the sun had set before them that first night in Italy.

My light, she had thought, dazed by him as if he were all the fire and song of the stars above. "Why am I your light?" she had asked. She'd meant, how can you love me when you are you and I am me?

"These eyes," he had murmured, kissing one closed lid and then the next. "They are as blue as the summer sky. How could you be anything but light, with eyes such as these?"

She had lingered over strong espresso in a café near her hotel after she woke, putting off the inevitable for as long as she could. With every bone in her body, every fiber of her being, she had not wanted to make the last leg of this journey. She had not wanted to travel the last few hours into the countryside, further and further into the past. Further and further into everything she'd wanted so badly and lost despite herself.

It seemed impossible that any of this was really happening. It reminded her of the dreams she'd had on and off since leaving Italy three years ago. She would dream that she had never left at all, that she had only imagined it, that she was still trying to bite her tongue and keep her feelings to herself like the dutiful principessa she had failed to become and that the hard, lonely years since leaving Leo had been the dream.

She had always woken in a panic, her face wet with tears, the bedroom seeming to echo around her as if she had screamed out in her sleep.

There was no waking up from this, Bethany thought now, feeling flushed, too hot with emotions she refused to examine. She stared at the ivy-covered wall before her as if it could help her—as if anything could.

She climbed out of the car and couldn't help the

deep breath she took then, almost against her will. The air was crisp, clean, and sweet-smelling. She fancied she could smell the Italian sun as it headed west high above her; she could see the Alps in the far distance, the vines and the olive groves. She could smell cheerful local meals spicing the early-evening air: rich polenta and creamy, decadent risotto, the mellow undertone of warming olive oil on the breeze.

It brought back too many memories. It hurt.

She was unable to keep herself from a brooding look up at the castello itself. It sat there, the high walls seeming to be part of the cliff itself, feudal and imposing, crouched over the town like a dragon guarding its treasure. She could easily imagine generations of Di Marcos fighting off sieges, bolstering their wealth and influence from the safety of those towering heights. She almost imagined she could see Leo, like some feudal lord high on the walls, the world at his feet.

Bethany almost wished she could hate the place, for on some level she blamed the stones themselves for destroying her marriage. It was a visceral feeling, all guts and irrationality, but the girl who had walked inside those walls had never walked out again.

She wished she could hate the thick, stone walls, the now-unused battlements. She wished she could hate the drawbridge that led through the outer walls of what had originally been a monastery, over the defunct moat and beneath the Di Marco coat of arms that had first been emblazoned above the entryway in the fifteenth century.

"It is so beautiful!" she had breathed, overcome as she'd walked through the great stone archway at the top of the drawbridge. He had swept her into his arms, spinning them both around in a circle until they had both laughed with the sheer joy of it right there in the grand hall.

"Not so beautiful as you," he had said, his gaze serious, though his mouth had curved into a smile she'd been able to feel inside her own chest. "Never so beautiful as you, amore mio."

Shaking the memory off, annoyed by her own melancholy, Bethany pulled her suitcase from the passenger seat and headed toward the entrance of the pensione. She had chosen this place deliberately: it was brand new. There would be much less chance of an awkward run-in with anyone she might have known three years ago.

She was reasonably confident she could avoid Leo as easily.

"It should not require more than two weeks of your time," Leo had estimated with a careless shrug. Two weeks, perhaps a bit more. She had survived the last three years, she'd thought, so what were a few more weeks?

But she couldn't help the feelings that dragged at her, pulling her inexorably toward that vast cavern of loneliness and pain inside that she could not allow to claim her any longer.

Just as she couldn't help one last, doubtful look at the castello over her shoulder as she pushed open the door to the lobby and walked inside.

"I am so sorry," the man said from behind the counter in heavily accented English. "The room—it is not yet ready."

But Bethany knew the truth. She could see it in the man's averted gaze, the welcoming smile that had dropped from his lips. It had happened the moment she'd said her name. It did not seem to matter that she'd used her maiden name, as she'd grown used to doing in Toronto.

Her hands tightened around the handle of her suitcase, so hard her knuckles whitened, but she managed to curve her lips into an approximation of a polite smile.

"How odd," she murmured past the tightness in her throat. "I was certain the check-in time was three o'clock, and it is already past five."

"If you would not mind waiting..." The man smiled helplessly and gestured toward the small seating-area at the far side of the small lobby.

Feeling helpless, Bethany turned from the counter, aware that her eyes were filled with a dangerous heat. She walked across the lobby with careful precision and then sat on the plush sofa, feeling as if she was made of glass, fragile and precarious. And then feeling broken, somehow, when the man picked up the telephone and murmured something she could not quite hear in rapid Italian.

Sure enough, not ten minutes later the front door was pulled open and two men in dark suits entered. Bethany did not recognize them personally, but she had no doubt at all about who they were.

They walked toward her, coming to a stop only a foot or two away. She stared straight ahead, willing herself to stay calm, adult, and rational, as she'd been so sure she'd remain. She fought to maintain her composure, though her stomach twisted and her heart beat too hard against her ribs.

"Principessa," the larger of the two men murmured in tones of the greatest respect—which made Bethany that much more furious, somehow, and that much more despairing. "Per favore...?"

What could she do? This was Leo's village. He was

its prince. She had been a fool to think he would let her return to it without controlling her every move. Back when she had felt more charitable toward him she'd told herself he simply knew no other way to behave, that he had been raised to be this dictatorial, that it was not his fault.

Today, she knew the truth. This was who he was. This was who he wanted to be. What she wanted had never mattered, and never, ever would.

So she simply rose to her feet with as much dignity and grace as she could muster. She let Leo's men guide her to the expected gleaming black sedan that waited outside, elegant and imprisoning, and climbed obediently into the back seat.

And then she sat there, furious, helpless and as brokenhearted as the day she'd left, as they drove her straight into the jaws of the castello.

It was all exactly as she remembered, exactly as she still dreamed.

The great castello was quiet around her—it was open to the public only on certain days of the week or by appointment—and felt empty, even though she knew that hordes of servants were all around her, perhaps even watching her, just out of sight.

Bethany felt a drowning sensation, as if she was being sucked backward in time, thrown back four years into that other life where she had been so miserable, so terribly alone. And it had been worse because she had not known how alone she was at first—she had still believed that she would recover from her father's death with Leo's help, that he would become the family she so deeply craved.

Instead, he had abandoned her in every way that mattered.

As if the stones themselves remembered that grief, that ache, they seemed to echo not just her footsteps as she walked but her memories of those awful days here when she'd been so isolated, scared and abandoned.

She barely saw the impressive entryway, the tapestries along the stone walls inside the grand entrance, the rooms filled with priceless art and antiques, each item resplendent with its pedigree, its heritage, its worth across centuries. Her silent escorts ushered her up above the public rooms to the family wing, then down the long, gleaming hallway toward her old, familiar door. But all she could see was the past.

And then it was done. Her suitcase was deposited just inside her chamber and the door was closed behind her with a muted click. She stood inside the bedroom suite that had once been hers, her luxurious cage, quite as if she had never left.

Bethany let her head drop slightly forward, squeezing shut her eyes as she stood there in the center of the grand room. This was the principessa's historic suite, handed down over the ages from one wife to the next. It boasted the finest furnishings, gilt-edged and ornate. The bed was canopied in gold, the regal bedspread an opulent shade of red. Everything was made of the darkest, richest wood, lovingly crafted and polished to a high shine. There was never a hint of dust in this room, never an item out of place—except for Bethany herself, she thought wryly.

She did not have to investigate to know that all was precisely as it had been the last time she'd been here. She did not have to walk to the towering windows to know what she would see through them: the finely sculpted gardens and beyond them, the rooftops of the village and the gentle, inviting roll of Italian countryside reaching for the horizon. All of it was beautiful beyond measure, and yet somehow capable of making that ache inside of her grow so much more acute.

And she did not have to turn when she heard the paneled side-door open because she knew exactly who would be standing there. But she could not seem to help herself, her gaze was drawn to him as if he were a flickering flame and she no more than a moth. She wished even that did not hurt her, but it did. It still did.

Leo lounged against the paneled door frame, his long, lean form packed into dark trousers and a cashmere black sweater that emphasized his whipcord strength. His eyes seemed nearly black, and she fought off the urge to rub at the back of her neck where the fine hairs there whispered in warning.

He looked dark and powerful, like one of the ancient Roman gods that had once roamed this land, capricious and cruel. And she knew he was bent on vengeance just the same. He did not show her that sardonic smile of his, that mocking twist of his sensual lips.

He did not need to. Her very presence was enough.

Already she felt as if she'd lost everything. Again.

"Ah, principessa," Leo said, his tone laced with irony. "Welcome home."

He took a moment to drink in the sight of her, back where she belonged after all of this time. Finally.

It almost eased the three years' worth of simmering anger and the deeper current beneath it he felt when he looked at her. She crossed her arms over her middle, as if it hurt her to stand there in the ancestral bedroom where she had once lived. Where—he knew, whether she did or not—she would live again.

He would allow for no other outcome.

She looked tired, he thought, eyeing her critically. She was unusually pale, though her head was high with the same kind of quiet pride she had showed in Toronto. He did not want her pride, he thought; he wanted her passion. And then her acquiescence.

Because he could think of no other way to reach her. And he had exhausted his futile attempts to pretend that that was not exactly what he wanted.

She wore a tight white T-shirt that clung to her pert, full breasts and a sweater wrap that hung down to her thighs in a soft blue that made her eyes glow even brighter than usual. She still wore those faded denim jeans. In some kind of deliberate rebellion, he had no doubt, though the triumph he felt that he had managed to bring her home far outweighed any disapproval he might have felt about her choice of wardrobe.

He wanted to touch her, taste her. Trace the shape of her graceful neck, sink his fingers into her dark curls. Welcome her back to her home, her responsibilities, him, in the way they would both find most pleasurable. In the only way he knew would bind her to him without having to touch on all that seemed to threaten from beneath the certainty of the fire that raged between them.

If he could only have that fire again, he thought, he would know better how to tend it. He would not let it go again so easily.

The vast room seemed smaller suddenly and her eyes widened with awareness. He smiled slightly. Bethany looked away and swallowed. Leo let his gaze trace the fine column of her throat and saw the wash of red that began to climb there.

"I do not understand why I was dragged from the inn of my choice," she said after a moment.

"I see you are starting at once on the offensive," he murmured, mildly reproving. "Are you not tired of it yet? I feel certain we have enough to discuss without any unnecessary histrionics."

Her brows rose in astonishment. "There is no reason for me to stay here. It is hardly histrionic to say so." Her voice was matter-of-fact, and rubbed him entirely up the wrong way.

"Why?" he asked coolly. "Other than the fact you'd made your usual dramatic proclamations about how you would never return, what objection can you possibly have to staying in the castello?"

She stared at him with a curious expression that Leo had never seen before—one that suggested that he was not very bright. It made him feel…restless. A slow beat of that same old anger and a very familiar frustration began to hammer in his gut, mixed with a new edge that had everything to do with the calm, cool way she looked at him. As if he was the person outside the bounds of propriety and self-control when that had always been her role.

"I do not want to be here." She said it very deliberately, her gaze still on his in that insulting manner. "I need no other objection than that."

Leo straightened from the doorway, coldly amused at the way she jerked back, as if she expected him to lunge at her. He wished he could. He wished he could simply throw her over his shoulder and take her down with him to the soft mattress of the bed behind her. But he knew that, as delightful as it would be to lose himself in her body, it would only delay the inevitable.

Sex had never been their problem. It had been a

weapon, a hiding place, a muddying of already murky waters. He knew with a sudden, devastating insight into the part of himself he preferred to ignore that he could not let it be used as such any longer.

He wanted her back where she belonged, and this time he would have all of her.

"Let me be clear," he said, his voice clipped. Authoritative. "You will not stay in the village. The fact that you attempted to do so after the childish stunt you pulled with your flight—without my ring on your finger or my name, though you are easily identifiable and must know the shame that casts upon this house—only underscores your selfishness."

He watched that red flush on her skin deepen one shade darker, then two. Her soft mouth firmed into a hard line he found unaccountably fascinating.

"How incredibly patronizing you are, Leo," she said coolly, though he could hear temper and something else crackling through her voice. "Patronizing and dismissive."

Leo shrugged. "If you feel you must call me names because it is difficult for you to accept that you have returned here, I will not blame you," he said.

Whatever it took, she would truly be his wife again, he vowed. She would be the principessa he had imagined she could be. He would not allow for any other outcome. Not this time.

Her blue eyes blazed into hard sapphires.

"I am having no difficulty at all accepting that I am here," she bit out. "I am, however, unable to process the fact that you feel comfortable speaking to me as if I am a child."

"I am well aware that you are not a child," he said.

His gaze met hers and held. "It has always been your behavior that causes the confusion."

Her eyes narrowed. He could sense her temper sky-rocketing, but could not imagine what it was that so enraged her. The simple truth? He was surprised she had not already thrown something at him, or launched her own body at his, nails like claws, as she would have done in the past.

He watched, fascinated despite himself, as she visibly fought for control. This was not the Bethany he knew. His Bethany was a creature of passion and regret, rages and tears. She threw precious china against the wall, screamed herself hoarse, threw tantrums that shook the ancient stones beneath their feet. She was not capable of reining in her temper once it ignited, like the woman before him.

He could see it in her eyes, the rage and the passion, the fury and the heat. But she did not move to strike him. She did not scream like a banshee. She only faced him.

He did not know if he admired her unexpected fortitude, or felt it as a loss.

"I will not be spoken to as if I am a recalcitrant adolescent or a lowly member of your staff, Leo," she told him, her voice tight and hard. "I understand that you live in a world where you need only express a desire and it is met, but I am not your underling. I am a grown woman. I do, in fact, know my own mind."

Leo let out a short laugh. "I am delighted to hear it," he said. "Does that mean the antique vases are safe from your rampages? I will notify the household staff."

Her face darkened, but she did not scream at him. Against his will, Leo's fascination deepened.

"Treat me like a child and I will treat you exactly

the same way," she said instead, her words very precise, very pointed. "And I very much doubt your exalted sense of self could handle it."

She was an adult? She had outgrown her childishness? He was thrilled, he told himself, eyeing her narrowly. Overjoyed, in fact. Wasn't that why he'd allowed her to run off to Canada in the first place? She had been so very young when he had met her; far younger than her years. Hadn't he wanted her to mature?

He had only himself to blame if he did not quite care for the specific direction her show of maturity had taken—if he found he preferred the angry child to this unknowable woman who stood before him with unreadable eyes.

"You are still my wife," he said after a long moment, his tone even. "As long as that is true, you cannot stay in the village. It will cause too much comment."

"Thank you for speaking to me as an adult for once," she said. Her chin tilted up and her bright eyes sparkled with a combination of defiance and a certain resignation that made his hackles rise. "What does that say about you, I wonder, that it was so hard to do?"

CHAPTER FIVE

"I TRUST that was rhetorical," he said mildly enough.

But Leo's gaze was too sharp, and Bethany knew that she could no longer maintain any pretense of calm if she continued to look at him.

She moved, restless and more agitated than she wanted to admit, wandering further into the room. She let her gaze dance over the painting that dominated the far wall, a richly imagined, opulently hued rendition of the view outside these very windows, give or take a handful of centuries, painted by no less an artist than Titian.

Murano glass vases glowed scarlet and blue on the dresser, picking up the light from the Venetian chandelier that hung from the ceiling high above. Bethany knew that one of this room's more famous occupants hundreds of years ago had been the daughter of a grand and noble Venetian family, and this room had ever since been adapted to pay homage to her residency.

What legacy might Bethany have left behind, she wondered, had she stayed? Would she have left her mark at all or would she have been swallowed whole into this castle, this family, this history? Annoyed by her sentimentality, and that wrenching sense of loss that inevitably followed, she shook the thought away.

She pretended she was not aware of Leo still standing in the doorway that connected his suite to hers. She pretended she could not feel the weight of his gaze and the far heavier and more damaging crush of the memories she fought to keep from her mind tugging at her, pulling at her, making her feel as if she waded through molasses.

Yet, despite herself, she was attuned to his every movement, his every breath.

"Dinner will be served at eight o'clock," he said in his inexorable way when the silence in the room seemed to pound in her ears. "And, yes, we still maintain tradition and dress for dinner."

She turned back toward him, hoping the fact that she was wearing jeans annoyed him as much as it had three years ago, when he had had his social secretary admonish her for her relentlessly common fashion-sense. She had been seen wearing them in the village, where anyone might have recognized her—oh, the horror.

"As you are not a student but the *Principessa di Felici*, it would be preferable if you dressed in a manner more befitting your station," the dry, disapproving Nuncio had told her.

She reminded herself that she had only moments ago claimed to have grown up; such spiteful, petty thoughts rather undermined that claim.

She smiled with as much politeness as she could muster and waved a hand toward her bag where it stood near the door.

"As you can see, I brought very little," she said. "I doubt I have anything appropriate. I am more than happy to take a tray in my room."

"There is no need," Leo said smoothly, a smile playing near his sensual lips.

He moved then, his long strides bringing him far too close to her until he stopped at the large dressing-room that led away from the bed chamber itself. He opened the door and indicated the interior with a slight nod.

"Your wardrobe remains intact."

Bethany felt her mouth open and snapped it closed.

"You cannot mean…?" She blinked. "I have been gone for three years."

Leo's smile deepened. "Eight o'clock," he said softly.

She did not know why she should feel so…disarmed. She did not know why it felt as if he had kept her things out of some sense of emotional attachment to her—when she knew such a thing to be impossible. Leo did not have emotional attachments, to her or to anyone. It was far more likely that he had simply forgotten this room existed the moment she'd left and the contents of her closet along with it.

Still, she felt a fluttering in her stomach and a kind of ache in her chest.

Leo was too close now, within a single step, and she knew the exact moment that both of them realized that: the air seemed to disappear even as it heated. His eyes grew darker, more intent. His smile took on an edge that made a tight coil of need twist inside of her.

"No," she said, but it was little more than a whisper. Need. Longing. She did not know which was worse.

"What are you refusing?" he asked, taunting her. "I have offered you nothing."

Yet, was the unspoken next word. It seemed to shimmer between them. Bethany could imagine his hands cupping her face, his hard, impossible mouth on hers. She knew exactly how it would feel, exactly how deeply and fully she would feel it.

But she knew better than to let him touch her. She

knew better than to trust herself this close to him. It was not him she feared, it was herself. Once she touched him again, how could she ever stop?

"I am here for one reason, Leo," she said, wanting to back away from him but worried that doing so would make her look weak, and encourage him to push his advantage. "I am not here to dress in fancy gowns for lavish dinners I do not want, much less to play bedroom games with you."

"Bedroom games?" His voice was like chocolate, dark and sweet. "I am intrigued. What sort of games do you have in mind?"

"A divorce," she said, feeling desperate. He still had yet to move! He simply looked at her in that knowing, shattering way, and it made her shiver. Her body wanted everything he had to offer and more. It always had. "All I want is a divorce. That is the only thing I have on my mind."

"So you have mentioned, I think," Leo said in that low, rich voice that seemed to connect directly to her nerve endings, sending sensations rippling throughout her limbs. "Repeatedly."

There was no magic, she told herself fiercely. He was not magical. It was simply because she was here, in this room, in this castle, in Italy. It was not his voice. It was not *him*. It was only the past, yet again.

If she turned her head too quickly she feared she would see her own ghost and his entwined together— on the thick rug beneath their feet, up against the door, on the window seat. They had always been insatiable. As their marriage had worn on and worsened, that had often been their only form of communication.

But those were ghosts, and this was now, and she knew exactly what that light in his eyes meant.

"I am sorry if I have begun to bore you," she managed to say. "A solution, of course, is to allow me to remain in this room until we go to court. You need never see me until then."

She sounded desperate to her own ears, yet Leo only smiled, a lazy, knowing smile that sent heat spiraling through her until her toes curled inside her shoes. It would be far too easy simply to move toward him. She knew he would catch her. He would sweep her into his arms and she would lose herself completely in that raging wildfire that was his to command.

A huge part of her wanted that, needed that, more than she wanted anything else—even her freedom. And that terrified her.

If she touched him, if she pressed her lips to his, she would forget. She would forget everything, as if it had all been a nightmare and he was the light of day. Wasn't that exactly what he'd done for her after her father had died? But she had no idea how she would ever fight her way out of it—not again. Not whole.

And she could not be this broken again. Not ever again.

"That would not suit me at all," he said, his attention focused on her mouth. "As I think you know."

"I don't want you to touch me!" she threw at him from the depths of her fear, her agony and her broken heart. Because she knew beyond a shadow of a doubt that she could not trust herself, not where he was concerned. She still wanted him too much. She bit her lip but then pulled herself together somehow, even as his arrogant brows climbed high.

"I beg your pardon?" He was all hauteur, untold centuries of nobility.

"You heard me." She looked around as if there was

anything that might redirect her focus when he was standing so close. She sucked in a breath and returned her gaze to his. "The chemistry between us is damaging. It can only lead to confusion."

"I am not confused," he offered, smirking slightly.

"I do not want you," she lied, in a matter-of-fact voice. She did not smile; she met his gaze. "Not in that way. Not at all."

She expected his temper. His disbelief. She was unprepared for the full force of his devastating smile. He crossed his arms over his tautly muscled chest and gazed at her almost fondly. Somehow, that was far worse than any sardonic expression. It made her almost yearn.

"You are such a liar," he said softly, without heat. Flustered, she began to speak, but he cut her off. "You want me, Bethany. You always have and you always will, no matter what stories you choose to tell yourself."

"Your conceit is astonishing," she said even as her heart leapt in her chest and her legs felt shaky underneath her. Even as she felt the roll and sway, the seductive pull, of all that grief just beneath.

"Just as I want you," he said, shrugging as if it was of no matter to him—as, she reminded herself forcefully, it doubtless was not. "It is inconvenient, perhaps, but nothing more dangerous than that."

"Leo, I am telling you—" she began, feeling flushed and edgy.

"You need not concern yourself," he interrupted her, his words casual, almost offhand, though his gaze burned. "I have no intention of seducing you into my bed. In fact, I will not touch you at all as long as you are here."

She stared at him, letting those unexpected words sink in, telling herself that this was exactly what she wanted to hear, that this would make everything easy, that this was what she wanted. Though she could not entirely ignore the empty feeling that swamped her suddenly, nearly taking her off her feet.

"I am happy to hear that," she said. His eyes seemed to see straight through her and she was as terrified of what he might see as of what she might feel. What she already felt.

His smile took on that edge again and the tension between them seemed to crackle with new electricity, making it hard to breathe.

"I will leave it to you," he said in that compelling voice of his that slid like whiskey and chocolate over her, through her, inside of her.

"To me?" She could hardly do more than echo him.

"If you want me, Bethany, you must come to me." His deep-brown eyes were mesmerizing, so dark and rich, with that gold gleam within. His voice lowered. "You must be the one to touch me, not the other way around."

"That will work perfectly," she said, her voice betraying her by cracking even as her breasts and her hidden core grew heavy and ached, yearned. "As I have absolutely no intention—"

"There are your intentions and then there is reality," he said smoothly. His gaze sharpened suddenly, catching her off-guard. "You cannot keep your hands off me. You never could. But you prefer to pretend that the passion between us is something I use to control you. Is that not what you said so memorably? That I would prefer it if I could keep you chained to my bed? It certainly makes you feel more the martyr to think so."

Bethany's mouth fell open then. There was a heat

behind her eyes and a riot in her limbs as she tried to make sense of what he was saying—what he was doing or, more to the point, deliberately not doing.

"I am not a martyr," was all she could think to say, instantly wishing she could yank the words back into her mouth. She did not feel like a martyr, she felt adrift and unsteady, as she had always felt here.

"Indeed you are not," he said softly, deliberately, that gleam in his eyes growing hard, seeming to take over the room, her pounding heart. "What you are is a liar. It is entirely up to you to prove otherwise."

He thought she was a liar. He had said it before, and she had no doubt he meant it. It was almost amusing, she thought, unable to look away from him for a long, searing moment. It should have been amusing, really, and she wanted to laugh it off, but she found she had no voice. She could not seem to find it.

She could not reply in kind, or at all, and she did not know why that seemed to highlight everything they'd lost. What was being called a liar next to all of that?

"Eight o'clock," he said with a certain finality and evident satisfaction. "Do not make me come and fetch you."

Then he walked from the room and left her standing there, shocked, trembling and lost again, so very lost— as he had no doubt planned from the start.

There was so much she had forgotten, Bethany thought as she made her way through the castle's quiet halls toward dinner moments before eight o'clock, as requested.

She had not expected to find so many memories when she'd ventured into her former closet and searched for something simple to wear to dinner. It was not quite a homecoming, and yet every gown, every bag, every shoe had seemed to whisper a different half-forgotten story to her.

They had all come flooding back to her without warning, leaving her raw and aching for a past she knew she needed to keep firmly behind her if she was to escape it. But the memories had rushed at her anyway.

A night out at the opera in Milan, where the glorious voices had seemed to pale next to the fire in Leo's gaze that she'd believed could burn out everything else in the world. A weekend at a friend's villa outside of Rome, replete with sunshine and laughter—and with her growing fear that she was losing him a constant sharpness underneath.

A rare public eruption of his fiercely contained temper on a side street in Verona while walking to a business dinner, quick, brutal and devastating. A passionate moment on a quiet bridge in Venice; the explosive, impossible desire that still shimmered between them had been the only way left to reach each other across the walls of bitterness and silence they'd erected.

So many images and recollections, none of which she had entertained in ages, all of them buffeting her, storming her defenses, making her feel weak, small, vulnerable in ways she hadn't been in years.

She ran her hands along the swell of her hips as she walked, smoothing the silken, kelly-green material that flowed to her feet, trying to calm herself. The simple cowl-necked dress was the only item she'd been able to find that was both relatively restrained and unconnected to any of the explosive memories she had not known she'd been carrying around with her.

But it was not only the memories connected to her forgotten clothes that had unnerved her.

More than that, she'd realized during that confusing

interaction with Leo that on some level she had forgotten who she was back then. The woman Leo had referred to so disparagingly—the one who had behaved so appallingly, who had, she was humiliated to recall, more than once destroyed more than one piece of china while in a temper—was not her.

That was not who she was, not anymore. It made her stomach hurt to think of it. To think of who he must see when he looked at her. To think that she remembered her isolation and the loss of all she had loved, but he remembered nothing but a termagant.

It had been that last night that had changed her, she realised, as she descended the great stone stair that dominated the front hall, rising from both sides to meet in the center and then veer off to the east and west wings. That last, shameful night. It was as if something had broken in her then, as if she'd been faced with the depths of her own temper, her own depraved passions. She'd lost that fiery, inconsolable part of herself, that wild, violent, mad part. For good? she thought.

Or perhaps it is Leo who stirs up all those dark and disgraceful urges, an insidious voice whispered. Perhaps he is the match. Perhaps without him you are simply tinder in a box, harmless and entirely free of fire.

"I am shocked," came his lazy drawl, as if she'd summoned him simply by thinking of him.

Bethany's head snapped up and she found Leo standing at the foot of the great stair, his brown eyes fathomless as he watched her approach.

"I had anticipated you would ignore what I told you and force me to come and deliver you to the table myself," he continued, and she knew there was a part of him that wished she had done just that. Because there was a part of her that wished it too.

"As I keep attempting to explain to you," she said, forcing a smile that seemed to scrape along all the places she was raw, "You do not know me any longer."

"I am sure that is true," he said, but there was an undercurrent in his rich voice that made her wonder what he did not say.

It was so unfair that he was who he was, she thought in a kind of despair as she continued to walk toward him, step by stone step.

The walls were covered with heavy tapestries and magnificent portraits of the Di Marco family from across the ages. Every step she took was an opportunity to note the well-documented provenance of the thrust of Leo's haughty cheekbones, the fullness of his lips, the flashing, dark richness of his gaze, all laid out for her in an inexorable march through the generations. His height, his rangy male beauty, his thick and lustrous hair: all of this was as much his legacy as the castle they both stood in.

And he was not only the product of this elegant, aristocratic line—he was its masterpiece. Tonight he wore a dark suit she had no doubt he had had made to his specifications in one of Milan's foremost ateliers, so that the charcoal-hued fabric clung to his every movement. He was a dream made flesh, every inch of him a prince and every part of him devastatingly attractive. It was hardwired into his very DNA.

How could she explain to this man what it was to feel isolated? He was never alone; he had servants, aides, dependants, villagers, employees. Failing that, he had some eight centuries of well-documented family history to keep him company. He was always surrounded by people in one way or another.

Bethany had only had her father since she'd been

tiny, and then she'd had only Leo. But soon she had lost him too, and it had broken her in ways she knew that he—who had never had no one, who could not conceive of such a thing—would never, ever understand. She only knew that she could not allow it to happen a second time or she was afraid she would disappear altogether.

"Why do you frown?" he asked quietly, his gaze disconcertingly warm, incisive—dangerous.

"Am I?" Bethany tried to smooth her features into something more appropriate as she finally came to a stop on the step just above him—something more uninviting, more appropriate for a divorcing couple. "I was thinking of all these portraits," she said, which was not untrue, and waved a hand at the walls. "I was wondering when yours will grace the walls."

"On my fortieth birthday," he replied at once, his brows arching. He smirked slightly, and his tone turned sardonic. "Do you have an artist in mind? Perhaps your lover is a painter. What a delightful commission that would be."

Bethany pulled in a long breath, determined not to react to him as he obviously wished her to do. Determined not to feel slapped down, somehow—after all, she was the one who had introduced the concept of a lover into this mess. She was lucky Leo preferred to make sardonic remarks and was not altogether more angry, as she'd expected him to be. She was somewhat mystified he was not.

She forced another smile, hiding the sharp edges she did not wish to feel, pretending they did not exist.

"I only wondered how odd it must be to grow up under the gaze of so many men who look so much like you," she said. "You must never have spent even a moment imagining who you might be when you grew up. You already knew exactly what was in store for you."

She looked at the nearest painting, a well-known Giotto portrait of one of the earliest Di Marco princes, who looked like a shorter, rounder, eccentrically clad version of the man in front of her.

"I am my family's history," he said matter-of-factly, yet not without a certain resolute pride. She could feel the current of it in him, around him. "I am unintelligible without it."

He spoke in an even sort of tone, as if he expected her to fight him about it. Had she done that before? she wondered suddenly. Had she argued simply for the sake of arguing? Or had she simply been too young then to understand how any history could shape and mold whomever it touched? She wondered if some day she would think about their complicated history without the attendant surge of anger and the darker current of grief.

"I can see that living here would make you think so," she agreed and turned her attention back to him in time to see a curious expression move through his eyes, as if he felt the same currents, then disappear.

"Our dinner awaits," he said softly. "If you are finished with my ancestors?"

She descended the last few stairs and fell into step with him when he began to walk. The castle seemed so immense all around them, so daunting. Shimmering chandeliers lit their way, spinning light down from the high ceilings, showcasing the grace and beauty of every room they walked through.

"Do we dine alone?" she asked in the same quiet tone he had used, though she was not certain why she felt a kind of pregnant hush surround them. She cleared her throat and tried to contain her wariness. "Where are your cousins?"

He glanced at her, then away. "They no longer call the castello their home."

"No?" So polite, Bethany thought wryly, when she had nothing at all courteous to say about Leo's spiteful, trouble-making cousins. She had been so delighted when she'd met them; as the only child of two deceased only-children, she'd been excited she would finally experience 'family' in a broader sense. "I was under the impression that they would never leave here."

Leo looked down at her, his gaze serious as they moved through a shining gold and royal blue gallery. They headed toward the smaller reception rooms located in the renovated back of the castle that, as of the eighteenth century, opened up to a terrace with a view out over the valley.

"They were not offered any choice in the matter," he said, a trace of stiffness in his voice. Almost as if he finally knew what she had tried to tell him back then. Almost as if…

Bethany searched his face for a moment, then looked away.

Both the cruel, beautiful Giovanna and the haughty, unpleasant Vincentio had hated—*loathed*—Leo's spontaneous choice of bride. And neither had had the slightest qualm about expressing their concerns. The noble line polluted. Their family name forever contaminated by Leo's recklessness.

But Leo had not allowed a word to be spoken against them, not in the year and a half that they had made Bethany's life a misery. And now he had banished them from Felici?

She was afraid to speculate about what that might

mean, afraid to let herself wonder, even as that treacherous spark of hope that still flickered deep inside of her threatened to bloom into a full flame. She doubted she would survive placing her hopes in Leo again. The very idea of it was sobering.

He did not lead her to one of the more formal rooms as Bethany had anticipated. She had not, of course, anticipated they might dine in the great dining hall itself, which was equipped to serve a multitude, but had imagined the more intimate family dining-room that was still elegant enough to cow her. But Leo did not stop walking until they reached the blue salon with its bright, frescoed ceilings and high, graceful windows.

Through the French doors that opened off the room, Bethany could see a small wrought-iron table had been set up on the patio to overlook the twinkling lights of the village and the valley beyond. The Italian night was soft all around her as she stepped outside, alive with the scent of cypress and rhododendrons, azaleas and wisteria. She could not help taking a deep, fragrant breath and remembering.

The table was laden with simple, undoubtedly local fare. Bethany knew the wine would be from the Di Marco vineyards, and it would be full-bodied and perfect. The olives would have been hand-picked from the groves she could see from her windows. The bread smelled fresh and warm, and had likely been baked that morning in the castello's grand kitchens.

A simple roasted chicken sat in the center of the table, fragrant with rosemary and garlic, flanked by side dishes of mushroom risotto and a polenta with vegetables and nuts. Candles flickered in the night air, casting a pool of warm, intimate light around the cozy, inviting scene.

Bethany swallowed and carefully took the seat that

Leo offered her. She felt a deep pang of something like nostalgia roll through her, shaking her. It was worse in its way than the usual grief, but by the time Leo took his place opposite her she was sure she had hid it.

"This is by far the most romantic setting I could have imagined," she said, a feeling of desperation coiling into a tense ball in her belly.

Why was he torturing her like this? What was the point of this meal, of their elegant attire, of this entire charade?

She met his gaze, though it took more out of her than she wanted to admit, even to herself. "It is more than a little inappropriate, don't you think? This is the first night of our divorce, Leo."

Leo did not respond at once, letting her words sit there between them. There was something almost brittle in the way she sat opposite him, as if she were on the verge of shattering like glass. He was not certain where the image had come from, nor did he care for it.

The Bethany he knew was vocal, mercurial. She did not break; she bent until she'd twisted herself— and him—into new and often contradictory shapes. He was not at all sure what to do with a Bethany he could not read, a Bethany whose temper he could not predict with fatalistic accuracy.

He was even less sure how it made him feel.

He reached over and poured the wine, a rich and aromatic red, into both of their glasses.

"Can we not enjoy each other's company, no matter the circumstances?" he asked. "Have we really fallen so far?"

He let his gaze track the flush that tinted her skin slightly red, and made the deep, inviting green of her dress seem that much more beckoning. He wanted to reach across the table and test the curls that fell from the twist she'd secured to the crown of her head, but refrained. When he gave his word, he kept it.

No matter what it cost him.

"It is questions like that which make me question your motives," she said, a vulnerable cast to her fine mouth. She kept her gaze trained on him as he lounged back in his chair and merely eyed her in return, trying to figure her out, trying to see beyond the facade.

He was starting to wonder why she was so determined to divorce him—and why she refused even to discuss it. It was almost as if she feared he would talk her out of it, should she allow the conversation. Which, of course, he would.

Talk or no talk, there would be no divorce. He wondered why he did not simply announce this truth to her here and now and do away with the suspense. He knew he would have done so three years ago without a second thought.

Was it a weakness in him that he was content to let this play out—that he was intrigued despite himself by this new version of his wife? Her return, her uncertainty, her obvious response to him that she worked so hard to conceal…he found himself fascinated by it all. He did not want to crush her with a truth he suspected she would claim to find unbearable. He wanted to see what happened between them first.

He did not want to investigate why that was. He did not want to look too closely at what felt more and more like an indulgence with every passing second.

He began to realize exactly what he had done by vowing he would not touch her. Perhaps she was not the only one who had hidden in their explosive passion.

Perhaps he too had used it as a shorthand—a bridge. It was an unsettling notion.

But this time, he thought with a certain grimness, he would make sure that there were no shortcuts taken. They would achieve the same destination, but this time they would both do it with their eyes wide open. It was the only way he could be sure that there would be no more years of estrangement, no more talk of divorce. And the more he let this play out, he told himself, the less likely that there could be arguments from Bethany about compulsion and manipulation, and all the rest of the accusations she levied at him.

"You are so focused on our divorce," he said after a moment. He selected a plump, ripe olive from the small bowl, swimming in oil and spices. He popped it in his mouth. "Don't you think we should first discuss our marriage?"

She let out a startled laugh. Her blue eyes looked shocked, which irritated him far more than it should have done. As if *he* was the unreasonable one, the hysterical one!

"You want to…talk?" she asked. Her tone of amazement set his teeth on edge. "You, Leo Di Marco, want to talk. Now. After all this time."

Something that looked like pain washed through her extraordinary eyes—but it could not be; how could it be? Then it was gone, hidden once more behind that brand-new armor of hers that she wore far too comfortably for his tastes.

"There was a time I might have killed to hear you say such a thing," she said after a moment, her voice husky. Her mouth twisted slightly, wryly. "But that is long past, Leo. It is too late for talking now, so far after the fact. Surely you see that?"

"Three years have passed since we were last together," Leo said, unperturbed, keeping his attention focused on her face. She looked away and he felt the loss, as if she had deliberately shut him out. "I imagine that ought to provide us the necessary distance."

"The distance to do what?" she asked—almost wistfully, he thought. She was still gazing out at the dark gardens, a faint frown between her brows. "Rake over the old coals? Poke around for old wounds? I do not understand the purpose of such an exercise. What will it accomplish? Our scars are our scars. Must we compare them?"

He searched her face, so much like a stranger's, when he had once thought he'd known it and its secrets far better than he knew his own.

He did not understand his own feelings. He wanted to go to her, to comfort her, and he could not understand the urge. The need for her body, for that addictive fire that raged between them—that he comprehended fully. But why should he want to chase the shadows from her eyes? Why should he yearn to make her smile? He wanted to focus on her duties, her obligations, the role he expected her to play. The rest of it, these softer urges, led directly to places within himself he had no desire to visit. He had walled them off long ago.

"You have returned after a long absence," he said, feeling as if he moved across shards of broken glass, buried mines. As if any wrong move might shatter them both.

He was aware of the tension rising between them and aware that it was not sexual in origin. He knew better than to let down his walls and feel, as he had once allowed himself to do so disastrously in the seductive tropics of Hawaii. Yet he could not seem to block her as he knew he should.

She shifted in her seat and her fingers crept up to her neck, as if she held her own pulse in her hand. Her eyes seemed huge and bruised, somehow, in the candlelight.

"I have not exactly returned, have I?" she said quietly, her gaze mysterious, compelling, more like the sea now than the summer sky. "Not really. Soon it will be as if I never came to this place at all."

"If that is what you want," he replied just as quietly, aware of the soft night all around them and the sense of change, of some kind of promise, in the air.

He wanted to see into her. He wanted to know her secrets, finally, and in so doing vanquish the ghost of her that haunted him even now while she sat within reach.

He wanted to reach out, but did not.

Could not.

He would not let himself, because it felt too much like it had so long before in Hawaii, when he had fallen too hard and trusted too much, and he had vowed he would never give into that weakness again. Not even for her.

CHAPTER SIX

"I WANT a great many things," Bethany said, lulled by the strangest sensation of something almost like peace that hovered between them. It made her wonder. It made her reckless. It tempted her to forget. "But I am finally old enough to understand that not everything I want is good for me."

If she expected him to smile, or nod in agreement, she was disappointed. He only stared at her for a long moment, then shook his head slightly, dispelling the odd feeling.

"From that I am to gather that it is your marriage you find… What is it?" He affected a total lack of understanding, as if it was perhaps the English she knew very well he spoke fluently that eluded him. She felt it like a slap. "Bad for your health?"

It was Leo at his most patronizing and it reminded her forcibly of the reason why she was here—not to understand what had happened between them, but to put it behind her once and for all.

She sighed, annoyed at herself for her momentary lapse, and busied herself with filling her plate. At least she knew that everything that was offered to her in this place would be excellent. Nothing else would be tolerated. She took a few slices of the chicken, and could not resist a large helping of the creamy risotto.

"No answer?" he asked quietly. He let out a sound somewhere between a laugh and a sigh. "Why am I not surprised?"

Bethany straightened her shoulders and took a calming breath as she picked up her fork. "As it happens, I have given the matter some thought," she said evenly. As if she was unaware he was coiled in his chair, waiting to strike. "I believe that when a marriage diminishes and degrades the people in it—" she began.

He actually laughed then, cutting her off.

"Such strong words," he taunted her. "You feel degraded, Bethany? I degrade you?" He shook his head, his eyes glittering, as if she had accused him of a terrible crime—as if was not the simple truth.

"You are the one who wanted a discussion, Leo," she threw back at him, exasperated, and unable to completely repress her reaction to him even under these circumstances. What was the matter with her? "You should have made it clear you meant that discussion to be entirely on your terms, as ever! I can do without your scorn."

"What you would like to do without is the truth," he said, all pretense of laughter gone from his hard face. The candles cast his features into harsh angles, forbidding shadows. "Because the truth is that you do not come out the victim in this scenario. The fact that you have cast yourself in that role is one more example of the infantile behavior you claim to have left behind you."

"You are proving my point," she said, unable to keep the faint tremor from her voice. Even so, she kept her spine ramrod straight, determined to look strong no matter how she might feel when he ripped into her.

He studied her for a moment and Bethany felt her face heat. Anger, she told herself. It was nothing more than anger, and never mind the twisting ache inside. Never mind the contradictory, baffling urge to reach out to him, to bridge the gap between them, no matter what it cost her.

"Perhaps it is simply that you are too fragile to face up to who you really are," he said softly. Deliberately.

She let out a small laugh and then put down her fork, no longer able even to pretend to enjoy the food, no matter how perfectly prepared.

"Who are you to tell me who I really am?" she asked with a kick of temper, clenching her hands into fists below the table, where he could not see. She had longed for him to know her, to see her, for years—but he never had. She shook away the old wants, the old needs, even as they seemed to sear through her, leaving deep marks behind. "When you are the person who knows me least of all?"

"I know you," he said, with that terrifying ring of finality, of certainty, that she could sense meant things to him that she was better off not knowing. "I know you in ways no one else could."

"If that was ever true, it has not been true for a long time," she replied, choosing her words carefully. Trying to ignore the part of her that still desperately wanted him to know her the way he claimed he did, the part of her that wished so deeply that somehow, some way, he could.

She shook her head, trying to ward off her own turmoil and his accusatory glare.

"Let me guess," he said icily. He did not move, and yet she could feel the way his gaze, his attention and temper focused on her, narrowing in on them both, trapping them in the grip of this roiling tension between them. "No doubt you have spent the past three years coming up with the perfect, bloodless fantasy to use as a comparison to our relationship. No doubt your supernaturally forgiving lover aids you in this. Anything to avoid looking at yourself with any form of honest appraisal, is that it?"

Her temper flared. And for once she could think of no particular reason to keep it locked up. She told herself she had nothing to lose—it was all already lost. This was simply a pointless dance around the bonfire of what they had been. An opportunity to watch it all burn away into ash.

So why should she bite her tongue?

"I do not think marriage should be a monarchy, with you installed as king by divine right while I am expected to play the role of grateful, subservient subject," she told him, the words three years in the making. For a brief moment she felt just as she sounded. Calm. Deadly. "It cannot even be called a marriage. It is an exercise in steamrolling, and I am tired of feeling flattened by you."

They stared at each other for a long moment. His expression was frozen, arrested. She was aware of the slight breeze against her bare skin, the dance of the candles in their crystal holders. She was not holding her breath, not quite. She felt as if she watched the scene from on high.

She had never dared say such things to Leo before. How could she? Their relationship had been entirely based on his acknowledged superiority. What room had there been for her to call his actions or his assumptions into question?

And she knew that her own appalling behavior had

only made everything worse. Who would have listened to an out-of-control maniac who smashed things? Who would take the emotional mess seriously? Certainly not Leo.

And not even herself, Bethany acknowledged with no little pain. That had come later.

"You say the most extraordinary things," he said coldly.

Because Leo did not explode. Leo did not rage, yell or allow things to become messy. Leo did not, could not, feel.

"I understand that this is all a foreign concept to someone who has issued orders to his minions from his cradle," she said, her voice stiff from her own revelations, and only partially a response to his chilly glare, no matter how it pierced her. "Who has priceless paintings on his walls of his own family members. Who lives in a castle."

"You quite mistake me," he bit out. "I am astonished that you would have any thoughts at all on what might make for a good marriage. Real relationships are not conducted according to your every melodramatic whim and tantrum, Bethany."

"That's taking the concept of the pot calling the kettle black to the level of farce," she replied, blinking away the avalanche of emotion that threatened to drag her under. There was no room for that here, now. And she could not be certain what lurked just on the other side.

His mouth flattened with displeasure, but she did not back down. Because, no matter what he believed, it was true.

He had left her to die of loneliness, and she nearly had.

"I am not the one who issued ultimatums and then,

when they were not met, threw temper tantrums," he said then. His mouth twisted; his dark eyes were condemning. "I am not the one who stubbornly refused contact for years in an extended fit of pique."

"Stop it!" she hissed, but he gave no sign of hearing her. She had the sense that he had been waiting to say these things as long as she had. She could see the way he held himself, all that power and ferocity tightly leashed and controlled, even now.

"I am also not the one who issued a demand for a divorce instead of the polite greeting one might give a stranger on the street." His eyes seemed to glow with his cold, consuming fury. He was, she realized, more angry than she had imagined. More angry than she had ever seen him. Was it sick that she wanted that to mean something? "And having done all of those things, seemingly without shame, I am not the one to sit here now and lecture on about successful marriages."

She wanted to scream at him, to protest what he'd said, but how could she? She had done all of those things. Could he not see how he had driven her to it? How she had never had any other choice? How she had felt forced to flee—or she might have withered away to nothing but an empty shell?

"I have always been right here, Bethany," he said, the anger she had never imagined she would see in him lighting him with a cold glow, making her yearn to warm him somehow, despite herself. "Right here, awaiting your return, should you ever condescend to recall your commitments."

"I don't know why you would expect—" she began, but cut herself off, her mind reeling. How could she ever imagine he might see these things from her perspective?

He saw only her abandonment of him. He never saw his own abandonment of her, because he had not physically left her. He had only disappeared in every other possible way. Yet he still considered himself firmly on the moral high ground.

"You to keep your promises?" he finished for her, his voice heavy with irony. When his gaze met hers it was too intense and angry, kicking into her and making her stomach clench and her breath catch. "Because you gave your word."

She wanted to fight him, deny his condemnation— but she was much too afraid that was not what she really wanted. That beneath it, she only wanted those dark eyes to shine at her again, as they had once. And she could not let herself down that way. Not this time. Not again.

"You gave your word too," she said in a determined undertone. "But that did not prevent you from conveniently—"

"Did I beat you?" he asked, his voice raw, yet still so fiercely controlled. Only his eyes showed any hint of the wildness within, so dark and stormy, bittersweet and on fire. "Did I take other women to my bed? Did I abuse you? Demean you? Did I fail to attend to your every need?"

He waved a hand at the castello.

"Is my home not big enough? Is it too rural? Would you prefer the house in Milan? Exactly what is the root of all this bitterness and hostility?" he demanded. "What did I do that was so terrible you punished me in the only way you could—by running away?"

She could not breathe for a long moment, could not manage it past the swell of agony that swept through her. When she could, she had to fight off tears. Was that truly how he saw her—no more than a spiteful little brat? She knew with a sudden, unbearable certainty that it was. He believed she'd left him on a whim—rather than in pieces.

"I can't imagine why you ever wanted me in the first place," she managed to say, her voice trembling, shaken to the bone.

"Oh, I want you." His voice was far too raw then, with too many undercurrents, and spoke to all the sins she dared not name—all of which he had taught her. The look in his eyes set her afire. His expression was almost brooding. Something deeper, more painful, than simply *wry*. "It seems there is nothing at all you can do to keep me from wanting you, and you have certainly put that to the test."

He did not move, he only watched her, and yet he seemed, suddenly, to be everywhere. It was as if she had forgotten the danger of being this close to him—of talking to him, of allowing him to weave his way into her psyche again—until this very second—and now she could notice nothing else.

Her heart beat in a jagged rhythm. Her mouth was far too dry. She felt as if her entire body was short-circuiting, shutting down. Readying itself for his touch.

It did not matter how much it hurt. She still wanted him. She always wanted him.

Blindly, she shoved away from the table and lurched to her feet. She knew only that she had to escape. She had to put distance between them, because he might have made a promise not to touch her of his own volition, but she knew all too well that she was the one who could not be trusted in that area.

She moved toward the French doors and she knew even as she reached for the handle that he was behind her. She did not have to turn and confirm it, not when she could *feel* him.

She stopped with her hand on the ornate handle and felt the heat of him at her back, so close she could smell the faintest hint of his cologne—so near that if she shifted her weight backward she would be nestled beneath his chin, her back against the hot, hard wall of his chest.

"You promised!" she whispered, desperate to run away and yet frozen in place. She wanted him, but she also wanted the comfort of his heat, his closeness, his scent.

He had been her man, her family, her love. She still did not know how to let go of any of that, only that she must.

Even so, her eyes drifted closed. "You said you would not…"

"Am I touching you?" he asked in that low, stirring tone that seemed to roll through her, quietly devastating her, reducing her to little more than mindlessness and need.

She turned then, before her knees collapsed beneath her, and found her back against the door with nothing before her but Leo. As if he was all the world.

He leaned closer, resting his hands against the paned glass on either side of her head, a move that brought his mouth nearly flush with hers.

And though she could feel him in every part of her—in her swollen breasts, her taut belly, her molten femininity—he did not touch her. He kept his promise. He only gazed down at her, his eyes hard with a passion she recognized all too well.

"I cannot stop wanting you," he said then, his mouth a breath away, his sensual lips close enough to kiss. "And

I have tried. Nights I lay awake, cursing your name, and yet here I am—as ready for you as if there was no history between us, no years apart, no demands for a divorce."

"Leo…" But she could not seem to form any words save his name, even then, when she knew she should end this moment, whatever it was.

She should not let him speak these things out loud, making both of them remember. Making her yearn. Ache. *Want*.

But all she could do was stare up at him and hope her heart did not beat so hard, so frantically, that it might break through her own ribs as she half-feared it might.

"You are under my skin," he whispered as if it was torn from him. "You are like a poison. You cannot seem to kill me, but I cannot seem to be rid of you."

He had said too much, Leo thought, and yet he did not step back.

He could not seem to make his own body obey him, not when she was so close. He could feel her breath against his skin, close enough that he could smell the unique scent of her. Like lavender and vanilla—her own delectable perfume.

He could count the freckles that splayed across her nose, and knew what the larger one on her clavicle tasted like. He felt it when their breath began to move in sync, as it always had—as if their bodies insisted on synchronizing even as they dedicated themselves to remaining at war.

This close to her, he could not even remember why.

"You…" She could not manage to speak. He watched,

fascinated, as she wet her soft lips and swallowed. "You must let me go."

"How many times must I let you go?" he heard himself whisper. Worse, he heard the emotion that was underneath it. The jagged pain. What was more horrifying was that he did not immediately move away from her. Not even then.

"You say you want me," she said in a low, urgent voice, her impossible blue eyes wide with a sheen that told him he was not the only one rubbed raw by this encounter, no matter that they were not actually touching.

"I do," he agreed. "Just as you want me, Bethany. I can feel it. I can see it."

"You say that," she continued as if it hurt her to push the words out. Her eyes searched his, something desperate there reaching out to him. "But you only want me if you can keep me in a convenient box of your choosing. If I behave, if I conform, if I act according to your rules, then I am treated like a queen. But it's still a box."

"You are confusing a box with a bed," he said. Her mouth was so close and her skin would be so soft and he could not believe he had made such a foolhardy promise, much less that he intended to keep it—even now when he was so hard it bordered on the painful.

"With you they are often the same thing," she said.

No matter how much he yearned simply to sink into her, he could not miss the reproving tone she used. He tilted his head back slightly and gazed at her, taking in that high red flush across her neck, the determined set of her jaw, the cool gleam in her eyes.

"I am only telling you the truth," she said after a long moment. She took a breath that lifted her breasts alluringly, but he refused to be sidetracked. "Nothing I did happened in a vacuum, Leo. You were as responsible for what happened in our marriage as I was. But I suppose it's easier to look only at me, isn't it?"

"I looked for you for three long years," he gritted out. He was so close to her it bordered on madness, yet he still did not touch her. "But you were never where you were supposed to be. Tell me what I was meant to do. Beg? Plead? Weep?"

"Why not?" she whispered fiercely. "Why not all of the above, if that is how you feel?"

"I am not you," he whispered back in the same hard tone, shoving through the things he refused to admit, even to himself. "I cannot flash my every emotion for all to see."

"You cannot or you will not?" She moved then, only slightly, but it brought her shoulder into glancing contact with his arm. They both froze, focused on that single, accidental touch. He watched her swallow, the long, graceful column of her throat begging for his mouth, his tongue, his teeth.

"Tell me to touch you," he ordered her huskily, their history forgotten in that moment like so much smoke. "Tell me to hold your face in my hands. Tell me to kiss you."

Her lips parted on a soundless breath, but he felt it fan across his jaw. Her eyes widened, darkened. He could feel that shimmering electricity arc between them, hot and wild.

"Tell me…" he whispered, moving his mouth to hover near her ear, so very close, just out of reach. "Tell me to take you in my arms and make you mine. Again and again. Until you cannot remember your name. Or my name. Or why you left."

* * *

She was almost his, until that last whispered sentence.

A chill snaked through her, and it gave her the strength to force open her eyes and remember. Why she was there. Why she could not simply surrender to him as every cell, every breath, every part of her longed to do. Why she could not let him cast this spell around her.

Not again.

"I think it is time for me to get some sleep," she said, keeping her head turned and choosing her words so carefully, so desperately. "I think the traveling is catching up with me."

He murmured something in Italian, something lyrical that she did not have to understand to know was all sex and command. She could feel it move between her legs, coil low in her belly and spiral along her skin until she shivered in reaction. But she did not look at him. She knew, somehow, that gazing into his eyes just then would be the end of her. She knew it.

"If that is what you wish," he said eventually, and he pushed away. The night air seemed to rush at her, cooler than it had been moments before; shocking.

He stood only a foot or two away, his beautiful face shadowed, though his eyes burned with a fire she dared not touch. Or even acknowledge.

"I will see you in the morning," she said with absurd, unnecessary courtesy.

His brows arched with a dark amusement, and she did not wait to see what he might say. Instead, she fled.

Again, she fled from him. She had spent her whole life running away from this man, it seemed. Was he right to accuse her as he had? Was he right to lay the blame at her feet?

She moved through the quiet halls as if pursued,

though she knew he did not follow her. Not then. She closed the heavy door of her bedchamber tight behind her and did not so much as glance at the other door.

She did not let herself think about where it led or how easy it would be to simply walk through the doorway and succumb to what her body wanted—and what would be, she knew, so very easy. So deliriously easy. Far easier than these conversations that ripped apart scars she had thought long-healed.

She pulled off her gown, changed into the comfortable pajamas she had brought with her from Toronto, scrubbed her face until there was no hint of color left in her skin and crawled into the wide, empty bed.

It was as soft and inviting as she remembered. No place for terrifying, unwieldy emotions. No room for a very old grief.

But she did not get to sleep for a long, long time.

CHAPTER SEVEN

HE WAS waiting for her in the breakfast room the next morning.

She walked in, her head still a confused muddle from the night before, and there he was. The sunlight poured in through the high, arched windows and surrounded him with a golden halo, despite the fact he looked forbidding and unapproachable at the head of the table. His gaze rose to meet hers over the top of the paper he held before him, cool and remote, in direct contrast to the pool of light around him.

She knew perfectly well he was challenging her, and it hit her hard and true, like an electrical charge, sizzling directly into the coiled tension low in her belly and between her legs.

Somehow, Bethany managed to keep herself from stumbling in the high, wedged sandals she had foolishly opted to wear beneath a casual knit sundress. She could feel his gaze in every cell, along every nerve. She had to fight to breathe normally.

Pressing her lips together, she let the ever-present servant seat her with a solicitousness that struck her as an absurdly formal manner to take with the soon-to-be ex-wife. The room was bathed in light and seemed to shimmer with promise, from the painted medieval ceiling with its long, dark beams to the bright friezes that decorated the walls above the wainscoting.

She could sense more than feel Leo's long legs stretched out beneath the polished wooden table, too close to her own, and wished that it was bigger or that she was further away from him instead of having to share a corner with him. As it was, she sat at a diagonal to Leo. But her body was not about to let her pretend she was not attuned to every single detail of his distressingly perfect appearance, the power he exuded as easily as he drew breath and the incredible, undeniable force of the pull he seemed to exert upon her.

Even now, when she had vowed to start anew this morning. When she had vowed not be so affected by him.

"Good morning," he said, and she was all too aware of the amusement that lurked in his gaze, his voice, the slight twist of his sensual lips.

Settled in her seat, the thick white linen napkin draped over her lap, Bethany faced him fully, to offer the expected polite greeting that would prove her to be as unaffected as he was. To present him with the cool and calm façade that she knew she needed to use if she was to survive any of this intact.

But she froze when her eyes met his. The dark, passionate, starkly sexual dreams that had kept her half-awake and tormented with longing the whole of the endless night rose again in her head, taunting her. Shocking her. She could see all of that and more in his black-coffee gaze.

He did not merely look at her—he devoured her, his eyes hot and hard.

Hungry.

Her lips parted slightly as her breath deserted her.

She felt her eyes glaze over, and that same tell-tale flush begin to heat its way along her breasts and neck.

It was as if he'd touched her, as if he was touching her *right now*—as if he'd reached over, yanked her into his lap and finally fixed that wicked mouth of his to hers. When all he had really done was greet her and then watch her, hard male satisfaction gleaming in his eyes and stamped across his beautiful, impossible face.

She did not need to be a mind reader to realize that he knew exactly what her flush meant—that he suspected she had tossed and turned, her body aching for him, all night long. Leo knew exactly what he did to her—what she felt—simply because of his proximity.

He knew.

"All you need to do is touch me," he said now, his intoxicating voice slightly hoarse, as if his own *want* shook him as it shook her. "It would take so very little, Bethany. You need only reach your hand to mine. You need only—"

"Leo, please," she said, trying desperately to sound stern instead of weak, all too aware that she fell far short. "The only thing I want right now is coffee."

"Of course," he said, not even attempting to hide his sardonic amusement. "My apologies." He did not even need to call her a liar. It hung between them like a shout.

Bethany scowled at her plate as the efficient staff poured her thick, aromatic coffee and placed the toast and jam she had always favored before her. She did not want to think about the fact that her preferences still registered here. She would not consider the ramifications of that.

Instead, she somehow managed to keep her hands from shaking as she lifted her delicate china coffee cup to her lips and drank the rich brew. Only after she'd taken a few bracing, head-clearing sips could she bear to look at him again.

He had placed his newspaper to the side of his plate. He lounged back against his chair, his expression brooding, one hand supporting his jaw. He looked every inch the prince, the magnate, the duly crowned emperor of his vast and ever-expanding personal empire.

He wore another perfectly tailored suit, the charcoal fabric molded to his shoulders, pressed lovingly to his fine chest. He was freshly shaved, newly showered—his dark hair glossy, begging for her fingers to run through it. He was like a dream made flesh. Her dream, specifically. The explicit, delicious dream that had tortured her all night long.

But she could not reach across the divide between them, no matter how much she longed to do it. She could not allow herself to fall again, not when she knew exactly how hard that landing was. And how impossible it seemed to her that she would ever truly climb back to her feet and walk away from him.

"I must go to Sydney," he said into the simmering silence. She had the sense he picked his words carefully, for all his voice remained cool and unemotional. "There are fires to put out, I am afraid, and only I can do it."

"You are going to Australia?" she asked, jolted from her own depressing cycle of thoughts. "Today?"

"I am interested in some hotels there," he said. Again, with care. "We are at a delicate stage in the negotiations." He shrugged, though his gaze did not leave her face or soften at all. "I did not expect that I would have to attend to this personally."

Her mind raced. What exactly was he saying? But then, she knew. Hadn't she been here before? Repeatedly?

There was always something, somewhere, that required his attention. A day here. A week there. Always at the last minute. Always non-negotiable.

"How long will you be gone?" she asked with as little expression as she could manage. She picked up a piece of perfectly toasted bread then dropped it again, unable to conceive of putting anything in her mouth when her throat felt too dry and her stomach clenched.

"It should not take long," he said, his own tone measured. He watched her, his expression cool.

"Which, if memory serves, can mean anything from an evening to two weeks," she said crisply. "A month? Six weeks? Who can say, when duty calls?"

He only lifted a brow and gazed at her, his expression inscrutable. After a moment he lifted his hand and with a careless wave dismissed the hovering servants. The way he had always done—as a precaution, he had said once, so condescendingly,should she fly off the handle.

She gritted her teeth and shoved aside the humiliating memories. The tension that always swirled between them seemed to tighten, to pull at her, hard and hot.

"I sense this is a problem for you," he said with exaggerated patience.

He had said such things before, she recalled. *A problem for you.* The implication being, as ever, that only a hysteric like Bethany would ever dream of finding his business affairs personally objectionable. It made her want to scream.

But she would not give him the satisfaction of reducing her to that. She would tear out her own throat first.

"Why am I here?" she asked quietly. A sudden

thought occurred to her and she could not hold it back. "Did you plan this?"

"It is business, Bethany," he said, his voice dismissive. "I know you choose to concoct plots and conspiracies wherever you look, but it is only business."

Any pretense of an appetite deserted her and she stood, pushing her chair back with a loud screech as she rose to her feet. The high shoes she'd worn to make his height seem less impressive compared to her own now seemed precarious, but she refused to show it.

"I might as well go home to Toronto and continue living this mockery of a life," she began, as angry that she had not foreseen something like this as that he was behaving in the same manner he always had: putting his title above his wife.

"I cannot control the entire world, Bethany," he said in that tone she loathed, the one that made her feel like an out-of-control, embarrassing infant—the tone that had so often goaded her into becoming exactly that. "I would prefer not to have to leave you now that you have finally returned to Italy, but I must. What would you have me do? Lose billions because you are in a snit?"

She fought off the haze of fury that descended on her then, and did not care if he could see that her hands were clenched into fists at her sides. She wanted to do more than simply ball up her hands in futility. She wanted to scream. She wanted to reach him, somehow. She wanted to make him feel this small, this unimportant, this useless.

But that would be descending to levels she never planned to visit again. She did not care that he stared at her while she fought her own demons. When she had battled herself into some semblance of control, she dared to look at him again.

"I understand that you need to speak to me this way," she said after a long moment. She was proud that her voice neither wavered nor cracked. "It even makes sense. Heaven forfend you treat me like an equal. Like a partner. That might make your own behavior subject to scrutiny, and the *Principe di Felici* cannot have that. Far better to manipulate the situation—to manipulate me into acting out the only way I could."

"You cannot be serious." He even let out a scoffing sort of laugh. "Is there nothing you are not prepared to throw at me? No accusation too big or too small?"

"You got to remain the long-suffering adult, while I got to be the screaming child," she continued as if he had not spoken. "It was a great disservice to both of us." She spread her palms wide as if she could encompass everything they'd destroyed, all they'd lost. "But I am not the same person, Leo. I am not going to break down into a tantrum so that you can feel better about yourself."

"All I have ever wanted is for you to act as you should," he threw at her, no longer quite so languid. His jaw was set, his dark eyes glittering as he rose to his feet. They faced each other across the table, too close and yet, as ever, so very far apart. "But it seems to me I was nothing more than a replacement parent for you."

A surprising wave of grief for her lost father washed through her, combined with a different kind of grief for the things she had not realized she'd wanted when she had married this man.

The things she had not realized she had inadvertently asked for, that she had not liked at all when he'd provided them. Like this impossible, disastrous, circular dynamic that seemed to engulf them, that she could not seem to fight off or freeze out or flee from.

"But what about your behavior?" she managed to get out, fighting for control, her hold on her emotions tenuous as things she thought she'd never dare say flowed from her mouth. "Never a husband. Never a lover. Always the parent. What could I be, except a child?" She shook her head in astonishment—and censure. "And then you wanted to actually have one, too?"

"I must have an heir," he snapped, his expression frozen. "I never made any secret of that. You are well aware it is my primary duty as the *Principe di Felici*."

"Let us not forget that," she threw back at him, her voice uneven to match the heaviness and wildness in her chest. "Let us not forget for even one moment that you are your duty first, your legacy second and only thereafter a man!"

"Is this what you learned in your years away, Bethany?" he asked after a brief, tense pause, his tone dangerous. Hard like a bullet. "This apportioning of blame?"

"I don't know who to blame," she admitted, the sea of emotion she'd fought to keep at bay choking her suddenly. "But it hardly matters anymore. We both paid for it, didn't we?"

When he did not speak, when he only gazed at her with fire and bitterness in equal measure, his mouth a grim line, she sighed.

Did his silence not say all there was to say? Wasn't this the tragic truth of their short marriage? He would not speak to her about the things that mattered, and he would not listen to her. She could only scream, and she could never reach him.

It hurt to look at it, so stark and unadorned in the bright morning sunshine. It hurt in ways she thought might take her lifetimes to overcome. But she would overcome this somehow. She would do more than simply survive him. She would.

"Go to Sydney, Leo," she said quietly, because there was nothing left to say. There never had been. "I do not care how long it takes. I will be here when you deign to return, ready and waiting to finally put all of this behind us."

Leo was in a towering rage, a fact he did nothing to conceal from his aides when they met his jet in Sydney and whisked him away to the sumptuous suite that awaited him at the hotel he no longer cared at all if he owned. He had stewed over Bethany's words the whole way from Milan, and had reached nothing even approaching a satisfying conclusion.

He started to worry that he never would—which was entirely unacceptable.

The picture she'd painted of their marriage had enraged him. It had infuriated him that night over dinner, and it had further incensed him this morning. Who was she to accuse him of such things, when her own sins were so great and egregious? When he was the one who had remained and she the one who had abandoned their marriage?

But his rage had eased the further he'd flown from the castello. His reluctance to be parted from her grew, no matter how angry she made him, and he found himself unable to maintain that level of fury.

Partly, it had been the brash courage written all over her face, as if she had had to fight herself to confront him in the way she had. He could not seem to force the image from his mind. Her remarkable eyes, blazing with bravado and no little trepidation. Her spine so straight, her chin high, her mouth set in a fierce line.

Did it require so much strength to speak her mind to him, however off-base? Was he such a monster in her mind, after all they had shared?

What did that say about the kind of man he was? But he was afraid he already knew, and he did not care for the twist of self-recrimination that the knowledge brought him.

He could remember all too well his father's thundering voice booming through the halls of the Di Marco estates, the shouting and the sneering, his mother's bowed head and set, miserable expression. He remembered the way his mother had flinched away from the strong, cruel fingers on her upper arm. He remembered the curl of his father's lip when he had referred to her, when she'd not been in the room—and, worse, when she had been.

Leo did not like the juxtaposition at all.

But it was impossible, he told himself grimly. He was not Domenico Di Marco, the bully. He had never laid a finger on his wife. He had never done anything that should make any woman cower from him in fear, much less this particular woman. He had spent his life ensuring that he was absolutely nothing like his father.

Except… He remembered the look in Bethany's eyes three years ago. That misery. That fear. He had found it infuriating then—unacceptable that she could be so desperately miserable when he had given her so much and asked for so little in return. It had never crossed his mind that she might have had the slightest reason to feel that way.

She'd had no reason! he told himself angrily. Just as she has no basis for her accusations now!

Later, he sat in a boardroom packed with financial advisors and consultants who were paid to impress him. He pretended to watch yet one more presentation with the discerning eye for which he was so renowned. But he could not seem to concentrate on dry facts and figures, projections and market analysis. He could not seem to think of anything but Bethany.

I do not think marriage should be a monarchy, he heard her say over and over again on an endless loop in his brain. *I am tired of feeling flattened by you.*

His instinct was to dismiss what she said out of hand. She would say anything to try to hurt him. She had proven that to be true over and over again. She was interested in scoring points, that was all.

But he could not quite believe it.

It would have been one thing if she'd lapsed into her customary hysteria. It was so easy to ignore what she said when it was screamed or accompanied by a flying missile in the form of priceless china or ancient vases. But the Bethany who had faced him this morning had not flown off the handle, though she had been visibly upset by one more round in their endless, excruciating war.

She had fought for calm instead of succumbing to her temper and emotions, yet even so he had seen exactly how much that fight had cost her. He had seen the defeat and the pain written across her face as if, once more, he had disappointed her.

He wished that did not eat at him, but it did.

You only want me if you can keep me in a convenient box of your choosing, she had said. It resonated within him in a way he hated. She had accused him of wanting to be the father figure, the parent, the adult in their relationship. He had never wanted that, had he? That had been a reaction to her, hadn't it? *Never a husband*, she had said. *Always the parent. What could I be, except a child?*

A feeling he did not like at all snaked through him then as he accepted the fact that three years ago, he would not even have tried to figure out where she was coming from. He had not bothered.

He had simply let her go when it had occurred to him that perhaps the polish and experience of a few years' growth might work wonders for the brand new, far-too-young wife he had inexplicably taken, upsetting a lifetime's worth of expectations. He had been weary of all the fighting, all the wild uncertainty and drama. He had wanted her to turn into the wife he had been expected to marry all along, the wife he'd always been told he, as the *Principe di Felici*, needed to marry to fulfill his obligations. He had wanted her to be dutiful and unobjectionable.

What was that, if not a box? The very same box, in fact, in which he had lived his whole life?

The day's business was concluded in due course, and Leo sat through a tedious dinner with his soon-to-be new partners, forcing himself to play along with the expected joviality when he could not have felt less disposed to do so. Finally, after an endless round of drinks and toasts—that he found slightly premature, given the contracts that had yet to be signed and his lawyers' ability to ferret out objections to every clause they viewed—he was able to retire to his rooms and drop the act.

He had long ago stopped questioning how Bethany could haunt him so thoroughly in places she had never been. And yet, as he sat out on the balcony and soaked in the mild Sydney autumn night, it was as if she sat beside him, astride him. It was as if he could smell the rich, sweet scent of her skin, as if he could hear the cadence of her voice echo all around him, as if from the city itself.

Was every man doomed to become his father? He rejected the idea, but it was harder to push away than it should have been. Because, if he cast aside his own anger and frustration long enough, the view into their marriage from Bethany's perspective was not at all pretty. He had failed her.

He faced the truth of that and sighed slightly.

He had not protected her from his spiteful cousins, when he should have known the trouble they would cause with their insinuations and their ingrained snobbery. He had not properly prepared her for how different his daily life was from their Hawaiian idyll. And he had been the older, experienced one. He still was. It had surely been his responsibility to make sure she felt secure, safe, at home in a place that he knew had been wildly foreign to her. And he had not done it.

He had not done it.

He had been so quick to accuse her of all manner of ills, but he had never thought to examine his own behavior. Who was the child—the woman who had been so sheltered and naïve? Or the man who had such a high opinion of himself it had never occurred to him to see what responsibility lay at his feet for the mess of his own marriage?

Leo sat in the dark for a long time, staring out at the lights of the city, lost in his own thoughts. In the past. Deep in a pair of bright blue eyes he was determined he would see smiling once again, if it killed him.

CHAPTER EIGHT

"I DO NOT wish to put you in a box," Leo announced, striding into the small drawing room off the principessa's suite.

Bethany was so startled she dropped the book she was reading, letting the heavy first edition thud to the floor beside the gracefully bowed legs of the scarlet and white settee.

"Quite the contrary."

She had not seen him in days. Four days, to be precise.

She sat up, swinging her legs to the floor and straightening her shoulders as her eyes drank him in, as they always did and always had, no matter how angry and hurt she had been when he reappeared. She could not seem to help herself. Her heart leapt, no matter how sternly she lectured herself against such foolishness.

Since she could not control it, she tried instead to ignore it, and focused on him instead.

He looked…different, somehow. Bethany's senses, more attuned to him than she was at all comfortable with, whispered an alert.

Leo's dark eyes glittered in a way that made the edgy need in her belly punch to life and roll lower, setting her alight. His mouth was set into a firm, determined line.

He was dressed impeccably in a black jacket over a soft cashmere sweater, his legs packed into dark trousers. Even relatively casually dressed, he was fully the prince. Only he could look so regal so effortlessly.

"I am delighted to hear it," she said, eyeing him warily.

She felt vulnerable, somehow, as if she'd arranged herself on the settee simply to tempt him, with her curls in wild abandon and a soft wool throw over her bare feet. When, of course, she could not have known he would appear today. If she had, she would not have worn the casual denim jeans she knew annoyed him, much less the skimpy, tissue-thin T-shirt that she was afraid showed far more than it should.

She would have chosen far better armor to ward him off, to keep him at arm's length where he belonged.

As if he could read her as easily as she'd read the novel at her feet, Leo's full lips quirked slightly, knowingly. Mockingly, she thought, and frowned.

She did not understand the tension that rolled through the room, seeming to rebound off of the elegant wall-hangings. She told herself it was no more complicated than his sudden return, his unexpected appearance before her.

The castello had been a very different place while he'd been gone. She could remember what it had been like before, every time Leo had left on another one of his business trips. He had gone to Bangkok, New York, Tokyo, Singapore—and she had been trapped.

In retrospect, it was so easy to see how well the cousins had played on her fears. While Leo had been in residence, they'd been nothing but charming—yet once he'd left, they'd attacked. But this time the castello had been empty of their negative voices.

Bethany had been able to wander through it at her leisure, with no one whispering poison in her ear or pointing out her unsuitability at every turn. It was as if she'd come to the place brand new. As if it were scrubbed free of ghosts.

She had not cared for the softening she had felt as she moved through the place, exploring it as if it were a beloved museum of a house she'd once known, a home. As if, given the opportunity, she could truly fall in love with it as she had when she'd first laid eyes on it so long ago.

She did not feel so differently about the man, she thought as she studied him now, and that shook her, down to her bones and back again. Her frown deepened, even as her heart began to pound.

"You look as if you have seen a ghost," he said with his usual inconvenient perceptiveness. Bethany actually smiled then, very nearly amused at her own predictability where this man was concerned, but covered it by leaning down and reaching for her book.

"Quite the opposite," she murmured.

She straightened and pushed her curls back from her face with one hand. She wished she had tamed the great mess of them into an elegant chignon or a sleek bun. She wished she had it in her to be appropriate. But then, she reminded herself, she had no need to seek his approval any longer. She told herself she did not want to, in any event, no matter the quickening in her pulse.

She placed the book next to her on the settee, and took her time about looking up at him again. "I hope you have come to tell me it is time to visit the divorce court?"

His expression darkened. He was still propped up against the doorjamb, yet somehow he had taken over the whole of the small room in that way of his, using up all the air, stealing all the light.

"I am afraid not," he drawled. There was something she couldn't quite understand in his tone, something she did not want to comprehend in his gaze. "Though your impatience is duly noted."

"I have been here for days and days," she pointed out mildly enough. "I did not ask you to travel half the world away. Once again, I must remind you that I have an entire life in Toronto—"

"You do not need to remind me, Bethany," he interrupted silkily, her name like some kind of incantation on his lips. She shivered involuntarily. His gaze slammed into hers. "I think of your lover often. It is a subject I find unaccountably captivating."

Her breath deserted her then, and she realized that she had actually forgotten all about that seemingly harmless lie. She wrenched her gaze away from his and contemplated her hands for one moment, then another, while she attempted to remain calm. Why did she have the near-overwhelming urge to confess the truth to him? Did she really believe that would change anything?

"My lover," she repeated.

"Of course," Leo said, his gaze never leaving her face. "We must make sure we do not forget him in all of this."

She fought off the flush of temper that colored her face. None of that mattered now. And she knew why he pretended to care about any lover she might have taken—he sought to own her, to control her, because she bore his name. It was about his reputation. His honor. Him—and that damned Di Marco legacy that he saw as being the most important part of himself.

"I am surprised that you have taken the news of him

so…easily," she said, holding herself too still. "I rather thought you would have a different reaction."

"The fact that you have taken a lover, Bethany, is a grave and deep insult to my honor and to my name," Leo said softly, a thundercloud in his coffee eyes—confirming her own conclusions that simply. But then his brows rose. "But, since you are in such a great hurry to divest yourself of that name, thus removing the stain upon the Di Marco name, why should I object?"

She stared at him, a mix of despair and fury swirling in her belly, making her flush red. He would never, ever change. He could not change. She even understood that salient truth differently now, having had these past days to really investigate the mausoleum where he'd been raised, and having finally, belatedly understood the kind of life he must have led.

He had been carefully cultivated his whole life to be exactly who he was. He'd been educated, molded, primed and prepared to assume his title, his wealth, his lands and his many business concerns. She was the idiot for having ever expected something different.

And if his belief that she could have betrayed him would help her gain her freedom, that was what she wanted. What she needed. She did not really believe that she could hurt him—that it was possible to hurt him. She told herself the softening she felt inside, the longing to explain herself, was no more than a distraction. She took a deep breath and refused to allow herself that distraction.

"What is your excuse this time?" she asked finally.

She raised her gaze to his and was surprised at the expression she found there. Not the fury she might have expected. Something softer, more considering. More dangerous. Her pulse skipped, then took on a staccato beat.

"For not going to court immediately?" she hastened to add.

He shrugged, a wonderfully unconcerned Italian gesture that should not have warmed her as it did. What was the matter with her? Their most recent parting had been bleak, and yet she practically fell at his feet simply because he'd bothered to return?

She was aghast at her own weakness. Her susceptibility. She knew that his vow to keep from touching her was a godsend. It might very well be the only thing that saved her from herself.

"It is Friday afternoon," he said. When she stared at him blankly, he laughed. "The court is not open on the weekend, Bethany. And Monday is a holiday. I am afraid you must suffer through a few more days as my wife."

She could not understand the undercurrents that swirled between them then. It was as if he'd changed somehow, as if everything had changed without her noticing it—but why should it have? She remembered his bitter expression in the breakfast room, the things he'd said, the same old cycle of their frustrating conversation. Blame, recrimination and that ever-tightening noose of shame and hurt she carried inside of her, made all the more acute when she was with him.

She'd had days to ponder the whole of that interaction, and had come away none the wiser. Yet somehow she was even further determined to simply put an end to the back and forth. What was the point of it, when it got them nowhere, when it only made her feel worse?

He moved farther into the room and Bethany had to fight the urge to rise to her feet, to face him on a more equal physical level. The room was too small, she told herself, and he too easily dominated it. That did not mean he dominated her. She would not let it. She would not let him.

"Have you ever wondered what would happen if I did not, as you say, keep you in a box?" he asked, his voice so smooth, so quiet, it washed through her like wine. Like heat. It took her too long to make sense of what he'd said. She blinked. If he had produced a second head from the back of his sweater and begun speaking with it, Bethany could not have been more surprised.

"Of course I have," she said, too shocked to be careful. "Just as I wonder what the world would be like if Santa Claus were real, or if all manner of magical creatures walked among us."

He did not take the bait. His inky dark brows rose, daring her, and she felt herself flush. Then, unaccountably, an edgy kind of anger swept through her, cramping her belly and making her pulse pound.

"I am not going to play games with you, Leo," she said stiffly, a sudden, terrific storm swirling inside of her, clouds and panic and thunder. She shot to her feet and found her hands in tight fists at her sides. "I am not going to have fairy tale conversations with you, or salt the wounds with discussions of 'what if.'"

"Coward."

It was such a little word, said so softly, almost kindly—yet it set Bethany ablaze. She felt the kick of her temper like a wildfire and clamped down on it desperately. She would not implode. She would not give him the satisfaction of making her do so. She would not crack, not now, not after she had worked so hard to remain calm and cool around him. She only glared at him mutinously.

"You are a coward," he repeated with a gleam in his eyes that she could not mistake for anything save what it was: satisfaction. That he was getting to her. That he could poke at her. He was not the only one with the ability to read things he should not be able to see. "You have complained at length that I did this thing to you, that I insisted upon it—but, when I ask you to imagine what it might be like if I did not, you lose your temper. You cannot even have the conversation. What are you afraid of?"

"I do not see the point of hypothetical discussions," she said as icily as she could.

She recognized on some dim level that she wanted to scream. To let everything out in a rush, like a tidal wave. But why should she feel this way? Surely there were any number of things that he'd already said to her that were far, far worse than this game he suddenly wanted to play.

"Then by all means let us not dwell in hypotheticals," he said smoothly—almost, she thought with sudden suspicion, as if he had planned this. He opened up his hands and spread them wide, as if between them he held all the world. "Consider yourself out of the box, Bethany. What happens now?"

She knew then, with shattering insight, why her reaction was this unwieldy surge of rage, this piping-hot furnace of anger—it covered up the dangerous longing beneath. The quicksand of her long-lost dreams, her once-upon-a-time, naïve wishes, the epic and impossible hopes she'd pinned on this frustrating man. Her prince.

For a long moment she felt suspended in his knowing

gaze, lost in it, as if he was truly offering her the things she was afraid to admit she still wanted.

Wanted once, she amended quickly, but no more. I want nothing from him any longer—this is only a memory. Just a game. It's not real.

It could not be real. What she felt as she stared at him was an echo, surely? Nothing more.

"Why would you want to do this?" she heard herself ask as if from afar. As if someone else had said it.

The drawing room, with its scarlets and golds, its exquisitely crafted furniture and graceful wall-hangings, disappeared. She could not feel the floor beneath her bare feet. She could not see anything but his fierce, focused gaze. There was only Leo and the vast sea of things she wanted from him that she could never, ever have.

"Why not?" he asked in the same tone, as if they stood together, yet still not touching, on the edge of a vast precipice and below them was nothing but darkness and turmoil. "What is left for us to lose?"

Bethany understood in that moment that she was every bit the coward that he had called her, and it galled her. Deeply. She felt her temper dissipate as if it had never been, leaving her slightly nauseated in its aftermath. But she took a deep breath, blinked away the sheen of anger and panicked temper in her eyes and confronted the facts. They were steadying, somehow, for all she would have preferred to ignore them.

There was truly nothing left to lose here, just as he'd said. So why was she so determined to protect herself? Why did she imagine her girlish, silly fantasies about who they could have been would matter once these strange in-between days were finished? Why did she act as if it would kill her to let him know how much she had once wanted him, and how desperately?

None of this had killed her yet, after all, and she had spent long nights wishing it would, hoping it would, so she would no longer have to live like such a broken, ruined thing. So she would not have to face herself and figure out how to survive him. The likelihood was that she would live through this, however unpleasant the process might be. And if that was the case why should she keep up the fruitless pretenses that had never protected her from him in the first place?

What did she have left except the truth, no matter how unvarnished?

"I cannot bear it if you use this as one more weapon against me," she said, feeling stripped and naked in a way she never had before, not even in the worst ugliness of their previous battles. Her hands fell, empty, against her thighs. "I cannot bear it if you mock this too."

His dark eyes glittered with something heavy and intense, but he did not look away. She respected him more, perhaps, because he did not rush to give her assurances she would have questioned anyway. She did not know why she trusted him more in this strange, bare moment than she ever had before. She did not know why it mattered, but it did. Something hard and bright kindled to life in her broken, battered heart, though she refused to look at it closely.

"I cannot promise you anything," he said after a long moment, still looking at her as if she was made of glass that only he could see through. "But I can try."

Bare feet and a picnic basket, of all things.

Those were her first two demands the following morning when she met him at breakfast with a sparkle in her bright summer eyes. Leo had not seen her eyes dance like that, merry and mischievous, in far too long. He did not wish to speculate about the surprising depth of his own reaction.

"I beg your pardon?" he asked, but he was only feigning his customary hauteur. She smiled, that lush mouth curving in a way that sent heat straight to his head, his groin. Oh, the ways he wanted her. But he could not take her as he yearned to do. He could only wait, though it rankled more with each passing second. "You wish for me to scrabble around in the dirt?"

"Like the common peasant you will never, ever be," she confirmed with no little satisfaction and arched her fine, dark brows challengingly when he laughed.

"And just like that a lifetime of assumptions about the fairer sex disappears into the ether," he said dryly. He let his eyes trace a longing pattern along her delicate neck, deep into the shadow between the breasts her blouse concealed. His fingers twitched with the need to touch her, to suit action to yearning, but he shoved it aside. "One would think they'd all prefer the prince to the frog, but not you, Bethany. Of course not you."

His words sat there between them on the gleaming breakfast table, shining in the morning light, weaving in between the platters of food and carafes of steaming coffee, hot tea, and freshly squeezed juices. He had meant them playfully enough, but her expression changed, becoming more guarded as she gazed at him. She cleared her throat and shifted slightly in her chair.

"There is no point playing these games," she said, her voice stiffer than it had been before. And, he thought, far sadder. He wished he did not feel both as a personal loss. "I don't know why we are bothering. Nothing will change the facts of our situation."

"Indeed, nothing will," he agreed, aware that he and she had very different ideas about what those facts entailed. But this was not the time to explore those differences. This was no time to feel.

What was the matter with him? This entire situation was about the fulfillment of obligations—hers. He did not know why he was entertaining her requests, worrying about whether or not he had treated her fairly. It did not signify; no matter how she had been treated, it was time to take her rightful place at his side. He was not a man who failed twice and, having accepted his first failure, he knew he would not repeat it. He should not allow anything else to keep him from securing her—or, at the very least, explaining to her exactly what he planned.

Annoyed with himself, and his own inability to say what he should, he rose and headed toward the door.

"Where are you going?" she asked. He was sure it said things about him he was better off not examining that he was pleased to hear the uncertainty in her voice.

Why should he be the only one left unsettled by these seething, unmanageable, unspoken issues that swirled between them, making every moment fraught with tension? History? Longing? Perhaps that was why he did not call this ill-conceived game of hers to a halt. Perhaps that was why he continued to indulge her.

He turned at the door and let his gaze fall on her. She was so artlessly beautiful, this faithless wife of his, with the light streaming in to light up her face, make a symphony of her glorious eyes and wash her dark curls with gold. He had never been able to control this need for her that ravaged through him, that compelled him, that never, ever left him.

She bit at her lower lip, and he felt it as if she'd sunk those white teeth into his own flesh. He wanted to taste her more than he could remember wanting anything else. But first he was going to play this game of hers. And he was going to win it.

Then, perhaps, they could compare their facts and discuss a few home truths he was certain she would not like at all.

Leo shoved the burning desire as far down as he could and forced himself to look at her blandly, politely. As if he could not imagine six separate ways to take her right here, right now. On the table, on the floor, up against the windows with the light bathing them in—

But that was not productive.

"I must have my valet prepare the appropriate attire to complement bare feet," he said instead, lazily.

He gazed at her until her neck washed red, and then he smiled, because he knew exactly how she felt. Winded. Hungry. And resentful of both.

This was about crawling out of boxes and removing boundaries, Bethany reminded herself, and that was why she pushed her way into Leo's bedchamber not long after he'd disappeared into it.

He had never encouraged her to treat his chamber as her own, unless they were naked. And she had heard more than enough from his cousin Vincentio on the topic of appropriate behavior for the wife of such an important man as the *Principe di Felici*, so she had not attempted it.

She shook off the past with effort and stepped into the principe's master suite.

It befitted the noble ruler of an ancient line. It was magnificent and profoundly male. Deep reds and lustrous mahoganies dominated the great room and the four-poster bed that rose in the center like an altar.

Bethany's throat went dry, and she found herself wringing her hands like some kind of virgin sacrifice before she caught herself and stopped.

The rugs at her feet were old, impressive. They whispered of wealth across the centuries, of ancient trading routes and princes long past whose regal feet had stepped where hers did now. She wished for a moment that Leo could be just a man, just the simple man she had imagined him to be when she'd first met him in the Hawaiian surf. But even as she wished it something in her rejected the thought.

He had called himself 'unintelligible' without his family's history, and the truth was she could not imagine him separate from all that sweeping past entailed. As awe-inspiring as even his bedchamber might be, a paean to Renaissance architecture and aesthetics, she could not deny that it suited him. He was every inch a prince. He always had been.

Then he walked into the room and Bethany froze.

Her breath caught in her throat and her knees felt like water. He was wearing clothes that Bethany would have sworn this man did not own. On some level, perhaps, she had imagined that her request for bare feet and casual clothing would catch him out—would force him into some kind of awkwardness, make him something more normal, more ordinary.

She should have known better. She should not have forgotten.

Leo sauntered toward her, his eyes hard on hers, alive with a glittering heat that made her body shake with helpless response. Her nipples hardened against her soft cotton shirt, while everywhere else she melted.

He wore a pair of low-slung, faded denim jeans that clung to his mouthwatering form in a way that made her feel light-headed. And he wore nothing on his magnificent torso save one very, very tight black T-shirt.

Even dressed like the simple man of her old fantasies, Leo Di Marco was completely and totally at ease, fully in command.

It was impossible to drag her eyes away from his toned and rangy body, especially when he moved. His smile was sharp, hungry, his eyes all-seeing, all-knowing. Bethany realized at once that, as ever with this man, she had miscalculated.

She had forgotten how lethal Leo was, how elemental.

If anything, the sleek business suits and predictable finery of the *Principe di Felici* distracted from Leo's essential male charisma, no doubt allowing him to do business without sending all those around him into fits of the vapors.

How could she have forgotten what lay beneath?

This was the man who had swept her off of her feet, altering her life completely with one slow smile. *This* was the man she had seen in the warm, soft waters of Waikiki, this confident and dangerously attractive man, all hot eyes and a hard body, who had shorted out her mind, her body, her heart.

This stripped-down, lean and hungry creature was the one she had followed all the way to Italy. *This* was the man she had married and had loved with every fiber of her being, only to see him swallowed whole into the great, vast mouth of his family, his history, his endless obligations.

The last time she had seen this man, he had convinced her over the course of two heady, passion-drenched, impossible weeks to turn her back on everything she had ever known, marry a stranger and ride off into a sunset she had trusted him to provide.

What would he do this time? When she knew better and still, her heart stopped at the sight of all that casual, male grace? When she hadn't managed a full breath since he'd walked through that door?

This was not a game at all, Bethany realized, far too late, astounded at the breadth of her own stupidity—her own great weakness. This was everything she'd lost. This was everything she grieved for.

This was a huge mistake.

CHAPTER NINE

"You have been at pains to tell me what you are not," he said in that rich, low voice that for all its gentleness still seemed to Bethany to take over the whole of the Felici Valley. "Perhaps it is time to tell me who you are."

They walked along the cypress-studded footpath that wound down from the castello toward the valley floor and which would, Leo had promised, lead them to a secluded lake just over the crest of the next hill.

It was like a dream, Bethany thought, feeling as if she watched them from some distance—as if that was not her who walked on a warm autumn morning with this dark, brooding, impossibly handsome man, but some other woman. One who was not afraid that her slightest move might shatter this unexpected, fragile accord. One who knew nothing of the long war that had come before and scarred them both.

Oh, the people they could have been. The people they should have been! Bethany could feel the bite of that loss, that tragedy, all around her in the air like the hint of a changing season.

Or perhaps it was simply that they were free of the castello today, free of its heavy stone walls and the great weight of its history—free of the people they had to be when they were inside it.

She darted a glance at him, at his high cheekbones and flashing eyes, at that satyr's mouth that had once felt so decadent against her skin, yet could flatten into such a grim and disapproving line when he was disappointed with her. And he had so often been disappointed in her.

Next to her, his long legs keeping pace with her shorter ones with no apparent effort, he swung the basket laden with delicacies from the kitchens in one large hand. He seemed as easy with his bare feet stuck in the dirt of his family's land as he did in full princely regalia at the head of the massive banquet table in the castello's great hall. For some reason, that observation made her heart seem to expand inside her chest, almost to the point of pain.

"You finished a degree at university, I believe?" he prompted her when it became clear that she was not going to speak of her own volition. Bethany laughed slightly, flustered.

"Yes," she said, struggling to collect herself, to cast aside the enchantment of the countryside, so green and gold and inviting in the sunshine with the great expanse of the cerulean sky arched above them. To forget what had not been, and could not be. "I studied psychology."

To find out what was so terribly wrong with me that I could disappear so fully into you, she thought, but did not say. As if I'd never existed at all.

"Fascinating," he murmured, and though she shot a sharp look at him his expression was mild. "I had no idea the human mind was of such interest to you."

Only yours, she thought with some fatalism, but then pulled herself together. That was not entirely true, in any case, and this was a day without lies or pretense, she decided. She could act as if they were suspended out of time, as if they had escaped their history today, their tangled and heavy past.

"Human interaction interests me," she said. "My mother was an archaeologist, which is something similar, I suppose. She wanted to figure out human lives from the things left behind in ruins. I am less interested in the remains of societies and more interested in how people survive what occurs in their own lives."

She thought that was too much, that she'd gone too far, revealed herself. She pulled her lower lip between her teeth as she waited for an explosion, a reaction. Leo shot a dark, unreadable look at her, from beneath lashes that were frankly unfair on a man of his physical size and indisputable prowess, but did not strike back as she'd expected.

"You do not normally speak of your mother," he said. Did she only imagine his hesitant tone? Was he as loath to disrupt this fragile peace as she was?

"She died when I was still so young, just a baby," she said. She shrugged, wrinkling her nose up toward the sun, tilting her head back to let the warm rays caress her face. "To be honest, I cannot remember her at all." His silence, his somehow comforting presence beside her, encouraged her to continue. "My father never spoke of her when I was growing up. I think it caused him too much pain. But then toward the end he could not seem to speak of anything else."

She looked down at her feet, slightly chilled against the rich earth, but it felt good to be barefoot, to act as if she was free of cares, regardless of the truth. "I think he was afraid that if he did not she would disappear when he did."

The path along the valley floor meandered through

the vineyards before beginning an easy climb toward the next rolling hill. They walked side by side, as if they had all the time in the world, Bethany thought. As if they were under enchantment. As if this game of theirs was real and they could live this day forever.

What did it say about her that so much of her wished that they could?

"When I returned to Toronto..." she began, sneaking a look at him and flushing slightly when he met her gaze, his eyes sardonic. "I wanted to finish my degree," she continued hurriedly, jerking her gaze away. "And I suppose in some way I wanted to honor her, too. It felt like a continuation of her studies, somehow."

"I am glad for you," he said simply when she stopped talking and returned her attention to the path in front of them. "I know you wanted very much to maintain ties with your family however you could."

She did not like the way he said that—as if he had spent time pondering her. As if he knew things about her that she might not, as if he cared in ways she was not prepared to accept. It made her feel restless in a way she could not name.

"That cannot be something you ever worry about," she said, changing the focus of this odd, out-of-body conversation, pushing the spotlight away from herself and the panic that she desperately wanted to hide. "You cannot take a step without coming face to face with the Di Marco history."

He smiled slightly.

"Indeed I cannot," he agreed. "But it is not necessarily the voyage of discovery you seem to imagine, I think." He let out a short laugh. "My father was not an easy man. He believed absolutely in his own dominion over all things. His wealth and estates. His wife and family. He was neither tolerant nor kind."

"Leo..." But he did not hear her, or he did not choose to stop.

"I was sent to boarding school in Austria when I was barely turned four," Leo said in that same matter-of-fact, emotionless voice. "It was a slightly more nurturing environment than my father's home. I was raised to think that nothing and no one could ever be as important as the Di Marco legacy. My responsibilities and obligations were beaten into me early." His eyes met hers, and she could not read what swam in those bittersweet, chocolate depths, just as she could not identify the mess of emotion that fought inside of her. "There is a certain liberty in having no choices, you must understand."

"That sounds horrible," she said, her eyes heavy with tears she could not shed where he could see her. "Cancer took my mother too soon, and my father grieved for her the rest of his days, but he loved me. I never doubted that he loved me."

"I was raised to disdain such foolishness," Leo said, something indefinable across that mobile, fascinating face before he hid it behind his customary mask of polite indifference.

She knew she should recognize that odd expression—that something in her swelled to meet it, to match it—but her mind shied away from it before she could properly identify it. She found she was holding her breath.

"The Di Marcos, no doubt, had more important things to concentrate on," she managed to say, forcing herself to breathe past the knot in her belly.

"My duties were very clear from a very young age, and there was never any point in rebelling or arguing," he continued, his voice hushed, his eyes clear. "I must never forget myself and act with the recklessness of other young men. I must always think of the Di Marco legacy first, never my own needs or desires." He shrugged. "If I forgot myself, there were never any shortage of people around to remind me. Especially my father, using any means he deemed necessary."

"That seems so cruel." Bethany could not look at him; she was afraid she would try to do something she should not, like hold him, or soothe him, or try to make something up to the little boy she was not certain he had ever been. "You were a child, not a tiny robot to be programmed according to a set of archaic demands!"

"My father did not want a child," Leo said quietly. "He wanted the next *Principe di Felici*."

There did not seem to be anything she could say to such a simple yet devastating statement. It hung there with them, as if it ripened on the vines that stretched out beside them and climbed the hill along with them.

Bethany could not bring herself to speak because she was afraid the tears she fought to keep at bay would spill over and betray her, and the worst of it was, she was not entirely certain what emotions these were that held her so securely in a tight, fast grip. She only knew that things were clear to her now that had not been clear before, though she could not have articulated what she meant by that.

She only knew the truth of it, and that that truth was painful and seared her right through to the bone.

But then they reached the top of the second hill and her breath caught in her throat for an entirely different reason. The path delivered them to the banks of an absolutely perfect, kidney-shaped lake. The water gleamed like crystal and glass in the autumn sun, basking in the late-morning light. All around, birds called from the shade trees, and sweet-smelling grass swept along the banks.

"This is beautiful," Bethany breathed. But a different set of tears stung her eyes now. How could she have missed this place, in a year and a half spent only a hill away? How was that possible? She had the strangest sense of vertigo—as if everything she had accepted as fact, had acted upon, was spun around before her, out of focus and somehow not at all what she had believed it to be.

"My mother might have been an artist," Leo said in that low, irresistible voice of his, velvet and steel, whiskey and chocolate. He gazed out over the postcard-perfect setting, though the look in his eyes was far away. "Had she not had the misfortune to be the *Principessa di Felici*. When she provided my father with the necessary heir, he provided her with a token of appreciation for services rendered. This lake."

He crossed his arms over his leanly muscled chest, making the black T-shirt strain against his well-formed biceps.

"He had it made to resemble a lake on an estate in Andalucia where my mother spent summers as a girl." He sent her a dark look beneath a sardonic lift of his brow. "But do not cast my father as a romantic in this scenario. He had not one sensitive bone in his body. He did, however, care deeply about public opinion, and the birth of a new prince was certainly an event worth celebrating in an ostentatious manner."

He waved a hand at the enchanting, peaceful view. "And he built her a lake so that forever after Domenico Di Marco might be hailed as the great romantic hero he was not."

"It is beautiful," Bethany said again, more firmly, past

the lump in her throat, the ache in her heart. "However it came to be here."

She moved toward the water, that same deep restlessness making her feel edgy, nervous. She stared out over the sparkling surface for long moments, only half-aware that he was moving around behind her. She needed to think, to calm herself. She needed to rein in the wild, chaotic emotions that buffeted her. This was supposed to be a different kind of day—no wildness, no upset.

Surely she could handle that? Surely she could manage to keep her cool if Leo, of all people, could bring himself to talk to her like this?

She would not let herself regret that it could happen only now, when it was all over between them save the legalities. She would not imagine what might have been between them if this day had occurred three years ago, four years ago, instead of now. She would not ruin this, whatever it was, with the things that could not be changed no matter how this day went. No matter what she felt.

When she turned back around, he had set out a large, square ground-covering and had unpacked some of the hamper's tempting items. Cold chicken, a bowl of olives. Wine and two glasses. Cheeses and slices of meats— *carpaccio*, *prosciutto*—and a selection of pâtés. Slices of apple and plump bunches of grapes.

He lounged across the blue and white blanket, his jeans-clad body on deliberate display, every inch of him clearly a delectable and dangerous male animal, for all that he appeared so indolent. She could not seem to look at that tight black T-shirt without losing her focus, much less the tanned, taut ridge of his abdomen that was revealed beneath the hiked-up hem. She had to swallow twice.

The look in his dark eyes, when they met hers, made her temperature soar. She felt feverish, too hot and too cold all at the same time.

"Come sit with me," he said, the wolf to the foolish girl.

And, because she had never been anything but a fool when she was near him, no matter what else she might have been or wanted to be, she did.

Bethany knew the moment she lowered herself to the ground beside him that something had changed. She wanted it to be no more than a shift in the light breeze that danced in the trees above her head, or in the temperature of the day around them, but she was afraid she knew better.

She tucked the white cotton skirt she'd worn because it felt far too casual for a *principessa* tight around her knees, and tried to keep her attention trained on the beautiful water in front of her rather than the raw sexual energy emanating from the man lounging next to her.

"Are you not hungry?" he asked after one heated moment bled into another. She could not help herself— she turned to look at him, as if his very body commanded her and she was helpless to do anything but obey.

And he knew it. She could see that smug, male satisfaction in his dark gaze, the faint smile that toyed with the corner of his mouth.

She did not know what to do. She knew how she might have handled this moment even two hours ago, but that had been before they'd walked through fields of green and gold and he'd told her things that still made her feel raw. Unsettled.

That had been before her traitorous heart had let itself yearn for him so fully, as completely as if he had never broken it in the first place. What was she supposed to do now?

"How did your meetings in Sydney go?" she asked, because it seemed so innocuous a question and because it could not possibly make this tension between them any worse. And perhaps because she was every bit the coward he had called her.

Leo's smile deepened, and he reached down to capture a piece of hard cheese with his long fingers. He took a bite, considering her, and she could not have said why she found all of it unbearably erotic.

The lake was so quiet, the breeze so sweet against her skin. The sun above them was so warm, caressing. Her breasts felt heavy, aching behind her thin shirt. She felt a faint sheen of moisture break out across her upper lip.

She knew he missed nothing. His head cocked to the side. "I do not often lose the things I want, Bethany. But perhaps you knew this already."

"I know you take your business very seriously, if that is what you mean," she said, unable to look away from the dark seduction of his gaze, unable to keep herself from imagining what might happen if she tilted forward and let herself fall across that hard, rangy body spread out before her like a buffet of sensual delights.

But of course she already knew what would happen. She could already taste the salt and musk of his skin against her tongue. She could already feel his long, smooth muscles hard beneath her palms. She could hardly breathe for the images that chased through her head, memory and imagination fused into one great wave of ache and want and need.

She knew that he knew it, too.

"I take everything seriously," he said, his voice a low

rumble she could feel as well as hear, moving through her, leaving heat and fire in its wake. "I am known for my attention to detail. Renowned for it, you might even say."

"Leo…" She did not know what she meant to say, but she felt so snared, so captured, as if he'd trapped her here. The truly terrifying part of that was how little she cared. What was happening to her? How could she let him cast this spell over her just by lying there?

But she had the lowering thought that she'd left the fight somewhere back at the castello. That he had finally disarmed her and she was more vulnerable now than she had ever been before. Mostly because she could not bring herself to care as she knew she had even this morning. As she knew she would again when this dangerous moment was past.

Still, here—now—there was only his hot gaze and her helpless melting deep within.

"I can see the way you look at me, Bethany," he whispered, his eyes intent on hers, his voice a seduction, a caress. "You are eating me alive with all that blue heat, all of your desires written like poetry across your face. I can see that your breathing has gone shallow and your hands tremble."

"Perhaps this is disgust," she breathed. "After all."

He smiled, but it was a predator's smile, and it connected hard with her core, sending heat searing through her. Electric. Shattering. Leo.

"You are the student of psychology," he said. "You tell me what it means, these physical signs and your continued denials that they mean what we both know they must mean."

Bethany looked away then, the word 'psychology' managing to break through the haze. You have another life, a different life, she told herself fiercely, trying to breathe through the tightness inside of her that mounted with every beat of her heart. This is just a dream by a lake that should not exist in the first place.

"I do not need to be a psychologist to know that touching you would be a monumentally stupid thing to do," she said in a low voice, her attention trained on the lake's clear waters as they lapped against the shore.

"If you say so," he murmured, sounding neither offended nor put off. Hyper-aware of him, she could practically hear every shift of his body.

She knew when he reached for the succulent cuts of salami and prosciutto crudo, when he tore off a piece of fresh-baked bread and slathered it with an olive tapenade. She knew when he relaxed back on his elbows, when he licked his fingers, when he let that hungry gaze of his eat her up instead.

"Why did you never bring me here?" she asked finally when she could no longer stare at the lake without driving herself insane.

Was it worse to imagine what he was doing or watch him do it? All these years later, and she still did not know. She twisted around to look at him, not surprised to find him watching her with that same intense regard.

"Before," she amended.

He looked at her for a moment, then out toward the opposite bank of the lake where leafy green persimmon trees rustled in the slight breeze.

"This was never a happy place," he said finally. "It did not seem appropriate to bring a new bride to a place made from one man's ego and a woman's tears."

Bethany swallowed. "And now?"

Why did she ask? What did she want from him?

But she knew what she wanted. She had always

known: everything. That was why the little she'd received had hurt so very badly. That was why she had haunted that house in Toronto for so long, hoping in the dark of night that he might return even as she hated herself for that weakness in the light of day.

She was merely feeling the echoes of all of that now, she told herself desperately. Just the echoes, nothing more.

"What answer do you wish me to give?" he asked softly, turning that brooding yet fierce gaze back upon her. "What must I tell you to make you touch me as you want to do, Bethany? As we both want you to do? Tell me what you want and I will say it. Just tell me."

It was as if there was a sudden earthquake beneath her—as if the earth tumbled and rolled, cracked and heaved all while she sat there, not moving, not touching him, not even fighting with him—which was, she acknowledged in some far-off part of her brain, far easier than whatever this was.

This…aching regret. This longing. This undeniable need and this deep, wrenching fear that if she did not reach over and place her hands on him he would truly disappear as if he had never been.

Because he never should have been. He never should have noticed her in the first place. He had never been meant for her—he had always been on loan, and some part of her had recognized that from the start.

Was that why she had thrown tantrums, indulged her inner lunatic, done everything possible to push him away? Had she done it all to hasten along the inevitable day when he looked at her and saw nothing but his worst mistake? Why not rush to that end, when she'd known they were always destined to get there one way or another?

"You look at me as if I have become a ghost," he said, his eyes narrowing. "Before your very eyes."

"Sometimes I think that's all you ever were," she heard herself say as if she had no control over herself any longer—as if all the things she had only ever admitted to herself in the dark of the night were suddenly free to tumble from her lips. As if this secluded, unnatural spot, so pretty and so calculated at the same time, was somehow the safe haven she had searched for all these years.

"That is all you allowed me to be," he said quietly. "It is all you would give me—your body, your protestations of love. But the real woman? The flesh and blood? That was never on offer."

Any other day she might have thrown something back at him, tried to hurt him in return. But today was too different. Too out of time, as if their usual rules did not apply. Or perhaps it was this odd place, this peaceful lake hidden away on a hilltop, yet never meant for happiness—just like us, she thought.

She could not bring herself to do anything but reply honestly.

"Whose flesh and blood did you want?" she asked, her voice as soft as his. "You wanted something I could never be. You wanted the woman you should have married. The woman you would have married, had you not met me instead."

She did not know what she expected from him. Protestations? Denials? Some part of her yearned for him to storm at her that she was mistaken, to demand that she tell him who had put such thoughts in her head. But he did neither.

Instead, his dark gaze seemed electric on hers, searing and hard, and his face darkened. A moment passed, and then another, and he did not speak.

"You were meant for someone noble, well-educated, refined and elegant," she continued, reciting from memory the words his cousin had hurled at her, trapped in Leo's gaze but unable to look away. "Every day I was none of those things, and every day you resented me more for it."

"No," he said, his eyes clear on hers even though his voice was gruff. "I did not. I did not resent you for that." He paused, then continued, his voice low and harsh. "If anything, I resented myself for trying to make you into something you were not."

She opened her mouth then, but nothing came out. She looked at him and it was as if she shook, or the earth shook, but nothing made sense. It was all a jumble of regret and misunderstanding; her own fears and his cousins' poison; his retreat into his title and her inability to reach out to him; resentment and anger, the wounds inflicted across the years, and her inability to dismiss him as she should. And she knew she should.

"The fact that you were not those things, could never be those things, was why I married you in the first place," he said, his voice softer, yet somehow more urgent.

She was astounded to realize that she believed him. Yet she remembered how it had been. He had been so cold, so distant, so disapproving, and she had not known how to handle that when the man she had fallen so far in love with had been so fiery, so deeply entwined with her at every moment.

"Why did you not tell me that then?" she asked, surprised to find she was whispering. Would it have made a difference? she asked herself now. Would it have changed anything?

"I could not tell you something I did not know myself," he said in a low voice.

But she could not get past what his words seemed to imply. And she was shaken by the wave of grief that washed through her, over her, making her feel too large and unwieldy, too exposed, too vulnerable.

"You wanted something different, is that it?" she asked, because she could not seem to stop herself, not because she really wanted to know the answer. Her voice was hoarse from the agony of this conversation. She was sure she had bruises, yet she still could not seem to stop. "You...what? Thought I could be the symbol of your rebellion?"

"I wanted you," he said, his voice as dark as his eyes, his expression as troubled as she imagined hers to be. His lips pressed together and she could see that tension radiating along the length of his body. "I wanted you. And I confess, Bethany, that I did not think of anything else at all."

She wanted to weep. To curl herself into a ball and sob until the great mess of the feelings that swirled around inside of her were purged from her once and for all.

But instead, responding to an urgency she dared not examine too closely, she leaned forward. She propped herself up on her hands and held herself above him for a long, trembling moment. Then she closed the distance between them and went to press her lips to his.

"Wait."

He stopped her just before she touched him and she froze, her mouth so close to his, so very close. She dragged her gaze up to his, so bright now, with desire glowing like molten gold. She shivered and he smiled, though his whole big body was as taut as a spring, coiled tight beneath her, so much raw male power leashed and ready.

"What is it?" she whispered just a breath away. Her heart pounded wildly in her chest, and she could see his hands in fists at his hips, digging into the blue and white blanket beneath them.

"If I taste you, I will take you." His eyes, glittering with that intoxicating heat, were hard on hers. His harsh promise hung between them and lit her on fire. She exulted in the flames, the burn. "Be certain, Bethany. Be very certain."

She was not certain at all. She felt reckless, compelled. She felt as if she had lost herself in quicksand. She felt too much, all of it so big, so terrifying, shaking her even as she sat.

I wanted you, he had said, and it made her shiver. Today of all days, here beside a lake that should not have been—a monument to a marriage disturbingly like the one she had walked away from—she would not let herself worry about the consequences.

She licked her lips and felt him sigh against her, felt that dark and intoxicating desire kick hard and hot between them.

Just for today, she promised herself. This is only for today.

And then, reaching across all of their history, across too many years and regrets, too much resentment and the space of one quick breath, she fit her mouth to his.

CHAPTER TEN

Leo let her kiss him, her soft, lush mouth hot against his. Once. Twice. Like heaven, her taste. A kind of paradise, the slide of her lips on his—tasting, touching. Needing him as he needed her. If this was his rebellion, he did not know why he would ever do anything but fall.

And then he could not help the thudding, pounding, heady mix of desire and triumph, victory and relief that flooded through him. He jack-knifed forward, never taking his mouth from hers, and took her face in his hands, angling her head for a better, hotter, slicker fit.

Oh, the taste of her. It was like the finest of his wines, like the heat of the summer sun, and he had been hard for her for days. Years. He went harder still when he heard the impatient, greedy sounds she made, her mouth opening over his, her hands spearing into the thickness of his hair to hold his head close to hers.

He felt her fine cheekbones under his thumbs, the soft swell of her cheeks. Still he tasted her, over and over, as if he could sate himself on this alone—as if he feared that should he stop, should they breathe, should they pause for even a moment, she would disappear from him all over again.

Not again, he told himself. Not now. Not while he captured her curls beneath his palms. Not while he tasted her as if he were dying of thirst and she was the coolest, sweetest, purest water he had ever known.

And then he could not think. He could not plan. He could only pull her close, crushing her breasts against the wall of his chest. But soon even that delicious pressure was not enough. Could anything be enough?

He shifted, sliding one hand down the enticing line of her spine, the other along the side of her body to trace her perfect, delectable curves—the side of her breast, the indentation of her waist, the fascinating curve of her hip.

When his hands reached the tempting swell of her bottom, he lifted her, shifting her up and toward him so she sat astride him, the heat of her nestled tight against the hardest part of him.

She gasped and pulled back, bracing her small hands against his shoulders, and for a long, fierce moment he gazed at her. Her curls tumbled around them, dark and wild, and her lips were swollen and slick from his. Her color was high and bright, and her eyes glowed like sapphires, dazed with the same dizzying, raging passion that charged through him, burning him alive.

She was the most beautiful creature he had ever beheld, like lightning and quicksilver in his arms, and she was his. She was his. She had always been his. Even when he had wanted her to be something other than she was, he had known that simple truth. Every curve, every sigh, every shiver that wracked her delicate body—all of it, all of her, was his.

Leo wanted to lick every single inch of her until she admitted the truth of it, until she screamed it, until she sobbed out his name like it was a prayer that only he could answer. And he would.

"Tell me you want me," he commanded her, his voice

a stranger's, no more than a growl as his hands retraced their journey and she squirmed on his lap, rocking her core against him, making them both sigh as the fire licked through them.

"You know I do," she replied, more groan than words, her hands testing the shape of his shoulders, the corded muscles she found there, the smooth skin that stretched across his biceps.

He found her high breasts with his hands and let them fill his palms, teased the hard nipples through her soft shirt until she rocked against him, her eyes dark with need, her breath coming in quick, shallow pants.

"Say it." It was a stark demand, a necessity for reasons he could not understand and did not care to examine.

As if she understood that on some primal level, she bent her head down and licked him, her small tongue tracing fire across the sensitive skin where his neck met his shoulder. He felt himself shudder with an elemental need as the storm within him began to howl.

"Bethany…" A warning. A plea.

"You know that I do," she whispered in his ear. "You have always known it."

He was lost. He found her mouth with his, hot and wet and perfect, as his hands worked between them. He tested her thighs beneath his palms, pushed her skirt out of the way and felt the scalding heat of her at her core. It inflamed him.

With a muttered curse, and more determination than skill, he released himself, letting his member free, proud and hard between them. Then he lifted her again, pulled her lacy panties to one side with an economy of motion and held himself perfectly still at her entrance for a breathless, shattering moment.

"Leo…" His name was a sob, a curse, a chant.

"Tell me." His voice was thick, tortured.

He could feel her heat, beckoning and promising, so close. So close. She squirmed against him, her hips wild beneath his hands. Desperate.

"I want to hear the words," he gritted out. "From your mouth. I want you to say it."

She wrapped her arms around his neck, pressing her breasts tighter against him, torturing them both. When she spoke it was as if it had been torn from her, as if she was as helpless in the face of this passion as he was, and he loved it.

How he loved it.

"I want you, Leo," she whispered, her voice broken, dazed, aching for him. He could feel it resonate in him, his chest, his head, his sex. "God, I want you."

He plunged into her, sheathing himself to the hilt, the fit tight and hot and as perfect as it had always been— like she was made for him, crafted expressly for this heat, this passion, *him*.

She shattered around him almost before he had finished that deep, perfect thrust. Her head fell back, her eyes drifted closed, her body rode his through tremor after tremor. He pulled back, shaking slightly with the effort, the control, reveling in the feel of her against him, so soft and wet where he was hard—all of it heaven and all of it his.

It was not enough. It was never enough.

But it was a start.

She could not breathe, she was in a thousand pieces, and yet he was still hot and hard inside of her.

Bethany managed somehow to pry open her eyes and found him watching her, his features tight and sensually intense as he gazed at her. She bit her lip as aftershocks rippled through her, making her nipples harden and her thighs clench.

Never breaking eye contact, he moved inside of her, guiding her over him.

She clung to his shoulders, loving the width and strength of them, letting her fingers caress the intriguing rock-hard muscle she found there. He held her hips in his capable hands and slowly, deliberately, he built the fire within her—stoking the embers, fanning the flames.

Bethany felt the tension she'd just released roar back, coiling with twice the strength inside of her. His thrusts were long, slow, deep, driving her mad with a need far greater, far more encompassing, than what had come before.

She could not think, she could only feel. His mouth on hers, his face against her neck. Her breasts pressed against his chest, his strong arms encircling her. She was swept away in his demanding rhythm until all she could feel was his possession.

Deep. Slow. Devastating.

Her head fell back, and his mouth was like a brushfire against the sensitive skin of her neck, hot and electric.

"Do not close your eyes," he ordered her, his voice low and sensual. It vibrated against her, through her. She could feel it deep in her core, where he slid into her again and again, so hard and hot where she melted all around him. "You have been away from me for three years. Stay with me now."

She forced her eyes open and met his. She could feel the air sizzle. Dark need arced between them, filled her vision, became the world. The fires burned high within, turned white-hot, and still he continued to move so slowly, so deliberately, so surely, each thrust almost more than she could bear until the next. And the next.

He was killing her.

"Leo..." she whispered, desperate, her voice strangled and her eyes bright with heat. "Please..."

As if he'd been waiting for exactly that plea, as if he'd planned it, he smiled and his thrusts grew faster, less measured. Wild and hot. Perfect.

"Now," he murmured, his voice a dark, deep command, and she shivered.

But that was not enough.

Leo reached between them, found the center of her with his sure fingers and then, as he licked her neck and took her mouth in a frank, carnal kiss of possession, he catapulted them both over the edge.

She came back to herself slowly, to find his mouth against the skin at her neck as she lay boneless against him, draped across him, her heart still pounding in her chest, her limbs, her ears.

He looked up as she stirred and she felt herself flush, whether from embarrassment or something far deeper, far more vulnerable, she could not say.

She opened her mouth to speak but nothing came out. He was still inside of her. She could feel the coarse material of his jeans against the sensitive skin of her inner thighs. She could feel his hard chest against her, his maleness deep within her, his strong arms all around her. There was a part of her that panicked at that stark evidence of his possession even as a darker part, a part she wished to deny even as she became aware of it, gloried in it.

If I taste you, I will take you, he had promised her. And he had kept his promise.

"That was…" But her voice trailed away and she realized she was still spinning. From a single kiss she had not planned to give, to him buried inside of her. She had no idea at all how to make sense of what had happened.

It felt cataclysmic. Life-altering. And, then again, perhaps it was simply Leo.

"Yes?" he asked; teasing her, she thought.

There was a smile in his eyes, if not on his lips, and she could not have said why seeing it made her chest ache. She only knew that it hurt, that she hurt. She knew she desperately needed to think about everything that had just happened in a critical, logical, unemotional way—which was unlikely to occur while they were joined like this, in the middle of the day, outside where anyone at all could happen by and see them on the banks of a lake that should never have been made in the first place.

Her discomfort grew, skittered through her, made her stomach clench and her breath come faster.

He only gazed at her, those eyes clear in a way that made her want to pull away, shield her own eyes, hide from him. But she could hardly do such a thing in this exposed position, so she was forced to simply gaze back at him, feeling that itchy flush work its way over her skin, her discomfort made real and red on her flesh.

She felt him move slightly, deep within her, and realized with a kind of amazement that he was becoming aroused. Again.

"But you…" Her voice was too high, too breathless, as if she was someone else. She felt like someone else, someone she was not at all sure she should permit herself to acknowledge, much less embody. Someone as silly and as profoundly thrown by him as she had once been, years before. "How can you...so soon?"

He laughed then, his hands moving along her back as if he was soothing her, settling her, using his touch to calm her. She had a vague memory of him doing this long ago, gentling her with that tremendous power he unleashed only when he chose to share it. She had thought it patronizing then; she had believed it an attempt to control her.

She wished she could summon the anger that had once stirred in her, but she could feel only her body's helpless response to him, as if it wanted him in ways she was afraid to face. She wanted to shake off his hands, but she was too captivated by his expression to do more than shift against him.

And of course, when she moved, she felt him—hard and hot so deep inside of her—and she felt her own melting, shivering response.

"That was but a taste," he said, that near-smile flirting with his mouth. "It has been a long time."

Her head spun, and then the world spun too as he swung her around, moving her with an effortless might and grace, rolling them both over on the blanket. He settled himself between her thighs and looked down into her face.

He never broke their intimate connection, and she told herself that was what made her heart hammer even harder against her ribs.

"Since me, you mean?" she stammered, gazing up at him, her eyes wide with a kind of desperation.

Why did she feel the overpowering need to run from him, to put any distance between them she could? But he was everywhere—inside her, above her—and there was no escape.

"You don't mean a long time over all—you mean since me? Since you and I...?" Her voice trailed away.

The laughter faded from his expression, and an enigmatic light gleamed in his dark eyes. She shivered, and he was still inside her, growing harder by the moment. She shifted, but it only drew him in deeper, closer, and she caught her breath as sensation arrowed through her, bathing her in heat and light.

"I mean that it has been a long time since I touched you," he said, his eyes pinning her to the ground as surely as his body did, offering no quarter, no compromise. "Which also means that it has been a long time since I have touched anyone." His eyes rose, challenging her. Shaming her. Reading her secrets and laying her bare. "I take my vows very seriously, Bethany. I did not break them."

Bethany felt dizzy. Her heart fluttered wildly in her chest and she thought—she hoped—she might faint. But instead one moment dragged into another, and he simply waited. Watched and waited, when she wanted to thrash and scream and howl out her reaction, no matter how little sense that might make.

She felt lost to herself. A stranger.

"Leo..." She could only whisper his name. She could not identify the emotions that swelled in her, rolling and pitching as if she were a tiny boat adrift in a great sea. "You should know...I mean, I never..."

Who had she become? she wondered in a mix of shame, panic and something else, something far deeper and more dangerous. She could not make it through a single sentence.

She felt her eyes fill and was horrified to think she might weep. Not now. Please, not now!

Still, Leo merely waited. He only watched her,

propped up on his elbows, his expression unreadable, though she could feel the great, humming power of him as if he connected her to some immense electrical storm—as if he was the storm, just barely held in check by the iron force of his will.

"I thought if I claimed to have a lover you would hate me," she said, forcing the words out, though her lips felt numb and she knew on some deep level that she could not understand, that there was no going back from this admission. This was new ground, shaky and insecure.

And still she continued on, face to face, more naked and more terrified than she could ever remember being before though she still wore her clothes.

"And I thought if you hated me," she managed to say, "You would let me go."

Something seemed to shimmer between them, bright and sharp, and he very nearly smiled. He moved closer to her, pulling a curl between his fingers and tucking it behind her ear. She was sure she saw something sad and resigned move through him before he laid a trail of soft kisses along her jaw.

He does not believe me, she thought in a dawning kind of horror, and it broke her heart.

"I never had a lover," she confessed, desperate that he hear her, that he listen, that he believe her. She was as desperate he believe this truth as she had been that he believe the lie, and even as she spoke she could not quite face the reasons she was so distraught. She only felt it, deep within, like a great abyss she had been pretending for years did not exist at all. "I made it up."

He looked up then, his eyes gleaming with a bone-deep satisfaction, bright and hard and triumphant. His mouth curved into a stark, male smile that made her shudder deep within.

"Believe me," he said, a ruthless heat in his voice, his gaze, his skin against hers, "I know."

"But..." she breathed, her voice catching in her throat, her mind a sudden tumult of 'how?' and 'when?' and 'why?' but he only laughed. It was a resoundingly wolf-ish sound, and she could not help the way she shuddered around him.

Then he began to move.

Later, Bethany could not pinpoint the moment she let go—the moment she stopped desperately trying to cling to the shreds of the persona she had built around Leo's absence and allowed herself instead to sink into the overwhelming, devastating reality of his presence, his body, his clever hands.

Leo made love to her with shattering intensity and ruthless, focused thoroughness. He stripped them both of all their clothes until they were naked in the sun, and then he fed her with his own fingers, olives and cheeses, salted meats and sweet grapes, and washed it down with wine and kisses.

Then he took her again, making her fall apart over and over, until she could hardly remember who she had been before that kiss of hers that had started it all again—this madness and fire, this need and heat.

When the shadows lengthened over the quiet water of the lake, Leo led her back to the castello along the same path that they had traveled that morning. Bethany felt as if years had passed since then—whole decades, perhaps, lost beneath the quiet, encompassing mastery of Leo's hands, his mouth, his hard and fascinating body.

She was not sure, she thought as he wrapped his hand around hers and tugged her with him through the vine-yards, if she would recognize herself if she came face to face with the woman who had set out on this walk. She'd been so determined to play a game, so sure that game would change Leo—never dreaming how deeply it would change *her*.

But she pushed that thought away because she had no other choice. He was too demanding, too enticing, and she could not seem to stop herself from responding to his smallest caress, his barest glance. And, if she was honest, she did not want to stop herself. She did not want to stop at all.

At some point, when the enchantment of the green and gold fields had worn away and he was not there to ensnare her with his rich, dark gaze, she might have to worry about that. *But not today*, she told herself, repeating it like a litany.

When they returned to the castello, Bethany was not surprised when he was pulled aside by the usual collection of aides and servants, all of them anxious to speak to him. She climbed to her chamber and ran a hot bath in the deep tub that stood before the high windows of her expansive private bathroom.

Feeling as if she was in a dream, she pulled off the clothes he had so recently put on her, her hands trembling slightly as she remembered his method of dressing her—his mouth against the tender underside of her breasts as he smoothed her bra into place, his fingers exploring every curve, every secret, making each and every one his. She felt a deep shuddering inside of her; she could not stop herself from shivering, though she knew she was not cold.

She knew it was him: the fever of Leo Di Marco, the flush of him still heating her skin. It was the same sorcery he had always wielded over her, rendering her his slave, desperate to do or say anything that would make him touch her, take her, bring her screaming and sobbing to the completion only he could provide.

She should be horrified with herself, with what she had let happen—with what she had made happen. She knew that, could see it objectively, as if from a great distance.

She stood naked as the tub filled, and let the bath salts run through her fingers into the foamy water. She understood that she should be appalled that there was not a single square inch of her body that he had not touched, not one part of her he had not claimed beneath the canopy of the Italian sky. She raised her arms to clip her heavy curls up on the back of her head and winced slightly. She could feel him still, in the slight aches in sensitive areas that were somehow more arousing than painful; in the ecstatic, left-over shivering that she could not control or deny.

That she did not want to control. That she did not want to deny.

Whatever that made her, she did not want to know.

She had just settled into the hot, silky water, letting out a blissful sigh and tipping her head back against the high porcelain edge of the tub, when something prickled across her skin like a breeze. She opened her eyes, not at all surprised to see him in the doorway, his dark eyes shadowed.

She thought he might speak, or that she should, but neither of them moved for a long moment. She felt the steam rise around her, heating her face, making her curls tighten and bounce. But she could not look away from him.

She could not, it seemed, do anything at all but gaze at this man, helpless, as her body reacted to him in the same, predictable manner it always had. As if he had not spent the afternoon having her again and again in a variety of clever and devastating ways. Her body did not seem to care. It only wanted more.

Bethany understood something then, something that seemed to drop through her like a stone while he stood there before her.

It had always been like this—this unquenchable thirst for him, this explosive passion whenever they'd touched. She remembered that shameful night in Toronto, the night she had held up for years as the very lowest point of her life, and realized that she had needed to think of it that way. Not because they had both been so angry, but because she had needed to demonize the sexual connection between them in order to think past it, in order to figure out who she might be without it. Because when he was near her she lost the ability to think at all.

She must have known, on some level, that to demonize it the way she had was the only way she was likely to survive the loss of it, of him, for so long.

She still did not dare think of why that was. She still shied away from the simple truth that her body knew, had always known, that moved through her, illuminating her.

Not today, she thought fiercely. It would be too much, that level of self-awareness. She could not quite do it. She would not allow it.

She opened her mouth to speak, but stopped when he moved. He came to stand beside the tub, still looking down at her, that same simmering awareness lighting up his dark gaze, making his sensual mouth move into something approaching a smile.

She found she could not tear her eyes away from him. She stopped trying.

He pulled the tight black T-shirt over his head, tossing

it carelessly to the floor. Bethany let her gaze travel over his rock-hard pectoral muscles, the tantalizing indentation between them, the ridged expanse of his abdomen. She let out a small sound when he stripped off the jeans as well, kicking them out of his way so that he stood fully naked and indescribably beautiful before her.

She could only stare. He was pure, masculine perfection, lethal grace and tightly controlled strength, and she wanted to touch him and taste him all over again.

"Move over," he ordered her with a regal tilt of his jaw in a tone that expected instant compliance. That demanded it.

She knew she should object. She knew she should set her ground rules, define her boundaries. She knew she should demand her space—she knew that she should want the space from him she ought to demand. But she did not say a word. Not now, she told herself, her own private prayer. Not today.

She sat forward so he could sink down behind her in the tub that had been built for precisely this purpose. She sighed in a contentment she opted not to question when he pulled her back against the wall of his chest, settling her between his thighs, bringing his strong, hard arms around her.

The water lapped against her breasts. She could not tell which was hotter—the steaming bath or his silk-and-steel skin against hers. His hardness pressed against the small of her back, making her core throb and ache.

When she tipped her head back against his shoulder, she saw something she could not quite define flash across his face. It made something deep inside of her shift, like a tectonic plate deep beneath the ground. Grief turned to something else, something less raw, more smooth. But before she could do more than note it he fit his mouth to hers.

Soft. Sweet. The fire raged anew.

Not today, she thought. Not today.

And then she stopped thinking altogether.

CHAPTER ELEVEN

LEO could not quite put his finger on the complicated emotions that held him in such a tight grip that it bordered on the uncomfortable.

He sat in yet another tedious meeting in the suite of rooms in the castello's west wing that he used as his corporate offices when he was in Felici. He lounged behind the massive desk that his father had bought as a match for his grand ego, and knew that he looked every inch the prince, as he ought to. He had been raised to wield his own magnificence as a weapon, and he had long done so without thought. He did not want to investigate why the mantle of it seemed so ill-fitting today. As if it was no longer his second skin, indistinguishable from his own.

The meeting should not have been tedious. There had been a time when the thrill of figuring out how best to beat a rival's offer, or managing to pull together a deal in the eleventh hour, would have kept him high on adrenaline and triumph for days.

He had never involved himself in the kind of extreme adventures that attracted so many of his wealthy peers, because he could not risk himself or the Di Marco legacy. He had therefore contented himself instead with the drama of high finance—the greatest poker game in the world, with the highest stakes—and it had always worked.

Yet today, even that familiar thrill seemed to have lost its appeal. He knew that Bethany was somewhere in the castello—not in Canada, as she had been. Not across the planet. Not even so terribly angry with him any longer. She was somewhere close and, more than that, agreeable.

He knew that she was nearby, and that was what thrilled him—not these papers, these debates, these strategies that he found so unaccountably boring these days. He knew that he could walk out of this meeting, go to her and he could have her. It would be as easy as a look, a touch. As simple as their presence in the same room.

He could, as he had done yesterday, simply enter the chamber she happened to be in, tumble her to one of the soft, plush carpets and be inside of her before she had time to greet him properly. He grew hard merely thinking about it.

He scowled at the sheaf of documents in front of him, trying to make sense of the financial portfolio before him when he could hardly make sense of himself. It wasn't the sex that was affecting him this way—though he was not above feeling deeply satisfied that, even after all of the time they'd been apart, he was capable of driving Bethany absolutely wild. Driving them both wild.

It was not that at all. It was…the rest of it.

A week had passed, then several more days, and Bethany had made no move to leave; she had not so much as mentioned their divorce. She had not even asked after the court as she had when she had first arrived. Leo wanted to view that as a victory, but somehow he could not.

She shared his meals, his bed. She shared her delectable body with a delight and an enthusiasm that he found alternately humbling and exciting. She talked to him. She laughed with him. There were no tantrums, no tears, no rages, not even the barbed exchanges he had come to expect since seeing her again in Toronto.

She was, in short, everything he had always imagined she could be, as if their tumultuous eighteen months of marriage three years ago had simply been a bad dream they had woken from together.

It should have been blissful—it was blissful—yet it was not, somehow, enough.

Leo could not rid himself of the feeling of unease that never quite left him—the sense that they were living on borrowed time, that there was a clock ticking, for all that he could neither hear it nor see it. It was the faraway look in her eyes sometimes when she thought he was not watching her. It was the sadness he sometimes sensed in her, though she would always smile when he said her name and pretend she did not know what he meant when he asked what troubled her.

He knew she was holding great parts of herself in reserve, and he told himself that was why he felt this edginess, this undercurrent of disquiet. It was at odds with the deep sense of contentment he sometimes felt when she was curled around him in the night. He felt as if he could never get enough of the feel of her softness next to him, the sound of her breathing in the dark room, the scent of her lustrous curls draped across his chest.

He felt. Perhaps that was why he felt that edge inside. It was so unusual. Not new, exactly, for this was exactly why he had married her. How had he managed to forget? This had been what had happened in Hawaii, what had brought them here in the first place. He had looked at her, touched her and it was as if he'd been reborn. Made new.

With Bethany, he was aware of himself as a man in a way he was with no one else. He was not the *Principe di Felici*. He was not the heir to the Di Marco fortune and executor of its storied legacy. He was simply a man. A man who wanted her, who she wanted in return, as if nothing else mattered. As if only that mattered.

He had hated that he'd felt this way. He could remember it all now with a clarity that had somehow deserted him during the years she had been gone. He remembered how bizarre he had found his own feelings when he'd returned to Italy, having acted out of character for the first time in his life.

He had felt as if he had dishonored himself. He had not known how to act like the man who had fallen so in love with her, so in love that he'd forgotten the history that had made him who he was until he was immersed once again in the seat of that history. He had instead tried to pretend that the man who had been so alive, so accessible, so vulnerable in the soft Hawaiian night had never existed.

Worse, he had tried to make her into the woman he had been meant to marry, the stiff and formal automaton that she had never been and could never be. He had tried to make the two of them into the image of the marriages he'd witnessed his whole life—fake and bloodless society arrangements, all manners and materialism, convenience and practicality. Why had he been surprised when she could not handle it? What had he expected?

The outer door to his office swung open then and Leo glanced up as one of his fleet of secretaries walked in. He could see out into the antechamber, and felt that spike of desire pound through him when he saw that Bethany was standing there, smiling at one of the attorneys who had left earlier to take a telephone call. He snuck a look at his watch and saw that it was nearing noon, when he had planned to meet her for lunch.

She looked fresh and pretty, her curls spilling toward her shoulders from a high ponytail, the dark gloss of her hair seeming to shine against the pale peach cashmere of the turtleneck sweater she wore. Her dark brown trousers clung to her curves, and made him think of more private venues for their meal than the excursion they'd planned into the village.

But when she turned toward his door her gaze met his for a split second across the antechamber and the spacious inner-office before the same secretary walked out and closed the door behind her.

The split second had been enough. Leo felt the force of her gaze as if it still seared into him through the heavy wooden door. Tortured. Bitter. Despairing.

Furious.

And he knew then exactly what he had feared, exactly what he had felt floating around them, undermining all the seeming perfection of their reunion: this moment.

This was what he'd been attempting to avoid all along.

Because he knew what the damned lawyer must have told her. He knew exactly what could put that horrible look on the face that had been soft and shining when he'd left her this morning.

He had taken his biggest gamble yet, he realized, and if that expression was anything to go by Leo Di Marco had finally lost. He had lost and this loss, he realized with a sudden flare of deep certainty, he could not tolerate.

He could not. He would not.

"Excuse me, gentlemen," he said, cutting off the consultant who was still speaking. He rose to his feet. Because he was the prince, no one argued—no one even commented. They merely stood respectfully. "Something has come up."

Then, with a growing sense of something he refused to call panic, but which shot through him too fast and too slick, he went after her.

He was a liar.

He was still no more than a liar.

Bethany could not breathe. She could not breathe, and she could not seem to stop making that choking sound in the back of her throat as she hurtled herself down the long, history-laden hallway that seemed to shrink around her as she moved. Oppressive, not beautiful. Dark, not graceful. A prison, not a castle—all over again.

How could she have forgotten how ruthless he was? How could she have done the one thing she had known better than to do and fallen right back into his arms, his bed? It was as if he touched her and she immediately contracted some kind of amnesia. What had she been thinking? Had she been thinking?

All the while, he had lied to her.

She reached her chamber and threw open the door, her breath coming in shallow, desperate pants. She was a fool, such a naïve little fool, even now. It was not her youth or her inexperience this time. It was him.

It was Leo, who had never intended to let her go. Who had talked her into coming to Italy simply because he'd grown tired of waiting for her to return of her own volition, because he wanted her here for whatever complicated reason of his own. And he was the prince—he did as he pleased. His wish was her command. Her stomach heaved.

But what other explanation could there be? The lawyer had told her the sickening truth about Italian divorces outside Leo's office: both spouses had to appear in court and declare they wished to separate. And only after three years of legal separation had passed could divorce be considered, much less granted.

"But I explained all of this to the prince..." the man had stammered apologetically. "Weeks ago."

She had no doubt at all that he had done precisely that.

Which could only mean one thing, she thought as she staggered into her bedchamber and then stood there, her head spinning around and around: Leo had brought her here under false pretenses. He had known the laws of his own country; of this, Bethany had no doubt. He had always intended to use her body against her, to lull her into a false sense of security.

She heard herself let out a low sound, a kind of sob, and then she bit it back, the pain too great, the anger leaving her as suddenly as it had crashed into her.

She was not his puppet. She was not some kind of marionette that he directed at his whim. She had chosen to kiss him at the lakeside. She had done this to herself, in full possession of her faculties, for all the good they had done her. She had abandoned herself as totally as she had years ago—as completely as everyone else had abandoned her over the years.

Her mother, who had died when she was so young, who she had never known. Her father, who had been wracked with grief, then so weak, then so ill, before he died. Leo, who had left her so alone when she had not known herself at all, much less him. But, above all, she had abandoned herself. She had lost herself again and again, and it was this that she thought she might never forgive. Leo was merely the catalyst.

This was no more than her latest great betrayal—the latest heartbreak she had perpetrated on herself with her own shocking inability to keep herself safe as she should, as any adult would. Leo's manipulations were almost beside the point. This was, after all, who he was, and she'd known it full well. She'd had no illusions at all about what sort of man he was, had she? So why was she so astonished? Why did it hurt so much that she could not manage to breathe as she should? Why did she feel so…bruised?

It didn't matter who was to blame, she told herself, pushing past the anguish. It only underscored what she had always known: she could not stay here. She should never have come here. She had known better, and yet she had done it anyway.

And she even knew why.

It was like a sickness, she thought, a great wave of despair crashing over her, so hard it nearly took her to her knees. She moved over to the great four-poster bed and leaned against it, her hands loath to touch the linens where she had lain with him, over him, where he had brought her to such great heights with his hands, his mouth, that all-seeing gaze and boundless need.

And all of it part of this lie, she thought, miserable. The lie she should have known he would tell, because this was who he was. Why did it hurt so much to have her worst suspicions confirmed?

But she knew. She loved him. Despite everything, she was in love with him.

She rubbed her hands over her face, but the uncomfortable and ugly truth did not dissipate. The love, fierce and tough and uncompromising, remained. It was why she had stayed in that house in Toronto, rattling around like a wraith. It was why she had let him talk her into coming here. It was why. It was that silken, unbreakable thread of hope that could not let him go. She did not want to love him, but she did. She still did. She always had.

She had loved him since she'd first laid eyes on him, wet and glistening in the Hawaiian sun, and nothing had ever altered that love. Nothing had changed it or diminished it. She had adored him, hated him, feared him, blamed him—and still she loved him.

These past days had been a fantasy of all they could have been; he had been, at last, the man she remembered from Hawaii so long ago. The man she had thrown away all she'd known to follow heedlessly across the globe. But even knowing now what she had not wanted to suspect—even now, she loved him.

There was no one else for her. She faced the truth of that, and managed not to flinch. There would be no 'moving on', no 'getting over it.' There was only Leo. He had broken her heart so many times she had stopped expecting anything else. Yet still she could feel the way she loved him swell in her, dance through her veins and slide deep into her bones. Even now, when she wondered how she would ever survive this moment. Even now, when she was not even sure she wanted to survive it.

She loved him, but he was still playing his games. He was still playing lord of the manor, the presumptuous prince. He was still manipulative and deceiving, patronizing and cruel. She had stopped questioning why she should love a man like that, who seemed sometimes to be so different, so good, so noble.

But there was no use in questioning it. She loved him,

but that did not mean she had to live with him and let him move her around like one more pawn on his chess board. She knew she could bear almost anything, but not that.

Something rolled through her then, something hot and arid—her love, her history and her heart so broken it could never be repaired. She straightened from the bed and marched over to the dressing room door. Wrenching it open, she stalked inside, yanked her roller-bag out and tossed it on the bench that ran along the wall. It would not take long to pack—after all, she had come with so little and she would leave as she'd always sworn she would: with nothing he had given her. With only what was hers.

You will be perfectly fine, she told herself, repeating the phrase again and again, though she knew better than to believe it. But she would survive. The worst had already happened three years ago—she had already lived without him, had already had to accept that he did not and could not love her in the way she loved him.

She could do it again. She would do it again. And, if it hurt her worse this time somehow—because she had expected she would keep herself safe and armed with all she knew—well, she had years and years ahead of her to explore that particular shame.

"What the hell are you doing?"

His voice came from the door, low and fierce. She did not look up. She did not trust either one of them.

"I think you know," she said in a quiet, controlled voice that cost her bits of her soul.

She tossed her jeans into the bag and then zipped it shut. Who cared what she left behind? She wanted to leave. She needed to leave, immediately. Before he could tell her more lies she would want so desperately to believe. Before she could betray herself further.

"You are leaving," he said, as if he could not believe it, as if his eyes must be deceiving him. As if—as usual—she was the villain in this piece. "You are packing up and running off again?"

She turned on him then and was slightly taken back when she saw an unexpected wildness in his dark eyes, a kind of raw fury she had never seen before. She had no idea what it meant, and so plunged ahead.

"Did you know?" she asked, her voice clipped. She glared at him, forcing herself to be fierce, refusing to show him the agony inside, much less that terrible, doomed love for him that made her act like such a colossal fool. "Did you know that we would have to register our separation and then wait three years? And did you convince me to come here anyway, knowing that I thought we could divorce immediately? Did you manipulate me in that way, Leo?"

His lips pressed together into a hard line. His eyes burned but he did not speak. One moment passed. Then another.

Bethany did not realize how much she had hoped he would have an explanation until he failed to offer one. She let out the breath she had not been aware she was holding.

"Well," she said unevenly, and it cost her not to show how deeply his silence hurt her. "There we are."

"Did I drag you here against your will, Bethany?" he asked fiercely, his features harsh with something like pain. "Did I kidnap you like the savage you love to tell yourself I am? Did I lay a single finger upon you before you asked me to do so?"

"No, of course not," she said bitterly, the pain of all

their years so heavy on her heart, that she thought her
knees might give way. Part of her wanted to collapse
beneath it, to be done with it finally. To be at some kind
of peace. But she could not allow that, and she knew it.
She felt her lips twist into something rueful. "You are
a saint."

"You are my wife," he said.

"What does that mean?" she asked, hearing her own
voice shake but not knowing what she could do to stop
it. "You still do not have the right to treat me this way—
like an asset you must manage, a pawn you must maneuver around according to your own Byzantine rules!
I am a person, Leo. I have feelings. And I am tired of
you treading them into dust beneath your feet!"

"You have feelings?" he demanded in a kind of furious amazement. "You dare to stand there, one foot out
of the door, your suitcase packed, and talk to me of your
feelings?"

"I do not want a lake from you some day once I finally *do my duty*," she threw at him, barely able to see
him through the sheen of tears she desperately wanted
not to shed, to keep hidden. But then they were streaming down her cheeks, and she could see the look on his
face—as if she'd hit him with something much too hard
in his gut—yet she could not seem to stop. "I do not want
your parents' marriage. I won't do it, Leo. You cannot
make me do it!"

"I love you!" he bellowed. She did not know what was
more astonishing—the words themselves or the tone in
which they were delivered.

Leo—shouting? Leo—with that color splashed across
his high cheekbones and eyes too wild to be his? Love?
He had not mentioned love since those heady early days

so lost to them now…. She could not take it in. She could not absorb it, make sense of it.

Though that traitorous part of her, that silver thread, pulled taut. Hoped.

"I love you," he said again more quietly, but somehow it had all the same kick and power of the louder version. It seemed to rip into her, ricocheting inside of her like a bullet and doing as much damage.

He stepped further into the room. She could see that he was not the man she knew—not the perfectly groomed, perfectly pressed prince. The man in front of her looked slightly out of breath, and ever so slightly disheveled—as if he'd run after her, which was impossible. As if he had not stopped to smooth his clothes back into line, which was unlikely.

As if he was finally telling the truth, a small voice whispered, and her heart began to kick painfully against her ribs.

"You…" She could not repeat what he'd said. It hurt too much. It made her yearn for things he had proven, time and again, he could not give. She shook her head. "If you loved me, you would not spend so much time trying to manipulate me. Surely you must know that?"

"Let me tell you what I know about love," he said, his voice ragged, not his at all. It seemed to strike her directly in the heart, paralyzing her. "Nothing," he snapped. "Not one damn thing, Bethany. No one was at all concerned with teaching me about something I was never expected to experience."

She wanted to go to him, to hold him, to mourn with him for the things that had been done to him, but she could not. She ached for him, for both of them, but she could not move. Neither toward him, nor away.

"Your parents treated you abominably," she said in a low voice. "But that does not give you the right to do these things to me. You cannot truly believe that it is okay. You cannot. If you thought you were in the right, you would not have hidden it from me."

"It never crossed my mind to do anything but my duty," he continued in that same rough, almost angry tone. "And then there you were. You were nothing like the woman I was expected to choose. You were too warm, too alive, and you expected the same from me. You saw me as a man. Just a man. And I loved you when I had never known I could love at all."

"And look what we have done with it," she said, her voice so rough she hardly recognized it. She used her fists to dash the tears away from her eyes and could not even hate herself for showing that weakness. "Look what we've become."

"Bethany," he said, his voice harsh; she could see to her amazement that he was pleading. This man, who only issued orders. This man, who did not know how to bend at all.

But she had already bent too much. She had bent and twisted and tied herself into knots, and she trusted neither one of them anymore. How could she? He had lied to her and, worse, she had lied to herself. She could not handle herself around this man. She never could. How many times must she prove this same failing to herself, in ever more catastrophic ways?

Three years ago she had dissolved into incoherent rages and tantrums, trying desperately to reach him. This time, she had simply dissolved into him as if she had no other existence of her own, as if her return to this place completely deleted all that had gone before.

She loved him, but he was no good for her, and she

was never going to become the person whom he should have married. Hadn't they learned all of this long ago? Why were they still here, still fighting, over the same futile ground?

"I do not want a lake," she said again, not sure why she could not let go of it.

She imagined the pretty stretch of grass where she'd found herself so enchanted that she'd lost her head and surrendered herself to him once more. It was the bait, perhaps, to the pretty little trap this life could be, but she did not have to accept that particular cage.

Who would she be if she stayed here? Leo's mother, whose name was never mentioned as if she had never existed outside of her prescribed roles? A woman who had merited a show of respect in the form of that lake, but no true respect at all? And no love.

Certainly no love. The woman's only son spoke of it as if it was an alien notion, profoundly foreign to him. How could she live with that?

"I am not willing to relive your parents' marriage," she told him then, aware that he was watching her with that terrible look on his beautiful face, as if she was killing him. As if she was doing it with her own hands. It made her ache, but she could not let herself stop. "I'm not willing to simply accept unhappiness."

"Why are you so certain that we will be unhappy?" he demanded, his voice still so raw. "Have you been unhappy since you came here?"

"It's like that lake..." she began.

"I will dredge it and pave it over with concrete, if that will make you happy," he gritted out, temper crackling in his voice. "If that will keep you from mentioning it again—as if I built it myself!"

"It doesn't matter how happy we are, or think we

are, because there is always something rotten underneath," she managed to say. "There is always another game, another lie. We cannot do this. It has been five excruciating years and we have proven repeatedly that we cannot do it, Leo. We simply cannot."

It was as if the pain was another entity, a vast sea, an agony both acute and dull ringing in her ears and cramping her belly. It seemed to fill the room, shining from Leo's drawn, ragged features and the very salt in the tears that she could not seem to stop, the tears that slipped down her cheeks unheeded.

"Then what do you want?" he asked starkly.

Bethany did not mistake the question for another shot in their long battle. It was a deeply serious question. He looked at her as if he could see into her, as if he knew the things she still kept hidden. As if he wanted to see everything.

She thought for a brief moment that she could do it—that she could say she loved him too and let that sit there between them. That she could let herself be that vulnerable, that honest, that open. That she could risk it—risk everything.

But all those empty years… All the times she had said she loved him and he had merely smiled and then used her desperation to make her do his bidding. All the nights she had tossed and turned, alone and ravaged with this terrible grief, tortured by the love she would have cut out of her own flesh if she'd been able to.

How could she trust this man with her heart when she could not trust herself with it? How could she possibly admit to that much vulnerability when she was already so shaky?

Nothing good can come of this, she told herself

bleakly, staring at him, her tears making his dark coffee eyes seem to shimmer and glow. Nothing ever has.

"Tell me what you want," he said gruffly, as if it hurt him too. "Tell me and it is yours."

She wanted so many things. She always had. But she was too beaten, too bruised by all of their epic and painful failures. She had given up too much and she was so afraid that she had no more left to give. She could not do it anymore. In that moment she wanted some semblance of peace more than she wanted anything else—even him.

"I want a divorce," she whispered, and saw his eyes go cold, his mouth tauten, his face pale.

But it was better to break what was left of her heart right now than to hand it to him and watch him smash it into dust again and again until nothing was left, not even that thread of hope that had kept her going all these long years.

She told herself it had to be.

CHAPTER TWELVE

Leo found himself standing in her bedchamber, the ancient room seeming to whirl around him. His heart was too loud in his ears and his chest, and he could not seem to force a full breath.

He could not believe the finality he had heard in Bethany's voice, had seen stamped on her face. He could not believe that after all of this—all they had been through, all they clearly still felt for each other—she still wanted to divorce him. He could not accept that she wanted to leave him. Everything in him rebelled at the thought!

He had told her he loved her, and it had not moved her at all, when the same words had once transported her entirely—made her smile and laugh and shine from within. He did not know where to put that sad reality, how to keep it from tearing at him.

If you loved me, you would not spend so much time trying to manipulate me, she had said. Her words still echoed in his head, sounding like an uncomfortable truth. Look what we've become.

He felt his hands clench into fists at his sides.

She did not want a lake, and he did not want to be a man like his father who would build such a monument to something he had never felt. He did not want her trapped and miserable, unhappy and dutiful. He did not want this woman who had wrecked him and exalted him, sometimes with the same small smile, to end up like his own mother. He did not want her to transform herself into the kind of woman he'd been supposed to marry. He did not want any part of the life he'd been lucky to be banished from as a small boy. Was that what he wanted for his own children?

He knew he did not.

And he also knew, though he wished he did not, that it was his pride that wanted to force her to stay, his pride that wanted to keep her no matter what it was she said she wanted. He might not believe that she was as finished with him as she claimed to be, but it was only his pride that would force her to confront that, wasn't it?

He had lived his life in service of his pride for far too long, he thought then. Because once he set it aside, all he could see was the expression on Bethany's pretty face, pale and streaked with tears. Did he love her so little that he could keep her here, his prisoner, when she wanted to leave? Did he want her close to him more than he wanted her happy?

He detested himself for how long it took to answer that question, for how agonizing it was to come to the only possible conclusion.

That was the kind of man he was, he thought bitterly. The kind of man she accused him of being. That was exactly who he was to her, and had always been: autocratic, conniving, manipulative. Just as she'd thrown at him, time and again—but he had excused it all away because he had told himself it was all about duty and obligation, when, in truth, he had simply wanted her.

Here. Now. For ever.

He had seen her and he had never looked at another woman again. He had never wanted anyone else. Only Bethany. He simply wanted her with him in whatever way he could have her, because without her he feared he would disappear forever beneath the crushing weight of his own vast history, his family's legacy.

He let out a breath and let it roll through him, the truth he had fought so hard, so long, to suppress, even from himself.

She was the only one who had ever seen him simply as a man. But she could not be happy if she was with him. This was finally clear to him. It was killing her—and he could not stand by and let something hurt her so badly, even if what was hurting her was him.

He had to let her go. He did not know how he would do it when every single instinct he possessed screamed that he must prevent this very thing at all costs—he only knew he had no other choice.

Bethany did not realize that she had sunk to the floor until she looked up to see Leo standing before her, a strange and unreadable expression on his face. She stared at him, aware then that she was on her knees. She had no idea how that had happened. She had told him she wanted a divorce, he had walked away from her and it had been over.

She had known, with some kind of primitive instinct that seemed to emanate from deep inside of her, that they had finally snapped that thread of hope. It was finally broken. They had finally ended this thing between them, whatever it was, and she was free. Free to go, free to live—free.

And it felt like dying.

"Did you fall?" he asked in a voice that sounded far away, as if it was a stranger's.

Or perhaps she had become the stranger, having cut the thread that tied them together. Perhaps that tiny little shred of hope had been the only thing that had bound them, after all. She tried to wet her lips, to speak, but nothing came out.

"Are you unwell?" he asked, his elegant brow furrowing as he moved closer. She had to blink to bring him into focus, and that was when she realized that tears still coursed down her cheeks unchecked.

"I want to walk out of here," she managed to say in a whisper that seemed to tear at her throat. She felt the hot sting of her tears, the clog of emotion in her chest, the threat of deep sobs from low in her abdomen. "I want to be free...of all of this."

A stark emptiness washed across his face, hurting her as surely as if he'd struck her, even when she would have thought that she could not hurt any further—that it was not physically possible.

"I told you that I love you and I mean it, Bethany," he said in a low, quiet, awful voice, his powerful hands in fists at his sides, his dark eyes bleak. "And I will love you enough to let you go, if I must."

His mouth flattened into that grim line. He looked... defeated, this strong, unbreakable man. It made Bethany feel like shattered glass, all jagged shards and fine dust scattered across the floor. It made her want to rewind, erase, do whatever it took to make him Leo again.

"If that is what you want," he said.

It rang in the air like a vow, and she believed him. He would let her go. He would do it. Only moments ago, she had known that was precisely what she wanted. She had been deeply hurt, but sure. Certain. Leo was finally acquiescing, and this time she knew that he was not playing one of his games. They had moved far past that.

This time, he meant it. Which meant that all she had to do was stand and walk out of this place, head high, heart battered, perhaps, but free—just as she'd wanted to be for so long.

All she needed to do was rise, climb to her feet and start for the door. Start the rest of her life as she'd believed she wanted to do for so long.

Stand up! she ordered herself, desperate.

But she could not seem to do it.

"I do not know how to let you go," he said, his voice darker than she had ever heard it, laced with all the pain and sorrow she knew was inside of her, spilling out of her. "But I will do it, Bethany. I promise you."

It seemed to reverberate deep in her heart. It made her feel weighted to the floor, heavy like a stone, when she kept telling herself she should feel lighter, should fly, should cast aside the shackles she had always believed he'd placed on her and make for the sun.

Was this how it ended for them? Was this how it felt?

But her legs refused to work. Her hands were clasped together before her as if she were praying, and she could not force herself to wrench her gaze away from his. She was not sure she was even breathing. Time seemed to stand still, fold in on itself, and all she knew was that sorrow in her heart and the way it reflected back at her from his bittersweet gaze.

She had cut that last silver line of hope, of the dream of him, and without it, she knew suddenly, with a deep certainty that seemed to echo inside of her and grow louder with every passing second, she was as unknowable to herself as he was without the great long parade of his history.

He was her history. He had made her as surely as she had made herself; they were entwined and entangled, and she did not know how to exist without it. Without him. She could as soon exist without air.

Thinking that, she released the breath she had been holding and inhaled deeply, as if for the first time.

"I cannot seem to leave you," she whispered then, something like grief washing through her as if it was overflowing from within, as if it was a poison, as if it had to get out. "I have been trying to do it for years, and this time even my legs have given out on me."

"I will carry you wherever you want to go, if you wish it," he said gruffly, and she could see that he meant it, this difficult man, however little he wished her to leave.

He would do it because he was honorable, for all she had longed to believe otherwise. He was not his father. He was not a monster. He was, perhaps, as conflicted and confused as she had always been.

Then she could not hold any of it at bay any longer— the sweltering heat and storm of all that sorrow, all that pain, all their years and wars and battles and passions— and she bent over with the force of it, sobbing it out into the plush carpet beneath her.

"Come now," he murmured, coming closer.

But still she wept, as if she would never stop, as if she was only beginning, as if she could make sense of the past five years through the salt of her tears.

"Bethany," he said softly as his arms went around her and lifted her. "Please."

But she sobbed against the wide wall of his chest, his scent and heat enveloping her like an embrace, warming her, caressing her, keeping her safe while the storm raged on.

"Come, luce mio; do not cry like this," he murmured close to her ear, pressing a kiss against the flushed skin of her cheek, soothing her the only way he could. "I beg you."

But she could not seem to stop. Not when he lapsed into crooning, comforting Italian. Not when he carried her to the window seat in the bedchamber and settled her on his lap, holding her close and murmuring into her ear. She cried and cried, and she could not make herself stop it any more than she had been able to make herself stand up and walk out the door.

Instead, she simply let him hold her.

"This is my fault," he said when she had been quiet against him, in his arms, for a time. Bethany tilted her head back and searched his face. He held her close to his chest, but for once she did not worry that this made her appear the child. She felt…comforted by the steady beat of his heart. By his warmth. By his muscled strength surrounding her.

"If there is fault," she said, her voice raspy in the aftermath of the storm that had shaken her, her eyes feeling swollen and bruised. "Then there is enough to go around."

"I am the perfect prince," he said, his tone heavily sardonic, and for once she knew he aimed it at himself. "I have spent my life practicing, so one should hope I've succeeded at it after all these years." His eyes blazed at her, alight with a kind of determination she had never seen before. "But I am not much of a man."

"I love you," she said unevenly.

The fear was gone, wept away. She was washed clean.

Only the truth remained, shining hot and bright inside her like a beacon. Like something profoundly, life-alteringly simple. She loved him. What else mattered?

She sat forward, turning so she could face him on the window seat. "That does not mean it is not complicated. That it is not painful. But I have always loved you."

"I know," he said, a ghost of his arrogant smile curving his sensual lips, though his eyes blazed and his face filled with an emotion that made her stomach clench. "But I did not think that mattered to you any longer."

"Of course it matters to me!" she whispered. He reached over and traced her mouth with one long, tapered finger, elegant as the rest of him. He smoothed his fingertip along the bow of her upper lip, the curve of her lower lip, and Bethany shivered slightly as that same familiar fire scorched her from within, as it always did. Always. Leo smiled slightly and drew his hand away.

Bethany stared at him for a long moment, as if she could see the answer to all of their problems tattooed across his beautiful, regal, beloved face. She was not sure what she felt, or how. All she knew was that once again she could not take the final step that would separate her from him. She could not do it. And every second that she did not leave, that she let him hold her, that she breathed in and felt him do the same beside her, that resilient little thread of hope stretched out between them. And grew thicker. Tougher. It would be that much harder to break the next time.

Maybe, a little voice whispered inside her heart, it is not supposed to break at all.

She had wanted him to be all things to her, when he had wanted the chance to be no more than a man. She had wanted him to keep her safe, but there was nothing safe about loving like this—so deep and so hard that it had altered her completely, changed her, made her into someone she had not recognized for years. She had feared it for so long, fought it, fought him, desperate to keep herself from disappearing in him. Because that was what she'd always been so scared would happen if she succumbed to the power of her feelings. He was so much bigger than life, so much more than she had ever dared dream... Of course she had thought he would consume her whole.

But what if that was not what happened at all?

Today she had seen Leo as she never had before. Perhaps he had always been this way and she had been too overawed by him to note it, but today she realized that she had the power to hurt him as much as he had hurt her. It did not make her happy or proud of herself. But, as she sat and looked at him, she felt that shifting once again, as if they sat on a fault line and the earth was readjusting itself beneath them. If he did not hold all the power, then that meant she could only disappear if she chose to let that happen. If she did it herself, to herself. But...what if she did not?

What then?

She was not a puppet, she thought, the words feeling almost nonsensical, impossible, in her own head even as they resounded like truth in her gut. But a partner. His partner.

The idea of it all but took her breath away.

"If you are leaving me," he said, his voice low and rough, his gaze intent on hers as if he was inside of her already, as if he could read her as easily as he read her body, as if he knew what she was thinking, "then you must do it soon, Bethany. I am only a man, and not a particularly decent one, I do not think. I fear my good intentions are few and far between where you are concerned."

She felt the tug in her heart, the silver string wrapping around her again and again, tying her securely to him as it always had. She understood, in a way she never had before, that she could choose.

Every moment of the day, every moment with this man, she could choose: hope or fear. One would help her fly and one would shut her down. She had spent three years in fear, all alone in that house in Toronto. She had spent all the scared and lonely nights she needed to spend. Did she really want to spend the rest of her life that way, loving this man and keeping herself apart from him because it scared her too much to be with him?

What kind of life was that?

She sat up straighter and could not look at him. She lifted up the hands that she'd kept clenched into fists while the sobs had wracked her body and she'd cried out all the years of sorrow.

"But what if I choose to stay?" she asked, her voice the barest whisper, though she saw each word hit him like an electrical bolt. His dark eyes blazed with a fierce hope she recognized. She felt it hitch in her own chest.

And then, slowly, she opened up her hands until he could see her palms and what lay in each of them—what she had scrabbled to find in the pocket of the purse where she'd secreted them. What she had held on to even as she fell to her knees.

In one palm lay a simple platinum band. In the other, an exquisite sapphire ring.

"I was given to understand you got rid of them," Leo said with an echo of his usual arch amusement, but he picked up the rings, holding them in his much bigger hands as if he was seeing them for the first time. As if he had not selected them himself from the Cartier boutique in Waikiki. As if he had not slid them onto her trembling fingers while she'd cried tears of joy through a smile so wide it had made her jaw ache.

"I refused to wear them," Bethany admitted, looking at him and pushing through the cloud of fear—because what was a little more vulnerability at this point? What was left to protect, if she lost him and herself? "But I could not be without them."

It was one more truth she had ignored. One more clue. One more part of a deep, abiding and painful love she had given up on, called hopeless, but had never quite managed to let go.

His eyes met hers then and Bethany felt exactly the same way she'd felt when they'd married on that private beach in Hawaii years ago. Holy. Sacred.

Right—despite everything.

They had stripped everything away, and here they still were. She could choose to fear, or she could choose to hope. She could choose—and the truth was that her heart had chosen long ago.

It had never wavered, even when she had—especially then.

"Allow me," Leo said.

Then, just as he had so long ago, he put the rings back where they belonged. One by one, he gently slid them onto Bethany's left hand. When they were secured, he laced his fingers tight to hers and drew her hand to his mouth.

"Do we start again?" he asked, his brown eyes calm and clear but so alive. So filled with hope, with a love she thought she just might dare to believe. To return. Bethany felt his gaze move through her, down to her toes.

Such a simple question, for such a complicated endeavor. But what else could they do? They could not seem to live apart. They could not seem to leave. Perhaps it was time to see what they could build together.

"We cannot seem to end," she said, but her heart felt full, and the threads that tied her to him felt intricately knotted, tangled and tight. At last, she admitted to herself that she wanted it that way. That on some level she always had.

"Then we might as well begin," he said huskily. A new promise. "Again and again."

"Until we get it right," Bethany vowed, her voice soft and sure.

He leaned closer and pressed his mouth to hers, making it right. Lighting the great fire that had always burned within them.

Sealing the promises they'd made so long ago. Sealing their fate.

Setting them both free.

Hot reads!

These 3-in-1s will certainly get you feeling hot under the collar with their desert locations, billionaire tycoons and playboy princes.

Now available at www.millsandboon.co.uk/offers

24 new stories from the leading lights of romantic fiction!

Featuring bestsellers Adele Parks, Katie Fforde, Carole Matthews and many more, *Truly, Madly, Deeply* **takes you on an exciting romantic adventure where love really is all you need.**

Now available at:

www.millsandboon.co.uk

Discover more romance at

www.millsandboon.co.uk

The World of Mills & Boon

There's a Mills & Boon® series that's perfect for you. There are ten different series to choose from and new titles every month, so whether you're looking for glamorous seduction, Regency rakes, homespun heroes or sizzling erotica, we'll give you plenty of inspiration for your next read.

By Request

Back by popular demand!
12 stories every month

Cherish™

Experience the ultimate rush of falling in love.
12 new stories every month

INTRIGUE...

A seductive combination of danger and desire...
7 new stories every month

Desire™

Passionate and dramatic love stories
6 new stories every month

nocturne™

An exhilarating underworld of dark desires
3 new stories every month

For exclusive member offers go to
millsandboon.co.uk/subscribe

WORLD_ M&Ba

Which series will you try next?